PHILIP McCUTCHAN

THE CONVOY COMMODORE

and

CAMERON
ORDINARY SEAMAN

PAN BOOKS

The Convoy Commodore first published in Great Britain 1986
by Weidenfeld & Nicolson Ltd
Cameron Ordinary Seaman first published in Great Britain 1980
by Arthur Barker Ltd (a subsidiary of Weidenfeld (Publishers) Ltd)

This omnibus edition published 2003 by Pan Books
an imprint of Pan Macmillan Ltd
Pan Macmillan, 20 New Wharf Road, London N1 9RR
Basingstoke and Oxford
Associated companies throughout the world
www.panmacmillan.com

ISBN 0 333 42061 5

Copyright © Philip McCutchan 1980, 1986

The right of Philip McCutchan to be identified as the
author of this work has been asserted by him in accordance
with the Copyright, Designs and Patents Act 1988.

135798642

A CIP catalogue record for this book is available from
the British Library.

Printed and bound in Great Britain by
Mackays of Chatham plc, Chatham, Kent

THE CONVOY COMMODORE
and
CAMERON Ordinary Seaman

Philip McCutchan served in the British Navy
throughout the Second World War.

THE CONVOY COMMODORE

ONE

The weather was cold, very unseasonable for early August, but the North Atlantic was as ever unpredictable. The Commodore, on the bridge of the former Mediterranean-Australia liner *Ardara*, wore his bridge coat, the shoulder-straps carrying the thick gold bar surmounted by the crossed-triangle 'curl' of the Royal Naval Reserve, hands clasped behind a broad back as he scanned the convoy, watching the ships astern and on either beam. They formed a great spread of bottoms mainly in ballast out of UK ports for a troop and war materials pick-up in Halifax, Nova Scotia, currently on the starboard leg of the zig-zag and some of them having trouble with their station-keeping.

The Commodore glanced aside as the *Ardara's* master, Captain Arthur Hampton, joined him at the bridge screen. 'Damn big target,' he remarked.

'It is, sir. We've been lucky – so far.'

Mason Kemp grinned. 'Don't tempt fate! Homeward bound . . . that's when it's more likely to come, when we're laden. I doubt if we'll be having much luck then, somehow. That's the way things go.'

Hampton nodded and turned away from the Commodore to pace his wide bridge wing. This OB convoy, which would turn into an HX convoy on the homeward route from Halifax, was the biggest ocean lift in terms both of ship numbers and the size of many individual ships that he had so far sailed in – no less than five liners, average 23,000 tons displacement apiece, liners that in pre-war days had sailed to Australia and South Africa, India and South America and the Far East; four deep-

1

draught tankers of around 17,000 tons which would detach once the convoy was past 40 degrees west longitude to head for Galveston on the Gulf of Mexico to take on their potentially lethal liquid cargoes; a dozen sizeable dry-cargo vessels on hire contracts from such companies as the Port Line, Clan Line, Union Castle and British India, together with eighteen smaller ships, tramps in peacetime mostly, that would load to their marks in Halifax with all manner of humdrum cargoes that would help to sustain life in war-torn, besieged Britain. The Battle of the Atlantic had begun only three months before; none of the men who sailed beneath leaden skies this particular morning had any notion of how long that battle against U-boats and aircraft and surface raiders was destined to last, no idea of the scale of the sinkings that were to come.

They had all, or nearly all, been in action before; some of them in the last lot, the 1914-18 war, as well as since September 1939. It was little more than a year since the period of the phoney war had ended with the threat of invasion following Dunkirk, and then the airborne Battle of Britain, but the months of continual sea-keeping had taken their toll of men and men's endurance and they felt as though they had been at war for a decade. Peace forgotten, war had already become a way of life. Not for the merchant ships alone: the men of the warship escorts had done their share and more, the destroyers and corvettes, always too few in number and driven to the limit, bringing biting cold and wet and extreme discomfort to their ships' companies as so often in the winter storms they rode gigantic waves that could make life aboard even the *Queen Mary* into a time of desolation. The North Atlantic could be hell, far worse than the Bay of Biscay, worse than the Great Australian Bight where the storm roared straight up from the southern ice or the westerlies bellowed round the globe in the High South latitudes. And always there was the potential threat of the lurking U-boats of Grand-Admiral Dönitz and, when the ships were within their range, the Nazi air armadas, the reconnaissance Focke-Wulfs and the bombers.

The escort apart, the best defence of the convoys was the zig-zag. The point was always made by the officers of the Naval Control Service and it had been made this time at the

2

convoy conference held before the bigger ships joining from the Clyde had left the Tail o' the Bank off Greenock. All masters of the Clyde contingent had attended, along with the Commodore of the convoy and the commanding officers of the naval escorts. So vital was the OB that additional escorts had been provided: four heavy cruisers and an old, slow, rusty battleship, a mixed blessing whose fifteen-inch guns might well be effective enough if the convoy should come under attack from a surface raider, a German pocket-battleship perhaps, but which the Commodore fancied would tend only to slow the convoy's advance into safer waters beyond forty west.

Commodore Mason Kemp lifted an eyebrow at Hampton as the latter's pacing brought him close again. 'I'm going below,' he said. He rasped at his chin, and yawned. He had been almost all night on the bridge as the ships from the Clyde, having made the rendezvous with those out of Liverpool, moved away from the Bloody Foreland at Ireland's north-western tip. 'Shave, if nothing else! You know the orders, Captain: I'm to be called immediately if anything happens. I'll be back in fifteen minutes in any case. Where's that assistant of mine?' He looked around, saw the RNVR lieutenant in the wheelhouse, and lifted his voice. 'Williams!'

A lanky figure emerged from the wheelhouse, clad in a duffel-coat, balaclava, thick woollen scarf and gloves. 'Here, sir.'

Commodore Mason Kemp grunted: there was a gleam of humour in his eye as he remarked, 'Warm life for some. Where's your normal sartorial elegance, Williams?'

'Sorry, sir –'

'Oh, don't apologize, it's not vital.' Kemp stretched. 'You can go below when I return to the bridge –' He broke off as a shout came from the signalman of the watch. 'What's that, MacCord?'

'Destroyer leader, sir, reports contact starboard. Submarine, sir.'

Kemp caught Hampton's eye. The long business of the convoy's defence had begun already. 'Sound action stations,' he said.

On the outbreak of war nearly two years earlier Captain Kemp, as he had then been, had brought his ship along the English Channel from Brixham, where he had embarked the pilot, to the Downs and Tilbury, homeward bound from Sydney. Soon after the ship had berthed in the basin the chairman of the line had come aboard and had been taken to the master's day cabin. He said, 'We're going to lose you, John. I'm more than sorry, I need hardly say.'

'Lose me?'

'Yes. You're RNR. And this has come for you.' The chairman handed over a buff envelope marked ON HIS MAJESTY'S SERVICE, with the Admiralty crest embossed on the flap. It was addressed to Captain J. Mason Kemp, RD, RNR.

Kemp said, 'Not unexpected, Sir Edward. But what'll they do with a captain RNR? They won't give me one of their battle-wagons, I'll bet!' He held the envelope in the air, quizzically, as though keeping himself deliberately in suspense.

The chairman said, 'I understand the Admiralty's bringing in the convoy system – right from the start this time. Carrying on where they left off in '18.'

'Commodore of convoys?'

'That's my guess, John.'

Kemp slit the envelope, using an ivory paperknife from his desk. The guess had been a good one. That afternoon Commodore Kemp left the liner to report to the Admiralty and then to proceed on a fortnight's leave before taking up his war appointment. The liner was the *Ardara*. Leaving the ship with much nostalgia for a life that had come to a sudden end, it never occurred to the Commodore that within two years, after many convoys, he would once again be upon her bridge. He went home, home being an olde-worlde cottage in Meopham in Kent, and broke the news to his wife.

Mary Kemp was no more unexpectant than he himself had been; one didn't join the RNR and expect to be left to carry on one's peacetime ways in war. Expectant, and accepting of the lot of a seaman's wife, though with sadness for all the

4

exposure to danger there would be.

'Tripe,' Kemp said, and grinned. 'We're all in it together. If I'd been left in the *Ardara*, I wouldn't have been protected by different gold stripes, would I? Look on the bright side, Mary.'

'What bright side?'

He kissed her. 'More leave. The RN's good at that.' The Merchant Service wasn't: an Australian voyage, then a week or so at home, and back again to Australia, world without end. Kemp had been married almost twenty years, and if he added all his leaves up he reckoned he's seen his wife and children for a little less than two years in all. Young Harry, nineteen and likely to volunteer now for the navy, and Rufus, sixteen and currently with a few more days left of his summer holiday from Pangbourne, scarcely knew their father other than as a fleeting and somewhat autocratic stranger who reappeared at intervals. They had taken to calling him the Ancient Mariner, unflatteringly . . .

Mary said, 'All right then, the bright side.' She said it determinedly, then added, 'I don't know about Granny.'

'Oh yes, Granny. How is she?'

'Better than she thinks she is. You'd better go up and see her, John, otherwise –' She broke off. 'Started already. Go on up, do!'

A walking stick was being banged on the floor; flakes of ceiling came down. Commodore Kemp left the drawing-room and went up the twisty staircase down which Granny could never again walk, being bed-bound with all manner of disabilities, some of them real. Granny Marsden was in fact Kemp's grandmother and had been inherited when Kemp's mother had died. His mother had died young; Kemp had been devoted to her and had accepted the burden she had left. Granny Marsden at ninety-six was something of a miracle, if a tiresome one. Everlastingly expectant of death, she continued to survive, smoked like a dangerous chimney and drank two weakish whiskies every evening to help her sleep. She came of seafaring stock and in her childhood had sailed in the square-rigged ship commanded and owned by her father. She had been round Cape Horn to Chile and Australia not far off as many times as her grandson had taken the Suez Canal route to Sydney. She still had all her faculties and her hearing was as

5

sharp as her voice; her eyesight was more than equal to the task of watching out that the right quantity of whisky went into her tumbler.

She was propped up in bed by what looked like half a dozen pillows when Kemp entered the bedroom. 'Well, Johnny,' she said.

Kemp bent and kissed her on the marble-like forehead. 'Well yourself, Granny.' It always struck Kemp as slightly ridiculous that a middle-aged shipmaster should be in the position of addressing anybody as Granny. 'You look it, I must say.'

'Look what?'

'Well.'

She gave a snort. 'If you did but know. No one ever listens to me! I keep telling Mary –'

'Yes, I'm sure you do. She does her best.'

'If you call –'

'Now, now, Granny.' Kemp began to use his master's voice, not wishing to hear criticism of his wife. It had its effect: Granny Marsden knew when she was being told to watch it.

'Well,' she said grudgingly, 'it's nice to see you again, Johnny. What are they going to do with you?'

'Do with me? I –'

'There's a war on, so they tell me.' Kemp didn't realize how many times he was going to be told there was a war on over the coming years. 'That man Chamberlain, such an idiot. And as for Hitler!' Words seemed to fail her, for she didn't go on. 'They'll call you up, I suppose.'

He told her the facts. 'Second time round,' he said. He had served right through the last war in the RNR, in Q-ships and later in minelayers, and he'd been torpedoed twice and had to swim for it. 'War to end wars my foot!'

'Your great-grandfather always said –'

'Yes, I'm sure he did,' Kemp broke in quickly, for his great-grandfather had evidently said plenty; his sayings never ran out. He made his excuses and left the bedside; he would be up later to say goodnight if she wasn't asleep.

'Huh!' Granny Marsden said scornfully. 'How *anybody's* expected to sleep in this house I *don't* know!' Kemp knew that the reference was to Harry, who possessed a bagpipe chanter

6

and made hideous noises on it, though, out of respect for the wrath that would otherwise descend on his mother's head, not unduly late at night. Kemp's view was that within reason there were times when the old had to give way to the young with their lives before them and Harry, curiously perhaps, had talent in a musical direction, or so he insisted. He was currently employed by the BBC . . . but when he came home that evening he confirmed what Kemp had foreshadowed earlier: he intended going along to the naval recruiting office within the next few days and joining up as an ordinary seaman. In the middle of this announcement Rufus turned up: it now being officially wartime, he had put on his Pangbourne cadet's uniform and this brought a lump to Kemp's throat. So young . . . and God alone could tell how long the war was going to last. Rufus expressed the hope that it would last long enough for him to join in.

One way and another, the home wasn't going to be the same. Only Granny Marsden went on for ever.

[iii]

Two years on now, from Kemp's first wartime homecoming: Paul Williams, lieutenant RNVR, looked at himself in the mirror in his bedroom at home in Hounslow. He liked what he saw: the second wavy gold stripe had only recently been sewn on to his uniform by Gieves on the Hard in Portsmouth, turning a sub-lieutenant into a full-blown lieutenant, and it gave him added importance, the equivalent of a captain in the army to whom in fact, being of the Senior Service, he would rank senior. More importance, in his view, was given by his new appointment to the staff of a convoy Commodore – even though he understood it to be normally a sub-lieutenant's appointment. Never mind: no doubt an important convoy, a very large convoy, needed the extra rank. The personal staff would consist of himself and two signalmen, plus telegraphist ratings. The Commodore was to be an RNR with the Reserve Decoration, an oldie from the liners and probably with a constipated mind, but Lieutenant Williams could cope with that. So far in the war he hadn't coped too badly, he believed, though his last 'flimsy' – the copy given all officers of their captains' personal and confidential reports – had made use of the expression self-assertive and bouncy. A previous one had indicated cockiness but both went only to show that senior RN officers were also constipated mentally. If he had been all that, he wouldn't have landed a staff job – which was how Williams thought of it.

He saluted himself in the mirror, smartly. Then he coloured as he recalled not so long ago overhearing a leading seaman in his last ship referring to him as being all wind and piss like the barber's cat. He had been mortified but had prudently turned a deaf ear. It wasn't the sort of comment you made a song and dance about to the extent of putting the man in the rattle and having the phrase repeated loud and clear at Captain's Defaulters. Anyway, wind and piss or not, it paid to be smartly turned out, since then you got noticed. Having saluted himself, the new lieutenant removed his cap and went downstairs, but not in time to hear the conversation between his father and mother. His mother had been fondly enthusing over her son's elevation and appointment.

'Staff,' she had said almost reverently. 'Isn't it splendid, Fred?'

'I don't know so much.' Williams' father didn't know the contents of the flimsies, but he would have been in some sympathy with the commanding officers. He knew his son pretty well.

'But *assistant commodore*!'

'Is that what he calls himself? I hadn't heard . . . and I wonder what the Commodore'll call him!' He filled in the blank for himself: 'Commodore's assistant, I reckon.' When Paul came in, his father heaved himself to his feet. He'd got his stint at Air Raid Precautions; he was on duty as a warden. Working in the City, chief clerk in a firm of insurance brokers, he often didn't get home till late but he was determined to do his bit to flatten out Adolf Hitler and teach the Nazis a lesson about ordinary Englishmen.

Three days later Lieutenant Williams left Hounslow and went north by train from Euston, speeded on his way by the air-raid syrens and then the falling bombs, bound for the naval office in Greenock's Albert Harbour to report to Commodore John Mason Kemp for the OB convoy.

Kemp and Hampton met at the convoy conference, duplicates of which were being held in the other assembly ports. Kemp and Hampton, both Mediterranean-Australia Line, were old friends; and two years earlier, when Kemp had been taken out of his command for war service, Captain Arthur Hampton had been appointed master in his place: Hampton had never bothered with the RNR and had thus been left in peace, if such was the word, in the liners, now converted as troopships and on loan to the government as hired transports in the official term. Kemp had been delighted to be told at the Admiralty that he was to hoist his broad pennant in the old *Ardara*.

'Just like old times, Arthur.' Hampton, some five years before, had been his staff captain in the *Aratapu*, which as it happened was another of the troopships in the OB convoy.

'Same but different, sir. No parties.'

'They won't be missed.' One of the bugbears of liner life had been the entertaining, the enforced giving of Captains' cocktail parties – the gin-palace aspect of the job – and the need to appear as often as his duty permitted at the Captain's table in the first-class dining-room where there were important passengers to be entertained with small talk, something John Mason Kemp was not good at and had had to force himself into. He would have been highly surprised had he known how popular he was with most of his passengers. One thing he did know: right through his career in the liners he had been the target of forward young women and some not so young: the liner atmosphere did funny things to women, especially once the ship had entered the Red Sea. It had been all right until he had met Mary and married her; after that the female attentions had to be fought off, the more so when he got his promotion to staff captain and then Captain in Command. Senior officers could not afford to be put in compromising situations.

Kemp was about to make a further remark to Hampton about the peacetime liners when the conference was called to order by a lieutenant-commander RNR. The conference, Kemp

9

reflected, was to be a high-powered one: as the conversation died, the Chief of Staff to the Flag Officer in Charge entered the room. The Chief of Staff was a pompous-looking officer, rotund, two pisspots high in Kemp's seafaring terminology, wearing a gold-rimmed monocle and carrying, of all things, a beautifully turks'-headed telescope. There was a good deal of other brass around: the Rear-Admiral commanding the cruiser squadron, no less than five four-ring captains RN from the cruisers themselves and the solitary battleship of the escort, each of them accompanied by his navigating officer. The remainder were a mix of commanders and lieutenant-commanders plus a number of lieutenants, mostly RNR or RNVR, from the smaller escort vessels – the corvettes – and the masters of the merchant ships.

The Naval Control Service officer was concise: time was not for wasting. As they all knew, the OB convoy route was normally south through the Irish Sea, the last pick-up being the ships out of Liverpool Bay. This time, they were going north about, taking their departure from the Bloody Foreland. Why? The answer lay in the intelligence reports. Some German cyphers had been broken and it was known that there was to be a concentration of U-boats lying in wait off the exit from St George's Channel. So the Germans were to be fooled: no convoy would steam into their periscopes this time. Instead, the U-boats would come under heavy depth-charge attack from Western Approaches command. The lieutenant-commander went on to give the precise route to be followed clear of the British Isles and beyond the range of the German bombers. He stressed the importance of the convoy even though the ships were in ballast. Bottoms were valuable even without cargoes, and the cargoes and Canadian troops that would be picked up in Halifax were very badly needed. As for the escort, the corvettes would break off for return to base at 19 degrees west longitude. The remainder, the destroyers, the heavy cruisers and the old battleship, would, exceptionally, remain with the convoy right through to Halifax to form part of the homeward escort which would if necessary be joined nearer home waters by a fleet aircraft-carrier being held in readiness in the Clyde. The destroyers would re-fuel as necessary from one of the tankers, a Royal Fleet Auxiliary

10

tanker which would be carrying sufficient oil fuel for replenishment. The RFA would break off with the other tankers for the Gulf of Mexico, escorted by destroyers of the Royal Canadian Navy, which would leave Halifax for the rendezvous.

Afterwards Kemp remarked to Hampton that he had the feeling something hadn't been said. Hampton shrugged. 'They always keep their cards close to their chests when there's –'

'When there's something else. That's what I meant. Apart from the sheer size, the convoy's not all that unusual. Why fall over themselves to provide an escort all the way when they're always so short of escorts? There's *got* to be some other factor.'

'I dare say we'll be told in due course,' Hampton said.

They made their way along the dockside at Albert Harbour, stepping over the usual clutter of any dock – coils of wire and rope, broken packing cases and the like – closely attended by Lieutenant Williams who was efficiently looking out for the drifter detailed to take the officers back to their ships in the stream. Kemp thought his assistant looked like an impatient bird, peering about for its nest. Back in London words had been uttered in the Queen Anne's Gate office of the Naval Assistant to the Second Sea Lord, known in brief as NA2SL, the officer responsible for appointments. Naturally, the confidential nature of Williams' flimsies had been respected; but the navy had ways of conveying information by facial gestures, waved hands and a minimum of words. Commodore Kemp had hoisted in that his new assistant walked with God, but was otherwise reliable and efficient enough. Williams needed to be sat on now and again, and Kemp was regarded at the Admiralty as someone who would sit hard when necessary.

'Training exercise?' he'd asked with a grin.

'You could put it that way, Commodore. Yes. Make something of him – what?'

Moving through Albert Harbour to the drifter, Kemp reflected on these words of wisdom. So far his contact with Williams had been of the briefest, a hurried introduction just before the convoy conference, but already he'd got the idea that his assistant was summing him up as a kind of blimp, a relic of the last war, and that he, the assistant, was going to

11

find it a bit of a strain keeping the boss up to the mark. Well, time would tell; Kemp wasn't the man to make pre-judgments. He had asked Williams a question that he knew the answer to already: was this his first experience of the merchant-ship side of convoys? It was; but Williams had served in the escorts, which should be of some help. Kemp had had, in the past, RNVR lieutenants who had never hitherto moved off their backsides in shore jobs, not as officers anyway: they'd done their sea-time as ratings and then promptly shifted out of discomfort and forgotten all they'd learned. Kemp had refrained from saying what Williams would learn for himself soon enough: that his job wasn't going to be so much that of assistant commodore, which his manner suggested he believed, or flag lieutenant, as of a kind of tea boy and general-purpose dogsbody.

Meanwhile Williams identified the duty drifter, not a hard task since so many officers were making for it, and reported the fact with a flourish and a salute.

'Well done, Williams,' Kemp said, keeping his face straight. Williams didn't seem aware of any irony. They embarked and proceeded out of the harbour. As senior officer present, Kemp was accorded the privacy, honour and fug of the wheelhouse where he did his best to interpret the Scots tongue of the skipper, a gnarled fisherman from Caledonia's wilder north-eastern shores. Kemp gathered that the skipper regretted his patriotism in making his drifter and himself and crew available to the English, like so many other skippers, for the duration when he could be making a damn sight more money by sticking to the fishing. Kemp saw that he was homesick: to the skipper, Clydeside was the south.

[v]

Leading Signalman Mouncey, together with his number two, Signalman MacCord, had already taken up his quarters aboard the Commodore's ship and was having his customary grumble about this, that and the other whilst waiting for the Commodore to come aboard. Their quarters, for one thing: a bloody great liner with hundreds of single-berth cabins and state-

12

rooms and they'd been shoved in a carved-up former nobs' suite on A deck together with the naval guns' crews, the gunnery rates who manned the two six-inch, one for'ard and one aft, that made up the *Ardara's* main defence and despite the strengthening would likely split the ship asunder if fired. Signal ratings, Mouncey said, didn't expect to be berthed with common seamen gunners.

'Handy for the bridge,' MacCord said. It didn't sound like that, MacCord being very Scots, and Mouncey had to ask for a repeat.

Mouncey said, 'Bollocks. Plenty of other spaces just as handy. Just some sod being awkward. When I was in the . . .' He went on and on, moaning about better ships and better billets. MacCord listened philosophically, letting the killick drip himself out. Even a tap must eventually empty the reservoir. After a while Mouncey, a small, dark man with a repaired hare lip and the screwed-up eyes that spoke of many a long year gazing through a telescope at flag hoists and Aldis lamps and the big signalling projectors, came back from the past and peered into the future.

'That there RNR. Commodore Kemp.'

'What about him, killick?'

'Looks all right. Spoke to me decent, almost as if I was yuman. I've 'eard 'e used to be in this ship – must be funny, coming back like with a bloody great thick stripe on 'is cuff.' Mouncey sniffed and wiped the back of a horny hand across the end of his nose. 'That wavy bloke gives me the bloody creeps, though. The lootenant – Williams.'

'Looked all right to me, killick –'

Mouncey jeered. 'Call yourself a bunting tosser! Blind as a bat, you are. Tarted-up little ponce. Stuck up as a pr –'

MacCord never heard the rest of it. Mouncey was interrupted by the broadcaster coming on suddenly, almost in his ear. A voice said, 'Leading Signalman on the bridge. Leading Signalman on the bridge, immediately.'

That meant the Commodore of the convoy was aboard. Mouncey went up the ladders at the double. On arrival he got a bollocking from the Commodore's assistant, which didn't please him: he should have been on the bridge waiting for the Commodore, Williams said, not skulking below. Mouncey

13

didn't answer back, you didn't answer officers unless you liked being put in the rattle, but he fizzed and muttered like a bomb. For his part, Lieutenant Williams didn't like that. He said something hasty, about dumb insolence. Mouncey's mouth fell open in astonishment. Daft young bleeder . . .

A moment later Kemp called Williams across for a quiet word. 'Laid yourself open, haven't you?'

'Sir?'

'Dumb insolence went out of the crime sheet years ago – as you must surely know.'

'Sorry, sir. Heat of the moment –'

'Well, don't let us have any more such moments, Williams. You did right to utter a reprimand, but don't overdo it. I like a happy signal staff. Understood?'

Williams, red-faced, said, 'Yes, sir. If I might explain, Mouncey strikes me as a –'

'All right, Williams, that's all.' Kemp turned away, walked with Captain Hampton to the port bridge wing. Signals were passing between the King's Harbour Master and the battleship, and between KHM and the senior officer of the close escort. The moment of departure had come. Five minutes later the great concourse of shipping was on the move, the battleship and the cruisers going ahead to be followed by the Commodore and the other ships in convoy, with the destroyers and smaller escorts bringing up the rear, proceeding in line ahead; the ships would remain in single column until the waters of the Clyde opened out beyond the Cumbraes, widening into the firth between Holy Island and Ardrossan so that the convoy could begin to move into its ocean formation. On the bridge of the *Ardara* Kemp stared ahead through binoculars, towards the anti-submarine boom strung across from Cloch Point to Dunoon, a strange stirring agitating his mind. This, he believed for no real reason beyond a hunch that he avoided thinking of as psychic, was going to be no easy convoy.

14

TWO

Signalman MacCord reported again: 'Lost contact, sir.'

'Thank you, MacCord. Scared off by the depth-charges.'

'Likely, sir. No apparent damage to the bastards, sir.'

Kemp nodded. That was convoy work: attack, draw off, come again. Alarms that were not false, but led to no result. A lot of it was boredom and fatigue, but you could never let up, never drop your guard, never allow yourself to miss the smallest feather of water that would indicate a watching periscope. Hampton, as the morning wore on into afternoon and the convoy left Ireland well behind, had a feeling of deteriorating weather: the wind was increasing from the south-west and heavy cloud was extending. White horses were forming on the water and soon there would be spindrift. That was good: the U-boat packs didn't attack when the weather was bad and if the wind strengthened to gale force, and stayed with them beyond the range of the hunter packs, then they would have a good chance of getting through unscathed. And before long they would be coming to the limit of the Nazi aircraft range, the bombers anyway.

Not the recce boys, the FW Condors. So far, by some stroke of sheer luck, nothing had appeared in the sky, but the convoy was not yet in the clear.

[ii]

Every convoy had its arse-end Charlie, the ship that couldn't keep up the speed and fell everlastingly astern to become the

15

bête noire of the Commodore and even more so of Captain(D) in the destroyer flotilla leader, whose job it was to detach one of his escorts for the job of chivvying. This time, arse-end Charlie was the ss *Stephen Starr*, one of the smaller steamers whose official maximum speed was said to be a fraction over the mean speed of the convoy which had therefore allowed her inclusion in what was a semi-fast convoy insofar as the outward run was concerned. The *Stephen Starr*, along with all the other smaller ships, was due to detach in Halifax and return at a later date with a slow convoy, while the Commodore and the troopships and armaments carriers formed a fast HX convoy for home waters.

But for now the OB convoy was saddled with her. Her master, Captain Peter Redgrave, saw the impatient signalling, saw one of the destroyers turning out of formation on the starboard beam and bearing down on him with a big bone in her teeth. As the destroyer passed along the steamer's side a loud-hailer boomed irritation across the water.

'What's it this time, Captain?'

'Trouble in my engine-room,' Redgrave called back.

'What sort of trouble?'

Redgrave set his teeth. 'Worn-out bloody machinery, that's what! If it's not one thing it's another. My chief engineer's doing his best.'

'He'd better do it fast,' the destroyer Captain said. 'Much longer and you'll be astern of the corvettes.'

The destroyer turned away, making back at speed for its position in protection of the main body of the convoy. Captain Redgrave thought: astern of the whole God-damn escort, right out on a limb! NCSO at Liverpool, where the *Stephen Starr* had sailed from, had put it very plainly: stragglers would have to lump it. The speed of the convoy would not be reduced and escorts couldn't be spared, not unless one of the big ships happened to become a straggler, which wasn't likely. Redgrave knew his ship was expendable, a casualty that could be accepted. Had it not been for the war and the need to keep as many ships as possible at sea, she would have gone to the breaker's yard long since. As it was, just so long as she could stay afloat without becoming an inconvenience, she could carry cargoes around the world and help to keep Britain fed.

Redgrave was well aware of the facts: neither the poor old *Stephen Starr* nor any of the other former tramps of uncertain years would have formed part of this convoy if it hadn't suited the Trade Division of the Admiralty to shove them in, tag them along with the big stuff and thus save on escorts. It was insane, and it was probably murder.

But didn't they all know there was a war on?

Redgrave knew, all right. Not just because he had sailed the war-torn seas right from the start. Because his home had been in Liverpool, or Birkenhead to be precise. In peacetime Liverpool had been his home port and he had sailed out of it for more than twenty years as second mate, mate and master. He had bought his house on a mortgage at the time he'd met his wife. When Clare had said she wouldn't marry unless he started buying a house, he had been in full agreement. That was – what? – ten years ago, just under. The house hadn't been much to start with, but it had become a little palace in those years, the happy years before Hitler had mucked everything up. Clare had done wonders with decorations and he'd spent almost all his leaves with a paint brush in his hand. A lot of hard-earned money had gone into it as well, and what with that and three children in due course, Redgrave had never had so much as twopence to scratch his own bottom with. But he hadn't minded that; though a seafarer, he was a home-lover and the mere thought of home, the satisfaction of owning his own place, had been his mainstay during days of boredom on the bridge, taking cargoes around the world from Liverpool to Sydney, Sydney to Japan, Japan to San Francisco and virtually anywhere else you cared to name.

And what had been the end result?

Extinction. Back in May the Luftwaffe had come to Liverpool in an attempt to put the city and docks out of commission. The result had been terrible but Redgrave's house had been all right. Then a sneaky raid had taken place, nothing very big, only a fortnight before Redgrave had sailed on the present run to Halifax, and this time his house had taken a direct hit in his absence on a coastal convoy. There had been nothing left when he'd come home, nothing but a heap of rubble. Somewhere underneath it all had been Clare and the children. He'd been told it was impossible to get them out. Maybe they'd got the bodies out by now; if so, he didn't know. He didn't much want to. Probably they hadn't; too much else to do – and if they had, then presumably he would have been told.

Since then there had been nothing left but the sea, and the *Stephen Starr*. There was something very personal about the ship now: Clare and the children had come aboard whenever he was in Liverpool and he had the memories of them all about him, in his cabin, in the saloon, on the decks.

And now he was being a nuisance to the escort and the Commodore. Light signals were being flashed from the *Ardara*, admonitory messages similar to the amplified words of the destroyer captain, messages warning him that he would soon be on his own. The Commodore wished him luck and added his regrets. Redgrave knew the regrets were sincere; no seafarer liked the idea of leaving men to the mercy of the sea and the enemy, and Commodore Mason Kemp was RNR, had been a merchant shipmaster himself and would thus have an intimate understanding.

Redgrave sighed and moved to the engine-room voice-pipe.

'Chief? Bridge here. What's the score?'

'Heap of old iron.' The voice came hollowly up the pipe, and sourly. Mr Hankins, chief engineer, knew he could never get through to the deck officers, they were blind and deaf when it came to machinery and always expected miracles – like now.

Redgrave asked, 'Can you get just half a knot more out of her?'

'No, I can't. She's flat out now . . . too many worn bearings. Too many other things. It's hell down here. Talk about the Dustbin Line!'

Redgrave snapped the cover shut and stood back, looked across the increasing sea towards the other ships, steaming solid and in station, lifting and falling to the mounting waves. His thoughts were bitter – not as regards Hankins, for the chief was obviously doing his best since, to take the lowest viewpoint, his life was as much at risk as anyone else's – but about shipowners, peacetime shipowners who had let things slide, kept the repair bills down and let ships deteriorate in times that were admittedly not prosperous. The years of depression couldn't be shrugged aside, of course; but too many tramp owners had sent men to sea in coffin ships, uncaring so long as their own personal living standards were not affected. The rot for such old-timers as the *Stephen Starr* had set in and they were virtually beyond refitting, but the country needed them now and they still went to sea . . .

Captain Redgrave sent a final signal to the Commodore and Captain(D): Regret cannot maintain station and must drop astern.

[iii]

'*Stephen Starr* dropping out, sir.'

'Thank you, Williams. Make another signal: Our thoughts and hopes are with you.'

'Aye, aye, sir. Mouncey?'

'Yessir?'

'Signal to the *Stephen Starr* . . .'

Kemp, his back turned to what he preferred not to see, heard his assistant pass the message to the leading signalman. There was something in Williams' tone that suggested he found the words smug. Well, perhaps they were, but they were not meant to be. The *Stephen Starr*'s master would understand that, better than Williams could ever hope to. Mason Kemp's jaw was out-thrust, his face set hard and grim. His whole instinct urged him to turn his ship to stand by the drop-out himself, but that was manifestly not to be done, and as regards detachment of an escort the orders had been clear, unequivocal.

Williams, however, had something to say on the point.

'Commodore, sir –'

'Yes, what is it, Williams?'

The RNVR lieutenant gave a cough. 'Escorts, sir. I know the orders, but –'

'So do I. They stand – to my regret.'

'Yes, sir. But as Commodore –'

'I'm aware of my duties as Commodore.'

'Of course, sir.' Williams was at least dogged. 'But you have an option, sir. The officer on the spot and all that?'

'I have no option, Williams. If I had, I'd use it.'

'But –'

Kemp turned, sharply, angrily, caught a sight of the *Stephen*

19

Starr already well behind the convoy. He shifted his gaze to Williams' face, stared him in the eye. 'That's all, Williams. No more to be said. Except this: orders are to be obeyed and you're learning your first lesson in the conduct of a convoy. I am the *convoy* Commodore – I don't command the escort. Remember that.'

Kemp turned away again. Hampton had gone below now and the liner's bridge was in the charge of Hampton's chief officer, Marcus Whitehead. When Mason Kemp had served in the line, Whitehead had been a senior second officer. Now he caught the Commodore's eye and said, 'I'm sorry, sir. I know how you feel.'

'Thank you, Whitehead.'

Whitehead had overheard the remarks offered by Williams. He said sourly, 'Saturday-afternoon sailors . . .'

'No criticism, Whitehead. He's spoken his mind. That showed guts.'

'I suppose so, sir.'

Kemp didn't say anything further. He was thinking about Redgrave, the story of whose recent loss had permeated even the Clyde conference. A hard-luck story, so close to sailing. Redgrave could have got out of this convoy; even in wartime there was such a thing as compassionate leave, but apparently he'd preferred to sail. Redgrave, of course, wasn't the only one who'd lost everything to Hitler and there were going to be hundreds of thousands more such sufferers before the war was won. Redgrave was one of those who was going to ensure that it was. Standing four-square on the *Ardara*'s bridge Kemp found himself wondering if Redgrave would find death came easy if the *Stephen Starr* should fall victim to the Nazis. As for himself, he knew that if enemy bombs destroyed his own family he would find no more joy in living but would hang on in the hopes of driving a few nails into Hitler's bloody coffin. Probably Redgrave felt the same way.

[iv]

Below decks, far below in the working alleyways beneath the passenger accommodation – passenger accommodation now converted to troop decks much used as such over the last eighteen months and now ready for the reception of the Canadians – Mr Portway, second steward, was in his cabin, an inboard compartment with no outlet to the fresh air other than by way of the forced-draught trunking. Mr Portway, the stewards mustered and detailed for the day's work by this time, was making up his overtime bill for eventual presentation to the purser. War or no war, the routine of a liner went on notwithstanding, if in a less glamorous way. Troops were passengers of a sort, and the first-class saloon, officers for the use of, was still a somewhat superior place and with an air of distinction, though Mr Portway had found that some so-called officers were not quite what would have worn stars and crowns in pre-war days. Some of them didn't know how to treat stewards – chucked their weight around and were rude and dismissive. Once, Mr Portway had been first-class head waiter in the *Aramac* on the Australian run. The passengers had been ladies and gentlemen then; they treated you decently and also they tipped well. Often on arrival in Sydney Mr Portway's pockets had bulged with five-pound notes, and in those days five nicker was five nicker and bought a lot. Of course he didn't keep it all himself: like the table waiters, he passed some of it on to the pantry and galley. The waiters did it because if they didn't, then they would get rotten pantry service and passengers kept waiting didn't tip well.

Mr Portway did it for similar reasons: the galley was the primary producer as it were, and their chagrin would reflect upon the head waiter.

Somewhat the same with the overtime. Overtime was in the second steward's gift and a lot went down, in fact, that had never been worked at all. Mr Portway knew that the stewards called him a fat-arsed bastard who put most of the overtime down to his blue-eyed boys but he wasn't worried by that. No one ever liked second stewards, and he knew that the best way to get efficiency was to encourage the good hands and then, when the message penetrated, add some of the improvers to the overtime bill. It worked. Other things worked too: the chief steward was accustomed to receiving a bonus at the end of each voyage based to some extent upon the muster of

21

crockery when back in Tilbury. One of the lowest of the low categories aboard a liner was that of dishwasher, a lazy lot and inclined to chuck huge quantities of dirty china into the hogwash via the gash chutes rather than wash it up. That cost the Line money and it was cheaper to grease the palm of chief stewards – not only cheaper, it also meant that the passengers didn't have to go without plates, since a lot could go overboard between Tilbury and Sydney. The next stage in the game, of course, was for the chief steward to farm out his bonus so that next voyage he didn't lose the lot.

Wheels within wheels, all of them turning over very nicely, even in wartime. You didn't often come across a penniless chief or second steward. Mr Portway, the overtime totted up, pushed himself back from his desk, reached into a drawer, and brought out a bottle of whisky and a glass.

He was pouring out his tot when the balloon went up. Or anyway, the alarm rattlers sounded. Bloody Jerries around, evidently. Mr Portway put the bottle back in its safe stowage and lumbered to his feet. In action – or defence stations, in the case of a virtually unarmed troop transport – Mr Portway had a place to go to, in charge of the stewards' fire parties. He put on speed, shouldering his way through a rush of men, eager to get higher up in the ship before the bridge shut the watertight doors.

[v]

Captain Hampton was on the bridge again within thirty seconds of the alarm being sounded, and found the Commodore staring into the sky astern, using his binoculars.

'Aircraft report, Hampton. Picked up by the rearguard.'

'How many, sir?' Hampton brought up his own glasses as the close-range weapons' crews doubled up the ladder to man the machine-guns in the bridge wings.

'They think just one. So far unidentified. I'm thinking of the *Stephen Starr*.'

'Yes indeed. But it's very likely a recce Condor.'

Kemp nodded. 'Could be, at this range. But some of the Condors have cannon, Hampton. All the *Stephen Starr*'s got is

Oerlikons and a 3-pounder.'

Kemp said no more; they all listened for the sound of aircraft engines. Kemp swept a glance around the convoy, still keeping good station, the ships large and small steaming in apparent unconcern through the increasing waves. The warships of the escort were at action stations, their ack-ack armament trained on the reported bearing. Two destroyers had turned, following upon signalling by light between them and Captain(D) in the flotilla leader. Hampton said, 'It looks as if they're going back to stand by the *Stephen Starr*.'

'Let's hope so.' In such circumstances, so long as the straggler was still close enough, the orders could be ignored. The two destroyers were now making back at speed, throwing up great swathes of North Atlantic from their bows, the White Ensigns nearly rigid in the wind. They were joined by a corvette, already astern of the convoy. The cruisers and the rest of the destroyers maintained their station as close escort, and astern of the centre column the old 'R'-class battleship came on ponderously, like some huge, camouflaged block of flats, surrounded by foam as the sea surged along her anti-torpedo bulges.

A report came from the battleship a few moments later, flashed by light, the all-round masthead lamp, addressed to all ships. Leading Signalman Mouncey reported, 'One aircraft, sir, Condor, bearing green one-seven-oh.'

The binoculars swung. 'Recce,' Kemp said. 'Got it!' They could hear the engine beat now. Hampton picked it up: it was at a distance, and high, but he believed it was losing height. That could be to come down on the straggler, arse-end Charlie. Hampton glanced at the Commodore: Kemp was thinking the same. There was a haggard look in his eyes, as though, foolishly, he was blaming himself. As the convoy moved on-ward, the sharp crack of anti-aircraft gunfire was heard. Puffs of smoke appeared in the sky. Lieutenant Williams, still wrapped in wool, was alongside Kemp, giving what he considered a useful commentary.

'High but losing height, sir –'

'I've seen that.'

'Gunfire, sir, heavy. But having no effect.'

'Ditto.'

Williams gaped. 'Sir?'

'I mean I've seen that too. We can all see it. Save your breath.' Williams looked put out. 'You're not covering cricket for the BBC,' Kemp added with a grin. He watched out astern. The Focke-Wulf had come a good deal lower, obviously over its target, and the fire from the destroyers was hairy to say the least, going nowhere near the aircraft. A moment later there was something else to worry about: Captain(D) reported a contact. His Asdic had picked up an echo. Leading Signalman Mouncey read off the lamp.

'Submarine bearing red three-oh, sir!'

Already the escorts on the port beam of the convoy were swinging round.

THREE

The attention of the bridge staff was now on the coming
underwater attack – coming, unless the speeding destroyers
could intercept and frustrate. Mr Portway was supervising the
laying out of the fire hoses along the alleyways that in
peacetime had seen nothing more lethal than the involuntar-
ily-ejected contents of passengers' stomachs in bad weather.
That, and at other times the smartly-dressed ladies and
gentlemen, or the inevitable cabin-crawlers, mostly east of
Suez, in pursuit of sex. There was none of that now, it was in
the past for both passengers and crew: no women aboard
beyond the two nursing sisters, officers for the use of. Not that
Mr Portway cared. There never had been much opportunity
for a fat, middle-aged second steward whose only hunting
ground had in any case been the tourist end of the ship: second
stewards were not permitted the freedom of the first class
other than on duty, and the tourist end was never quite the
same. Their morals were different, they weren't so forthcoming, even to the brassbound ship's officers who had the run of
the whole ship including the first class . . . and anyway Mr
Portway had his own arrangements made at either end of the
run and in some of the ports – if ever there was the time *en
route*. Mabel in Grays, near Tilbury – Mrs Portway was frigid
and lived in Thurrock – Daphne in Melbourne; Lou in Sydney,
down by the Cross and desperate for it: she wasn't too good-
looking, it had to be admitted, and it was a case of any port in a
storm for both of them, but Mr Portway got by and it didn't
cost him anything beyond the odd meal in a café. While he
carried out his defence duties his mind roved ahead of the

convoy's track to Halifax. They would be in port the best part of a week, or so he believed, and with luck he might get fixed up fast. Mr Portway hadn't been in Halifax before so had no organized up-homers.

When a broadcast throughout the ship from the bridge told him there was now a U-boat in the offing as well as an FW, he forgot about his sex life. The bowels of a liner was a poor sort of place to be if a torpedo should hit.

[ii]

From the bridge of the *Ardara*, in the lead of the centre column behind the extended escort, they could only watch, wait and pray. A troopship had no part in submarine attack other than to be attacked. All she could do was to take appropriate avoiding action at the right time, which could only be when the torpedo's trail was seen approaching. Under certain circumstances the convoy could be ordered to scatter so as to diffuse the target. But scattering was never something you did other than as an extreme measure. Ships of all sizes, of all speeds and with varying manoeuvrability, could be an awesome sight when scattering. This way and that, a disorganized rabble in effect, with collisions being avoided by a hair's-breadth or not avoided at all. And afterwards they had to be shepherded back into formation again, a job that could take a very long time and cause oil fuel problems to the escorts, who had only a certain range at the best of times.

Captain(D) was signalling again: only the one contact so far.

'Thank God for that,' Kemp said heavily. He and all the bridge personnel were watching the bearing where the U-boat had been reported. In the breaking waves the periscope would be almost impossible to pick out; it would be raised only just far enough and just long enough to give the U-boat captain a sight of his target. In a flat sea the feather of spray should be visible if the lookouts were alert, but not now. They were watching the bearing when the destroyers reached the point of attack and Kemp saw the depth-charges ejecting from the throwers and being dropped from the racks, but it was a little late. Without warning a loud explosion came from half-way

26

down the port column of the convoy and a flash appeared over the port bow of a former Clan Line cargo vessel and she began to dip by the head.

Williams consulted a list which he had ready in his hand. '*Clan MacWishart*, sir. Captain J. R. Rawlings, master –'

'Thank you, Williams.'

'P. V. Dunhill, chief engineer.'

Kemp nodded, his attention on the damaged ship and on the huge spouts of water coming up from the explosion of the depth-charges on the port beam. Hampton glanced at Williams, still scanning his list. Captain Hampton had an urge to ask the RNVR lieutenant for the name of the ship's cat but knew this wasn't the moment. More explosions came from the attack area, now drawing astern as the convoy continued on its course. The *Clan MacWishart* had slowed and her stern had swung out to starboard. She was causing confusion to the next astern and the next abeam to starboard, but not for long.

'She's going,' Kemp said suddenly.

She was, and quickly. The bow went down, the sea could be seen climbing the fo'c'sle towards the island superstructure, the stern rose high in the air, the screw still spinning, and there was a rush of steam from somewhere aft, and then she was gone, a steel finger lifting to the sky and then going down with a rush.

Kemp said, 'Mouncey?'

'Yessir?'

'Make to the *Clan MacWishart*'s next astern, you may ease engines to pick up survivors.'

'Aye, aye, sir.' Mouncey got busy with his Aldis lamp. While the signal was being made the lamps were busy between Captain(D) and the attacking destroyers, and soon after the message came for Kemp. Commodore from Captain(D): Got the bugger.

Kemp rubbed at his eyes and blinked: getting old, he thought, binoculars were becoming a strain. He said, 'Well, one for one.' He didn't add that it was also one up for the convoy in a sense: a U-boat was a more valuable kill than the *Clan MacWishart* since if it had lived, that U-boat would no doubt have sunk a good many more cargo vessels in the future. That was the way to look at it, though the survivors wouldn't be looking at it like that. Kemp watched as the *Clan MacWishart*'s next astern slowed right down, put out nets and cast heaving lines attached to lifebuoys. Like anglers from a pier, Kemp thought. Unlike the majority of lines cast from piers, however, these made their catches. When the report came in for the Commodore it indicated twenty-three survivors out of a complement of thirty-two, none of them injured. Kemp remembered the *Stephen Starr*. He asked, 'Any word of the straggler?'

Williams said, 'Detached escorts rejoining now, sir.'

Kemp turned to look aft. The two destroyers and the corvette were coming up fast, the corvette taking up her station astern and the destroyers weaving through the convoy to their own positions, a lamp flashing as they came. Mouncey read it off for Kemp's benefit. The FW Condor had got away but before turning for home had come down to strafe the decks of the *Stephen Starr*, killing the semi-trained merchant guns' crews manning the ship's pathetic armament, sweeping the bridge and colandering the helmsman – the actual signal was a good deal briefer but that was the picture Kemp received. The master had a flesh wound; medical assistance had been offered but refused. The ship herself was sound. She was carrying on for Halifax. Or staggering on.

Kemp said, 'You know what the Scots' toast is, Hampton?'

Hampton raised an eyebrow. 'Which one?'

'The one that goes: here's tae us, there's nane like us. Boastful . . . but why not? I feel the same way. Master mariners, Hampton – *all* mariners, come to that. We've lost too many men like Captain Redgrave.'

The convoy moved on; there was no further attack. Defence stations were fallen out but Kemp made a warning signal to the convoy masters, even though they probably didn't need it. The Condor, he said, would already have reported their position and their anonymity as it were was gone. Any number of U-boats could be in the area and could be moving in to attack. Extra vigilance and alert lookouts were the order of the day.

Deep down in the ship, Mr Portway was seeing the fire hoses returned to their normal reel stowages. This done and some of the watertight doors opened up, he returned to his cabin and his bottle of whisky and after a couple of measures he returned to his ponderings on sex. He didn't know much about Canada or Canadians, still less about Nova Scotians in particular. Cold country, warm women – or not? All done up in fur, parkas and all, you wouldn't get a fair summary just by looking, no idea of the figure beneath. Mr Portway ticked off names on pudgy fingers: Mabel, Daphne, Lou, not to mention Mrs Portway and the *en route* popsies. Quite a lot to miss him if that Jerry U-boat had struck. But he'd always been lucky and he reckoned his luck would hold.

He put the bottle away again and went up top to the purser's office, clutching his overtime sheets.

[iii]

The night fell. There had been no further attack. With the ship's first officer and senior third officer on bridge watch, with Lieutenant Williams strutting from one wing to the other in the role of Commodore-of-the-Watch as he regarded it (though Kemp didn't), Kemp and Hampton took it easy for half an hour once dusk action stations had been fallen out. They went to Hampton's day-cabin and eased dead-weary limbs in comfortable chairs beneath shaded light behind the blanked-off square ports that looked out on the Captain's deck. Two years earlier this had been Kemp's own cabin. On joining the *Ardara* as Commodore of the convoy he had been offered Hampton's accommodation. He had refused. He would not, he said, turn out the ship's master. He never did. So he had taken up the spare cabin and was comfortable enough – he was seldom able to use it in any case, for his place was mostly on the bridge when at sea. But, the day he had joined in the Clyde anchorage, he had been attacked by a strong nostalgia for his old quarters. He had made no less than five Australian voyages in the *Ardara* and there were many memories. Like Captain Redgrave aboard the *Stephen Starr* he had brought his family to his quarters on many occasions. Now, at sea in wartime, he could see Mary sitting in the chair he himself was sitting in, could see her pride in him, aboard his own ship with the four gold rings on either cuff, the brass hat

29

chucked into another chair. Very nearly the senior master of the company, in line one day for Commodore – of the Mediterranean-Australia Steam Navigation Company, not of a convoy. He could see the boys, having a whale of a time rushing about the decks, yarning with the bosun, old Frank Bush who was still, this day, aboard the ship, still bosun. The younger boy, coming up for Pangbourne, had been overawed the first time he'd visited his father's ship and had treated all the officers down to the junior fourth officer almost as God.

But it wasn't only the family: it was the different voyages too. Each one had been just that – different. Different problems, different passengers, different crew members. When Kemp thought of crew members he meant his officers and senior ratings rather than the rank-and-file, not from any sense of superiority but simply because inevitably in a ship carrying some six hundred crew he never met some of the categories other than on Captain's Rounds: the scullions, the dishwashers, the kitchen porters, the firemen and greasers in the engine-room. It had to be a case of the chef and second chef, the engine-room storekeeper and his number two, and so on. Even so . . . the master was always Father to his officers, as in the RN – just a handy sobriquet but it had always meant, to Kemp, much more than was intended, and he extended his fatherhood to every man in his crew, whether he knew them or not. He was always available to them through their heads of department and often without the benefit of the proper channels – he was never stuffy or stand-offish and frequently passed the time of day with ratings on deck or along the alleyways or on the bridge. They were all doing the same job in basis, taking a great ship half across the world, and each man did his job – for the most part – with pride. Each had to be accorded his own dignity in Mason Kemp's book. Many of them had been with the Line, even in the one ship, for years, and even now when trooping under war conditions and government charter so many of them were there still. But now that he was Commodore, they were no longer his responsibility or of his seafaring family. They were Hampton's, and thus in good hands.

Kemp and Hampton chatted, mainly of the old times. 'A bit of a change from the Indian Ocean,' Hampton said.

Kemp laughed. 'You can say that again.' He thought of the sunlit days, the first-class passengers around the swimming pool, or in the tavern bar at the after end of C Deck which abutted the pool, and men and women sitting around with long, iced gin-and-somethings, in their swimming gear, the young girls largely surrounded by off-watch ship's officers, though the latter usually contrived to look as though they were only duty-socializing if they saw that the Captain's eye was on them. The assistant pursers were the worst, Kemp remembered – they had more opportunity than the deck officers.

Hampton, seeming to sense Kemp's thoughts, said, 'A different world, sir.'

'It'll come back when this lot's over.'

'I doubt if it'll ever be quite the same again.'

'Don't be so pessimistic! The Indian Ocean'll still be the same, so will the romance – it's human nature, isn't it?' Kemp could remember back to when he'd been a junior officer, young enough to appreciate the possibilities raised by the deep-sea moonlight, the balmy night air, the slow, gentle roll of the ship, and the undoubted attractions of a brass-bound uniform – mess dress, for the ships of the company changed for dinner every night except in port or on the first night after departure. Bow tie, wing collar, starched white bum-freezer and shoulder-straps of rank. Kemp had in fact met his wife on board one of the company's ships, going out to Sydney with her mother to visit an aunt who'd emigrated years before. Mary had returned alone to UK by the homeward voyage: it had been one of those whirlwind romances associated with the sea, and it had been a success from the start. They'd married before the ship sailed again, and next voyage Kemp had brought his mother-in-law back. That had been the one snag: mother-in-law had had a flea in her ear on account of the whirlwind element, but it had stopped biting after a while. Now, looking back after many years, Kemp could understand. The young were thoughtless.

Kemp got to his feet. 'I'm going to take a look around, Captain. Coming up?'

'Yes, sir.'

'After that I'm turning in for a spell.' He repeated, from force of habit, the order that officers in wartime knew by heart.

31

'I'm to be called immediately if necessary.'

The two men climbed to the bridge. Looking aft and to either side, Kemp could see the shadowy shapes, large and small, beamy and slim, moving in their formation through the night, following the zig-zag pattern, each ship darkened and showing no steaming lights other than the shaded blue stern lights that were needed to assist station-keeping. The wind had increased again and was now blowing, by Kemp's estimate, a Force Six on the Beaufort Scale. The more wind the better, at any rate until they had passed beyond the likely U-boat range.

Kemp remained on the bridge for a while, went into the wheelhouse for a word with the Officer of the Watch and the quartermaster, then went below and turned in, having told Williams he too could get some sleep.

[iv]

Andrew Pemmel, purser, had a drink or two too many with his deputy purser and Sister Jacqueline Ord who, with the second nursing sister, was one of the only two females aboard the troopship. Obviously, they would be in much demand, at least until more nurses, army nurses, embarked with the troops. The nursing sisters were usually considered the hunting ground of the deck officers, though humankind being what it was this was not always strictly adhered to, and Pemmel had currently more than an eye for Jackie Ord. After a while he looked at his watch and said, 'Well, lads and lassies, the time has come: bed.'

His guests took the hint and left. Ten minutes later Miss Ord was back. Pemmel said, 'Good ol' Jackie.'

She gave him a look, a raking one. 'Not so much of the old. Or the good either, not tonight. I only came to say you've had too much. You don't need me, you need the surgeon.'

'That old has-been.'

'Which is what you are at this moment. And you know what I mean, Andy. Do I have to spell it out?'

'Shut up,' Pemmel said.

'All right. I'll leave you to your Scotch bottles.'

'You bloody bitch,' Pemmel said. He said it without any particular emotion. Jackie Ord left his cabin, her retreating footsteps overlaid by the sound of the forced-draught blowers. Pemmel went for his cupboard and poured another whisky, which he took fast and straight. Then he looked at himself in the full-length mirror behind the door of his wardrobe. Tall and slim yet, no stomach, he looked years younger than forty-five. Even his face . . . well, no, perhaps not. No lines or wrinkles certainly, but there was a puffiness and a nasty pallor behind the suntan and in the morning his eyes would look like pissholes in the snow. But drink was part and parcel of a purser's life: so much duty entertaining of passengers, and he had been too conscientious. It was too late now to kick the habit, he was more or less immersed. He knew the line would say a polite goodbye once the war was over and for now he was going to make hay.

Pemmel shrugged, had another whisky, and dropped fully dressed on to his bunk. In the morning he would feel like death warmed up.

[v]

The *Stephen Starr* was now many sea miles astern of the convoy, way out of the helpful reach of the escorts even if they had been permitted to turn back. Captain Redgrave carried no doctor: the Nazi bullet was still embedded in his right thigh and he was in a good deal of pain and general discomfort: the climb to and from the bridge was difficult to say the least, and he had given up the attempt and now sat permanently on a hard chair in the starboard wing of the bridge, a case of watch on stop on. Hardy, his chief officer, had done what he could with a knife supplied by the galley and sterilized, more or less, by a naked flame. The result had been horrible. The bandages were bloody but Redgrave believed the flow had stopped. The bullet seemed to have missed veins and arteries, which was something to be thankful for. He would make it into Halifax and hospital. As the painful hours passed, however, Redgrave began to regret his quick dismissal of the aid offered by the escorting destroyer that had turned back to the *Stephen Starr*'s assistance. That doctor could have made all the difference, but Redgrave hadn't wanted to be the cause of any ship hanging about in dangerous waters. Nor had he wanted to be yanked off the ship, which had been to say the least a possibility. The *Stephen Starr* had become home now; even back in Liverpool he would remain aboard all the time and then sail again, quite likely without setting foot ashore except on duty. There were those memories of the family . . . now he would guard them personally all the way across the North Atlantic wastes, come gale or sunshine and enemy attack.

His steward came to the bridge, bearing a can of water, a tin hand-basin, a flannel, bandages and some sort of white powder.

'What's all that, Flynn?'

'Bathe the wound, sir.' He pronounced it 'sorr'. Flynn was from County Galway in the west of Ireland, a good and loyal steward who had once been a soldier, a lance-corporal in the Connaught Rangers, a regiment disbanded in 1922 when the British had left and the Irish Free State had come into existence. 'Keep it nice and clean, sir.'

'It's clean enough. Mr Hardy did a good job.'

'Ach, maybe he did, sir. But it'll need attention. We don't want to lose you, sir.'

Redgrave managed a smile. 'In case you can't find the way across without me, no doubt.'

'Ach, that'll be it, sir.'

Redgrave knew it wasn't just that. Flynn looked after him like a nanny, anticipated his every whim with true devotion. Redgrave had lost count of the times he'd bailed Flynn out in the various ports of the world they'd visited. Flynn had been his steward in every ship he'd commanded and Redgrave knew his ingrained habit of drink. Once ashore, Flynn made for the nearest bar. His drink was either Guinness or whisky, usually both, but he was willing to drink the wine of the country when he couldn't get either. The results were often appalling. Redgrave paid the fine, argued the toss with the local police when they wanted to put Flynn in a cell, had even been known to make a metaphorical rude gesture at the Line and hold the ship in port when Flynn had been given an unavoidable week in gaol. Flynn was always grateful. There

34

was nothing he wouldn't do for the Captain.

'Have your way then, Flynn,' Redgrave said.

'Yes, sir. Hold still now – it'll hurt.' Redgrave felt a prize charlie: in the wheelhouse now, trousers down, shirt-tail flapping . . . deftly Flynn removed the bloodied bandage and got to work with the flannel soaked in salt water. It bit and stung, felt as though it must be doing some good. Redgrave could feel the bullet when Flynn pressed, however gently, a red-hot lump boring into his flesh. Flynn clicked his tongue.

'Now what?' Redgrave asked.

'It has an angry look, sir. Red and swollen. Maybe it's heat it needs.'

'What about a poultice?'

'Ach now, a poultice, sir, yes. I'd not be knowing how to make a poultice, sir.'

'You don't *make* a poultice, Flynn, you apply it. It's ready made. That's if there's any kaolin in the medical kit.'

'Kaolin, sir . . . no, there's not. I did happen to notice nothing called kaolin, sir –'

'It's great to be Irish, Flynn. Go and check through, just to be sure.'

'I'll do that, sir, I'll do that right away.'

'And if there's no kaolin, get some bread from the galley. Heat it.'

Flynn looked puzzled. 'Toast, sir, would it be?'

'Not toast. Hot bread. Crumbled, I fancy. Applied and bandaged.'

In truth Redgrave had no idea; nor had Flynn or anybody else aboard. Hardy had been unable even to find the statutory copy of *The Ship Captain's Medical Guide*, which should have been with the first-aid kit. Maybe the rats or cockroaches had eaten it. Redgrave felt as though rats were gnawing at his thigh as he waited for Flynn to prepare some sort of poultice. As he waited he thought of the convoy ahead – far ahead and steaming fast for Halifax. Those big liners . . . himself, he would have detested the life, detested passengers. He was dedicated to the carrying of inanimate cargoes, crates and bales and so forth without tongues to argue with, complain with, ask silly questions with. They could keep their passengers, Redgrave thought, but he could have done with a bit of

35

the plush now, the sheer comfort below and the high bridges that didn't often get swept by spray or solid water. That, and the ship's surgeon. They were mostly a pissy-arsed bunch, but they did know more than Flynn with all his devotion.

The weather was worsening now. Nearly gale force already, and the spray was coming over, drenching the bridge wings, sounding like machine-gun fire on the wheelhouse screens and bulkheads. The ship was lurching heavily from time to time and water was cascading through one of the glass screens shattered by the FW's gunfire. Redgrave shivered, suddenly began feeling hot and cold by turns. Fever? If it was, there was nothing to be done about it except take aspirins. And whisky.

Flynn came back with a dirty-looking tin. He had found the kaolin after all and had sought help as to its administration. He brought a pad of pink stuff, lint. He was making his final preparations when the voice-pipe from the engine-room whined. The second officer, who had the watch, answered then spoke to Redgrave.

'Chief, sir. Wants to stop engines.'

'What for? Never mind, I'll have a word with him.' Redgrave hobbled across to the voice-pipe. All chief engineers were fairly impossible and Hankins rated high in impossibility: this was a fine time to stop engines, in worsening weather and with the glass falling so fast it was going to clang against the bottom. Redgrave knew that the closer enemy was no longer Hitler; it was the elements.

FOUR

Now it was another morning and a grey one. The sky and sea were bleak, the horizons close and seeming to merge with the sea itself. Mason Kemp went to the wheelhouse as soon as he woke, in his pyjamas and dressing-gown. He had found he couldn't sleep, had tossed and turned all night, woken right up at intervals, switched on his light and smoked cigarettes. He was thinking about the *Stephen Starr*: just one ship out of many that were his responsibility, but as important to him as any of the others. The ship was, of course, right out of contact: you didn't break wireless silence at sea in wartime. So Kemp had no notion of what was going on other than that the *Stephen Starr* had shaky engines and a wounded master. Redgrave had been a fool and a remiss one not to have taken advantage of the destroyer's surgeon lieutenant, but Kemp could understand what he knew would be the reasons behind the refusal. Masters stood by their commands. Redgrave had probably thought a lodged bullet not too serious, something not to make a fuss about – at the time anyway. During the previous afternoon Kemp had asked Hampton to send for the ship's surgeon so that he could pump him about lodged bullets, but the result had been unsatisfactory. The surgeon had never seen a lodged bullet and hadn't operated for more than a dozen years. God help passengers with appendicitis, Kemp had thought. He'd served with some first-class ships' surgeons in the Mediterranean-Australia Line; this particular medico was unknown to him until now, had apparently joined the Line from another shipping company just before the war – years ago he had been in general practice somewhere up in

Westmoreland, until his drink problem had eased him out of it, or so it was whispered according to Captain Hampton. Certainly he looked as though he might even clean his teeth in gin in preference to plain water . . .

The wheelhouse door opened and Lieutenant Williams came in.

Kemp turned. 'Morning, Williams.'

'Good morning, sir.' Williams was brisk, rubbing his hands together and smiling. The weather didn't seem to depress him – nice to be young, Kemp thought. 'Poor visibility, sir.'

'Yes, bloody awful. But some protection.'

'We're beyond the Nazis' range by now, sir, I imagine.'

'I wouldn't bank on it,' Kemp said. He reached into his dressing-gown pocket and brought out a silver cigarette-case: a wedding present from Mary and he was never without it. Opening it he handed it round. Williams and the Officer of the Watch, First Officer Wells, accepted. Williams flicked a lighter, always the attentive Commodore's assistant. 'Thank you, Williams.'

Kemp sucked the smoke in deep and blew out a grey-blue cloud. What men at sea would do without cigarettes . . . life savers, stopped you going round the bend, eased tensions, the first thing wounded men in both world wars asked for and were given. And they always kept up the supply to ships at sea, duty-free price sixpence for twenty, half a crown a hundred in sealed, airtight tins.

'Sea's increasing, sir,' Wells said. He looked up at the brass clock above the fore screen: ten minutes to eight bells and the reliefs were moving around the ship, on deck and in the engine-room, ready to take over and send weary officers and men below for breakfast. Wells was writing up the deck log at the end of his watch when the flagship of the cruiser escort began flashing a message to the Commodore.

[ii]

Purser Pemmel didn't feel at all well; it went beyond the expected hangover. He'd vomited and felt better, but only for a short time, after which he felt worse. He was shivering and

38

had a terrible headache and the cabin had spun in circles when he got up from his bunk to visit his bathroom. The symptoms were not unusual and it could be just a hangover but he didn't think it was. This time, there was an extra dimension. Approaching death?

Pemmel tried to pull himself together. It wasn't as bad as that, but there was something wrong. His mind reeled and he had weird thoughts, like visions almost, visions that receded and were replaced by a kind of blank blackness.

Pemmel was dead scared. There was a griping pain in his gut and his stomach felt bloated. When his steward came in with his early-morning tea Pemmel sent him for the doctor. The doctor took his time and came in looking like the wrath of God.

'Thank God you've come,' Pemmel said, looking at his watch.

The doctor sat beside the bunk. 'What seems to be the matter, Pemmel?'

'I'm bloody ill, Doc.'

"M-h'm.' The doctor reached out a shaking hand, holding a thermometer which he thrust beneath the purser's tongue. With the other he felt for the pulse. He was noncommittal as to the result of his investigations. 'What are the symptoms?'

Pemmel told him.

'A simple hangover, that's all.'

'No, it's more than that, Doc, I'm certain. Those queer visions . . . could it be DTS?'

The doctor shook his head. 'Oh, no, you're not a candidate for that. You'd have to be drunk consistently for something like three weeks, never let up, never *sober* up. You haven't reached that stage yet, have you?'

'Of course I haven't.'

'If I were you, I'd make sure I didn't.' The doctor caught the expression on Pemmel's face, the expression that said clearly: look who's talking. He didn't mind; there were few secrets at sea and he and Pemmel had shared many a gin session. There was little work for a doctor to do in all conscience, aboard a ship. He was really only there because the regulations said a doctor had to be carried – two doctors aboard the *Ardara* in fact, and he had an assistant not long out of Bart's, no experience to speak of, mostly seasick, but as sober as a judge, fortunately. 'I do understand. You know that, don't you?'

'Yes.'

'There's not much I can do. I'll have a powder sent along from the surgery – that'll put you right. Better stay turned in for the rest of the day, perhaps – you haven't much to do till we reach Halifax. You can be spared.'

'Yes.'

The doctor looked at him quizzically, bloodshot eyes narrowed above a purple nose. 'You really should cut it down. Think of what can happen. Cirrhosis of the liver for one thing, very nasty indeed.'

Pemmel said, 'It's an occupational hazard.'

'Up to a point. I know what passengers can be like. But use some will power. You must have the strength of mind. You'd not have got a full purser's berth unless you had.'

'For God's sake,' Pemmel said, 'don't preach!'

'I'm trying to help. As I said, I understand. I'm looking for a reason.' The bloated face hung close, like an engorged moon, but the look was kindly, as was the intent. 'Tell me something: is it Sister Ord?'

Pemmel gave a start. 'What's Sister Ord got to do with it – or with you either? What are you suggesting?'

'I'm not suggesting anything. But you can't expect these things not to be talked about. I've been at sea long enough to know that. I'm not moralizing either – it's not my concern other than as a medicine man. It's between you and me. I'm still looking for that reason, old chap. If you'd like to – to unburden yourself –'

'Are you after Jackie too?' Pemmel asked angrily. 'Is that it?'

The doctor wasn't offended. 'Goodness, no! I'm past all that sort of thing, a long time past. Don't worry on that score. If you'd just like to talk, I'm very willing to listen.'

I'll bet you are, Pemmel thought, dirty old man. Vicarious sex . . . the doc was after the gory details, would listen to all revelations with flapping ears, after which he would see Jackie Ord through different, lascivious eyes. Pemmel said, 'Just bugger off, Doc. If you're not going to treat me, just bugger off.' The doctor shrugged, looked sad, got to his feet and left the cabin. A few minutes later Pemmel got up. He felt better, quite suddenly, and no thanks to the quack. He believed it had been a mild case of panic and all he needed was a morning stiffener of brandy and ginger ale.

The signal from cs29 – the abbreviation for the Rear-Admiral Commanding the 29th Cruiser Squadron – though sent openly by lamp, was in naval cypher. It carried the Most Secret prefix and in addition to the convoy Commodore it was addressed to the senior officer of the destroyer escort and the captain of the battleship. Aboard the *Ardara* Lieutenant Williams had the decyphering tables in the safe in his cabin. One of his action duties, if the *Ardara* should look like being sunk, was to take the codes and cyphers in lead-weighted bags to the open deck where he would throw them over the side – just in case. An abandoned ship could stay afloat after all, and could be searched. Now, with Leading Signalman Mouncey's numeral-filled naval message form safely in his pocket, he went to his cabin to begin what was going to be a long job of decyphering.

Mason Kemp paced the liner's bridge, out in the open wing, facing the gale, bracing himself against the roll and pitch of the ship beneath him, pondering on the unexpected cypher. That it must be important was obvious. Even so, Kemp thought it was carrying security to extremes not to use plain language between ships out at sea with no enemy present. No U-boat captain would come so close to the surface in this weather that he could read a signal through his periscope. Was there, could there be, a lack of trust in the merchant-ship masters or their officers? Scarcely; but there was a parallel thought insofar as ships could be torpedoed when the weather moderated, and survivors could be interrogated, and the Nazi methods were far from civilized. Admirals had to have a care. Kemp paced on, felt the wind and spray, and now the rain, stinging his face; he willed his assistant to make fast work of the decyphering.

But below in his cabin Lieutenant Williams was having difficulty and was smoking one cigarette after another and looking distracted. He had always found decyphering – or

41

encyphering come to that – a hard task and this time there appeared to be some corrupt groups since some of it wasn't making sense. The originator of the signal was the Admiralty, not unexpectedly, and that was about as far as Williams had got so far. It was probably the fault of Leading Signalman Mouncey in not taking down properly the repeat flashed by light. Williams got a little further and decyphered the words Prime Minister. There was an obvious importance and Williams wrestled on, trying not to let himself get rattled by his slowness.

[iv]

Away astern of the convoy, the main body of which was now beginning to approach the longitude of Cape Farewell at the southern tip of Greenland, though well to the south, the *Stephen Starr* lay with her engines stopped, heaving and rolling to the deep-sea swell and the waves brought up by the increasing wind. That wind was now at gale force. Captain Redgrave was still in the wheelhouse, the chair having been brought in from the bridge wing after Flynn had finished his first bathing and poulticing exercise, an exercise that had been repeated several times since. Redgrave was in considerable pain and the wound looked nasty. Flynn was a worried man, and cursed engineers under his breath but not so low that Redgrave didn't hear.

'The chief's doing his best, Flynn. Criticism doesn't help matters.'

'That's right, sir.'

The Irish were a weird lot, largely: there were two physical types of Irish, one lugubrious and dark and with a long upper lip, the other fresh-faced and merry, always smiling. There were two mental types as well, one argumentative, the other tending to agree with everything that was said. Physically Flynn was group one; mentally, group two. A tiresome group; Flynn, having agreed that what the Captain said was right, went on muttering as he fixed the fresh bandage.

Redgrave said, 'Put a sock in it, Flynn. Not the thigh, your mouth.'

Flynn grinned. 'Yes, sir. Sorry, sir. It's you I'm worried about, sir.'

'Then don't be. You've done your best. The rest is up to God.'

'And the chief engineer, sir.'

'Oh, get away with you, Flynn.'

Flynn departed; Redgrave stared through the rain and the spray-slashed glass of the fore screen. He had an idea the engines would never start again; they needed the assistance of the shore, of the shipyard. Worn out, past it, and, according to Hankins, not the right spares aboard, not the ones he needed for the job. Hankins had tried to explain to the bridge but neither the Captain nor any of the deck officers seemed to hoist in the technical details and he'd given up. The screw wasn't turning over and that was all they were interested in, and it was his job to make the repair before Hitler found them wallowing and helpless. With his second engineer he worked like a slave, covered in grease and muck, perspiring and feeling savage and wanting to take a crowbar and smash the whole show up. He was as conscious as anyone else aboard of the potential dangers of lying stopped on the convoy routes, though very likely by this time the gale had blown them away to the north of the track, somewhere up towards Greenland and the Denmark Strait.

The voice-pipe from the bridge whined and the second engineer answered, then called out to Hankins.

'Bridge, Chief. Skipper wants a word –' The second engineer broke off, swore as his feet slid from under him on the greasy steel deck. 'Bugger!'

'D'you mind?' Hankins asked coldly.

'Sorry, Chief.' Hankins was religious, a member of the Elim Tabernacle, and swearing and such was a sin. 'Such' included almost everything a seaman indulged in: fags, booze, women. The second engineer thought what a hell of a life the chief must have had, always in the company of sinners; but no doubt it meant he saved money.

Hankins was at the voice-pipe. 'Chief here. No progress yet, Captain.'

'As long as you're doing your best, Chief.'

'Of course I'm doing my best. And it doesn't help to keep

pushing.' Ill-temperedly, Hankins banged back the voice-pipe cover. At once he regretted it: the skipper was all right and he was said to be in pain. Nasty, that bullet wound. Hankins had half a mind to call the bridge and apologize, but he didn't. It might show weakness. He lurched across the engine-room from the starting platform, fast and slow by turns as the deck heaved beneath his feet, and fetched up hard against a big handwheel. Not a tall man, he banged his face against the metal. His lips worked: often he wished he wasn't a member of the Elim congregation. At times like this a good, hearty 'bugger' would have been an immense relief. But as it was he had no intention of messing up his chances with the Almighty, whom he might be about to meet face to face at any moment.

[v]

When Williams had finished his task he had brought the result to the bridge, post-haste, doubling up the ladders, his expression urgent. Saluting Mason Kemp, he passed over the transcript on a naval message form. He couldn't wait to impart the news in person. He almost gabbled it out. 'It's Mr Churchill, sir!'

The Commodore nodded. 'All right, Williams. Thank you.'

He read. The Admiralty's signal as summarized by cs29 was very informative: 'The Prime Minister is currently aboard *Prince of Wales* steaming to the south of the convoy en route for a meeting with President Roosevelt in Newfoundland waters. *Prince of Wales* is strongly escorted but intelligence reports indicate two German commerce raiders proceeding north from the South Atlantic. One is believed to be *Scharnhorst* the other a converted merchantman. I am ordered to detach with all escorts except two destroyers and steam towards the Germans to intercept. Commodore will assume command of remaining escorts. The priority is obvious and the situation most urgent.'

Without comment the Commodore handed the message to Hampton. He said, 'This won't be Winston's wish. Very likely he doesn't even know. He wouldn't leave a convoy without protection.'

'An *empty* convoy,' Hampton said.

Kemp gave a hard laugh. 'Not quite empty! Just add up all the crews, Captain. However, those are the orders. We just push on. No option!'

Williams said, 'We're moving into safer waters, sir. Beyond U-boat range.'

'We won't count too many chickens, Williams. And the information about Churchill is to be kept to the bridge.' Kemp moved away, paced the bridge wing as he had done so many times. To reduce the escort so drastically was an extreme measure whether or not the convoy was moving into safer waters; it was going to be bad for morale, would leave a very naked feeling as the warships turned to the south and steamed away. The little ships, the corvettes, had already withdrawn for home waters as indicated by NCSO in the Clyde, and even their departure had left a gap both in the defences and in the minds of the merchant crews who had watched them go. Soon the tankers would be detaching for the Gulf of Mexico – soon, but not yet. As this thought came to Kemp a light started flashing from CS29's signal bridge and Leading Signalman Mouncey banged the shutters of his signalling projector in acknowledgement. This time the signal was in plain language, and Mouncey read it out to the waiting officers.

'Commodore from CS29, sir. Tankers *British Light*, *British Lantern* and *British Leader* will accompany me for refuelling destroyers in suitable weather conditions and will then detach in accordance with previous orders.'

'Thank you, Mouncey. Williams –'

'Sir?'

'Make to the tankers: You are to detach with CS29 and then come under his orders.'

'Aye, aye, sir. Mouncey?'

'Yessir!'

Kemp listened to the rigmarole, the repetition to Mouncey of what he had just said to Williams. The RN was something of a marvel insofar as it found time to work at all amidst all the bull and flannel. All the niceties had to be observed, and that wasn't just as between Williams and the leading signalman. It was as between CS29 and himself. The Rear-Admiral could more expeditiously have made the signal direct to the tankers himself, but no, that would cut out the Commodore of the

45

convoy, rip across his responsibilities. Sometimes Kemp thought he was just a messenger, a signal link between the escort and his merchant ships. Very largely that was so; but not any longer, not this time, not all the way in to Halifax.

In a few more minutes the convoy would be on its own and so would he, the Commodore. He would be in total command of thirty-four merchant ships plus two destroyers. They would succeed or fail, arrive in Nova Scotia or sink *en route*, depending upon his yet-to-be-proven ability to outwit any enemy that might be in the vicinity.

[vi]

Pemmel had gone along to the main office after all, but had skipped breakfast as he usually did, making do with a cup of strong black coffee to follow the brandy and ginger ale. He found his deputy purser in conference with the chief and second stewards. They all looked up as Pemmel entered. Mr Portway thought there was one thing about the purser: even when his eyes looked red in the whites he was always well turned out dresswise – he had his steward largely to thank for that, of course.

'Morning, sir,' the chief steward said.

'Good morning, Mr Sandys. Anything you want of me?'

'Not really, sir. Just a reminder: Captain's Rounds, 1100 hours.'

'God damn . . . what day of the week is it?'

It was the deputy purser who answered. 'Saturday, sir.'

'Ha!' Stupid of him to have asked. Captain's Rounds was always on Saturday. Pemmel banged his way into his private office, sat down and put his head in his hands. He felt ill again, his stomach heaving. He was losing his grip and hoped it wasn't becoming obvious. A knock came at his door and the second steward entered. Pemmel looked up.

'What is it, Mr Portway?'

'Permission to alter the last lot of overtime sheets, sir.'

'See the deputy purser. You know the drill.'

'Yes, sir. But Mr Lewis said to see you, sir, seeing as the sheets have gone through the Portage Bill.'

46

'Already?' The Portage Bill was the account of the crew's wages, overtime payments, allotments, fines, income tax and insurance deductions and so on. Even with no passengers aboard, there was still work for the purser's department to do. 'Someone's been conscientious, evidently. All right, Portway, tell Mr Lewis he can make the alteration.' He paused. 'What's it all about?'

Portway coughed. 'Dispute from some of the bedroom stewards, sir.'

'Dispute?'

'Bit of a moan, sir.'

'They haven't got enough overtime – even though the cabins are empty, and they haven't enough work even to fill the normal hours of duty?'

Mr Portway shuffled his feet. 'Well, sir. You know how it is, sir.'

'Yes, yes, I do. They have to keep their families in the style to which they've become accustomed – by way of unworked overtime. All right, Mr Portway, go ahead and work your ungodly fiddles only don't make it too obvious, eh?'

'Thank you very much, sir,' Mr Portway said, and backed out of the door obsequiously. Bedroom stewards were only bedroom stewards but when they banded together they could be a flaming nuisance to a second steward who liked peace and quiet – and good bonuses for himself. He looked at his watch: early yet, but he had things to see to, and if he spun them out he'd be right on time to bum a noggin off the chief steward at 1030. He went about his work, ponderously, carrying a sheaf of papers: you always looked busy when you carried a sheaf of papers and never mind what the subject matter happened to be. Sharp at 1030, which he knew from experience was the exact moment the chief steward relaxed on Saturday mornings with a bottle of beer before Captain's Rounds, Mr Portway knocked at the cabin door and went in, trying to look surprised at how well he had timed his arrival.

'Sorry to butt in, Chief –'

'Save your lying breath,' Sandys said amiably, 'and shove your arse in a chair.'

'Well, don't mind if I do. Thanks.'

'All ready for the skipper, are we?'

47

Portway nodded. 'All ready. Nice and easy when the ship's empty.'

'Still get accumulations of dust.'

Portway nodded and took a tankard of beer from the chief steward's hand. Dust. He knew captains, and he knew Captain Hampton in particular. Dust was his hobby and he knew instinctively where to look, where to draw his hand across the top of a steam pipe or similar and have it come away dirty. Then the rocket went right down the line: staff captain, chief officer, purser – if the dust was in the accommodation – chief steward, second steward. Mr Portway did his own bollocking afterwards until the actual miscreant was discovered and taught a thing or two. This time he'd been round all the accommodation twice, just to make sure. He was about to tell Mr Sandys this when the Tannoy came on, informatively, from the bridge.

'This is the Captain speaking. The naval escort is about to withdraw. There is no cause for any concern, the situation in regard to the convoy is in hand.'

That was all. The chief steward gazed blankly at Portway and said, 'Well, luv-a-duck, eh? What's all that in aid of?'

FIVE

If so many of the convoy crews were thinking in their quiet moments of home, of wives and girlfriends, parents and brothers and sisters, then an equal number of thoughts were winging out across the seas from the home front. Naturally, the tightest possible security screen had been thrown around the mission of HMS *Prince of Wales* and the fact of the vital meeting between Prime Minister and President. A handful of persons were in full possession of the facts; Mr Churchill had embarked in total secrecy and the *Prince of Wales*, Britain's newest and most powerful battleship, had slipped away into the dawn mists from Scapa Flow, as anonymously as was possible, carrying the hopes of a war-torn country across the seas to the New World.

Much secrecy: so the families knew nothing, had no knowledge that now their menfolk were being left unguarded. But no matter: they would have worried anyway, since they worried all the time when their minds were not otherwise occupied. One of them was Patricia Redgrave, Captain Redgrave's sister, a spinster of thirty-five who looked after her father, a widower. They lived in York, a house off the main road running into the city from Harrogate and Green Hammerton. Peter Redgrave filled Patricia's life: the father was tiresome, demanding, rude and unloved, and the fact of his continued existence had kept the daughter chained to spinsterhood. That, and nothing else: she was attractive enough to have married and she'd had her chances but she'd been loyal to her father, who was an invalid, and had never felt it fair to ask any husband to take him on.

The news from Liverpool earlier had been shattering: she had wept for Peter and prayed for him to come to York but beyond one quick visit he had not done so. Now she prayed for his safe return, knowing nothing of the current state of affairs aboard the *Stephen Starr*. She knew her father worried too, though he didn't say much. He was too preoccupied with his own state of ill-health, had too much to say on that subject to have speech for anything else. There were only so many hours in a day . . .

Mary Kemp worried too, down south in Meopham. John had a hard job to do, mentally and physically wearing, always at sea – but he'd been at sea all his working life. She believed he would come through the war: she had a strong belief in God and she knew her prayers were going to be answered, so her worries were more for John's day-to-day life than his safety and eventual homecoming.

In Thurrock in Essex Mrs Portway, as frigid as ever, had no idea that a girl called Mabel in Grays, not so far away, was worrying about her husband, although, when on Herbert Portway's last leave she'd been shopping with him in Grays, there had been a curious incident that had bothered her for a while and had then been forgotten: Herbert, not looking where he was going, had bumped stomachs with a fattish young lady outside the Co-op, quite an accident, but there had been some confusion, startled looks from both of them and the young lady's face very red, more as if they knew each other than reciprocal apologies between strangers over a bit of clumsiness. Had she but known it, that was Mabel. Mabel – a case of fat calling to fat perhaps, plus a certain mutual unattractiveness – was in love with Herbert Portway. They saw quite a lot of one another when his ship was in Tilbury: Mabel worked in Tilbury and it was comparatively easy for a second steward to find business ashore, comparatively easy for a second steward to find good excuses why he couldn't get home to a wife in Thurrock and by no means impossible for that second steward to bring a popsie aboard to his cabin in the bowels of the ship. A shade more difficult in wartime perhaps than it had been in peace, but not impossible. As for Mabel, she had no ties and could always take time off work on the ground of feeling seedy. It wasn't as though Herbert Portway was continually on the scene.

Mabel was one of the worriers, whenever Mr Portway was at sea. She always feared the worse: he had come into her life some four years earlier, – she worked, as now in a laundry and Mr Portway had come ashore to negotiate for the laundering of the stewards' gear, or the gear of such as were not on leave, the liner's own laundry being temporarily out of commission due to a recalcitrant electric fault. It had been a case of love at first sight through the steamy mist of Mabel's working environment, at any rate on her part. To Mr Portway she was just another bit of fluff that might prove willing and did. He seldom thought about her when he wasn't with her, other than to hope to goodness she never got a bun in the oven and tried to pin it on him . . .

He wasn't thinking about her or any of the others now, as the *Ardara*'s staff captain made Rounds in the place of Captain Hampton who was otherwise occupied on the bridge as the warship escort withdrew to the south.

[ii]

The naked feeling had come. Commodore Kemp watched as more signals were made between cs29 and the rest of the escort. A flag hoist crept colourfully to the cruiser's starboard fore yardarm. Leading Signalman Mouncey trained a telescope on to it. Within the minute it was hauled down and Mouncey reported to the Commodore.

'Executive, sir.'

'Thank you, Mouncey.'

That was when the warships made their turn to port, increasing speed when they had done so. They steamed away through the gale, taking the three tankers with them. Kemp was lucky, he supposed, to be left with the RFA.

'Williams?'

'Sir?'

'Make to cs29: Good luck go with you all.'

Mouncey said suddenly, 'Rear-Admiral's signalling, sir.' He read it off. 'May God have mercy on us all.'

Williams asked, 'Do you still wish to make your signal, sir?'

'Yes,' Kemp said.

He looked around at the bridge personnel – Hampton, Williams, the two Officers of the Watch, Leading Signalman Mouncey, the ship's quartermaster and the bridge messengers and telegraphsmen. He looked out across the gale-torn sea at the accompanying ships plodding along for Halifax, all now wide open to attack. He felt very lonely. The two remaining destroyers steaming ahead of the convoy to port and starboard brought little feeling of security. There was a similar sense of loss throughout the ship: all personnel not on watch or caught up with Captain's Rounds were on deck, watching the inexplicable retreat of the heavy cruisers and the destroyers and the old battleship wallowing in the troughs and cutting through the wave crests to fling the tons of water back over her fo'c'sle to swill around the fifteen-inch turrets now moving to the defence of the Prime Minister. Not that anyone other than those on the *Ardara*'s bridge knew anything about that; Kemp's order had been strictly adhered to and no rumours had spread, no rumours, that was, that came anywhere near the facts. There was a similar situation aboard the rest of the ships of the convoy. Only the Commodore had been told; the masters and their crews were left to speculate. Aboard the *Ardara* there was a lot of speculation. To say that everyone was dazed would have been an understatement. It was unbelievable. Not unnaturally in the circumstances, the navy itself was taking the blame. A crowd of galley hands right aft on E deck, hanging over the guardrails of the open deck-space accorded the lower orders, were loud in their condemnation.

'Bloody yellow-bellies –'

'Pissin' off and leavin' us to it!'

The voice of common sense was there as well, insisting that there had to be a good reason, but it was shouted down. The only reason was the navy's own safety. The anti-navy sentiments took no time to reach the naval ratings who manned the ancient six-inch LA guns and the close-range weapons. Twelve DEMS – Defensively Equipped Merchant Ships – gunnery rates plus two leading seamen qualified as captains of the guns first class, with the assistance of some members of the *Ardara*'s own crew trained for the job by naval gunnery instructors. These latter mostly manned the ship's anti-aircraft armament, which

52

consisted of three Lewis guns and four 40-mm Bofors, mounted along the boat deck, plus two light machine-guns mounted in the bridge wings. The six-inch were manned only in action but there were always four ack-ack gunners on watch. In general charge was a petty officer with the non-substantive rating of gunlayer – PO Frapp, a pessimistic man, a pensioner of the Royal Fleet Reserve, three good-conduct badges, indigestion, and elderly to be still at sea. He had first seen service as a seaman boy before the 1914–18 war, back in the *Dreadnought* days.

A deputation waited on Petty Officer Frapp, complaining of hostility.

'I know, lads.' Frapp pushed his cap back and scratched at his head, grizzled grey in a fringe around a bald top. 'Only to be expected, I reckon. Me, I'm looking for a reason too. Could be anything.'

'Another convoy . . . under attack somewhere south?'

'No, that won't wash. Each escort to its own convoy, that's the flaming rule, lad. You don't shift things around like that, rob Peter to pay Paul.'

'There's going to be trouble, PO. Some of us . . . we're going to hit back if that bloody galley rabble don't shut their traps –'

Frapp shook a warning finger. 'Cool it. We don't want that sort of thing aboard. Tell you what. I'll go and see that Williams, see if he knows anything. Or Mouncey, maybe.'

[iii]

Frapp's journey to the bridge proved unnecessary. He was on his way when the Tannoy came on again – Kemp's voice, speaking to the crew with the formal permission of Captain Hampton. He confirmed: no reason to be alarmed. The escort was required elsewhere, in waters more liable to contain German forces, and the convoy was not expected to steam into any difficulties. A situation report had just been received from the Admiralty: there was nothing indicated on the plot, nothing between the convoy's position and Halifax. But as a precaution escorts would be leaving Halifax and were expected to rendezvous in forty-eight hours and take them over.

53

That, as Frapp said, was something. Things weren't so bad that they couldn't get worse, he said with a misguided attempt at humour. Anyway, Kemp's words had improved the atmosphere and the resentment against the navy simmered down. Then, just after the midday dinner, Frapp was sent for to go to the bridge.

He went up at once and reported to Lieutenant Williams. 'You wanted me, sir?'

'The Commodore.' Williams turned about, approached Kemp and saluted. 'Petty Officer Frapp, sir, reporting.'

Kemp came away from the bridge screen, returned Frapp's salute. 'Guns, Frapp.'

'Yessir?'

'As I said on the Tannoy, there's absolutely no cause for alarm. But we must be prepared for any emergency, naturally. I know you've been carrying out exercises on passage, but now I want gun-drill stepped up. Exercise action twice each watch – day and night. Get your guns' crews right on the top line – understood, Frapp?'

'Yessir.'

'And another thing: I want you to reorganize your watch and quarter bill. I want both the six-inch manned with skeleton crews from now until we make the rendezvous with the escorts out of Halifax. It'll no longer be good enough to have just the close-range weapons manned.'

'Aye, aye, sir,' Frapp said.

'If anything does happen, the convoy's going to be largely dependent on the naval guns' crews embarked aboard the merchant ships – that's obvious. The destroyers can't cover the whole convoy. All right, Frapp, thank you.'

When the PO had left the bridge, Kemp told off Williams to signal all ships that they were to bring their guns' crews to a similar state of readiness. By nightfall that day the weather had shown signs of moderating, returning to more seasonal conditions. The glass, which had started a slow rise, went up fast during the night and by dawn the sea had flattened considerably, with all the ships riding more steadily. Kemp, who had remained on the bridge throughout the night, remarked to Williams on the change.

'Not so good, in certain circumstances.'

'No, sir.' There was no need to spell it out: they both knew what better weather could bring.' The convoy was not, in fact, wholly in the clear yet. Hitler had some very long-range U-boats; also, it was not impossible, as Kemp knew, for a German surface raider to steal down through the Denmark Strait past Greenland's eastern coastline and emerge into the North Atlantic to head for the convoy tracks. Not impossible, but perhaps not likely: in theory such a raider should encounter the armed merchant cruisers of the British Northern Patrol. The poor old AMCs . . . they might be sunk but at least they would make a report and the main battle units of the Home Fleet could then be sent out from Scapa and the Firth of Forth.

Kemp looked around: there was no one close enough to overhear. In a low voice he said to Williams, 'I wonder what this meeting's all about. Any ideas?'

'Not a clue, sir. At a guess, I'd say Mr Churchill's trying to prod the Americans into the war.'

'That's my idea too. A kind of grand alliance, reaching across the Atlantic. Well, I wish them luck!'

Williams nodded. 'Yes, sir, very much so. If the Yanks come in . . . well, it would make all the difference. I suppose they'd share the escort duties for one thing?'

'Yes. Just what we need. The poor bloody country's bleeding to death . . . and then there's their army, all those fresh troops. Not good for Hitler at all!' Kemp paused, lifted his binoculars and scanned the seas ahead and to either bow. Flattening out, but leaving the usual swell behind the departed gale. That sea still looked empty without the escort's protection. He said, 'D'you know, Williams, I've a feeling we're on the coat-tails of history – of history about to be made.'

'Perhaps we are, sir.'

Kemp looked at his assistant's somewhat blank face. 'Does that do anything to you, Williams?'

'Do anything, sir?'

Kemp gave a sigh. 'No. I see that it doesn't.'

'Well . . . not really, sir.'

'Pity.' Kemp had plenty of imagination; he believed young Williams hadn't any beyond his sense of self-importance and the dash he might cut with the girls when they reached

Halifax. There was something of a Brylcreem image about Lieutenant Williams, as though the creases in his uniform trousers were of more importance than the conduct of the convoy. He was always very well turned out beneath the layers of wet-weather gear and this morning, with the weather so fine, he was simply beautiful. Kemp turned away and went into the wheelhouse for a word with the watchkeepers, still thinking about history, which meant a lot to him. Twenty-odd years after the event, he was still glad he'd been present when the German High Seas Fleet had steamed under escort of Admiral Beatty to its final anchorage in the waters of Scapa Flow: that had been history, so had the act of scuttling when a whole navy had opened its seacocks and gone down to oblivion in the hour of its total defeat. Kemp, as a seaman, was glad enough that he hadn't witnessed *that* sad scene. There had certainly been no gloating from the British Fleet that day.

[iv]

Petty Officer Frapp had been allocated a cabin, all to himself, something he'd never been accorded before. In HM ships, you slept in a hammock unless you were the master-at-arms or managed to survive the rigours of the lower deck and the attentions of the enemy so far as to achieve the rank of warrant officer and above. Frapp really spread himself: it was almost like home. In peacetime some nob would have paid the earth for what he was getting for nothing, a nice single-berth cabin with a wash-basin on B deck . . . talk about posh! On the chest-of-drawers – much better than a ditty box or locker for stowing personal things – he had set up his family photographs. Doris and the kids, though they weren't kids any longer. Ron was twenty-one and already in the Andrew himself, if only as a leading writer in the Commodore's office in RNB Pompey. PO Frapp thought writers a smarmy bunch, not unlike that Williams the convoy had been lumbered with, thought a lot of themselves and filed their fingernails and had smarmed-down hair. Very uppish with common seamen, especially when the latter had any queries about their pay and allowances. They talked double-dutch mostly, baffled brains

56

with bullshit and implied that you had no education. They treated even seaman petty officers as idiots and many a time Frapp had wanted nothing in the world so much as to take one of the pansy little sods by the scruff of the neck and kick his arse all the way across the parade ground from the Pay Office to the seamen's blocks and then stuff his face down a pan in the heads. It irked him continually that Ron was one of them.

The girl, Else, was all right. Risen in the world – married a pilot officer in the RAF! Not that Petty Officer Frapp had any more time for the RAF than for writers, they were such a scruffy and indisciplined shower and never around when wanted, but an officer was a catch. Pilot Officer Pinkney, when they had met, had told Frapp rather grandly that he needn't call him sir and had himself addressed Frapp as Dad, which Frapp liked – being called Dad by an officer was quite something. He had responded by calling Pilot Officer Pinkney son, after a bit of embarrassment and a tendency at first for the 's' sound to be followed by 'ir'.

Petty Officer Frapp, down from the upper deck to catch up on some sleep, looked at his watch, a pocket-watch he'd bought for five bob in Gibraltar years before when serving in a battleship of the Mediterranean Fleet, the flagship *Queen Elizabeth* no less. Just about now, Leading Signalman Mouncey would be coming off watch, his place on the bridge being taken by his side-kick, MacCord. The bunting tossers were berthed with the guns' crews, in a converted stateroom one deck up. Frapp left his cabin and went up the stairs – real *stairs*, in a ship! – and hung about in the vicinity of Mouncey's accommodation, looking busy by shuffling a fistful of lists. Mr Portway wasn't the only one who knew the game.

Mouncey appeared. Frapp looked up. 'Oh – you, Bunts.'

'As ever was, PO.'

'Better up top, eh? Weather, I mean.'

'Yep.'

'Going to turn in?'

'You bet I am,' Mouncey said.

'Don't blame you, but . . . look, sleep comes better after a tot, right?' Frapp edged closer and gave Mouncey a wink. 'Not a word to anyone, Bunts, but I got a bottle of Scotch in my cabin.' Mr Portway, a power in the ship where the bar staff were concerned, had been co-operative. 'Care for a nip, would you, eh?'

'Don't mind if I do,' Mouncey said. 'Thanks a lot, PO.'

They went down and Frapp shut the door firmly, waved Mouncey to a chair and brought his bottle from the cupboard that in peacetime would have held only the bedroom utensil, which in fact was still there. There was a chink of china as Frapp removed the John Haig. In the meantime Mouncey had been studying the photographs.

'Nice-looking girl,' he said, flipping a thumb towards Else. 'Daughter, is she?'

'Married to an RAF officer.'

'You don't say! Cor.' Mouncey shifted target. 'That your missus, PO?'

'Yes.' The less said about Doris the better; she was pure vinegar and her tongue was busy acid, never still. Scraggy as a daddy-long-legs with it. Frapp, his back turned to Doris, poured two tots. They all missed the daily rum issue, the lack of which was the principal drawback of being in a liner rather than a warship.

'Cheerio,' Mouncey said. 'And thanks again.'

'Bottoms up. Don't mention it.' Frapp drank, folding his lips one over the other in appreciation. Then he approached the reason for his hospitality. 'Funny business, all this.'

'What, PO?'

'Withdrawing the escort like.'

'Yer.'

'Commodore doesn't go much on it, I'll bet.'

'No. 'E don't.'

Frapp coughed. 'I heard there was a signal . . .'

'That's right. Cypher. Officers only.'

'Course, yes. You wouldn't know what was in it, would you?'

'No.'

There was a short silence. The curtains over Frapp's scuttle swayed inwards to the *Ardara*'s roll: the swell was heavy still. Firing the six-inch from a ship with such a roll on her would be like trying to train and lay the turrets aboard one of the old County Class cruisers, the 10,000-ton three-funnellers with so much freeboard they rolled their guts out in a flat calm. Frapp tried again, all his curiosity, his innate seaman's urge to pick up the latest buzz, consuming him.

'Dare say you may have heard something, Bunts,' he said. 'Being up there on the bridge, like?'

Mouncey shook his head. 'Not a thing. Not a bloody thing. Commodore, he don't say much.'

'Williams, though?'

'Likewise. Williams don't know he's born, half the time.'

'Not even a buzz?'

'Not even a buzz,' Mouncey said firmly, tongue in cheek. He'd heard all right – enough to have some idea at any rate. He'd heard Lieutenant Williams speak the name, Winston Churchill. That was about all in fact, apart from the Commodore's order that nothing was to be mentioned thereafter. Maybe Winnie had some special task for the escort, but if he had, then Mouncey didn't know what it was. And he wasn't going to open his trap about Churchill. If Frapp talked around the ship, which he would, the Commodore would know very well who to pin it on: himself, Leading Signalman Mouncey, who had no intention of risking his rate. He finished the second whisky and looked hopefully at his empty glass for another, but in vain.

'You can bugger off,' PO Frapp said sourly, having developed a sudden dislike for the sharp-faced little leading signalman, 'if you've got no bloody buzzes.'

Grinning, Mouncey left the cabin. 'Useless bloody article,' Frapp said as the door closed.

[v]

Williams had been with Kemp on the bridge for the latter part of the night and remained there when the Commodore went below for a wash and shave and a change of clothing. And breakfast, which Williams had already been down for. Wartime or not, the food was good. No rationing for those who ploughed the waves in merchantmen or warships. Williams had tucked into grapefruit, cornflakes with condensed milk, kipper, fried egg, bacon, sausages, hot rolls and marmalade and several cups of steaming coffee. Now he felt good as he paced the bridge, back and forth like Kemp, really feeling the assistant commodore and in charge of the convoy until Kemp returned. If anything should happen, it would be up to him to deal with it in the first instance and he rehearsed in his mind what he should do – not for the first time: it was the duty of an officer to think ahead, to visualize situations, use his imagination; and in that imagination Lieutenant Williams had dealt with all manner of emergencies. Fire below, the appearance of a periscope, sudden aircraft attack, the advent of a German pocket-battleship, man overboard, collision between ships of the convoy, some hiatus in the engine-room, defective steering for one reason or another, the sudden and unheralded impact of a torpedo. There was potentially any amount of drama at sea and Williams knew that his list of rehearsals could never be complete; it was always the unexpected, the unrehearsed, that tended to happen and then you were liable to be caught out. Nevertheless Williams went on dreaming, seeing himself as the saviour of the convoy, the one who had in fact thought out the unexpected in advance and had dealt with it, his sense of the dramatic and the heroic dimmed only a little by what would prove to be the fact: his immediate reaction would be to obey the Commodore's standing order: *If anything should happen, call me at once.* And in the meantime, the transport's Officer of the Watch, if not her master, would have acted.

After a while Williams' thoughts shifted elsewhere: they shifted homeward to Hounslow. He thought of his father, travelling daily to the City in a crowded District Line train, carrying his gas-mask dutifully – his father had always been dutiful. If anybody asked him to do anything, he did it, like sacrificing the iron railings in front of the house in aid of the war effort, fondly imagining they'd be turned into guns to blast off at Hitler. Williams believed that to be nothing more than a ploy, something dreamed up by Lord Beaverbrook, or Churchill himself, to make the man in the street, the civilian, feel he was doing his bit. His father had been angry when he'd suggested that on his last leave, telling him he shouldn't belittle what the civilians were doing. Look, his father had said, at the Home Guard and, come to that, the ARP wardens like himself. He'd got in such a state that Williams had banged out of the house, calling out to his mother that he would be back late, and had gone to the pictures and sat through Deanna Durbin.

He'd gone by himself, wishing he had a girl to take. He hadn't got a girlfriend and really he couldn't understand why. He'd tried hard enough but somehow things never seemed to click, or not for long. It wasn't as though he was a freak: he knew he looked smart in his uniform, top button always undone, handkerchief tucked into left sleeve, stiff collar, cap at a Beatty-ish angle, never a hair out of place. To think of some of the scruff girls went out with! But whenever he found a girl who seemed likely, he never had the right conversation. Perhaps it was too naval; even the odd Wren in Portsmouth or Greenock or wherever seemed to tire of naval slang and his yarns about old so-and-so and how tight he'd got last time in port. It always petered out, generally by way of a broken date followed by excuses, but once by more direct methods. A leading Wren called Judy, in Greenock.

She'd stopped suddenly one early evening, in the main street while they'd been on their way to the Naval Officers' Club for a drink.

She said impatiently, 'Oh, for God's sake, Paul!'

'What d'you mean?' He'd stared, blankly. He hadn't done anything that he was aware of.

'Stop looking at yourself, can't you?'

'I –'

'You haven't missed a shop window yet,' she said, really angry. 'Talk about Narcissus! Looking over your shoulder all the way along.'

He was hurt; his face flamed and he blurted it out. 'Oh, piss off, why don't you!'

Then she had slapped his face. There happened to be a naval patrol passing, trudging along the gutters wearing belts and gaiters, watching out for ratings who failed to salute officers. The seamen had grinned openly; Williams had been mortified. Of course, he could have run the girl in – a leading Wren, striking an officer, a Court Martial offence if ever there was one! Anyway, that was the last he'd seen of Judy. She had been fairly recent, not long before he'd got his present appointment as assistant commodore, and he wished she'd lasted. It was nice to have a girl at home to think about when

61

upon the lonely wastes of the sea. It wasn't the same, having only his parents to think about, the romance was absent.

But a time would come; Williams thought ahead to Halifax. Canadian girls might be more forthcoming, less inhibited and less formal than their English counterparts. After all, Canada had been a pioneering country with wagon trains, gold rushes, saloons and doxies. Some of that spirit must linger yet.

Williams was thinking un-naval thoughts when the escorting destroyer on the port bow of the convoy began flashing back towards the Commodore and was answered by Signalman MacCord, who reported to Lieutenant Williams.

'Contact, sir, bearing red two five!'

Williams went into the wheelhouse at the double and, wrenching back the voice-pipe cover to Kemp's cabin, called the Commodore to the bridge.

SIX

Aboard the *Stephen Starr* the engines were turning over again but Captain Redgrave's condition had worsened and Flynn was a worried man. The wound was an angry red and the flesh was very swollen and there was a lot of pus. Flynn began to worry about gangrene: could you get gangrene of the thigh? You probably could, and being high up made it the more serious. It wouldn't have far to go to reach the torso, which was something you couldn't very well chop off. Flynn consulted with the chief officer and the chief steward, out of the Captain's hearing – Redgrave was continuing to insist on remaining in the wheelhouse and was shivering most of the time like a castanet.

The chief steward reckoned he had a smattering of medical knowledge; it had been he who had advised Flynn over the preparation of kaolin. Now he confirmed Flynn's worst fears.

'Gangrene,' he said. 'Gangrene for sure. Only one cure.'

Flynn knew what that was. He looked up at the chief officer, his face crumpled with anxiety. Hardy said, 'We can't do that. Amputate, I mean. We could be wrong, and anyway we haven't the know-how.'

'No, sir, nor the anaesthetic.'

The chief steward said, 'There's always Scotch. That's how they did it in the sailing ships. Fill 'em up, uncorked bottle in the mouth.'

Hardy said, 'No, we can't possibly do it. It'd kill him.'

'He'll die if we don't, sir.'

'You really think so?'

'Yes, sir, I do.' The chief steward went on, 'I've seen gangrene before now. In the trenches, in the last lot – I was a pongo then, and never no more, that's why I came to sea the moment I got my demob back in '19. Gangrene took 'em off like flies if they didn't get back to the base surgeons fast. Which they didn't half the time.'

Hardy nodded, faced with a wicked decision – what to advise the Captain. And suppose he went unconscious? Then it wouldn't be a case of advice but of making up his own mind to it. Flynn was thinking of what they hadn't got aboard: scalpels. Or if they had once, they hadn't any more. Of course, the galley had knives and the chief steward could procure something, say one of the big cleavers used by the ship's butcher. Or maybe a nice slim carving knife . . . but that wouldn't go through a thigh bone, it would have to be a cleaver. Flynn shuddered. He made a suggestion even though he knew Mr Hardy would have thought of it already. He asked, 'How about sending a message, sir? Ask for assistance . . . or medical advice, sir, maybe?'

Hardy was definite. 'The Captain would never authorize breaking wireless silence. Nor could I.'

'But that Focke-Wulf, sir. They know we're here.'

'A while ago now – we've moved on, back into anonymity. We can't jeopardize that, Flynn. In any case, where would the assistance come from?'

There was no anwser to that; the convoy, presumably the nearest ships to them, wouldn't send a doctor back, not now. There was just a chance they might pick up a homeward-bound HX convoy but that was very slim, it would be like the needle-search in the haystack, since they had no idea of the sailings out of Halifax date-wise. Anyway, it would take too long. Flynn had an idea that if the chief officer didn't decide to operate mighty fast, then the Captain was going to join his wife and kids – and maybe he'd not be minding that at all.

[ii]

When Mason Kemp reached the *Ardara*'s bridge the action alarm was sounding and the guns' crews were already doubling to their stations while down below Mr Portway once again supervised the running-out of the fire hoses. Kemp, through his binoculars, watched the escorting destroyer on the port bow of the convoy breaking off to make its attack on the reported bearing and a few minutes later felt the heavy thuds as the depth-charges exploded deep down. Spouts of water rose and the destroyer on the starboard bow raced across under full power to join in the attack, and there were more explosions. So far as Kemp could see there was no result: no patch of oil, no black, sinister bows or conning-tower emerging hurt, just nothing.

Then there was a shout from Williams. 'Port beam, sir! A periscope, I'm almost sure.'

Two seconds later confirmation came from Leading Signalman Mouncey. 'Torpedo trails, sir, port beam, two of 'em coming straight for us!'

Kemp saw them, between the two leading ships of the port column. He spoke to Captain Hampton, urgently. 'Turn towards, Captain –'

Hampton gave the order: 'Port twenty!'

Ponderously, the big transport swung to point her bows to the torpedo trail and give a smaller target. Hampton watched closely, ready to check the swing. Kemp said, 'Hoist the warning signal, Mouncey.'

'Going up now, sir.' Mouncey had the flags already bent on. A colourful hoist sped fast to the signal yardarm. Now it would be up to the individual ships to take their own avoiding action; Kemp held his breath, gripped the bridge rail until his knuckles stood out white. The trail of the tin fish was now plain to see, coming down on them to pass along their port side.

'I think we're in the clear, sir,' Hampton said.

'Yes. But some other poor bugger probably isn't.' Kemp waited in anguish. Astern of him now that he had turned, the ships of the convoy were moving on. The *Aratapu*, also of the Mediter-ranean-Australia Line, was one of those coming up to dead astern. Behind her was a 15,000-ton ammunition ship, fortun-ately with empty holds ready for Halifax. Farther out to the north were the one remaining tanker and a number of cargo vessels. The double explosion came within the next two minutes and Kemp swung round to see a sheet of flame and an outpouring of thick, black smoke from the 15,000-tonner. A few more seconds and another explosion came, from farther aft this time – the convoy was drawing ahead of the U-boat now. Kemp passed the word to Hampton to bring the *Ardara* back on her course, and as he did so he saw the escorts racing back along the convoy's flank, about to go into another attack.

Williams made his report to the Commodore. 'First casualty, sir, ss *Bellman*, master, Captain Harkness. Two torpedo hits. Second, ss *Cerberus*, Captain –'

'Yes, all right, Williams. Hampton, I'd like you to take her in and stand by the *Bellman*, if you please.'

'Aye, aye, sir. Boats away?'

Kemp nodded. 'She's going. And we can leave the U-boat to the escort. But keep way on – circle round.'

Hampton passed the orders. The staff captain and chief officer left the bridge at the rush and along the boat deck three nested boats were swung out on the davits and run on the falls to the waterline, their crews embarked at the davits. Slipped, they pulled away fast as the troopships circled, a rescue fleet making for the ammunition ship, which was well down fore and aft and settling in the water, an obvious loss, as was the *Cerberus* which was being attended by boats from another cargo vessel.

Two more gone . . . Kemp's face was sombre. There would be more casualties, more families back at home shattered. He watched as later the *Ardara*'s boats came back to be hooked on to the falls and hoisted to the embarkation deck. The moment they had been hooked on, Kemp had given the order to increase speed again. As the shivering survivors were lifted out Kemp heard screaming, a sustained high note of agony. He clenched his fists, fought to resist an urge to put his hands over his ears. He was thinking that the ship's doctor was going to be a busy man and hoped he'd be found sober enough to cope. Looking aft from the bridge wing he saw the doctor with his assistant, the recently qualified man from Bart's, bending over the injured men, then his attention was distracted by Lieutenant Williams.

'Message come from the radio room, sir. Another Admiralty cypher. Addressed Commodore, sir, prefix Most Urgent.'

'Very well, get on to it.'

'Aye, aye, sir.' Williams turned away and went at the rush down the ladder to the boat deck and his cabin, where he brought the naval cypher tables from the safe and got down to work. It was not a long signal like the previous one. From the bridge Mason Kemp watched as the torpedoed vessels disappeared in a swirl of sea, both of them abandoned just in time. The escorts carried on with their attack. The convoy proceeded, the columns sorted out again. No collisions: that, Kemp thought, was something to be thankful for. He looked out towards the *Aratapu*, steaming majestically in her grey paint, and wondered how many years would have to pass before both she and the *Ardara* would be back in the company's colours of light blue hull with dark blue boot-topping, and brilliant white upperworks. Or whether indeed either of them would survive the war.

[iii]

The embarked survivors had been sorted out now. Those who were fit were allocated cabins by Purser Pemmel's staff and arrangements were made for them to be provided with dry clothing and a meal, plus hot drinks or brandy. One of the seriously injured was the master of the ammunition ship, who had been taken by the blast as he had leaned from his port bridge wing just at the moment one of the torpedoes had hit. There was little left of his face and the head injuries were bad. With the other wounded he was carried below to the sick bay. The ship's surgeon had never known the place filled up. In peacetime the casualties had been mainly seasick passengers and they hadn't needed the sick bay's facilities, or the hospital as it had been called then. There had been the occasional heart attack or stroke, and those had usually remained in their own staterooms, at any rate if they were travelling first class. The hospital's inhabitants when there were any had tended to be tourist class, the sharers of cabins, who paid less than the first class for the ship's medical facilities and surgeon's fees. And since the outbreak of war and the requisition by the government, the *Ardara* had been lucky in her convoys. She had sailed mainly south around the Cape of Good Hope for Australia, returning with Australian and New Zealand troops. Down there the threat had been principally from the German commerce raiders, surface ships that the *Ardara* and her consorts had mercifully not met.

So the doctor was unprepared mentally and was shaking like a leaf at the thought of his own inadequacy to cope. Just before the boats with the survivors had been hooked on to the falls, he had taken a stiffener and he knew the result was on his breath even

67

though he had sucked a couple of peppermint tablets. Everyone else knew it too: peppermint on the doctor's breath had only the one meaning.

Sister Jackie Ord took him in hand. 'Dr Barnes can manage, Doctor.'

'Are you sure?'

'Yes. He's very competent.'

'If there's any difficulty . . .'

'He'll have your advice, Doctor, naturally.'

'Yes, well.' The surgeon dithered, hand pulling at his jaw. 'Frankly, you know, I don't feel too well. My stomach . . .' He laid a hand on it, and grimaced. He wove a path towards the lavatory, entered and locked himself in. Sister Ord reported to Dr Barnes and the junior sister that the boss was suffering the squitters due to pressure of events and would remain glued to the lavatory seat until the drama was over. At least he could do no harm there but was technically available.

Just before luncheon, the *Bellman*'s master died; soon after this two more of the survivors, men with widespread burns who had been among those screaming out in agony as they were embarked, also died. There was in fact nothing more that could have been done had he been present and *compos mentis*, but the doctor was seen to go to his cabin with tears running down his cheeks.

[iv]

Before the deaths had taken place Lieutenant Williams had reported to the Commodore with the plain-language version of the Admiralty's signal. It was stark enough. Interception of German wireless traffic and patient work by the cypher-crackers of the British intelligence services had produced some vital operational information: two large U-boat packs were in station across the track of the OB convoy, between their current position as estimated by the Admiralty and the coast of Nova Scotia.

'No orders, Williams. In the signal.'

'No, sir. Just the warning.'

'And no indication how far off the packs are.' Kemp's face was set hard. 'We're moving westwards of the meridian of Cape

Farewell now – this is totally unexpected so far west. And more than I'd ever have expected anyway, against a convoy in ballast!'

'Yes, sir.' Williams paused. 'It occurs to me, sir, they may have been moved into position ready to attack us homeward.'

'Unlikely. Time at sea, time submerged and all that . . . and they're at risk from our escort. The Asdics . . . they'd be giving the game away, surely?'

Williams said, 'They could lie doggo, down deep. Or they may not be right across the track. The Admiralty won't be that sure, sir. They could be well out to either side, north or south . . . just waiting.'

'Waiting for what, Williams?'

'Well, sir, our homeward run. Attack the HX.'

'Or something else.'

'Yes, sir. That did occur to me.'

Each avoided implication of the Prime Minister by name or office. Kemp turned away and began pacing the bridge, up and down on the strip of coconut matting. Always he thought better on the move; at the convoy conferences he was always restive, sitting on his bottom and listening to other men giving detailed instructions and assessments and so on. In a similar fashion to a piper who played best when on the march, Commodore Mason Kemp found that motion helped his decisions.

And this was a big one.

He saw three alternatives: one, he could hold his course and speed and rely on the escort and the zig-zag; two, he could order an alteration north or south and hope to elude the hunting packs, if the OB convoy was their target, but either choice could be the wrong one; three, he could turn the convoy and steam back on a reciprocal of his present course. That would keep them in the clear, at least as regards the reported threat ahead. But it didn't take Kemp many seconds to reject this alternative. It would be an act of cowardice and one that would be likely to upset the overall strategy of the North Atlantic and its intricate convoy system, the shuttle back and forth. And the U-boats, frustrated in their plans, might find that other target, Winston Churchill heading west aboard the *Prince of Wales* – if they didn't know about that already.

'Williams?'

'Yes, sir.' Lieutenant Williams, apprised not long after leaving the Clyde that his lord and master didn't like being followed up

69

and down the bridge, had hung back in the port wing. Now he came forward, the dog given its bone.

'Pass the signal by lamp to the escorts.' The destroyers had broken off their attack some while earlier and had reported no luck. 'When they've acknowledged, make: Intend to maintain my course.'

'Aye, aye, sir. A word about full alertness, sir?'

Kemp snapped at his assistant. 'For God's sake, Williams, they don't need that!'

Williams, red-faced again, passed the word to Mouncey, who began clacking the big SP in the bridge wing. As the signals and acknowledgements were made, Kemp's mind was busy. His own belief was that the U-boats were after bigger game than an empty convoy, a point he had already made to Williams. True, they might, just might, be awaiting the homeward run with all the Canadian troops embarked, all the ammunition and guns, all the other war materials and supplies for the civilian population that was facing the possibility of starvation if the merchant fleet was too far decimated.

It might be that, or it might not.

Surely, Kemp thought, the biggest prize of war for Adolf Hitler would be the despatch of Winston Churchill. The mind boggled at what the result would be back home and overseas, in every part of the world where British and Allied troops were fighting, backs to the wall in a war that wasn't going all that well, when the BBC News bulletins and the world's press blew the shattering facts, HMS *Prince of Wales* sunk, Winston Churchill dead. They might try to hold the truth, anyway for a while. But it wouldn't be possible to keep up a pretence for any length of time. With that towering personality gone the facts would show in dither, in a lack of direction, in a terrible weakening of the war effort.

If necessary, the OB convoy must be the decoy.

SEVEN

Mason Kemp believed, had always believed, in keeping his ship's company informed of all matters affecting or likely to affect their welfare. This time it was their lives, and he gave them the facts whilst remaining silent as to the presence, not so far off by now probably, of the British Prime Minister and his entourage. He used the Tannoy and spoke of the information received that a large concentration of U-boats was somewhere ahead. There would be no interruption of the convoy's progress and every man was to be ready in his own sphere of action.

'Which means to be bloody sunk,' Petty Officer Frapp said, thinking of his museum-piece guns in action against a U-boat, a small enough target at the best of times. The convoy was wide open and they all knew it. The merchant ships would just have to steam on stoically, taking independent avoiding action as and when necessary, and hope for the best. There had been more signalling between the Commodore and the senior officer of the escort and when the visual signalling became heavy, Kemp, with the need for secrecy in mind, suggested that the senior officer lay alongside and be embarked by breeches buoy for a conference.

The senior officer concurred; and the destroyer turned sharply, heeling over to port to cross the columns with a big bone in her teeth and make her approach along the starboard side of the *Ardara*. When she was in position and the breeches buoy's gear ready, the two ships equalized their speed, maintaining way throughout, the ropes were sent across and the senior officer, one Commander Phillips, was hauled across the gap, legs protruding like those of a spider through the breeches part of the buoy,

71

hands holding fast to the ropes above his head, an undignified performance.

He was brought to the bridge, where he saluted the Commodore. Kemp walked with him to the port wing, where they conferred together with Captain Hampton and Lieutenant Williams.

Kemp spoke his thoughts about Mr Churchill. 'He's the first priority. Agreed?'

Phillips said, 'Yes, indeed he is, sir –'

'So my intention is to engage the attention of the U-boats. You understand?'

'A sacrifice?'

'Yes,' Kemp said directly.

'A big one.'

'A big reward, Commander. A big man. A vital one! In any case, I have no alternative. We are at sea, so are the U-boats.' Kemp returned to an earlier thought, the one that hadn't lasted. 'I can't turn the convoy back.'

'No, no, that's true, sir. And of course I take your point about the Prime Minister. But –'

'Then let's consider it settled, shall we?' Kemp said briskly. 'It's going to be up to you and your destroyers, I need hardly say – we're just the sitting ducks, but if some of the buggers can be brought to the surface, we have guns to fire at them. And sometimes a lot can be achieved by ramming, as we all know.'

Commander Phillips was sent back to his ship and as soon as he was aboard the destroyer moved away at speed to resume her position on the starboard bow of the convoy. The weather, unkindly enough, was improving all the time; apart from the swell, the sea was virtually flat as the sun began to go down the western sky. There was going to be a brilliant sunset, Kemp thought, blood-red amongst many other colours. Blood was on his mind: he was putting so many lives at risk. Just how many? Give or take a hundred or so, the convoy contained around three thousand souls. Churchill himself would not have considered his own life worth three thousand possible deaths, if the worst came to the worst – taking the most pessimistic view, that was. But this wasn't Churchill's decision and he wouldn't have been the best judge of his own value to the Allied war effort. Kemp fought down strange feelings that rose in him, feelings of acting God, taking Prime Ministerly decisions in a very wide interest. He must not think that way. He was just the convoy Commodore, doing his duty as he saw it. But his heart bled for the lives at risk.

Walking the bridge after the departure of Commander Phillips, Kemp looked aft along the boat deck and for an instant that seemed a lifetime he saw it as he had seen it in peacetime, as master of what had then been a luxury liner homeward bound from Sydney. Those nights in the Indian Ocean, the drifting music that used to come to him as he took a late-night turn up and down the master's deck below the bridge, the gentle hiss of water streaming away into a tumbling wake, the moon's beams slanting across the funnel and the lifeboats, touching the masts, bringing light and shadow across the first-class passengers, the gay evening dresses of the women, the dinner jackets of the men. The bridge watch changing at midnight, the off-going officer filling in the deck log and giving the course and speed to his relief, a similar changeover taking place at the wheel and down below in the engine-room, a never-ending routine at sea where the whole ship never slept all at once. In the passenger alleyways the cabin-crawling taking place, for passengers were human and never more so than when east of Suez . . . the night stewards patrolling in uniform blues even when the rest of the crew were in whites, blue tunics buttoned to the neck, brass buttons, men of special status, reliable and discreet. One of them had once been a colour-sergeant of the Royal Marines . . . where was he now? Still aboard, or recalled to Eastney Barracks and a draft to a warship? Most likely not the latter; he would have been too old.

In point of fact ex-Colour-Sergeant Crump was still aboard the *Ardara* in his peacetime capacity of night steward and had not yet found an opportunity of making his number again with the Commodore, or Captain Kemp as he thought of him still. Captain Kemp would remember him, he was sure, and wouldn't snub him when the occasion arose. There was no bull about Captain Kemp, no snobbery, he had always been man to man, and a man's man with it. Crump had a lot of time for Captain Kemp, as had almost everyone else; even those who had felt the weight of his tongue from time to time recognized that he was fair and that they'd asked for it. Crump as night came down to end that day moved on along the darkened alleyways, the alleyways lit at night by only the police lights. Coming out from a cross alleyway, Crump all but bumped into the ship's master-at-arms, prowling

73

in soft-soled shoes. Master-at-Arms Rockett, an ex-RN regulating petty officer also too old for recall, was a soft-soled-shoe sort of man and had a face to match, pale and lowering and with eyes that didn't meet another man's gaze. Big feet, the prerequisite for the navy's regulating branch, the ship's police – big feet, so it was said, that crushed cockroaches whilst on the snoop at night, hence their sobriquet of crusher.

'Well, Crump?'

'All well, Master.'

'Huh! Look down there, purser's alleyway.'

Crump turned and looked aft, just in time to see a nursing sister's uniform turn into the passage leading to Pemmel's quarters.

'Sister Ord,' MAA Rockett said with a sniff. 'That on again, is it?'

'Not my business to know that, Master,' Crump said.

'Oh yes, it is, you're the night steward on this section –'

'Not for snooping on the ship's officers I'm not. Not unless there's a complaint. Which there never has been. Anyway, Mr Pemmel, he's been sick, a day or two ago, had the doctor, so –'

'Sick my backside,' Rockett said with a short laugh like a bark. 'Pissed to the gills, is Pemmel, half the time. Think Miss Ord's taking his temperature, do you? Time you grew up, Crump.' He paused, said, 'So just watch it, all right?' and moved on, hands clasped behind his back, soft soles shuffling over the polished corticene. Crump shrugged, made a rude gesture towards the departing back, dismissed the 'just watch it' as a bit of bull designed to cover up the fact that Rockett didn't know quite how to disguise the irrelevance of his earlier remarks, or innuendos, about Sister Ord and the purser vis-à-vis Crump's duties, and went along to his pantry. Just as he reached it the purser's buzzer sounded.

Crump knew Mr Pemmel's habits: he already had the sandwiches and coffee ready, two cups and saucers, two plates. A mixed lot of sandwiches, tastefully decorated with parsley which Crump grew himself in a couple of flower pots that lived in the pantry and were taken on deck to get some sun and air whenever possible. He went along to the purser's cabin and knocked discreetly.

'Come in, Crump.'

Crump went in, stood at attention, one hand holding the tray,

74

the other stiffly in line with the seam of his trousers. When speaking to officers, Crump was still the colour-sergeant and training died hard. 'You rang, sir. The usual I don't doubt, sir. Good evening, miss.'

Jackie Ord smiled at him; Pemmel said, 'Thank you, Crump. A man in a million. You'd be ready with the sandwiches even if the ship was going down.'

'That's right, sir.'

'Care for a drink, Crump?' Pemmel asked suddenly and surprisingly. The purser was not normally a generous man and he'd never offered Crump a drink before, though he tipped reasonably enough at the end of each voyage. 'Whisky, is it?'

'On duty, sir –'

'Never mind that and if there's any trouble from Mr Rockett, refer him to me. Sit down, man!'

'Well, sir, I don't mind if I do. Whisky, please, sir.' Crump sat on the settee, his bottom right on the edge and his long, good-humoured face showing that he was ill at ease because he had sensed that both Mr Pemmel and Sister Ord were also on edge. He didn't know why, unless they were worried about the nests of U-boats said to be ahead, and they were all more or less worried about Hitler's antics. At a time like this Crump himself would have given his Royal Marines pension to be back aboard a battleship, say the *Nelson* or the *Rodney* with their bloody great sixteen-inch gun-turrets.

Pemmel got up and brought out a bottle of John Haig, poured Crump a measure and after some slight hesitation added some to his cup of coffee, glancing at Sister Ord as he did so. 'You?' he asked.

She shook her head; her answer was abrupt. 'No, thanks.'

'Suit yourself,' Pemmel said. He raised his cup towards Crump. 'Bottoms up,' he said.

'Your good health, sir.' Crump drank, feeling more and more uncomfortable. He was sure something was up, felt something in the atmosphere.

'You were in the navy,' Pemmel said.

'Royal Marines, sir.'

'Same thing, more or less – no, don't bother to explain the difference, Crump. Point is . . . you were in the last lot, weren't you?'

'I was, sir. Gunner Royal Marine Artillery in them days, sir, the Blue Marines. Royal Marine Light Infantry, they were the Red Marines –'

'Yes, Crump. You were in action, I believe.'

'Yes, sir.' Crump drank some more of his whisky, and wiped the back of a hand across his lips. 'On Y turret I was, sir, aboard the *Good Hope* – armoured cruiser, sir. We got it. I ended up in the drink for a bit, sir. Got picked up, of course.'

'Yes. So you know what it's like.'

'To be in action, sir?'

'To be bloody well sunk, Crump!' Pemmel voice was high, very much on edge.

'Yes, sir. It happens. Nothing you can do about it. Except swim, sir.'

'You were all trained men – seamen. Trained for war, Crump.'

'We were that, sir, yes –'

'Not aboard the *Ardara* we're not.'

'I don't know about that, sir. I don't honest. We've no passengers embarked – *that*'d be scary. But we've faced it ever since the war started, sir. Nothing different now. And you can rely on the deck officers, sir. Specially now Captain Kemp's with us.'

Pemmel gave a nervy laugh. 'Captain Kemp can't stop torpedoes. He may be a bloody marvel but he can't jump overboard and ride 'em away like a horse.'

Crump didn't like that, didn't like any sort of implied disrespect towards Captain Kemp. His normally kindly eyes hardened a little. He didn't know quite how to react; he was about to drink up his whisky when the nursing sister got to her feet and said she was going to turn in. Pemmel nodded, and she left the cabin. There was a funny look in the purser's eyes and after Sister Ord had gone he seemed to lose interest in Crump, who took the hint, drank up, thanked Pemmel again, stood briefly at attention, and went away. Odder and odder, he thought; it was as though he'd been brought in to defuse a delicate situation, be a sort of gooseberry to prevent something developing. When Sister Ord had gone, Pemmel had no further use for him. Crump moved along the alleyway, thinking, his face puckered. What Rockett had said – of course it was basically true. The purser was, or had been, running a hot affair with Sister Ord, Crump couldn't help but be aware of that. Likewise, Mr Pemmel's drinking habits – they were common knowledge, of course. Could be just the whisky, Crump supposed, and the purser was looking for a way out of bedding the girl just because he was incapable.

[ii]

Still some distance to the east of the OB convoy's position and a little south, HMS *Prince of Wales* with her destroyer escort headed at speed for Placentia Bay in Newfoundland. The security was still one hundred per cent and would remain so if the combined efforts of British and American Intelligence could enforce it. Even the American press had been diddled: it was believed that President Roosevelt was aboard the *Potomac*, the presidential yacht, whereas in point of fact he was aboard the USS *Augusta* which would rendezvous with the *Prince of Wales* in Placentia Bay.

With the British Prime Minister aboard the battleship were Harry Hopkins, Roosevelt's confidential aide, together with Field Marshal Sir John Dill: a useful bag for Adolf Hitler. Winston Churchill, revelling in being aboard a warship at sea, seemed to have no worries about his safety. His curiosity was intense: he explored every part of the battleship, asking probing questions, gesticulating with his cigar as he put officers and ratings through analytical interrogation. He worked or played cards in what would normally have been the Admiral's quarters or he watched films in the ship's cinema or he walked the decks as the great screws thundered him westwards for a vital meeting. He was usually awake early, turning out to smoke a cigar on the quarterdeck and chat to the after turrets' crews and breathe the morning freshness; either that, or get down to some early work before breakfast.

During one of these quarterdeck walks, something seemed to be happening. The Prime Minister became aware of signalling between the extended escort and the flag deck of the *Prince of Wales*. He asked what was going on: no one appeared to know. It could be that a U-boat had been reported, an Asdic contact. But there was so sign of the battleship going to action stations.

The Prime Minister climbed many ladders, making his way to the compass platform, where he found the Captain, the navigator, the Officer of the Watch and the chief yeoman of signals staring through binoculars towards the destroyer escort.

'Good morning, Captain.'

The Captain swung round. 'Good morning, sir. I –'

'What's going on, pray?' Cigar smoke drifted across the compass platform. 'A submarine?'

'No, Prime Minister. A merchant ship fallen out from the last OB convoy – she's been having engine trouble, but that's been sorted out. Now there's other trouble – her master's in a bad way.'

'Sick, Captain?'

There was a nod. 'Suspected gangrenous leg. High up in the thigh. Probably not much hope, if the diagnosis is correct.'

'But all possible must be done.'

'Yes, sir. It will be. One of the destroyers will embark him, and he'll be attended by a doctor.'

'Ah. What sort of doctor, Captain?'

'A surgeon lieutenant, sir.'

'Yes. And the medical facilities aboard a destroyer?'

The Captain shrugged. 'Bare necessities.'

'And little room or comfort for an injured man. I beg to suggest, Captain, that your sick bay and your surgeon commander might be more welcome . . .'

'With respect, sir, I think not.' It was not reasonable, the Captain said, to hazard either the Prime Minister or the *Prince of Wales*. To embark a sick man would mean reducing the speed of the battleship and if there were undetected U-boats in the vicinity she would be placed at much risk. Then there was the known presence of surface raiders to the south, who might well elude the heavy ships detached from the OB convoy and make a sudden appearance at a moment when the *Prince of Wales* was unready and not immediately manoeuvrable. The Prime Minister, knowing very well that only the Captain commanded the ship, that only the Captain could make the decision, grew visibly angry. The pugnacious jaw came out, the cigar made stabbing motions. Churchill's mind was made up: the merchant Captain must have the best attention, and that attention was aboard the *Prince of Wales*. Surgeon lieutenants were no doubt competent but their experience was not that of surgeon commanders, and there was presumably a chance that the leg might be saved.

The Captain assessed the situation as a destroyer detached from the escort towards the *Stephen Starr*, now visible to the naked eye. Winston Churchill would seethe and fulminate all the way across the North Atlantic and would arrive at his rendezvous in a fractious mood, and he might quarrel with Roosevelt, himself often not an easy man. The ramifications of a quarrel, of ill temper, would be catastrophic, all Britain's hopes shattered. The Captain conceded: signals were made accordingly and the smile came back to the Prime Minister's face.

[iii]

Redgrave was a very sick man; he was delirious almost all the time now, with just brief periods of lucidity, and in those periods the pain was more than agony. Chief Officer Hardy had still not taken the decision to operate, to amputate. He had agonized himself, sweating blood in an attempt to reach the right decision. Then his problem had been resolved when the lookout high in the foremast had reported a strong force coming up astern. They might be Germans in which case the *Stephen Starr* would be sunk. If they were British there would be succour. It was in the lap of the gods. Hardy recognized the British destroyers with relief, and answered the challenge on his Aldis lamp.

EIGHT

'Mouncey!' Kemp's voice was sharp.

'Yessir?'

'Look alive, man! Destroyer signalling.'

'Sorry, sir.'

Kemp glowered: inefficiency depressed him; signalmen were the eyes of the convoy and they couldn't afford to blink. He had a premonition as to what the signal was: already the escort had indicated that the time was not far off when both destroyers would need to refuel from the tanker in company but there had been general agreement that the ocean swell was still too great for the manoeuvre to be successful. It was a tricky business at the best of times, to refuel at sea. The vessels concerned had to approach dangerously close – dangerously, that was, in adverse weather conditions. Now the swell had decreased and the U-boat packs might not be all that far ahead. It was time to take a risk. As always it was a case of weighing one thing against another, the Commodore's responsibility again.

Mouncey reported. 'From leader, sir, to Commodore: Request permission to make alongside oiler.'

Kemp lifted his binoculars towards the fleet oiler, RFA *Wensleydale.* She was a big ship, had been the Mediterranean Fleet oiler just before the war, but well down now to her marks so that her size didn't show other than in her length. Her master and ship's company would be well practised in oiling at sea, and she had something of the manoeuvrability of a cruiser – twin screws, for instance, to assist in turning short round when necessary, and plenty of reserve power to give her some twenty-two knots of speed. But she was dipping a little to the remains of the swell and

Kemp knew the job was going to be a matter of crossed fingers throughout.

'All right, Mouncey. Make to the leader: Approved. And make to *Wensleydale*: Stand by to fuel destroyers in succession.'

'Aye, aye, sir.' Mouncey operated his shutters, using the big SP. The signals were quickly passed: the *Wensleydale* carried signal ratings and was not slow to respond as so many of the purely merchant ships could be at times. The Royal Fleet Auxiliary vessels were a mixture of two services, RN and Merchant Service. Owned and managed by the Admiralty, they carried Merchant Service officers and men. When *Wensleydale* had sent the acknowledgement, Kemp signalled the destroyer leader to start the ball rolling, then watched as she turned under full helm to race back through the convoy lines, her bows thrusting the North Atlantic aside and bringing up a big bow wave that washed aft from her fo'c'sle-head.

'They're like racing cars,' Kemp remarked. 'All swagger and a sharp pull-up as if they'd rammed the brakes on hard!'

Williams said, 'Showing off, sir.'

'Well, I don't blame them. They have the power, and usually their judgment can't be faulted.' Surreptitiously Kemp laid a hand on the teak guardrail in front of him, touching wood: this was no time to tempt fate. A scrape of hulls wouldn't be any help. Aboard the RFA, as Kemp saw through his glasses, they were lowering heavy fenders over the starboard side, heavy beams with lines attached at each end, the beams themselves thrust through a continuous line of old motor-car tyres, a type of fender known as the *Brambleleaf* fender, officially noted and recommended as such in Admiralty Fleet Orders and named after the *Wensleydale*'s predecessor in the Mediterranean Fleet, whose master had invented it. Very effective, as Kemp knew from past experience, and very necessary even though the destroyers wouldn't approach the oiler's side so closely. Precautions were never neglected at sea.

By now the leader had come round the oiler's stern and was turning to make her approach along the starboard side. Already a big gantry had been swung out from the *Wensleydale*, carrying the fuel pipeline, and as the destroyer came into position and the speed of the two ships was synchronized the gantry was lowered over the warship's deck, where the engineer officer and an engine-room artificer were standing by with four stokers to take the pipeline and make the connection to the bunkers.

'Expeditiously done,' Kemp said as the pipeline was connected. He spoke to Captain Hampton, who nodded.

Hampton said, 'Not something I'd care to do myself. I don't like other vessels too close . . . being in convoy's bad enough as it is! Just one lift of the sea . . .'

'Quite. That's when the fenders come into play, of course.' Kemp was watching closely. Every now and again the destroyer's stem swung, either to port or starboard, and was quickly righted. Too large a swing to port and she could cut in and smash her bows into the oiler's side. If there was damage, then the Commodore would be faced with problems. Kemp had already considered this and had formulated his orders in his mind, but he knew that nothing ever went quite as visualized and he would have, as it were, to think on his feet if the unexpected happened. For now he thrust it from his mind and said to Hampton, 'It's something we never had to think about in the old days, isn't it? Fueling at sea.'

Hampton laughed. 'You're right, sir. I wonder we didn't really, or the company didn't – something to amuse the passengers!'

'Yes.'

Keeping the passengers amused was always important. They were all very well in small doses but there were a lot of them at the Captain's table, mostly elderly and often full of their own importance. Kemp had frequently envied the junior officers. Their companions tended to be much younger and much less important, and Kemp had grown inattentive at his table, looking across at laughing groups getting along splendidly while his own gaggle of decrepits munched steak with false teeth, thought about their digestions, and explained in detail to Kemp how they had got to the top in their various spheres. Often their wives did that for them and the husbands themselves were embarrassed. Of course there were exceptions. Kemp himself was happiest on the few occasions when he had carried a retired admiral or general out to Egypt or Ceylon or all the way to Australia. They had something in common with him, and his last-war medal ribbons had meant something to them, as had his then rank of Captain RNR.

He reverted to Hampton's last remark. He said, 'I doubt if I'll enjoy retirement when it comes, in spite of all. What about you, Hampton?'

They knew one another very well. Hampton said, 'Same as you, sir. I'll miss the sea. I'll miss the companionship of men who go to sea. I'll miss the Line – as such. They're a good outfit. But I won't miss the passengers. What was it the pursers used to say? One thousand passengers equals one thousand bloody stupid questions a day.'

'Yes, do I not know!' Kemp swept a hand around the convoy, the ships pushing into the North Atlantic, heading towards danger. 'All that . . . it makes the peacetime days fall into some sort of perspective, doesn't it? All frivolity, people with too much damn money wondering how to get rid of it in the most pleasurable way. That was cruising anyway – the long run to Sydney was all right.'

'There was a different element creeping in even to that. We'd started to become gin-palaces and floating brothels! Maybe the war saved us, I don't know.' Hampton paused. 'If I had my time over again, I'd go for the cargo liners, the twelve-passenger jobs. Best of both worlds. More variety and nicer people.'

Hampton turned as the senior second officer came up to him with the result of the noon sight. He excused himself from the Commodore and went into the chartroom, where the position had already been noted on the chart by a neat pencilled cross. The convoy was now well westward of Cape Farewell.

[ii]

Pemmel sat in his private office leading off the main office, with his head in his hands. Another hangover, headache, red-rimmed eyes, parrot's-cage mouth, white-furred tongue, and a general feeling of creeping death and dissolution. By some sort of alchemy or thought-transference his mind had been running along lines similar to Kemp's reflections on the pre-war days and he had thought of the depressing sameness of the stupid questions that Kemp had talked of to Captain Hampton.

Pemmel could hear them now.

'Oh, Purser, do tell me, how much is a penny-ha'penny stamp?' They all thought prices were different at sea, like duty-free.

83

'Oh, Purser, where's the next deck up and how do I get to it?'

On embarkation: 'Oh, Purser, is this the right ship for Fremantle?' Just like a bus stop.

'Oh, Purser, which is the tender between this and the next, and what time does it go?'

That sort of thing; it used to be said that passengers marked their brains 'Not Wanted On Voyage', like their heavier baggage destined for the holds. Nevertheless passengers, at any rate the female ones, had had their compensations and Pemmel was wishing for the days of peace and promiscuity back again. He was having a bad time with Jackie Ord, who was slipping through his fingers. His own fault – he knew that; he had no illusions. He drank too much but he couldn't stop it now, couldn't get by without it, couldn't face the day. The doctor had spoken to him about it again, reprovingly, doing his duty as a medico but not managing to avoid the suggestion of the pot calling the kettle black and thus having no effect. Yet it was a funny thing: the doc had cut it down a lot in the last twenty-four hours. Rumour had said he'd taken it badly when he'd failed to follow his Hippocratic oath in buggering off to the heads when wounded men needed him. Something had penetrated, it seemed; but it was early days yet and he would probably have a relapse before long.

Pemmel gave a low groan as a knock came at his door. It was the second steward. 'Yes, Mr Portway, what is it? Overtime sheets again?'

It wasn't the overtime: behind Mr Portway loomed Master-at-Arms Rockett. It was Rockett who reported: 'Case o' theft, sir. One o' them stewards.' He jerked a hand towards Mr Portway, managing to infer that all stewards were thieves and layabouts. 'Have to be investigated, sir.'

Pemmel groaned again: a purser was ship's dogsbody. Banking, catering, sports and pastimes, money changer, tour organizer at *en route* ports, passenger appeaser, Captain's secretary – CID, too, when something like this happened. He didn't feel up to it. 'Too busy,' he said. 'See the deputy purser.'

Neither Rockett nor Portway argued; but Pemmel saw the look that passed between them as they withdrew to the main office.

The oiling of the leader was successfully completed and she drew away to resume her protective station while the other destroyer prepared to take on bunkers herself. As the leader settled on the convoy's starboard bow, her consort turned and headed for the *Wensleydale* and the performance was repeated, the gantry going out and down and the pipeline connections made. Kemp, watching as before, could see the pulsing of the heavy pipe as the oil-flow was switched on aboard the *Wensleydale*. A breeze was coming up now, nothing much but enough to ruffle the water – nothing much yet, but it could increase. Kemp was only faintly concerned, however. The oiling should be finished long enough before there was any real weight of wind to bring danger and perhaps force the termination of oiling.

Kemp's assistant had something to say; Kemp knew Williams had had something on his mind ever since the leader had asked the Commodore's approval for oiling and now he came out with it.

'Mouncey, sir.'

Kemp turned. 'What about Mouncey?'

'Slackness, sir. Having to be told the senior officer of the escort was calling us.'

'Yes.' Kemp's tone was off-putting.

'I was wondering if he was up to the mark, sir.'

'His first lapse that I'm aware of, Williams.'

'Well, sir, I've noted signs before.' Williams coughed. 'Do you want him charged, sir?'

'What with?'

Williams said carefully, 'I've been preparing a charge as a matter of fact. I suggest simply inattentiveness to his duty whilst signalman of the watch in convoy, sir. Whereby he could have endangered ships and lives.'

'But didn't.'

Williams gaped. 'Sir?'

'I think you heard, Williams. I don't deal in ifs and buts. The matter was not serious – though I agree it could be if it happened again. But, you see, I've already dealt with it and it *won't* happen again.' Kemp was looking his assistant straight in the eye. 'I see you don't consider a rebuke to be an effective way of dealing with it. Let me tell you something. There is a tone of voice that carries in it more than the words of the rebuke. Remember that, Williams. There will be no charges. Mouncey is a good signalman. That's all.'

Williams realized that Kemp's tone of voice was being used once again, with intent. Kemp turned his back and concentrated on the refuelling scene. He had a shrewd suspicion that there was more behind Williams' wish to make a charge than had appeared on the surface. He was aware of a touch of surliness in Leading Signalman Mouncey when addressed by Williams: Mouncey was a shade bolshie when it came to Williams, a different Mouncey from the one who jumped to it when spoken to by the Commodore or the ship's master. Although that was to be deplored it wasn't up to Kemp to interfere: Williams alone had to earn Mouncey's respect, all by himself.

[iv]

Captain Redgrave was aware of very little now and was barely conscious of the great camouflaged side of the *Prince of Wales* as a motor-boat from the destroyer escort brought him alongside in a Neil Robertson stretcher and he was hauled to the battleship's quarterdeck. He was unaware of the identity of the stocky man in civilian clothes and a yachting cap who was watching the embarkation and smoking a cigar. When Redgrave had been taken below to the sick bay and the attentions of the surgeon commander and his staff, Churchill said that he was to be kept informed of Captain Redgrave's progress.

'Such brave men,' he said to the battleship's Executive Officer. 'Armed with popguns . . . and always at sea. Without them, Britain would starve.'

Already the *Prince of Wales* was moving at speed again, heading west with her escort, zig-zagging continually through the seas. The Prime Minister remained on the quarterdeck, his mind projecting ahead. A message came for him, brought by a surgeon lieutenant from the surgeon commander: there was no gangrene – it would have been unlikely at sea in any case – but there was septicaemia and it was now too late to operate. Recovery was not expected.

Late that afternoon Redgrave died. No time was lost in disposing of the body. The battleship's captain came down from the compass platform to stand with the padre, and watched by the Prime Minister, Redgrave's body slid from under the folds of a Red Ensign provided by the chief yeoman of signals. When the *Prince of Wales* reached safe harbour in Placentia Bay the news would be sent home to Redgrave's owners who would inform the family, what was left of it – the father and sister, that lonely pair in York.

[v]

Jackie Ord had worked tirelessly in the *Ardara's* sick bay, fighting off weariness as she looked after the injured men. The burns cases were horrifying, pulpy flesh all red and blue, burned through to the bone in some instances. Pain-killing drugs were having their effect but there would come a limit to their use: the build-up could be dangerous. The ship's surgeon had come back after a while to do his duty and no one mentioned his lapse, but he was useless: very likely he hadn't seen a serious burns case in his life, or anyway not since his student days many years in the past, added to which he was running again on alcohol power and the fumes were wicked, enough to set light to. Dr Barnes was the saviour – him and Jackie.

When he saw she was almost out on her feet he told her to go off and have a zizz.

'But I can't –'

'We'll manage. We've already done all we can – you know that.'

She nodded; from now on it was a case of watching and keeping them under and re-bandaging when necessary. So Jackie went along to her cabin and dropped on to the bunk fully dressed. But she couldn't get to sleep; she was over-tired and her mind was too restless. After a while she gave it up, sat up in the bunk and lit a cigarette. She picked up a book: *Gone with the Wind*, which she'd started back in the Clyde anchorage whilst awaiting the forming-up of the convoy. But she found she couldn't concentrate. She was thinking of the injuries, the burns, the terrible screaming when the merchant seamen had been brought aboard and transferred below. It had been harrowing. Jackie was young still, her experiences had not been those of war. Trained at Addenbrooke's Hospital in Cambridge, she had done time as a staff nurse in casualty after qualifying, and there had been traumas – road accidents, would-be suicides, burns too – but nothing to compare with this. She forced her thoughts to happier, easier days, which meant Cambridge: she was a local girl from Cherry Hinton, so she'd not been far from home, and she loved Cambridge and its particular atmosphere – the Backs in summer and winter, King's College Chapel and the Christmas carols, tea at The Whim in Trinity Street with a gaggle of probationers – or with Tom. Tom Bulstrode had been an undergraduate at Clare, doing medicine the long way round – BA first, three years at Cambridge then on to St Thomas's in London for his medical degrees. They were probably going to be married, though they'd both agreed not to rush it. Soon after qualifying Tom had joined the RAMC and had been killed at Dunkirk. So had ended – so young – a chapter of her life. She had been devastated.

She was thinking of Tom now. Had he been like her current patients, before he died, screaming in agony, perhaps calling for her? Of course she would never know: the official bulletins, the notifications of death in action, didn't go into that sort of thing. Even his parents wouldn't know. She'd been back to see them – they, too, lived locally, in a small house in Fenstanton on the old Roman road that ran from Cambridge to Huntingdon. It had been a sad and harrowing visit. There were so many memories, days off, when they coincided, often spent bicycling around the villages, Hilton, Elsworth, Conington or through St Ives to Needingworth and other places, sometimes as far as Ely and back along the A10 to Cambridge. It was good flat country for bicycling and always the sun had seemed to be shining on the dyke-crossed fens. In his last term Tom had bought a small car, an MG, and they had extended their range to King's Lynn and Hunstanton and Cromer. Tom had once deviated off the A10 to show her the flood-control system near Littleport, the Old Bedford and the New Bedford, and had bored her with a long explanation of how it all worked and what would happen if it didn't.

Tears came to her eyes: she would have given anything to be

bored again.

She lit another cigarette: chain-smoking, which was bad. She thought of Andy Pemmel, so different from Tom, so dissolute – though he could be nice. She had drifted into that, seduced by sheer loneliness and unhappiness and Andy's attentiveness, though she knew very well that the attentiveness was directional, one end only in view. Dr Barnes had tried to warn her off – purely disinterestedly she knew, since he was engaged to a girl, not a nurse, whom he'd met when at Bart's, and he was so obviously the patient, faithful sort, a plodder in love and medicine – conscientious but unimaginative . . .

In the end she found sleep, deep and dreamless, really flat out to the point of unconsciousness, as though drugged. She was aware of nothing, didn't stir when there was a knock on the cabin door and Pemmel entered, more or less on spec. But she did wake when she heard him shout at her.

'Jesus, what the *hell*!'

On the heels of his words she found herself being drenched with a fine spray of water, she saw the flame and smoke and she felt burning, a sharp pain in the flesh of her shoulder. The cabin seemd to be full of smoke and Pemmel was dragging her from the bunk. There was a fine mist of water: the sprinkler system had gone into automatic action. At first, coming so quickly from deep sleep, she thought there had been an enemy attack. Then she heard Pemmel shouting at her again, something about how bloody daft it was to smoke in bed.

[vi]

The alarm had gone automatically through the ship as the sprinkler operated: Mr Portway, who had turned in for a late-afternoon nap, woke instantly and ran out of his cabin pulling on his uniform jacket. The working alleyways were crammed with stewards and galley hands, bar staff, laundry staff, all the denizens of the bowels of the ship surfacing at the threat of fire. Mr Portway pushed through, shouting at the top of his voice and causing worse confusion until the junior third officer appeared at the head of a ladder and took charge, after which Portway gathered his hose party and once again ran out the flat reels of canvas from the fire hydrants. No one seemed to know quite what was happening, not until the senior nursing sister's cabin sprinkler was isolated as having gone off.

For a while the Commodore was equally in the dark. The fuelling operation was finished by this time and both destroyers were back in their proper positions ahead of the convoy and out to either bow and aboard the *Wensleydale* the gear had been stowed away and the tanks trimmed by use of the pumping system that allowed transfers between one tank and another. The report of fire below on C deck had come as a shock: fire at sea was one of the worst hazards, for fire, once it had taken a grip, was devilish hard to get under control and if the flames should reach the upper decks then they would be fanned by the wind beyond any ship's resources. When fire came as a result of enemy attack, that was one thing and had to be accepted. But when it came internally as it were, then nine times out of ten it was due to one thing only: sheer damn carelessness, unforgivable aboard a ship at sea.

Kemp was livid when the report reached him: fire in a nurse's cabin, due to smoking and falling asleep.

'Is the girl hurt?' was the first thing he asked.

It was Pemmel, making the report in person since he had been first on the scene. 'No, sir. Shaken but not hurt, apart from a little burning.'

'Doctor's report?'

'Nothing serious, sir. He's dusted her with boracic powder, I believe.'

Kemp said, 'Well, well! I shall dust her with something else, Purser. Send her up to the bridge.' He remembered his own position aboard and turned to the master. 'Have I your permission, Captain, or will you see her?'

Hampton made a gesture of negation. He preferred to leave this to the Commodore. He was as furious as Kemp; the girl deserved the weightiest of brass-bound wrath, and the Commodore was the Commodore, an extra sort of God. Kemp turned back to Pemmel. 'Thank you for what you did, Purser.'

'It was nothing, sir. I just –'

'You smelled smoke, did you?'

Pemmel hesitated: he'd gone to Jackie's cabin for quite different reasons. He said, 'Yes, sir.'

'And you took immediate action. I dare say that girl owes you her life, or anyway her lack of burns.' Kemp paused. 'I don't believe we ever met before the war.'

'No, sir.' Pemmel seemed suddenly embarrassed. 'Different ships . . . we didn't cross.'

'And your last ship?'

More embarrassment: Pemmel began to stammer. He had been, he said, deputy purser in the *Aramac* just before the war had broken out. Kemp remembered then, but said nothing. The DP of the *Aramac* – there had been a scandal, a minor one, involving a female passenger. Minor it might have been but Kemp was surprised that Pemmel had made full purser after it; the exigencies of war, perhaps. Other pursers – he knew a couple – who were paymaster lieutenant-commanders RNR had been called up to the fleet. The scandal wouldn't have been a scandal if Pemmel hadn't been caught in the act, of course – the one unforgivable crime was being found out. So to some extent it had been bad luck. But Kemp was old-fashioned and didn't approve of cabin-crawling, certainly not on the part of senior officers who had a responsibility to the Line. Now, as he gave Pemmel a dismissive nod, he came close to the truth: it hadn't, in all probability, been smoke that had attracted the purser to Sister Ord's cabin. He smiled, grimly. No smoke without a fire!

His remembrance of Pemmel's past did nothing to soften his attitude when Sister Ord reported to the bridge. He took her into the starboard wing; everyone else moved away discreetly.

'Now, Miss Ord.' She was pretty – damn pretty! Lovely figure – but that couldn't weigh. 'First of all . . . have you anything you wish to say?'

'No, Commodore Kemp.'

'No excuses?'

'No . . .'

He liked that, not that there could have been any possible excuse. But she'd probably been dead tired and could have said so. He went on, 'I see. No doubt you realize just what might have happened.'

She nodded but didn't say anything. Her eyes were very bright. Kemp began his rebuke. He told her what fire at sea could be like, the many deaths that inevitably resulted when a fire got a hold. The damage to the ship, a valuable ship in time of war, much needed for trooping. The fact that they were part of a vital convoy and that a fire aboard the Commodore's ship would have played havoc. The fact that the ship's company had already been warned that the enemy lay ahead across the convoy's track, that attack could for all anyone knew come at any moment.

She nodded, didn't meet his eye, held her hands clasped in front of her body, a schoolgirl getting a blasting from the headmistress. *Was* he becoming headmistressy, or was it just because he had a girl to deal with this time?

Anyway, he laid it on thick. It was heinous. So many lives at risk from thoughtlessness.

She began to cry and Kemp broke off in mid sentence. Now he was out of his depth. Did he bring out his handkerchief, say 'There, there,' and wipe away the tears? He coughed, cleared his throat, and lifted his voice.

'Williams!'

Lieutenant Williams approached at speed. Kemp inclined his head towards the girl and Williams took over, very efficiently. Kemp glowered as they went down the ladder, Williams' hand on the girl's undamaged shoulder. Williams was proving his use: crying women looked as if they were right up his street. Kemp gave an impatient grunt. All *he* did was scare the pants off them . . .

[vii]

Dusk began to descend, the approach of any convoy's worst hours, the night hours when the zig-zag became a nightmare for the officers on watch as they altered course according to the laid-down pattern and kept their eyes on a number of things at once, the shaded blue stern lights, the great black bulk of ships moving across their bows as the convoy altered its formation. The escorting warships were now at dusk action stations, as were the naval gunners aboard the merchantmen. The convoy had been steaming slap into the sunset, a brilliant one, all colours of the rainbow and great streaks to either side, almost like those you saw, Petty Officer Frapp thought, east of Suez, the sort that struck you with awe if you had any imagination at all. Frapp had not, in fact, a great deal of imagination but he'd always been very impressed with spectacular sunsets because in his view they said something about God. Their beauty was way beyond anything that man could produce. There had to be some power beyond this life and this world to produce anything like that.

And perhaps, coming tonight, it was an omen, or rather a promise that all would be well. Frapp removed his cap and stared into the last flickers of the dying sun, into a sort of purple look that lay over the water; to the leading hand of the gun's crew behind him it looked like an act of obeisance . . . perhaps old Frappy was a sun worshipper. In fact the cap's removal was simply to facilitate the scratching of an itch on Frapp's bald skull, as the leading hand realized a moment later. Frapp, forgetting sunsets, got to work on his guns, keeping the crews busy, exercising action, laying and training on different ships of the convoy, depressing the angle of sight to bring the gun to bear upon an imaginary conning tower which would in fact be the actual point of aim if they should go into action against U-boats during the night.

When the stand-down came half an hour after full dark Frapp relaxed, pushed his cap back from his forehead and felt for a fag which he didn't light, not on the upper deck: the strike of a match, even just the red glow from the fag itself, could be seen through a periscope. But it was nice just to feel the cigarette between his lips.

'All right, you lot, fall out. Stand fast the duty watch.' Frapp smacked a hand against the breech of the six-inch as though saying goodnight, sleep tight, hope the bed-bugs don't bite . . . Frapp didn't want to have to turn out during the night and he didn't want to have to fire his guns in anger. For why? Because he fancied they might simply blow up and fragment the gunners. They were poor old has-beens, stored in the arsenals for years and years, dragged out of ancient cruisers long gone to the breaker's yard. Not long after leaving the Clyde PO Frapp had been visited whilst exercising action by an old bloke from the liner's crew, a night steward who'd been a Royal Marine in the last lot – Crump by name. Ex-Colour-Sergeant Crump had almost talked to the after six-inch and said he believed it had come from the old cruiser *Glasgow*, built back in 1909 and present at the battles of Coronel and the Falklands and partly responsible for sinking the German cruiser *Dresden*. Well, if that was true, it was something, though Frapp didn't know quite what beyond senility. It certainly wasn't going to sink another *Dresden* . . .

A shaded signal lamp began flashing from the escort on the port bow and on the heels of the message the alarm rattlers sounded throughout the *Ardara*. Alongside Frapp the telephone from the bridge whined and Frapp answered. 'Six-inch aft –'

It was Lieutenant Williams' voice. 'Alarm port, Frapp – contact! All guns' crews stand by. I'll be down as soon as possible.'

'Aye, aye, sir,' Frapp said into a line that had already gone dead. He sounded sour and was; the Commodore's assistant, at exercise action, had fancied himself as a gunnery officer and gone into several flat spins yelling out such orders as 'Still, misfire, carry on,' and 'Shoot, shoot, shoot,' and 'Check gun-ready lamps,' just as though the *Ardara* was fitted with a director. It sounded efficient, or Frapp supposed it did to Williams, but he thought the two-striper was a right tit. Meanwhile the six-inch crew was coming back to the gun, fast.

Frapp said, 'All right, lads, this is it or looks like it.' They took up their stations and Frapp saw the gun trained round to port. He waited for the next order from the bridge.

NINE

The minutes passed. Nothing happened. The ships moved on.

Kemp asked suddenly, 'What d'you make of it, Hampton?'

Hampton shrugged. 'Getting into position?'

'The bugger's already in position. Just ahead of the convoy and ready for the flank. Perfect!' All eyes watched from the bridge but there was nothing to be seen. The night was dark; as yet there were neither moon nor stars to give some light; just the faint glow that was always present over the sea. Yet it would, Kemp believed, be possible to spot a torpedo trail unless the setting was exceptionally deep. So far there were no trails. They went on watching and waiting. The port escort had gone in to investigate but nothing seemed to be developing.

'It's a bloody mystery,' Kemp said.

'False alarm?' Hampton suggested.

Kemp laughed. 'Could be. Echo off a whale – it's been known before now!' With a massive attack foreshadowed in the Admiralty cypher, there would be jittery men aboard the escort, Asdic ratings who might jump a mile if they got an echo from a sardine. And there had been, so far as Kemp was aware, just the one contact. It didn't quite represent a whole U-boat pack. The starboard escort was still standing guard and hadn't reported anything, so it could be assumed the right flank was clear and nothing ahead either. The destroyer would be sweeping all round, through three hundred and sixty degrees.

Then the shaded signal lamp came up again and Mouncey reported to the Commodore. 'From the leader, sir: "Lost contact. This I do not like."'

Kemp said, 'No more do I! But it's somewhat cryptic I fancy. I wonder what's in Phillips' mind, precisely?' The question was rhetorical. Kemp moved over to the telephone to the after six-inch and got Frapp on the other end. 'Frapp, is Mr Williams there?'

'No, sir. 'E went for'ard, sir, to take charge there.'

Kemp rang off, went to the fore screen and called down in a carrying voice. 'Lieutenant Williams?'

'Sir?'

'On the bridge, please. Pronto.'

Williams came up. Kemp said, 'You've served in destroyers. So have I, but in the last lot. We didn't have Asdics then – lots of things we didn't have. I'm out of touch, you're not.'

'No, sir . . .'

'Get inside Commander Phillips' mind.' Kemp repeated the leader's last signal. 'What do you think he doesn't like about the situation? I don't propose asking him – the fewer signals the better, in regard to certain matters. But I want to make an assessment.'

'Yes, sir. You say he's lost contact . . . and there haven't been any more contacts.'

'Not yet, no.'

'Well, sir, of course it's easy enough to lose contact –'

'I know that, Williams. That wasn't what I meant. If you've no ideas, let's try this for size, shall we? I'd like your reaction. The packs have drawn off, they're not interested in an empty convoy – I don't know what that one contact was, maybe it *was* a false echo. But the Nazis could be waiting for something else.'

'The HX homeward, sir?'

'No. I answered that question earlier. They won't hang about. They could have had a report about other matters. The *Prince of Wales*, Williams.'

Williams' lips framed a whistle that didn't emerge: it was a tradition that you didn't whistle at sea and Kemp was the sort of man who would jump on a whistler, hard and fast. He said, 'Yes, that could be right, sir. That's what Commander Phillips doesn't like.'

Kemp grinned. 'Great minds! I think it's a fair bet. The U-boats just aren't around any more. *We* don't know the actual course or position of the *Prince of Wales*, but Berlin could have had their ears to the ground. We all know about their bloody spy networks,

Williams. And there's something else we don't exactly know but can have a damn good guess at: the Admiralty won't know the U-boat packs have drawn off and are heading for bigger game.'

Williams said, 'We don't know for sure either, sir. We can't be sure we were spotted by a periscope. That's really only guess-work too.'

'Wars are often won on guesses, Williams, they're the very stuff of decision! However, we'll know before long. If no attack develops, they've gone.' Kemp blew out a long breath. 'That's when I'll have to decide whether or not to warn the *Prince of Wales*.'

'She'll have been alerted same as us, sir. By the Admiralty.'

'Yes. But she won't know the U-boats' whereabouts or that an attack may be developing, Williams.'

'But wireless silence –'

'Yes, I know. It's not a decision anyone can make yet. I shall make another assessment at first light. If there's to be an attack, then it'll come during the night, I fancy. And if that happens, there'll be no need to worry about wireless silence. That's all for now, Williams, thank you.'

'Yes, sir.' Williams paused. 'Will you be remaining on the bridge, sir?'

'Yes, Williams.'

Williams turned away and went down the starboard ladder to the Captain's deck and on down to the boat deck, making aft for the 6-inch. From behind the gun-shield, PO Frapp saw him coming. Frapp sucked at a hollow tooth and spat disdainfully and skilfully over the side to leeward. 'Here comes Johnny-come-lately,' he said to the gun's crew. 'Watch out.'

Williams halted by the gun. 'We remain closed up, Frapp.'

'Yes, sir. All-night job, d'you reckon?'

Williams nodded. 'The Commodore expects an attack to develop during the night.' He didn't add that the chances were no attack would come: no point in encouraging the guns' crews to slack off, he considered them a sloppy lot at the best of times. What they needed wasn't Frapp but a rasp-voiced gunner's mate from the Whale Island gunnery school in Portsmouth. Frapp was something of an old woman and a bit past seagoing. Williams looked him over, superciliously. 'Keep them up to the mark, Frapp.' He peered closer. 'That man. He's not in the rig of the day.'

Frapp said, 'No, sir. It's night.' Then he, too, looked: Williams was right, one hand wasn't in night clothing – still had his blue collar on. It should have come off after 1630 hours, as though it mattered when the gun's crew were wearing their anti-flash gear. Frapp made a pretence at bawling the man out, more than ever convinced that Williams was a prat.

'See it doesn't happen again, Frapp. We can't have slackness in wartime, you know.'

He turned away to go for'ard again. Frapp said nothing; if he had done so, it might have been a mouthful that would have put him slap in the rattle and endangered his rate. He wouldn't chance his arm to that extent. Officers could be rude to ratings but not the other way round.

The *Ardara* moved on, the dark shapes followed in their columns, the destroyers' wakes streamed back on either bow. Stars began to show, and a moon. The convoy became silvered with light, standing out sharply to any watching periscope. Throughout the convoy the guns remained manned on the orders of the Commodore, their crews weary but watchful, walking up and down where there was space, keeping themselves awake throughout a long night, most of them thinking thoughts far removed from their present environment. Home, women and beer . . . the pubs of Queen Street and Commercial Road in Pompey, the dockside pubs in Liverpool and Birkenhead, Sauchiehall Street in Glasgow, pubs in other parts where at the start of the war the canny Scots had produced whisky made from wood alcohol that had sent seamen blind – literally. Ladies of easy virtue loomed as large in their thoughts as the pubs, since the one led frequently to the other, a natural progression for a seaman ashore. Throughout the convoy the collected experiences of the land would have been a guarantee of hell's everlasting fires, far too powerful to be redeemed by all the prayers of all the nuns and monks throughout the world since time began. But they were men and they were fighting a long, hard war against tyranny and dictatorship, and they had men's desires. Perhaps God would not use too heavy a hand when they mustered at the last Defaulters.

PO Frapp was one of those who might not make it: he hadn't always been what Lieutenant Williams thought of as an old woman. He'd been quite a lad with the girls, once, before the fires had died down. A sweetheart in every port, had Frapp: Pompey, Guz, Chatham, Gibraltar, Malta, Singapore, Hong Kong . . . currently he was thinking of Hong Kong, where there had been more than the one – Frapp had done two commissions China-side and the second time the first girl hadn't wanted to know, having got married to a cook aboard an RFA, and he'd had to find another. He couldn't even remember their names now, one had sounded like Hoo Flung Dung . . . but the Chink women were wonderful in bed, nothing like them anywhere else. When he was a young AB he'd been told the Chink women were built different, that it went athwartships rather than fore and aft, but he'd soon found out that was just bull.

Below in the bowels of the ship Mr Portway, whose experiences and far-flung womanizing were not dissimilar from Frapp's, was thinking, or rather dreaming since he'd sat himself down in an alleyway near his fire hydrant and had fallen asleep, of Thurrock and Grays, of his wife and Mabel. It was Mabel's fault that he awoke suddenly: he had an erection. Embarrassed, he shifted to conceal it, but went on thinking about Mabel and what they would do next time he was in Tilbury, and God knew when *that* was likely to be, what with the war having shattered all the schedules. Next time in, it would in all probability be the Clyde again, not that anyone ever knew until they got there since no one was told anything of that nature, you just arrived somewhere and that was that, and then you sailed again and you didn't know where for until you'd left port. The uncertainty made things very difficult for a man with two women to consider, both of them near each other and far south. Mrs Portway, once she had realized that Thurrock wasn't going to see much of her husband while the war lasted, had made noises suggestive of wanting to shift up to Greenock or somewhere else handy. Mr Portway had dealt with that easily enough by hinting darkly at official secrets and the death penalty for careless talk that cost lives, and Be Like Dad Keep Mum as all the posters advised. If she went north, Mr Portway said, they'd be sure to pin it on him: she wasn't supposed to know where the *Ardara* was.

He wouldn't in fact have said the same to Mabel, but Mabel had her job and he couldn't afford to keep two women. Mabel had to pay her way. Currently Mr Portway was racking his brains as to how he might get her a job somewhere on the Clyde; he'd made a few contacts up there, useful contacts in hotels and so on, and something might be brought about. Mr Portway, as it happened, had no regular woman in or around Greenock, though there had been a few odd nights in Helensburgh . . . Scots girls didn't really appeal to Mr Portway. They were too direct, too outspoken and often abrasive, and for some reason or other he'd found the ones he had pursued had been Scottish Nationalists with a dislike of the English and the way their country had been taken over for war purposes by the navy. One of them, the last of his forays, had poked fun at his stomach, and that had hurt him. She'd wondered when he'd last seen his little willy other than in a mirror . . .

The junior third officer came along the alleyway and Portway scrambled to his feet.

'All right, Mr Portway?'

'Yessir. All's well, sir.'

'Good. It's all quiet up topsides. With any luck . . .'

'Funny, no attack, sir.'

'It wouldn't be if there was.' The officer passed on, stepping clear of the run-out fires hoses. Mr Portway remained on his feet and decided it was time he made his rounds again. He did so; in the course of his tour of inspection he came upon Master-at-Arms Rockett with his long torch, seeking sin. Mr Portway reckoned that Rockett, too desiccated for the real thing, did it by proxy.

[ii]

The next day's dawn was as splendid as the last evening's sunset, a splendour of many colours. On the *Ardara*'s bridge the Commodore rubbed at tired eyes and stretched his arms, longing for his bunk. No attack: now the time for decision had come and couldn't be delayed. The fact that there had been no attack must mean there were no U-boat packs, at least not where the Admiralty had expected them to be.

'Williams?'

'Here, sir.' Kemp's assistant emerged from the wheelhouse, where he had just got up from a catnap on the deck.

'I shall have to warn the *Prince of Wales* – break wireless silence.'

'It's risky, sir. For the convoy, I mean.'

'Yes. But there's a greater prize for Hitler, Williams, as I've said before. Make a signal to the destroyer leader, by lamp: Propose warning . . . propose warning prisoners-of-war of likelihood of their getting what we did not. How's that?' He saw the look of incomprehension and added testily, '*POW*, Williams. Phillips'll get the drift. There's still a need for secrecy within the convoy. God knows why, but I have to assume there is.'

'Yes, of course, sir. I think that's fine, sir, if you really do –'

'Really do what?'

'Really do think it's wise to break wireless silence, sir. As I said before, the Admiralty's signal –'

'Yes. And as I said before, neither the Admiralty nor the *Prince of Wales* is aware of the current situation.' Anger grew in Kemp: he was desperately tired. 'I've already made my decision, Williams.'

'Yes, sir, but –'

'But what?' Kemp's voice cut hard.

Williams said stubbornly, 'It's my job to make representations, sir. Point things out.'

The tone irritated. 'You're an assistant, Williams, not a consultant.'

Williams flushed. 'I'm sorry, sir. I just –'

'That'll be all, thank you.' Williams went off to pass the signal order. Kemp knew he had been unfair and was already regretting it, but Williams was the sort who grated on a man when he was dead tired . . . so damn tired, Kemp thought, that there was a possibility he wasn't thinking straight. That was no use to anybody. In a gentler tone when Williams came back he said, 'Let's just hope it's going to be in time.'

'Yes, sir. Depends on how far off . . . U-boats haven't all that much speed submerged.'

'No. And they won't know the precise position.' Kemp waited for the response from the escort commander. If Phillips came up with some cogent reason for not breaking wireless silence even for the Prime Minister, then maybe he would accept it, though since Phillips was RN he was probably to some extent hidebound about the use of w/T at sea in wartime. Kemp paced the bridge, so weary now that he cannoned off the screen at the extremity of the bridge and saw the look Williams gave him, the look that said the

101

old buffer was past it.

The leader was flashing now. Signalman MacCord reported the reply. '"Your 0433. Concur, sir."'

'That's all?'

'Aye, sir.'

Kemp gave something like a sigh. He said, 'All right, Williams. Make: To *Prince of Wales* from Commodore OB 418, U-boat packs believed to be closing your position from west. All right?'

'Yes, sir. Prefix?'

'Most Urgent and Most Secret. Get it encyphered as fast as you can and transmit immediately.'

'Yes, sir.' There was something smug about Kemp's assistant and a moment later Kemp knew why. 'I've already encyphered it, sir, during the night, word for word as it happens . . . I anticipated –'

'You anticipated well, Williams. Well done!' Kemp was astounded and in a way humiliated: Williams had hidden depths of efficiency tucked away and Kemp thanked God for it. This was something Kemp should have thought of for himself; perhaps he really was getting past it. Every second was vital – yes, he should have been more on the ball. It wouldn't happen again. Williams, who had lost no time in taking the encyphered signal to the radio room, was quickly back to say the message had been transmitted. Naturally, there would be no acknowledgement: the *Prince of Wales* would not risk giving away her own position. The message had been transmitted three times to make as sure as possible that the telegraphists aboard the battleship picked it up.

'That's all, then,' Kemp said. 'Nothing more we can do now. I doubt if we'll know the result until we reach Halifax.'

But in that he was wrong. That same day, as the sun went down the sky to bring another brilliant painting to hang above the waters, the lookout at the foremasthead, sweeping round a full 360 degrees through his binoculars, reported a light signal from the rearmost ship of the convoy. Leading Signalman Mouncey read it off: ships, as yet unidentified, were closing from astern.

Kemp said, 'Sound the alarm, Williams.' Once again the *Ardara* went to action stations, the ship becoming a busy beehive of running men above and below. As the overtaking ships, moving at high speed, came within visual distance, the challenge was made and answered, and soon after this Kemp recognized the silhouette of HMS *Prince of Wales* behind her escort, bringing her massive gun-power to head straight through the lines of the convoy. On she came, her escort parting to steam up the flanks of the outer columns, the great battleship herself passing between the two port columns to come close by the *Ardara* and the Commodore's broad pennant that flew from the mainmasthead. There was enough light for those aboard many of the merchant ships to see the officers clustered on the compass platform, and to see someone else: a stocky figure wearing an overcoat and an odd-shaped black hat that was half-way between a bowler and a topper, standing for everyone to see, right for'ard in the eyes of the battleship, ahead of the centre-line capstan and the fourteen-inch turrets.

As a gale of cheering swept across the darkening sea, Winston Churchill lifted his right hand high above his head, two fingers standing out in the familiar gesture.

'And up Hitler and all,' Petty Officer Frapp said at the after six-inch. 'Good old Winnie!' He roared the last three words out with all his voice, and the shout was taken up all along the decks. On the bridge Captain Hampton was standing with the Commodore as the *Ardara*'s ensign was dipped in salute.

He said, 'He's blown it, sir. All by himself. Indiscreet?'

Kemp laughed. 'Not a bit of it! It's a grand gesture – and it doesn't matter now. He'll be in Newfoundland waters long before we make Halifax.' As he spoke the battleship's flag deck came alive with a flashing lamp. Mouncey read, and reported.

'From *Prince of Wales* to Commodore, sir. "Your 0445 appreciated. U-boat attack repulsed with bad news for the Führer. Surface raiders as reported earlier failed to show. Your escort will rejoin soonest possible."' Mouncey wiped a hand across his lips and added, 'Message ends, sir.'

Kemp nodded. 'Thank you, Mouncey. Make back: Good luck to all aboard you and a safe passage.' He turned to his assistant. 'Read *Prince of Wales*' signal over the Tannoy, Williams.'

As Williams went into the wheelhouse another signal came from the battleship: the *Stephen Starr* had been encountered, the master had been transferred but had died. Kemp felt a curious emptiness inside. Poor Redgrave, so much endured for so little purpose in the end, another of the war's heroes to be quickly forgotten, probably by the time the convoy reached Halifax.

TEN

Various domestic matters were to engage the attentions of a number of the men in the convoy once they had entered the blessings, the mixed blessings for some, of the land. One of the less fortunate was to be Mr Portway, for events had stirred up trouble back across the sea in Essex, trouble that arose for no other reason than the fact that there was a war on and Mrs Portway's laundry had been put out of action by a bomb. Mrs Portway had never done her own washing: it was infra dig for the wife of the second steward of the *Ardara*. The trouble was that hers had been the only laundry left in business in Thurrock and she had quarrelled with the only one she knew in Grays. But she knew there was one in Tilbury, for that was where the second steward of the *Ardara* had on occasions negotiated for the laundering of his underlings' white jackets, so Mrs Portway went personally to Tilbury: she had tried telephoning but the instrument was out of order; Hitler again, no doubt. But it wasn't far by train.

The moment she set eyes on the fat girl with the poor skin she had the feeling she'd seen her somewhere before but at first she couldn't think where. Then she had been asked her name.

'Portway,' she said. 'Mrs Portway. Thurrock.'

The girl's face had been a picture – a picture of guilt Mrs Portway knew, for suddenly it had come back. The girl outside the Co-op, and the funny look that had passed between the girl and Herbert. A pity she hadn't tackled him about it there and then. Her face suffused and her jaw came out and she grasped her umbrella like a lance.

'You seem to know the name,' she said.

'Oh no – no I never –'

'Never what?'

'Never heard the name,' Mabel said, almost in tears already.

'I don't believe you, girl. What's your name?'

'Miss Tucker.'

'Tucker. I'll remember that. Now let me tell you something: I saw you once, not long ago, in Grays. You all but bumped into my husband. I sensed something then, I did.' It was odd, the way things went, the way the human mind and memory, or awareness, worked: all of a sudden other things had all come back to Mrs Portway – the times Herbert, when in Tilbury between voyages in peacetime and when somewhere up north after the war had started, hadn't been home when he should have been. Always some excuse, harder to find once the *Ardara* had quit her Tilbury base, but he always found something and here before her, in the laundry, was the cause. It stood to reason and Mrs Portway was convinced she wasn't imagining anything.

'You little bitch,' she said. 'You dirty little whore!'

Mabel found strength, hidden reserves of pride coming to the surface. 'Old cow,' she said as the tears ran. 'Give it him yourself and he wouldn't have wanted me. I'm not all that attractive, I know that.'

'No, you're certainly not,' Mrs Portway said. 'In any case, you've seen the last of him now.' With that she marched out of the laundry, head high and followed by astonished and intrigued stares. Going home to Thurrock as fast as she could she wrote a letter to Mr Portway, addressing it HT *Ardara*, c/o GPO London. This was two days before the Prime Minister in the *Prince of Wales* left Scapa Flow; and the GPO, efficient as always, delivered the letter via the RN postal service to Rosyth in time for it to join the mail being placed aboard one of the cruisers of the Prime Minister's escort, joining from the Firth of Forth.

[ii]

Four days after the *Prince of Wales* had passed through the lines of the OB convoy, the telephone rang in Mason Kemp's home in Meopham and Mary answered with her heart in her mouth: in wartime the telephone could be an instrument of torture. You

105

never knew what the news might be.

'Mrs Kemp?'

She recognized the voice of the chairman of the Mediterranean-Australia Steam Navigation Company and she braced herself. She said, 'Oh – yes, Sir Edward.'

There was a chuckle: that was one hundred per cent reassuring. 'Home to roost, Mrs Kemp – not home exactly, but I'm sure you understand. All's well, anyway.'

'Thank you so much –'

'Rubbish, least I can do. Is everything all right your end – boys well?'

'Oh yes, Sir Edward, thank you. I –'

'Anything you want, any time. Just let us know.' Sir Edward said a brief goodbye and rang off. There were tears in Mary's eyes, tears of relief and gratitude. The Line was always caring, never more so since war had broken out – even though her husband was at least temporarily away from the Line, they still regarded him as one of their own, and herself as well.

She went upstairs to tell Granny Marsden the good news. The old girl was looking rather peaky she thought, but she was, as ever, as bright as a button mentally. She said, 'Well, I never doubted Johnny would get wherever he was going. *Where* is he, do you know?'

'Of course I don't, and you should know better than to ask.'

'I'm not likely to tell Hitler,' Granny Marsden said tartly.

'That's not the point and you know it. Careless talk –'

'All that rubbish! In the Great War –'

'That was a different war.'

'Yes, it was.' The old lady gave a heavy sigh. 'And even then I was an old woman. I doubt if I'll be here much longer, Mary.'

Mary laughed. 'You'll be here for ever. You know that too.'

'I don't,' Granny Marsden said, and all at once Mary Kemp realized she meant it. Something was up, but no use asking questions. Granny Marsden kept her own counsel. But she would ask Dr Ford to look in. Mary went downstairs, thinking that the old girl's age made the end inevitable soon and it was silly to pretend they couldn't do with the room and an end to constant attention that kept Mary largely tied to the house – help was getting harder and harder to find, with all the women doing war work of one sort or another, munitions, conducting buses and so on, or in the women's services. But Mary would miss her, she was often good company, and John would be really sad if anything should happen. She wrote to him that night, care of the GPO like Mrs Portway, but she didn't worry him about his grandmother. The letter was largely news of the boys.

[iii]

After arrival in Placentia Bay and the rendezvous with the USS *Augusta* carrying President Roosevelt, HMS *Prince of Wales* passed the news to the shore authorities that Captain Peter Redgrave, master of the SS *Stephen Starr*, had died aboard and had been committed to the sea. This was passed by the Admiralty to York in the form of a telegram addressed to Redgrave's father, but it was the sister who opened it and sat staring at it for a long time, in silence. Then she took it to her father's bedside and read it out.

He seemed uninterested, far away. He said, 'Now they're all gone. Just you and me left.'

'Just you and me,' she said, her voice without expression. There would be no help with her father now, no one to share the mental strain, not that Peter had come home much. But he'd always been available, could be contacted somewhere, and that had been something to hang on to. No more now. She wanted to cry but couldn't: she felt dried up inside. Damn this war! Where was it getting anybody? Past scenes moved across her mental vision, long-gone childhood days, excursions out in the moors and dales to the north of York, the whole family going out by train and bus until her father had bought an old car which made things easier. She remembered driving through Wensleydale from Bedale and Leyburn to the little market town of Hawes, where once they'd spent the night and next day gone on to Clapham and Ingleborough, by way of a wild, mountainous road, and had then climbed up through woodland and past a lake, all the way up to the huge pothole of Gaping Ghyll, deep enough, it was said, to take St Paul's Cathedral into its great stomach. Peter, adventurous even then, had gone close to the brink and they'd all held their breath . . . she and Peter had been great companions in those days. Wonderful days that would never come again. She had been about to write to her brother when the telegram had come and now the sudden realization that there was no longer any need came like an awakening blow and she began to cry. She envied her father, with his mind so far gone that the news would never really penetrate.

Without the *Stephen Starr* which had not so far rejoined, the OB convoy slid to its anchorage off the port of Halifax, Nova Scotia, under a grey, windswept sky with low cloud and an unpleasant, damp atmosphere though it was not currently raining. The Commodore remained on the bridge, watching as the ships' cables rattled out and the many anchors took the sea bed, watching a pinnace of the Royal Canadian Navy cutting across towards the *Ardara* from the port.

'Here comes the brass,' he said to Williams.

'Yes, sir.' Williams sounded eager and was wearing his best uniform: the starched white collar was elegance itself and he was showing a lot of cuff. Best cap too, but with the gold badge nicely tarnished to prove his sea-time: the young officers, Kemp was aware, frequently left a new cap-badge in a cup of salt water until it looked as though it had been round Cape Horn half a dozen times.

Kemp grinned. 'I said, brass. There won't be any Wrens aboard the pinnace.'

'No, sir. But later on –'

'If you're asking permission to go ashore, Williams, you'll have it the moment all the bumph and bull has been sorted out. Satisfied?'

'Yes, thank you, sir.' Williams, anxious for the shore's as yet unknown offerings, also wanted the mail to come aboard. You never knew: there might be something from a girl and hope sprang eternal in his breast. He stood there with Mason Kemp as the chief officer reported that the ship had got her cable. The Captain passed down the orders to secure the slips and stoppers; Kemp rubbed at his eyes and left the bridge after a word with Hampton, making for the latter's day-cabin put at his disposal for the reception of the naval brass, which consisted of a commander RCN and two lieutenants of the Royal Canadian Naval Volunteer

Reserve. Not, in fact, as brassy as all that; and, as it turned out, there was a Wren as well. She was an attractive girl and Kemp was aware of his assistant making what he believed were called sheep's eyes at her but without much success. Kemp was glad he was no longer young himself: it was an awful strain on young officers trying to fit the war around their love lives. Kemp knew: he'd been young in the last one.

[v]

The mail, sent across the water from Newfoundland by the Prime Minister's escort on its arrival in Placentia Bay, reached Halifax and was distributed by boat around the ships in the anchorage. Kemp read his letters after the navy had gone back inshore with his convoy report for forwarding to the Admiralty. A bill from Gieves, the inevitable accompaniment of life in the navy: uniform was not cheap but Gieves never minded waiting so long as you paid a little on account now and again. In fact they hated it if you paid it all off: that could mean you'd shifted your custom to Miller, Rayner and Haysom. A letter from his brother, who was a solicitor in Worthing, doing good business on wills in an area where the average age was sixty-five plus. Some bumph from the Officers' Federation and the Master Mariners' Association and a reminder about increased subscriptions to a golf club.

Nothing from Mary, which was the one letter he wanted.

Well, that was the war. She would have written, of course, but the letter could have missed the mail, just missed a sailing. It was largely a matter of putting home out of your mind, but you couldn't do that entirely and now there was a nagging worry that something could have happened. Bombs could come down even on such unlikely places as Meopham when the Luftwaffe bomb aimers jettisoned their remaining loads on the way home to report the flaring bonfires to Hermann Goering. But if that had happened he believed Sir Edward would find a way of letting him know speedily, faster than anything from the Admiralty.

In his cabin in the bowels of the *Ardara* Mr Portway, together with a bottle of beer, read his fate. He read it from two sources, his wife and Mabel Tucker, and he didn't care for what he read. Mrs Portway appeared to be in a state of shock at the time of writing her letter: she never wanted to see him again and she was going to find out about a divorce. The loss of Mrs Portway would in fact be less disastrous but she wasn't the only consideration: Mr Portway owned his house, or rather he and his wife owned it jointly; and that fact came in for heavily underscored threat in the letter. So did alimony. Mr Portway felt already bankrupt and turned for comfort to Mabel's letter. This he found to be a sort of Dear John: Mabel had had to go off work as a result of the attack in the laundry, she was ever so upset about what had been said in public, she was already finding the deception something of a strain, what with the war and all, and now she felt that it had better end.

Mr Portway, pale-faced, said, 'Bugger,' and screwed up both letters and flung them viciously into his waste-paper basket. Then, since his wife's had uttered those threats of divorce and sequestration, he retrieved that one and smoothed it out. It might be needed.

That evening Mr Portway went ashore on the binge.

[vi]

Lieutenant Williams also went ashore, his objective a little different. For him there had been none of the hoped-for letters from such girlfriends as his imagination could drum up as likely correspondents: just the usual long letter from his mother, full of nothing in basis. The war was dragging on and on, wasn't it, and the queues were awful and people were so rude in shops and on the buses. She had bumped into Mrs This and Mrs That and they'd asked so nicely after him and she told them he was assistant commodore of a convoy and that so much depended on him, she was really ever so proud, but it just went to show. Williams didn't know what it went to show but evidently it showed something to his mother. There was mention of his father: Dad was working ever so hard, what with the City and the ARP, he was dead on his feet most of the time and had become bad-tempered and, it was funny, but he seemed to get worse every time she talked about Paul being an assistant commodore. His mother thought he might be jealous – jealous of his own son, did you ever!

Shoving the letter into his pocket, Lieutenant Williams reflected that old man Kemp might get equally bad-tempered at mention of the title.

The mail for Petty Officer Frapp brought mundane tidings of home. Portsmouth hadn't suffered much just lately from the bombings but things were getting hard and the prices in the shops were enough to give the cat kittens and Mrs Frapp didn't know how she was going to manage, she didn't really. Frapp's allotment note went nowhere, neither did her wages – she'd just changed her job to get a bit extra and had got taken on at the Landport Drapery Bazaar as a cleaner, and *that* wasn't doing her arthritis any good at all.

'Moan, moan, bloody moan,' Frapp said angrily to himself. What a welcome to a sodding place like Halifax after sweating his guts out across the bloody North Atlantic . . .

[vii]

The mail brought real anxiety to Leading Signalman Mouncey and with a shake in his hands he sought out Lieutenant Williams, who aboard the *Ardara* could be considered his Divisional Officer and as such someone to turn to, though in all truth that wet weekend wouldn't be able to help a snail off a dandelion. But Williams, he found, had already pissed off ashore; and after that it became a case of an ill wind blowing a bit of good his way.

Leaving Williams' cabin door, he all but bumped into Mason Kemp.

'Sorry, sir,' he said, backing off.

'All right, Mouncey.' Kemp looked at him hard. 'Is something the matter?'

'Yes, sir,' Mouncey said. His voice, like his hands, shook. 'The mail, sir. I was looking for Mr Williams, sir.'

'News from home, is it, Mouncey?'

'The missus, sir. A neighbour wrote, like. She's poorly . . . in hospital, she is, in Devonport, sir.'

'I'm sorry to hear that, Mouncey. Come along to my cabin.' Kemp turned and strode along the alleyway. Mouncey followed, suddenly feeling a great weight easing off a trifle: the Commodore might do something.

In his cabin Kemp said, 'Sit down, Mouncey. Let's have it all.' He paused. 'Like a drink?'

'Thank you, sir. Thank you very much, sir.' Mouncey sat on the edge of a chair, his cap on his knees, his weather-beaten face screwed up like a monkey's, his eyes showing the gnawing anxiety. He took the glass of whisky, imbibed a large gulp, and coughed and spluttered. 'Beg pardon, sir –'

'That's all right, Mouncey. Now – tell me the facts and we'll see what we can do.'

'Yessir.' It all came out, the words tumbling over each other in a torrent, so fast that Kemp could make neither head nor tail of them. But he didn't interrupt, didn't hurry the man; when Mouncey paused for breath he asked if he could read the letter for himself.

'Course you can, sir.' Mouncey passed it over, a crumpled sheet of Woolworth's lined paper from a pad. Kemp read that Mrs Mouncey had been knocked down by a double-decker bus in Fore Street, Devonport, while it was turning short of the bomb damage. The neighbour didn't know the full extent of the injuries but she said Mrs Mouncey was still unconscious at the time of writing. An ambulance had come along fast; the neighbour had happened to see Mrs Mouncey being lifted aboard and fancied there were head injuries, a fact that had been confirmed to her by Freedom Fields hospital.

That was all; Kemp had a feeling the neighbour was softening the blow. So had Mouncey. Mouncey said, 'I reckon she's bad, sir.'

'She may not be, Mouncey. Don't jump to conclusions.' Kemp tapped the letter. 'This was written some while ago. If there had been . . . well, worse news, then you'd have been informed. A telegram from the Commodore at the Devonport depot.'

'Yes, sir.' That hadn't occurred to Mouncey; now he looked a shade happier, but he said, 'She'll be wanting me, sir.'

'Of course she will. I understand that, Mouncey. But the exigencies of war – you must understand that too. What I'm saying is, it's impossible to get you home faster than by remaining just where you are.'

Mouncey nodded. 'Yes, sir. But we're going to be in Halifax a fair time –'

'I've no comment on that, Mouncey.'

112

'No, sir.' Mouncey sat there, looking expectant since Kemp wasn't throwing him out yet and looked as if he might have some more to say. Mouncey looked at the broad gold band on the Commodore's cuff: if that meant anything at all, Kemp might be able to pull something out of a hat.

But all Kemp said was, in a kindly voice, 'Leave it with me, Mouncey. I'll see what can be done, though I don't hold out a lot of hope. I'll send for you later. I take it you won't be going ashore today?'

'No, sir. I'll wait for news, sir. Me and the missus . . .' He couldn't go on, there was something in his throat. He saw Kemp's sympathetic look and he left the cabin with a mist before his eyes. Commodore Kemp, he was all right; Mouncey knew he would be doing his best. Half an hour later he saw the Commodore leave the ship in a tender that had come out with some dockyard mateys or whatever they called them in Nova Scotia to attend to some job or other in the engine-room.

[viii]

There were no letters for ex-Colour Sergeant Crump: he had no relatives left. He'd been a widower for some years and had no children. The ship was his life and he didn't go ashore except when he had to. The shore didn't appeal; Crump didn't go much for the drink and he was well past women, and what else was there ashore? So he retired to his cubby-hole and looked after his parsley for the purser's sandwiches. That early evening, taking the air on deck, he watched the libertyboat leave from the starboard accommodation ladder, taking among others Master-at-Arms Rockett, who if past form could be relied upon, and it usually could, would return aboard late and blotto. With him was Mr Portway, looking distrait.

Purser Pemmel didn't go ashore: there was too much to do, things he should have seen to at sea. Pemmel wasn't much of a shore-goer any more than Crump, since drink was so much cheaper and more plentiful aboard. Most of the assistant pursers went, all except one who was required by Pemmel for duty aboard. Jackie Ord went ashore, not because she was on pleasure bound but because she felt she would go mad if she didn't get a

113

change of scene. Once the wounded men from the ships sunk in the convoy had been discharged ashore in a hospital tender she had nothing to do. The ship's surgeon went with her, leaving her at the jetty and mumbling something about paying a call on the hospital and his former patients, but she knew he would in fact make for the nearest hotel and sit boozing in the bar and trying to forget his session on the bog seat.

That was where Lieutenant Williams, who had gone ashore earlier, met him. Williams had looked in at the naval offices in the port, seeking Wrens and looking what he was, just in from sea, though he looked it differently from a man like Mason Kemp. He put on a sort of world-weary look as though he'd borne the whole weight of the convoy and wanted the Wrens to know it. It didn't work; he was being a nuisance and they all but said so, being busy.

Williams drifted away and tried some shopgirls with equal lack of success. They seemed to sum up his wants with an extraordinary accuracy. In the end, down by the sleazier areas around the docks, he found a prostitute. She was a gold-digger and he couldn't afford the all-night tariff: the British Navy wasn't paid on the same scale as the RCN. He settled for a short time, maximum half an hour and away whatever stage you'd got to, unless you brought out more cash. Romance over for the night, Williams made his way towards drink and found the doctor. The doctor seized upon him as a long-lost friend, though they'd met but briefly aboard, recognizing, perhaps, someone equally lonely and willing to get drunk.

'Delighted to see you, young feller. Delighted!'

'Nice of you to say so, sir.'

The doctor looked surprised but pleased. No one with a gold stripe had called him 'sir' for years. He offered Williams a gin.

'Thank you, sir.' They drank large gins, then more large gins, no suggestion that they might eat, eating being a waste of time when you were enjoying yourself. The gin began to cost Williams a great deal of money at shoreside prices, for after a while the doctor stopped paying. But Williams grew reckless and paid up, drowning his sorrows and looking more and more war-weary as the time passed. Eventually, bleary-eyed and smelling like a couple of distilleries, they staggered back to the docks and the last boat back to the *Ardara*. They arrived clutching at each other for

114

support and singing loudly. Something about the nocturnal proclivities of Old King Cole, who sent for his wife and his retinue in the middle of the night.

'Whop it up and down, up and down said the painters,
Move it in and out, in and out said the barmaids,
Screw away, screw away, screw away said the carpenters,
Throw your balls in the air said the jugglers,
Very merry men are we,
For there's none so fair as can compare
With the boys of the King's Navee . . .'

They were still singing as the boat came alongside the *Ardara* and the racket disturbed Commodore Kemp and Captain Hampton. It continued as the two officers staggered along the alleyways to their cabins. Master-at-Arms Rockett was unavailable: he, too, was drunk.

[ix]

Kemp himself was having a couple of large whiskies with Captain Hampton and feeling more relaxed than he had felt since leaving Meopham. He looked forward to all night in his bunk and waking refreshed but he had a good deal on his mind. Not just the dangers of the homeward run for the Clyde and the responsibilities of his appointment; there was the nagging anxiety about Mary and the boys – no letter. He could think up all the reasons in the world, and had; they were all logical but the nag remained and wouldn't go away. And he felt very much for Mouncey; his understanding was complete. Going ashore that day as seen by Mouncey, he had made for Naval HQ and had talked first to a Captain RCN and then to a Rear-Admiral. He had put Mouncey's case and had strengthened it by some observations of his own.

'He'll worry himself sick,' he said.

'So would we all, Commodore.'

'I know. But I'd rather not have to rely on a signalman with only half his mind on the job, sir. I don't need to stress how vital the Commodore's signalmen are.'

'No, I take your point.' The Rear-Admiral drummed his fingers on the desk in front of him. 'The same could apply to you, you know – God forbid, but if you had similar news . . . you'd have to carry on.'

'True enough. But I've been trained to it for so many years, and I think there's a difference between a commodore and a leading signalman. Hard to put it properly, but –'

'Yes, all right, I think I follow. The bigger responsibilities concentrating the mind more – something like that. Again I take your point. But what do you suggest, Kemp?'

Kemp looked down for a moment, studying his fingers, noting the heavy nicotine stains: he was smoking too much. Then he looked up directly and said, 'The Prime Minister's escort, sir. I don't know when they're sailing, of course, but Mr Churchill won't hang around for long, and they'll get home a damn sight faster than the HX will.'

'H'm. A transfer?'

Kemp nodded. 'So long as your drafting commander can let me have a replacement.'

'Well, we'll see. No promises at all. But if I can bring it off there's to be full secrecy – even your man himself is not to know where he's going till he gets there.'

Kemp had returned aboard feeling he'd done all that could be done. The war wasn't going to wait for a leading signalman and his wife but something might happen now, like a miracle. He wasn't going to say anything definite to Mouncey yet but since he knew Mouncey would be waiting to hear something he sent for him and told him to keep his fingers crossed. Just that. Kemp said nothing to Hampton either when they had their whiskies together: it wasn't his concern, the signal ratings were firmly on the Commodore's staff. From the master's accommodation they heard the racket as the boat from the shore came alongside. Kemp recognized the song and also believed he recognized his assistant's voice. He would be having a word with Williams in the morning.

Hampton said with a grin, 'Not all that different from passengers really!'

'Only when cruising – be fair! My God, they were a mob, some of them! Cruising was my idea of hell.'

They yarned as they had yarned before about old times and different days, reliving their early years at sea. Both Kemp and

Hampton had done their time in sail and both held square-rig masters' certificates. Master in sail – that had been something. Neither of them had held actual command in sail, even then sail had been on its last legs and in any case they hadn't stayed in the old windjammers for long enough before following the trend and going into steam for the sake of their careers. But both of them remembered the crash and thunder of the seas off Cape Horn, the days, sometimes weeks, spent beating into the westerlies off the pitch of the Horn, seeking a shift of wind to carry them on and past and eventually into the calmer waters of the South Pacific *en route* for Chilean ports and the long haul to Sydney. Those had been vastly uncomfortable days of wet and cold, with no hot food, days of laying aloft with the fo'c'sle hands, out along the yards with the windjammer rolling so far that the yardarms seemed about to touch the water, desperately keeping a hold on the foot-ropes with seaboots that slipped continually, one hand for the ship and one for themselves as they fought the gale-blown canvas, often enough stiff with ice.

Really, Kemp thought, they all had it soft now. Apart from the war, that was, and even that was worse for some than others: the men aboard the *Stephen Starr*, for instance, of which there was still no news.

[x]

Like Lieutenant Williams, Mr Portway, that first night ashore, had found women hard to come by. In fact he was more bereft than Williams, for there was a fastidiousness about Herbert Portway that wouldn't let him go to a prostitute. It wasn't just the dangers of disease: he saw no reason why he should pay for it when it was all there for free. Or mostly it was; not in Halifax, not yet anyway, but there was time yet, and he could bide it. Anyway, he had plenty of women in other parts of the world, currently minus two if you counted Mrs Portway, and he could practise abstinence as he was forced to at sea. That evening he moved around Halifax like a zombie, worrying about the Tilbury-Grays-Thurrock situation. Trust his wife to shove her proboscis in and stir up trouble, bloody bitch . . . and Mabel, caving in at the first obstacle! It made you sick. You just couldn't

117

trust women. They were all the same, married or single, you were just a meal ticket to them and when things got rough they upped sticks and away.

Just as he was coming out of a bar, rather the worse for wear by this time, shifting berth to another bar where there just might be a decent woman, he bumped into the senior nursing sister.

'Evening, Sister,' he said.

'Good evening, Mr Portway.' Jackie Ord looked him up and down, a smile on her lips. 'Been enjoying yourself, I see.'

'Not really I haven't. Not really like.'

'Oh. I'm sorry to hear that, Mr Portway.' Then she saw his worried look, the look of acute anxiety. 'Is there anything wrong?' She knew what the arrival of the mail could do to seamen in from deep water, sometimes good, sometimes bad.

Tears came to Mr Portway's eyes, maudlin, drunken tears with a basis of good, solid trouble behind them. He said, 'Oh, my, Sister, yes there is. It's the wife.'

'Oh dear, I'm –'

'Bitch. That's what she is! Bitch.'

'Really?' Jackie was shaken: she'd expected a tale of illness or worse. Perhaps Mrs Portway had been unfaithful and it had all come out. Often enough, nosey neighbours caused trouble with the best of intentions. She went directly to the point: nurses so often did, it was part of the training. 'Is it another man, Mr Portway?'

'Like fuck it is,' Mr Portway said, then realized who he was talking to and apologized profusely. She cut him short; the wind was cold and filled with creeping wetness and it was blowing round her legs and up her skirt.

'If you want to talk, we'll talk. But no more drink, thank you very much.' She looked around: she remembered she had passed a Salvation Army citadel some way back along the street. That would offer comfort and sobriety and perhaps a hot drink. She took Mr Portway's arm and propelled him up the road, more or less quiescent but having difficulty with his legs. Mr Portway was trying to visualize his wife with another man – trying without success. The two just didn't go together. He entered the doorway of the Salvation Army without protest. Jackie Ord sniffed: certainly the place was teetotal but only by the skin of its teeth. Drunk seamen were everywhere, sobering up. There was a strong smell of beer recently taken. There were a Major and Mrs Moline in charge and they seemed delighted to see Jackie, who had obviously not been drinking herself, and they produced steaming hot cups of tea.

'The cup that cheers,' Major Moline said, beaming through gold-rimmed spectacles. 'That's what I always say.'

Mr Portway gave him a glare, wishing he'd bugger off so he could open his heart. As soon as the Major had withdrawn, he did. And began to get ideas: after all, the nursing sister was a woman – a woman without a man. All women except his wife wanted it and you could often play on their sympathy. There was just one snag: their relative positions aboard the *Ardara*. He was of the lower deck, the rank and file, she was an officer. It was all right for male officers to hump female ratings, but not the other way round. The world was a funny and difficult place.

[xi]

Halifax absorbed them all: not the town but the fact of being there and having to make preparations for the homeward run, the forming up of the HX convoy and the embarkation of the troops, the loading throughout the ships of the stores, ammunition and general supplies for home. RFA *Wensleydale*, which had not after all detached – the returning naval escort ex-*Prince of Wales* had brought changed orders – filled her cargo tanks so that she could fuel the destroyers on the homeward run. Aboard the *Ardara* life became hectic as the days passed. Purser Pemmel was glued to the office, scanning regimental lists of officers and men, organizing the cabins and the troop-deck accommodation, his staff of assistant pursers making out the meal sittings and allocating tables to the military officers who would embark for the war in Europe. The chief steward's department worked around the clock, ordering and loading foodstuffs for the galleys, getting the ship cleaned through all ready to be made dirty again. The surgeon checked his medical supplies of drugs, bandages, splints, aperients – there was always much constipation at sea owing to lack of exercise – and ointments. After the first two or three days there was little shoregoing except as a duty for the Commodore and Williams, who seemed to be needed constantly at conferences and discussions of the convoy's tactics under the attack that they all knew was bound to come as they neared home waters and came within the range of the U-boats and the air armadas that Goering would send out to try to halt the army reinforcements in their tracks.

On the second day Leading Signalman Mouncey left the *Ardara*, bound he knew not where and by this time not caring all that much: the dreaded telegram had come, telling him the worst. Notwithstanding this, Kemp had held to what had been arranged: Mouncey should get home as soon as possible and he wouldn't have been much use to the convoy had he remained. A replacement joined, a leading signalman who had been landed sick into hospital from an earlier convoy.

Six days later the troops embarked: thousand upon thousand of them pouring up the accommodation ladders of the *Ardara* and the other hired transports, milling men in an unaccustomed world afloat, getting lost along the alleyways and up and down the ladders and main staircases, chivvied by raucous-voiced sergeants and sergeant-majors as lost as their charges, and by an OC Troops, a brigadier named O'Halloran, MC and Bar from the last war, a loud officer who announced to Commodore Kemp that, by hokey, he was no hanger back and intended to keep him company on the bridge all the way through. Knowing this would prove unlikely, Kemp responded in a friendly fashion, but took an instant dislike to a bellicose, blustering man who showed all the signs of believing that the OC Troops commanded the ship.

As soon as the troops were aboard the big ships of the convoy, the Rear-Admiral commanding the rejoined cruiser squadron asked permission to proceed. One by one the ships, their cables already shortened-in, weighed their anchors and secured them for sea; and one by one they moved out from the port, out into the North Atlantic behind the old battle-wagon and the leading cruisers of the escort. It was a grey day and there was some wind and rain. Kemp's prayer was that the weather would worsen by the time they came into the main danger zone past the longitude of Cape Farewell. But that was too much to hope for.

ELEVEN

More mail from UK had come aboard before the convoy's sailing and Kemp had heard from his wife, to his immense relief: one worry the less as he set out across the seas for home. It was a homely sort of letter, the sort he liked to get. The daily round, so far removed from his life at sea if not from the war: there had been some raids but not close enough to Meopham to worry about. The boys were well and sent their love; he wished they would write more often, but there it was, they were young and had their own concerns. Rufus, just finished with Pangbourne, was enjoying his last summer holiday before being appointed to the fleet as a midshipman RNR. His first appointment was likely to be for further training and courses, probably at one of the naval barracks. Harry, the elder, had been some while in the navy now, an ordinary seaman with a recommend for a commission as sub-lieutenant RNVR. He was finishing his qualifying sea-time in the flagship of the 15th Cruiser Squadron in the Mediterranean, no quiet place to be and another anxiety to nag away at a father. And the war looked like going on interminably, a long haul ahead yet. Kemp thought back to the outward voyage. Those losses – each ship that went down was a sad blow to Britain's heart, another nail in the coffin that Hitler saw for the British Empire. Starving out was no empty threat. The country was so vulnerable, so dependent upon its seamen and upon keeping the trade lanes open.

There was brief news of Kemp's grandmother: she'd worried about him but was happier now. From that Kemp understood that Sir Edward had been in touch and Mary knew he'd made it one way in safety.

And now they were back in it again. The *Ardara* was a different ship now, she had come alive again as compared with the emptiness of the outward voyage, alive with a huge complement of passengers as compared with pre-war days, far too many for comfort. The smell of sweaty serge had pervaded the accommodation from the moment the Canadians had embarked with their rifles and heavy packs, so had the language as the close confines of an overcrowded ship brought friction and temper – and seasickness. The *Ardara* had only just put her nose out into deep water when the seasickness had hit, and hit hard. Bodies were everywhere, so was vomit.

Four hours out and Kemp was still on the bridge. So was Brigadier O'Halloran, keeping his promise so far. He walked up and down the bridge with the Commodore, talking about his lads and what they were going to achieve, which was total victory. Fair enough; Kemp wouldn't dream of denigrating anyone's enthusiasm. But the Canadians aboard were fresh, no experience yet of war. Few even of the officers, O'Halloran said, had seen action in the last lot, certainly no one below the rank of lieutenant-colonel.

'A lot to learn,' he said, 'but they'll be okay. I guess Hitler's not going to like it.'

Kemp asked, 'Where d'you think your troops'll be used?'

'Wherever they're needed.'

'Yes. But have you any views? A new attack, a second front?'

O'Halloran shrugged. 'Can't say. Wouldn't say if I did, you know that. But I can make guesses, Commodore, and my guess would be raids, forays along the occupied French coast, keep the bastards busy and not knowing where they're going to be hit next.'

Kemp nodded. He had heard rumours that the Canadians were to be based in Brighton, or many of them were, and Brighton on the south coast was a good place from which to carry out raids across the Channel. The brigadier talked on and on and Kemp lifted his binoculars to scan the convoy, which by now had sorted itself out into its proper formation, with the cruisers disposed ahead and to either beam, and the destroyers acting as the extended screen, the old battleship ploughing along behind, a massive seagoing fortress to provide the heavy gun-power if any surface raiders should turn up.

Kemp caught Hampton's eye. 'I'm going below, Captain. Usual orders.'

'Aye, aye, sir.'

'If you'll excuse me, Brigadier.'

O'Halloran looked surprised: Kemp grinned inwardly, thinking that perhaps brigadiers were superhuman. He went below; paper-work awaited him. He left Williams on the bridge: Williams was officiously instructing the new leading signalman, by name Mathias, in the duties of a convoy signalman. Mathias was being polite but clearly knew it all better than Williams did. After a while O'Halloran called out to Williams.

'Hey there, sonny.'

It was Williams' turn to look surprised and a shade offended when he realized it was he who was being addressed. He went across and saluted smartly. 'Yes, sir?'

'At ease,' the brigadier said automatically. 'What's your job aboard here?'

'Assistant Commodore, sir.'

O'Halloran gave a whistle and said, 'Jesus Christ.'

[ii]

Jackie Ord had started something: Mr Portway was almost, she believed, paying court. The excuse was his marital problems but he was growing matey little by little, having started the morning after their chance meeting ashore and the cup of tea with the Salvation Army. Mr Portway, whenever the senior nursing sister was off duty, seemed to appear at her cabin door. If Purser Pemmel was there, which he was on two occasions, Portway made an excuse and vanished.

The second time, Pemmel asked irritably what Portway wanted and Jackie told him about the wife and Mabel.

Pemmel grunted. 'Nothing unusual,' he said.

'Perhaps not, as an abstract thing. When it happens to yourself, it looms large.'

'How do *you* know?'

She disregarded that. 'I'm sorry for him. It's all got too big for him.'

'Let him stew, Jackie. No one's fault but his own.'

'And Hitler's, for bombing the laundry in Thurrock. Or was it Grays?' She giggled.

'Well, never mind Portway. What about us?'

'*What* about us?'

'Oh, come off it. You know what I mean. Look, I'm sober –'

'Yes. You're busy again now. How long will it last?'

Pemmel shrugged: he was a man of few self-illusions. 'As long as I'm kept busy, I suppose. I don't get all that pissed anyway.'

'No?' Jackie lit a cigarette and drew a deep lungful.

'No.'

'We'll agree to disagree on that, Andy.'

'How about the doc? If I'm –'

'I'm not going to talk about my boss.'

'Loyal girl,' he said with a grin. He put a hand around her shoulder and was about to pull her towards him on the settee when there was tap at the door and an assistant purser came in. Pemmel said, 'Well, young Bates? Looking for a cough cure – or something more personal?'

'No, sir. It's you that's wanted. The troops – the orderly officer with a complaint about the troop decks. If you'd come to the office, sir –'

'God! Can't anyone else cope?'

'The orderly officer's creating hell, sir.'

'Damn.' Pemmel got to his feet; Bates held the door open for him and he flicked a hand at Jackie and left the cabin, with the AP following. Jackie gave a sigh, stubbed out the less than half smoked cigarette. Time to turn in; she was thinking she would do just that when another tap came at the door. It was Mr Portway, back again and smelling a little of whisky.

Jackie frowned. 'Yes, Mr Portway?'

Portway came in and shut the door behind him. He said, 'It's my problems, Sister.'

'Yes, and I'm sorry. But I don't see –'

'I just don't know what to do, I don't really. Soon we'll be home and I don't know what to do.'

'You'll have to face up to it then, won't you?'

'Yes, I know. That's what worries me.' Suddenly Mr Portway was slumped on the settee; he seemed almost to have collapsed on to it, a sack of potatoes that was coming apart at the seams. Jackie moved away a little. 'I'm all twisted up inside,' Mr Portway said piteously. 'People don't seem to understand. My wife, she never did.'

'Never did what, Mr Portway?'

'Understand me. And then there was the – other. What she never did either.'

He seemed, she thought, to be approaching some point and she didn't find it hard to guess what. Portway had not previously revealed what he was now evidently revealing – a lack of zeal for sex on the part of his wife. Before Jackie could utter the second steward spoke again. 'Frigid, she is. Frigid. Like a blooming codfish. Stood to reason I 'ad to find someone else.'

'Did you not tell her?'

Portway blinked. '*Tell* her? Tell her what? About Mabel?'

'No. That you found her frigid. It's better to come out with these things . . . and avoid the other complications, surely?'

Portway said, 'Try telling the wife she's frigid. Just try! She wouldn't know what it meant.' He paused and there was some heavy breathing. 'Not like you, Sister. Not at all like you.' He shifted closer, hefting a lard-like bottom along the settee. 'You and I –'

'I can be far more frigid than your wife, Mr Portway,' she said calmly though her heart was going like a steam-hammer. 'When I try. And right now I don't even need to try.'

'That's a change of tune.'

'It isn't! I've never . . . all I've done is listen and try to help. I think it's time you left, Mr Portway.'

'Come off it, Sister.' He moved closer, a lecherous whale with whisky breath and a pawing fin.

[iii]

Ex-Colour-Sergeant Crump was in his pantry and had the purser's sandwiches nearly ready, just in case. Now the ship was full the purser could be busy even at this hour and the sandwiches might have to go to the office and not to Mr Pemmel's cabin and if he was too busy to bother with them at all, then Crump would finally eat them if none of the office staff wanted them.

There was quite a roll on the *Ardara* by this time; she was well out into the North Atlantic and the weather was restless. Things shifted about in Crump's pantry and from beyond its confines there came sounds of distress as troops made for the lavatories or the upper decks. Crump grinned to himself. Pongoes at sea were a bit of a joke; they didn't appreciate a moving, rolling barrack-room at all. Not like the Royal Marines – His Majesty's Jollies as they used to be known – who, though it was true they were half soldiers, looked upon themselves as sailors first and reacted as such. Crump looked out from his pantry and saw an infantry sergeant staggering along the alleyway, bouncing off the sides, a handkerchief crammed into his mouth. The sergeant just made it into one of the wash-rooms, going in with a rush as the *Ardara* rolled heavily to starboard and the door clanged shut behind him. As Crump withdrew back into the pantry a bell rang: not the purser, but the senior nursing sister. No ordinary ring, not the sort that meant sandwiches. A long, long ring as though Miss Ord had collapsed against it.

'Oh, dearie me,' Crump said aloud, and moved fast for Sister Ord's cabin, his face crumpled in concern. Reaching the cabin he knocked hard and went in, to be confronted, if such was the word, with the second steward's bottom. Mr Portway was on the bunk, so was Sister Ord. The bottom was clad certainly, but the attitude was eloquent. Sister Ord was weeping, as Crump saw when Mr Portway did a fast shift and thumped off the bunk on to the deck, his eyes wild and hair all over the place.

'Now what's all this, Mr Portway?' Crump asked, using his colour-sergeant's voice. 'Are you all right, miss?'

Jackie Ord had sat up. 'Just about, Crump. You were just in time. And thank God for it.'

'Yes, miss. That's all right, miss. Now, Mr Portway, sir, if you'll kindly leave the cabin I'd be obliged. We don't want trouble. But it's my duty to enter this in my night report and inform the purser.'

'You bloody do,' Mr Portway said threateningly. 'Bloody do, that's all!'

'Leave it, Crump, *please*,' Jackie said in distress. 'I can cope. It won't happen again.'

'No, miss.' Crump's heart went out to her. Nursing sisters . . . angels of mercy they called them. She wouldn't want the talk, all the nastiness. Maybe he could forget about his report – maybe.

But it wasn't to be that way. There was a step in the alleyway and the purser came in. He took in the scene at a glance: the bunk was ruffled, so was Jackie Ord, and Mr Portway's flies were still undone.

[iv]

It was all left until the morning. Jackie was in a state of distress still. Mr Portway spent the rest of the night shaking like a jelly. He knew he was done for; Pemmel had called it rape, or anyway attempted rape. When the *Ardara* reached UK Mr Portway would be given a bad discharge, such as would preclude any future employment at sea, and projected like a spent cartridge towards Thurrock and his ruined love life. Very likely he would find himself subject to the call-up and forced to become a pongo. Pemmel had been adamant: the affair could not be glossed over, for the sake of discipline it had to be reported and dealt with. Jackie had pleaded as much as Portway, but to no avail. Purser Pemmel knew his duty.

On the other hand, Mr Portway knew his onions.

'Led me on, sir.'

'I don't believe that for one moment, Portway.'

'She did, sir. Honest to God she did! Took off her –'

'All right, Portway. You know that's a lie.'

'No one else does.' Portway's eyes, red-rimmed, gleamed with spite and fear. 'I can always say she did. If there's to be charges. No proof either way, and *you* know *that*. There's something else too.'

'Such as?'

'I reckon you know, sir.' Pemmel's eyes flickered at that; he knew he had his Achilles heel. Portway confirmed it. 'Always half pissed, you are. All the stewards know it. Maybe the Captain knows it too. If he doesn't, I can tell him. I can quote times and places. You'll only have yourself to blame. Sir.'

That was when Pemmel peremptorily ordered the second steward to his cabin and told him the matter was far from ended. Pemmel thereafter spent a night as sleepless as Portway himself, wondering whether or not the thing should go any further. He wasn't too worried about the threat re drink, that was just stupid, just fear talking, and Portway could never make it stick – Captain Hampton wouldn't take any action because he couldn't. It was in basis just hearsay. At the same time it was nasty and wouldn't do Pemmel any good in the long run. Hampton would remember. Pemmel would need to be superhumanly careful ever after, for he would be watched closely. No good saying captains didn't pass things on to their fellow captains – they did. And any scandal was a scandal, unwelcome to the Line: which brought him back to the main point of Portway's crime. Report it or not? Rake up dirt, or deal with the matter himself? So far as he knew, it was currently between himself and Portway, Jackie Ord and nightwatchman Crump, the latter being the soul of discretion. It would not necessarily have come to the ears of Master-at-Arms Rockett: in fact it couldn't have, since Rockett would have exploded into action by this time with the charge already framed.

It was a dilemma.

Pemmel had his duty and if he didn't do it Portway would think his threat had paid off and from then on Portway would have the whip hand. But do his duty and the chief sufferer would be Jackie Ord, and Pemmel didn't like that. He was fond of Jackie, could even be in love, he believed. Just the proximity, the being thrown together in war? She had never given him any real encouragement. Perhaps he was being selfish in even thinking he might one day offer himself in marriage to a girl like Jackie – he didn't see himself through rose-tinted spectacles these days – but he wasn't in the first flush of youth and the sea life would come to an end one day; a bachelor in retirement was always a pathetic sight. Selfish was probably the word. Anyway, he didn't want her to suffer on account of Portway.

In the end he dropped the matter quite unconstitutionally and unfairly on the shoulders of Commodore Kemp.

128

TWELVE

It had been Pemmel's own personal idea. He went to Kemp's quarters after 0800 hours, at which time he knew the Commodore usually left the bridge to wash and shave and have his breakfast, brought from the Captain's pantry by his steward. Pemmel knocked and was admitted.

'I hope you'll excuse me, sir?'

'Pemmel, isn't it?'

'Yes, sir.'

'Well, Mr Pemmel, what can I do for you?'

Pemmel began to explain, intending to leave out only Portway's threat about his drinking habits; but, not unexpectedly, Kemp cut him short. And Kemp was angry.

'What the devil d'you mean by coming to me, Pemmel? This is nothing whatever to do with me – I don't command the ship! This is Captain Hampton's business and in no way can I become concerned. You should know that. Why go behind your Captain's back?'

Pemmel said, 'For the sake of the Line, sir. I'm still a company's man. So were you, sir – and basically still are. I'm certainly not asking you to take any action. I only want advice, that's all. Without involving Captain Hampton, who might be forced to act.'

'From what you've said, he would indeed – I should say.'

'And there's the girl to be considered, sir.'

'H'm.' Kemp got to his feet, leaving the set table to move across to a large square port that looked out beyond the Captain's deck to the fo'c'sle and the heaving greyness of the North Atlantic: the bad weather was holding but Kemp had an idea that wasn't going

129

to last. After all, it was high summer. In his mind he cursed Pemmel and the antics of an over-sexed second steward. In the middle of a troop convoy in wartime!

Just then Pemmel struck the right note. He said, 'An enquiry of that sort, sir, aboard a troopship bound for the war zone. It wouldn't be a good thing.'

'But that's Captain Hampton's business to decide!'

'When it would become official –'

'Yes, yes, I know you made that point. Sit down, Pemmel. Fill me in properly.'

Pemmel did so, appealing to a former senior master of the Line, a kind of father figure and a much-respected one, who by good fortune was aboard a ship where so many had served under him. Kemp ate while he listened: a good breakfast, grapefruit, kedgeree, fried bacon and eggs, toast and lashings of coffee: he ate fast and then lit a cigarette with the coffee. Pemmel was long-winded and was still talking. Kemp thought about Sister Ord, the one he'd bollocked for setting fire to her cabin. Women aboard ship were a blasted nuisance but he'd been quite struck by this one. And Portway was going to say she'd asked for it – that was far from nice.

He cut in on the purser. 'You said only the four of you know.'

'Yes, sir.'

'You're sure of that, absolutely sure?'

'Positive, sir.'

'Right. Now, anything I say, any advice I give, is just that – off-the-record advice, which is what you came for. Understood, Pemmel?'

Pemmel nodded. As yet he had no idea as to which way Kemp was leaning but whichever it was he would act accordingly. Kemp was a wise man and very experienced, and Pemmel knew that he himself needed bolstering. Kemp was about to speak again when the voice-pipe from the wheelhouse whined and Kemp moved for it, fast. Pemmel heard the chief officer's voice.

'Commodore on the bridge, sir, please.'

'Coming up,' Kemp said, and went out of the cabin at the rush. Pemmel was left in the air. A moment later the alarm went.

Kemp lifted his binoculars: a bearing had been pointed out to him but so far nothing was visible. A signal had been made by lamp from a destroyer on the starboard beam of the convoy: the radar had picked up an echo, a surface echo so far unidentified. As a precaution all the ships of the escort and the convoy had gone to action stations. Lieutenant Williams went down to the guns to chivvy Petty Officer Frapp.

Frapp asked, 'What is it, sir?'

'Suspected commerce raider, Frapp.'

'One of them pocket-battleships, sir?'

'Don't know. Just keep on top line, that's all. It could be anything.' The term commerce raider covered a lot of ship types. Williams stared around, the eagle-eyed look of a genuine gunnery officer. 'Frapp . . .'

'Yessir?'

Williams pointed. 'The gun barrel, Frapp. Seagull droppings. Have it cleaned up.'

Frapp bared his teeth and muttered *sotto voce*, 'Need bloody stuffing you do.'

'What was that?'

'Nothing, sir.'

'I heard –'

'I said, needs some buffing up, sir. See to it right away, sir.'

'You do that, Frapp.' Williams moved away for'ard.

When Williams was out of earshot Frapp said to one of the guns' crew, 'You there. Officer has birdshit on his mind. Get rid of it, son.' He looked out to starboard. He couldn't see anything, except that the escort was redeploying. Three of the heavy cruisers were heading out for the bearing, moving fast, with great swathes of sea sweeping back from their knifing bows, and the old R-Class battleship was moving ponderously astern of them. Frapp said, 'If it's a bloody Hun out there it won't bloody linger. The raiders don't attack escorts the size of ours. Not unless they've gone clean round the bend like Harpic.'

On the bridge Kemp had come to the same conclusion. 'Just shadowing, I fancy.'

Hampton nodded. Brigadier O'Halloran, whose promise about bridge-keeping hadn't lasted all that long, had come up when the alarm rattlers had sounded; now he asked questions in a somewhat hectoring voice. He knew little of sea warfare, in fact he knew nothing, but was keen to learn.

'Mean they'll report back to Berlin, Commodore?'

'Most likely to the U-boat packs direct. Submarines can receive whilst surfaced for battery charging and so on.'

'Uh-huh. How come they shadow inside our radar range?'

'Because they have to, it's inevitable. They shadow by means of their own radar and the range is the same as ours. Or they catapult off their spotter aircraft and the effect's the same. They'll just have picked us up and now they'll be getting out at maximum speed.'

'Just buggering off, eh?'

'Yes.' The radar reports had confirmed this already: the range was widening fast, very fast. It was possible the raider was one of the German battle-cruisers, the *Scharnhorst* or the *Gneisenau*. If so she was going to get away; the escort wouldn't leave the convoy too far to the north, in case the German ship proved to be a decoy. The convoy was the main concern. But Kemp knew that from now on the unknown ship would remain in spasmodic contact, approaching to get its radar echoes and then making off again at speed, breaking wireless silence with impunity to report to the U-boat packs. With her presence already known to the convoy, there was no point in attempting anonymity . . .

There was a low rumble from across the sea, like thunder.

O'Halloran said, 'For Christ's sake. That's gunfire.'

Kemp nodded. 'Very distant. This begins to look like an attack on someone else, not us.'

'A westbound convoy?'

'I don't know. So far as I'm aware there shouldn't be an OB at sea just now. And the escort's radar would have –' Kemp broke off as an urgent report came from the radio room abaft the wheelhouse and chartroom.

'Mayday, sir. Reads: "Am under attack by heavy German ships."'

'Call sign?'

'Ss *Stephen Starr*, sir.'

'Oh, my God.' Kemp blew out his breath. Arse-end Charlie

from the OB – up to the time they'd left Halifax there had still been no news and the assumption had been, as day after day had gone by and the freighter had failed to show, that she'd fallen to a U-boat. Not so, evidently: she'd struggled on, plagued with her doddery engines, doing her best to reach Halifax and load for home, without her master who had died aboard the *Prince of Wales*. Now she was being blown out of the water . . . Kemp's grip tightened on the bridge rail and he cursed aloud into the teeth of the wind blowing across the North Atlantic.

O'Halloran asked, 'What's the *Stephen Starr*, Commodore?'

'A small ship. Just a small ship with not much speed and engines that should have been taken out and scrapped years ago.'

'Uh-huh. Not much loss, then. That's fortunate.'

Fury swelled in Kemp's head. The veins stood out, but he contained the explosion. It would be bad for the convoy Commodore to fall out with the OC Troops, very bad. There was plenty Kemp wanted to shout at the soldier, to talk of courage and guts and determination and a sense of duty to an island nation facing the threat of starvation if ships, small ships such as the *Stephen Starr* as well as the bigger ones, didn't get through Hitler's U-boat blockade. But he had the feeling O'Halloran wouldn't understand how seamen felt about these things. The brigadier had the look of a dug-out, a real relic of the last war, almost a blimp. Possibly he had served under Douglas Haig or the other top generals, men who accepted enormous casualties with a shrug of the shoulders, regarding the men as no more than cannon-fodder to form a vast platform of corpses over which one day the Allied armies would march in victory upon Berlin.

No more gunfire was heard after that single salvo, and within the next half-hour the cruisers of the escort were to be seen returning once more, appearing over the southern horizon. As they came closer the signal lamps began flashing from the flagship and Leading Signalman Mathias reported.

'To Commodore, sir. "Enemy out of range. No survivors ex *Stephen Starr.*"'

She must, Kemp thought, have gone in one God-Almighty burst of flame and torn metal. He felt deathly cold inside, imagining the horror of the holocaust. There was nothing unusual about it, in terms of the war at sea, but he felt a special responsibility for the game old ship that had been a lame duck almost from the start. As more signalling came from the flagship, Kemp passed another order.

'Secure action stations.'

The convoy moved on, once again under full close escort.

[iii]

'Beg pardon, sir.'

Pemmel, in his cabin, looked up from his desk. His visitor was Mr Portway. 'Well, Mr Portway?'

Portway shuffled and coughed into his hand. 'I was just wondering, like. What decision you've reached.'

'I haven't.'

'Still considering, like.'

'Yes.' Pemmel hadn't been sent for by Kemp as he had half expected to be, to receive the advice cut off by the action alarm earlier. No doubt the Commodore was busy: by all accounts Kemp wasn't the sort of man to forget conveniently. Pemmel said sourly, 'You'll be told in due course, Mr Portway.'

'Yes, sir.' Another cough. 'That young woman, she flaunts herself. It's not right. A man's a man all said and done.'

'That'll be all, Mr Portway.'

'Now look, don't you forget –'

'Out!' Sheer anger brought authority to Pemmel's voice, and a sudden red blaze to his eyes. Portway looked startled, opened his mouth, shut it again and backed away to the door. He went out. Pemmel sat on, chest heaving, face flushed, fists clenched on the desk top, hammering. Damn it, he was the purser, he wore three gold bands on his cuff with white cloth between, he was in charge of the whole catering department from the chief steward down. And now he believed he might have the measure of Portway. Fat and flabby and full of spurious bravery when he thought he had his superior in his grip – but a basic coward who could be put in his place by a show of authority? Or by a counter threat: Pemmel had had those earlier words with Jackie Ord and knew a thing or two. His hand shaking with the anger that was still in him he took up his telephone and called Kemp's cabin. He was in luck: Kemp answered.

134

'Commodore here.'

'Purser, sir –'

'Yes, Pemmel.'

'Thank you for seeing me, sir, and listening. I've found an answer, so –'

'I'm glad to hear it. The best way is for you to make your own decisions, you know. From now on, I don't want to know any more about it.'

Kemp rang off. When he had done so he wondered if he had sounded too peremptory, too much as though he was washing his hands. But it had never been his concern and Pemmel had vastly overstepped the mark by talking to him about it in the first place. On the other hand a fellow officer of the Line had been in difficulties . . . but what he had just said was true: a man in the position of a purser should make his own decisions without wanting his hand held.

Below in his cabin, Pemmel used his telephone again, this time to the main office. 'Purser here.' An AP had answered. 'I want a word with Crump, the night steward – when he wakes. No special hurry. See to it, please.'

[iv]

The rumours ran round the ship: word about the sinking of the *Stephen Starr* had spread and most of the ship's company felt as Kemp had done. Arse-end Charlie was a special mate, a flaming nuisance to the escort and the convoy's safety but a plodder who'd done his honest best to catch up. So there was a good deal of talk about the *Stephen Starr*'s fate and much speculation as to who had sunk the ship. There was no hard information about that, but it was obvious that something heavy was at large, and according to the navy as represented by Petty Officer Frapp the chances were that it was a pocket-battleship such as the *Deutschland* or the *Admiral Scheer*, carrying six 11-inch guns in her main armament, plus smaller guns and torpedo-tubes.

But according to Frapp, who was talking to Bosun Bush at the after end of C deck, even a pocket-battleship was unlikely to attack. 'Escort's too strong,' he said. 'The buggers don't like being out-gunned, Bose. I'm not worried.'

135

'Pongoes are,' Bush said, grinning.

'Sod them,' Frapp said disinterestedly. 'Brown jobs get on my wick, all that stamping and saluting!'

'And puking. My lads spend all day with the deck hoses, sluicing down. Still, you get used to it. Fare-paying passengers, they puke too.'

'Been long in the liners, have you?'

'Forty years, about,' Bush said briefly. He wiped the sleeve of his tunic across his nose. 'I was an AB in the *Titanic.*'

'*Was* you?' Frapp looked at Bush with a new interest. The *Titanic* was history and high drama, an unsinkable ship, a bloody great iceberg, the band playing and all those deaths – and succour in fact not all that far off if there hadn't been some sort of communications balls-up. 'What was it like that night, eh?'

'Bloody,' Bush said. 'You've no idea . . . and I don't ever want it to happen to me again.'

'Don't blame you, mate!' Frapp said with feeling. 'But at least there won't be any women and kids. That's apart from the nursing sisters, of course. But it's not going to happen anyway. Like I said – we've got a nice strong escort.'

Bush gave a sardonic laugh. He'd been in a sight more convoys than Frapp had, in the merchant ships at any rate, the sitting ducks, the main target for attack.

The day wore on, taking the HX nearer home, beginning once again to close the sea area to the south of Cape Farewell, moving homeward slowly through waters that would become more and more dangerous as the sea miles fell away behind, the wakes streaming back towards the New World. That New World was in evidence on the bridge throughout the afternoon watch; and with apparent peace around the convoy for a while Kemp took the opportunity to get a couple or so hours' sleep. He would be on the bridge throughout the night. For now he left the brigadier to Lieutenant Williams, who strode from one side to another briskly, at O'Halloran's military pace, like a dog trotting by his master's side. Williams tended to be rank conscious and although he regarded the brigadier as a has-been like Kemp the air was thick with sirs.

'Young, to be Assistant Commodore, son.'

'Yes, sir.'

'Responsible job . . .'

'Yes, sir.'

'A lot of sea experience?'

Modesty would be in order. 'A fair amount, sir.'

'RNVR. They call you the Saturday-afternoon sailors, don't they, son?'

'Er . . . yes, sir. But there've been a lot of Saturdays since the war started, sir.'

'Oh, sure there have. Still.' O'Halloran chuckled. 'Like God, maybe.'

'Sir?'

'Your navy. Moves in a mysterious way – get it?'

This was O'Halloran's idea of a joke; he chuckled again. Politely, Williams laughed. But he didn't like being patronized; and the brisk walk was wearing him out. It was, however, interrupted half an hour later when another message reached the bridge from the radio room, this time a cypher from the Admiralty. When broken down this proved to be another warning: as on the outward voyage, a strong presence of U-boats was believed to lie across the track of the HX convoy to the south-east of Cape Farewell, and this time no one at the Admiralty had any doubts that they would attack. Later an air strike might come. The fleet aircraft-carrier that had been standing by with fighter squadrons embarked had been ordered to sea from the Clyde to rendezvous with the HX convoy. In the meantime Kemp was to alter course to the south in an attempt to outflank the U-boat packs.

THIRTEEN

Kemp broadcast the word throughout the ship; after that O'Halloran addressed his troops. Everything was okay for the moment, but before the next dawn they might be in the thick of it, he said, repeating what the Commodore had already told them. They had to be ready for anything and before dusk action stations that evening there would be an extra boat drill to ensure that every man knew exactly where to go in an emergency. The ship's Captain, he said, would say a few words about that.

Hampton went to the microphone. 'Captain speaking to you all, but with special reference to the troops.' He paused: there was a silence around the ship, above and below. 'If we're hit, we may have trouble with the generators – that has to be considered. The alleyways could be in darkness. My ship's company will of course assist with torches if that happens, but some of you may have to feel your way to your boat stations. You should make very sure you're familiar with the ship's layout. Above all, act calmly. We don't want panic – I'm sure there won't be, but for the great majority of you this is your first experience of the sea, and I understand the difficulties of an unfamiliar background. There is a first time for every one of us. One more thing: if it should happen that I have to give the order to abandon, then there will be strict and absolute discipline along the embarkation deck – the deck from which you embark into the lifeboats. For the purpose of abandoning ship, or any other emergency in a sea sense, the orders of my officers, petty officers and leading hands will take precedence over those of your own officers and NCOs. There will be total obedience to those orders for the sake of every soul aboard. That is all.'

The broadcaster clicked off and throughout the ship the men took stock. To the troops, an unfamiliar world it certainly was, and one that wouldn't keep still. Some had got their sea legs, many hadn't. Almost to a man they were from the rolling Canadian prairies, a few from towns such as Edmonton or Calgary, none at all from the coastal areas. They had never before been confined in a steel can that rose and fell and lurched from side to side, criss-crossed with alleyways and filled with ladders and stairways, the air itself noisy with the continuous hum of dynamos and forced-draught blowers and vague engine sounds from deep below, and with the peculiar smell that always filled a ship at sea, compounded of wax polish, a vague oiliness, tinned air and, in a troopship, human sweat and its effect on serge uniforms.

There was a decided nervousness along the troop decks. Aboard a ship you couldn't get away. Not that many of the men would think of running from action; but if you did want to when aboard ship, there was nowhere to run to other than a leap overboard. That was something they might have to do anyway if the worst happened. One of the sergeants had had a word with a bloke who looked important and knowledgeable: Master-at-Arms Rockett, ex-Regulating Petty Officer RN. The pongo had asked a question: what would happen if any of the lifeboats got damaged by a torpedo explosion?

That got a sour answer: 'Use one o' the others, that's what. You'll be told . . . and no torpedo hitting below the waterline's all that likely to damage the boats. Though it could 'appen. What's more likely is that we'd get a list one side or the other and if the list's big enough, well, then likely we couldn't get the boats away on the *other* side, not unless we slid the buggers down the plates like a load o' kids on a playground slide. All right?'

'Then what?'

MAA Rockett moved up and down on the balls of his feet, like a bobby. ''Ave to jump, wouldn't you? But no panic, now. This is all 'ypothetical. We'll cope, you'll see. We're used to it, mate.'

Nevertheless the word spread. Not via the sergeant; but the conversation had been overheard and the galley wireless went into instant operation and there was just the tinge of a fear-smell as the *Ardara* moved on towards boat drill, dusk action stations, and nightfall.

A knock at the purser's cabin door and Crump appeared. 'You wanted to see me, sir.'

'Yes, Crump. Come in. Sit down.'

For the second time since leaving the Clyde Crump sat in the purser's cabin. This time, no drink: Mr Pemmel was being formal – formal yet friendly and a shade oily with it. Crump knew what it was all about. But he wasn't going to speak till he was spoken to.

'Crump . . .'

'Yessir.'

'You were a primary witness. You know what I'm talking about.'

'Yessir.' Crump sat with his hands on his knees, staring over the purser's head at the white-painted bulkhead behind.

Pemmel said, 'You saw it all.'

'From a certain point, sir, yes. My statement –'

'Yes, I know. You got there – at that certain point. You couldn't really say what had gone on up to then – that's to say, how it came about.'

'That's right, sir.'

'You know what Mr Portway's saying?'

'No, sir. I'm not party, sir, to Mr Portway's statement.'

'No, quite.' Pemmel fiddled with a pencil on his desk. 'Then you don't know – and this is strictly between you and me, Crump – you don't know that he's trying to make out Miss Ord led him on?'

'No, sir, I do not.' Crump stared back at the purser, shaken. 'That's a lie, sir. A dirty lie, and –'

'Of course it is. But can you shoot it down, Crump? In your fuller evidence, shall we say, if it came to an enquiry by the Captain?'

Crump seemed to consider; then he said reluctantly, 'No, sir, I can't. I only came upon the scene . . . later as you might say. Result of Miss Ord's bell, sir.' He paused. 'That bell, sir. Wouldn't that be enough? If the young lady had been a willing party, she wouldn't have pressed the bell, sir.'

'Not good enough if Mr Portway takes his line further, Crump.

She could have changed her mind . . . and that doesn't shoot down the lie that she led him on in the first place. We need something more substantial than that. I want the nearest thing possible to proof positive – something to stop Mr Portway.' Pemmel looked down at his desk, avoiding Crump's eye. 'A statement from you, Crump. It could save all the unpleasantness. Do you see what I'm getting at?'

'I think I do, sir, yes.'

'Well?'

Crump made a business of clearing his throat. He said, 'A statement, sir, that I saw Mr Portway . . . make a grab, sir, if I may put it that way.'

'Something like that.'

'A false statement, sir.'

'Not all that false, Crump. That's what happened in actual fact. That is, if we believe Miss Ord. Which we do – don't we?'

'Yes, sir, of course we do.' Crump was looking really distressed. 'I'd like to help all I can, sir –'

Pemmel pointed out, 'I'm giving you the way to do just that.'

'I know, sir. But it'd be a *lie*, sir! Bad as Mr Portway, sir. That's not right.'

Pemmel sighed: he knew he'd lost. He said, 'Only a *technical* lie, Crump.'

'Same thing, sir. And even if I did, Mr Portway might bowl it out. It's hard to tell a lie, sir, and not show it.'

Yes, Pemmel thought, it is, for a patently honest man, very hard indeed. Crump's face was too open. But that wasn't the point: as he'd already hinted, all Pemmel wanted was a lever to threaten Portway with. Maybe he was being too devious: and there was nothing devious about Crump. A little thick, perhaps: Pemmel couldn't get him to take the point. Perhaps he didn't want to, Jackie Ord notwithstanding. Lies were not in his character: obstinate old fool! Pemmel realized now that he should have known. And he had a feeling he'd fallen several notches in Crump's estimation. He dismissed the nightwatchman; there was another way and he would use it. Portway, it appeared from what Jackie had said, was a womanizer who'd just been caught out by his wife. It might be hard for a known womanizer to make anything stick about being led on in innocence . . . after Crump had left his cabin Pemmel suddenly wondered why he was

141

bothering. All everyone wanted was to have the whole thing hushed up. Portway certainly wasn't going to press for anything like an official enquiry. Pemmel knew that he was being propelled by his own obstinacy: he wasn't going to have the second steward believing he'd got the purser to back down, caught in the cleft stick of threat, of statements being made about his drinking habits. Portway was the one who had to be forced to back down.

[iii]

After the deciphering of the Admiralty's signal, the orders had been passed by lamp from the Rear-Admiral commanding the cruiser squadron and from the Commodore. The new course was indicated; and a new zig-zag pattern was put into effect once the vast body of ships had steadied on its southerly course and, after much backing and filling and some anxious moments as one ship cut across another, was back in its steaming formation under cover of the warships. The orders were that the convoy should head due south for four hours and then alter to the eastward. Kemp was doubtful about the effectiveness of the manoeuvre. As he said to O'Halloran, who was back on the bridge with him, the packs would be well extended to north and south of the track.

'You mean they'll be expecting an alteration, Commodore?'

'Very likely, yes. And it only needs a couple of U-boats to play merry hell.'

'How many have they out there?'

Kemp shrugged. 'Your guess is as good as mine. All I know is, Hitler has plenty and to spare.'

'So what do we do?'

'Follow orders, Brigadier. Nothing else we can do.'

O'Halloran said, 'Well, I guess that's right. But once again, talking about orders . . .'

Kemp said, 'Yes.' He knew what was coming because they'd had it out already, before the *Ardara*'s captain had made his broadcast, but O'Halloran was a sticker and as obstinate as a mule, a mule that wouldn't let things rest or take no for an answer. 'We've been into all that, Brigadier –'

'I know we have. Now we're going into it again, all right?'

142

'Not all right,' Kemp said, bristling beneath his bridge coat. 'Orders at sea must be given by seamen.'

'My officers –'

'I've nothing against them. But they're not seamen, Brigadier.'

'You've denigrated them by telling their own troops not to take their orders.'

'Not exactly what Captain Hampton said. And remember I don't come into that. Hampton commands the ship, not I.'

'You told Hampton –'

'I *advised* Captain Hampton – or would have done had I needed to. As it happened I didn't even need to do that. Hampton has sailed in plenty of convoys.'

O'Halloran persisted, as dogged as ever. 'I still say it's my officers and NCOs who know how to control troops. I'm not having you or –'

Kemp's interruption was crisp and authoritative. 'I repeat, Captain Hampton commands the ship. He also commands you while you're aboard. Your time will come after you're disembarked. Currently you're a passenger. I suggest you remember that, Brigadier. And I'll tell you something else: if you complain when you're safe in Britain, you'll get no support from any quarter at all. The conduct of convoys and of the individual ships in the convoys is very clearly laid down as a wholly naval responsibility under the orders of the Trade Division of the Admiralty.'

He almost felt like adding, so there. But he grinned to himself when O'Halloran, as if in anticipation of some such suffix, said angrily, 'God, how childish can you get!' and stumped away to the bridge wing on the other side.

Kemp thought good riddance and wondered which of them was being childish, though it didn't take very much wonderment in fact. And he thanked God he'd gone to sea himself. He was sorry for the troops, destined for bloody battle against Hitler's Third Reich under O'Halloran's command. He'd watched them embark in Halifax: they were young and eager, a fine-looking lot, leaving for the unknown but not letting the fear of it dampen their spirits. Kemp hoped they would manage to survive such as O'Halloran . . .

'Kye, sir?' The voice came from behind him: Williams. Kemp swung round. Kye, the navy's term for a steaming hot cup of

143

cocoa, was always welcome.

The mug in his hand, Kemp said, 'Thank you, Williams. You can turn in for a spell so long as you keep an ear and a half listening out.'

'That's all right, sir. I'll stay.'

'Just as you like.' Kemp's tone was noncommittal but he was pleased by his assistant's sense of duty, even though it was unnecessary – in Kemp's view no attack was likely while the convoy was on its southerly course. The U-boat packs would wait on their possibly extended station for the ships to steam into the net. That was how it usually went, when you didn't know where the net was. They were a shower of bastards, loosing off their tin fish from the depths against helpless merchantmen, but a shower of bastards who were only doing their duty. Kemp wouldn't want their job. To be beneath the surface in a steel canister under depth-charge attack, lying deep in the hope of avoiding the shattering explosions that would spring plates and open seams, damage the batteries to bring poisonous fumes to claw at throats – such a life was not, in Kemp's view, one for any man of the sea. Too claustrophobic, too confined. One of Kemp's own reasons for having gone to sea was his love of open spaces and the feel of wind and weather on his face. To watch the sunrise and sunset in all their differing moods, to see the scud of cloud before the wind, racing across a blue sky. Much as he loved his home he sometimes found even Meopham claustrophobic. Thoughts of home and family obtruded . . . day-dreaming as the night came down into full dark.

Williams stood silent by the Commodore's side. He had earned a rebuke from Kemp the morning after he'd staggered up the accommodation ladder with the ship's doctor, bawling out 'Old King Cole' at the top of his voice. Bad for discipline, Kemp had said. Officers didn't get so disgustingly drunk in the full view and hearing of ratings. Kemp was no killjoy and he'd said so. But some steam was best let off in private, and noise was an abomination wherever it took place. Always aboard a ship, there was a watchkeeper, many watchkeepers, trying to sleep during their watch below, and such excruciating dins carried. Williams hadn't tried to excuse himself and had apologized and Kemp had found a new liking for his assistant, who had obviously been suffering from a filthy hangover, looking like death warmed up.

Now, up there on the *Ardara*'s bridge, Kemp said suddenly, 'A penny for 'em, Williams.'

'Sir?'

'You're unusually silent.'

'Am I, sir? I didn't . . . I thought perhaps you didn't want to be bothered.'

Kemp laughed. 'A kindly thought, but misplaced as it happens. I wasn't thinking about the convoy, though no doubt I should have been. Thoughts of home, nothing more . . . I'm perfectly human beneath my brass hat, Williams. Just like any OD.'

'Yes, sir.'

'No doubt you think of home. I don't know much about you – another example of my remissness. Where's home to you?'

'London, sir. Hounslow.'

'H'm. Family?'

'Parents, sir, that's all.'

'Your father in the service – or retired?'

'Neither, sir. ARP warden.'

'I take my hat off to him,' Kemp said, and meant it. 'Those chaps have had a bellyful, all slog and plenty of danger. No doubt you worry.'

'Yes, sir,' Williams said, and sounded what he was: surprised. In point of fact he hadn't worried at all. Kemp's words made him realize something – that his father could be killed in an air raid over London. Strange he hadn't thought of that before, but he hadn't, his thoughts being all of women and his urgent desire to have someone he could regard as a girlfriend, worrying about him every time he went to sea. Silence fell again between the Commodore and his assistant; Kemp once again went through the actions of lifting his binoculars and scanning the darkened ships of the convoy and the water to port and starboard. Speed of spotting the tell-tale feather of water from a periscope scraping the surface was vital, though of course the Asdics would, or should, spot the presence of a U-boat long before the human eye. Tonight the sea was moonlit, very unkindly, and the weather was just right for attack, an almost flat sea with the wind having dropped away, but something of a swell that wouldn't bother the enemy much though it kept the *Ardara* rolling fairly heavily. Williams said, 'I'll make rounds of the guns, sir. Just to keep them on the hop.'

'Right. But not so much of the hop, Williams. Alert's a word I like better. Don't make good men hopping mad!'

'No, sir.'

'I trust you understand what I mean?'

'Yes, sir.'

'Off you go, then.'

Williams left the bridge, a little puzzled and ruffled. Old Kemp . . . one moment he yacked about discipline, the next he didn't want the hands chivvied. To Williams, discipline meant chivvying and being the efficient, soft-soled officer who caught ratings out. He had the idea Kemp would clump round in clogs, just so that the lower deck would know he was coming and crush out their fag-ends and get their arses off the deck. Williams saw no point in that. There was a lot of satisfaction in a sudden pounce and it was always effective. The men had a respect for you when you appeared suddenly and bowled them out, the officer with the eagle eye over whom nothing could be put . . .

'Watch it,' Petty Officer Frapp said to his gun's crew. 'Johnny-come-lately's on the loose again.' He had caught a glimpse of an RN cap badge as a moonbeam slanted across the deck, a cap badge emerging from behind a big bell-mouthed ventilator. 'Daft bugger – looking for birdshit again, I s'pose.'

That episode still rankled with Frapp: young Williams, he'd be better off and less of a liability if he spent the whole war on the parade ground at Pompey barracks, done up in sword and gaiters and marching matloes around and back again, practising ceremonial drill. Plenty of the RNVR officers, the Wavy Navy as they were known on account of their wavy gold stripes, were very good indeed and had done wonders in adapting quickly from civvy life to the war at sea, and all honour to them in Frapp's view. But Williams struck him as just a mobile uniform, a tailor's dummy with gold lace. Or maybe he was simply prejudiced – that birdshit again.

Williams halted, 'Well, Frapp.'

'All's well, sir. Any news, sir?'

'News, Frapp?'

Frapp was patient. 'Of the Jerries, sir. The packs.'

'No.'

'Ah. Just thought something more might 'ave come through, sir.'

'Well, it hasn't. Keep on top line, Frapp.' Williams moved away again. Low sounds came from Frapp and his lips mouthed the silent words: *Fuck off for God's sake and drop dead*. Suddenly and involuntarily Frapp emitted a very loud belch across the open deck and saw Williams halt, stiffen and look round. Frapp had difficulty in not splitting his sides. The officer had thought for a moment a gun had gone off somewhere and had almost shit himself.

[iv]

'I think,' Jackie Ord said carefully, 'the bridge believes there may be an attack tonight, Doctor.'

'Oh . . .'

'If there is, we're going to be needed.'

'Yes, yes.' The doctor's hand shook and whisky slopped over from the glass. The doctor looked at it without interest; at three and sixpence net to the ship's officers per bottle, the expense was no consideration at all. 'We shall be ready, Sister.'

You won't, she thought. She did her best without being too insubordinate. He wasn't a bad old stick and she was sorry for him, for the way he was sliding down the drain: no doubt he'd been a good doctor once, young and keen and efficient, and it was always sad to see this sort of thing. She said, 'If I were you, I wouldn't have another, Doctor.'

'A small one, Sister.'

'Think of your liver, Doctor.'

'I do. Though I try not to.'

Cirrhosis of the liver, she thought, it gets them all in the end, though gin would be worse. There was something therapeutic about whisky: perhaps the silly old bloke was practising self-therapy or something. And God knew, he *did* need his stiffener. Jackie sighed as the doctor reached unsteadily for the bottle and poured a shot that was scarcely small. She'd said her piece and that was that, she couldn't be his keeper. But she had a terrible vision of a torpedo taking the *Ardara* and causing an explosion inboard, deep in the ship, and all the burns cases, all the shattered bodies and broken limbs, and a drunken doctor

147

staggering about with a hypodermic and adding to the confusion and agony – but there were army doctors aboard, of course, and army nursing sisters too. Perhaps one piss-artist wouldn't be missed after all and he might as well make a job of it and pass out, out of the way. Jackie left him to it, tippling away in his cabin, and went back to the sick bay.

The doctor finished the whisky and poured another. He lit a cigarette, taking a long time over it, for the end of the cigarette appeared shy of the lighter's flame, veering away from it again and again. At last he managed it, dropped the result on his carpet, fished about for it, picked it up and put it between his lips, where it trembled up and down. Why had that woman mentioned his liver? It was a sore point; he knew he wasn't doing himself any good and despite what he had said to the girl he did in fact spend a good deal of time thinking of his liver. He read books about it, diagnosing himself after every likely, or possible, symptom – he was years out of date in his medical knowledge and he knew that too. Too many years at sea, vegetating. And drinking, of course . . . frontal lobes of the brain and all that, they wore out, eroded by the constant drip of alcohol or its effect. Very nasty: he could even be in for early senile dementia for all he knew. It could have started already. He never felt too good, at any rate until he'd taken a fair amount of whisky into his system. Fortunately the diminishing of his medical expertise didn't matter all that much: it was seldom anything difficult cropped up at sea. No childbirths, not even in peacetime since the Line always demanded to know about pregnancies before female passengers were booked. Few diseases – the days of shipboard epidemics were largely past. Gippo tummy, mal-de-mer, VD among the crew, these were the mainstays of the surgery. These and boils and so on, simple ailments that could be left to the assistant surgeon and the nursing sisters.

Of course it was different now that they were at war.

A little more whisky to drown the thought of what might happen at any moment. A stiffener was in a sense a duty . . . for a moment the doctor put his head in his hands, a prey to sudden and terrible depression. He felt very much alone, alone in a ship filled with seamen and troops, a ship whose alleyways were never entirely silent. He'd enjoyed that night ashore in Halifax, when he'd encountered that friendly young fellow – what was his name? No idea. But he was aboard. Assistant Commodore – that was the young man's job. The doctor slithered along his settee and took up his telephone.

On the bridge Kemp saw the blue-shaded lamp from cs29, an urgent look about it. Leading Signalman Mathias was on the ball, acknowledging. 'Number of contacts on the port bow, sir,' he reported.

'Thank you, Mathias.' Kemp went at the double into the wheelhouse where the senior second officer was on watch. 'Captain on the bridge,' he said crisply. The lid of the voice-pipe to Hampton's day-cabin was wrenched up: the Captain wouldn't be sleeping, he'd gone down for a call of nature only. Unusually, as Kemp started to pass the order for the alarm to be sounded every one of the telephones and voice-pipes demanded attention at once: radio room, gun positions, engine-room . . . and something else. Kemp himself happened to take up the phone on that one.

'Bridge, Commodore here.'

'I want the . . . the Ashishtant Commodore.'

Kemp's face was grim. 'Who the devil's that?'

'Ship . . . ship's shurgeon. I want –'

The telephone slammed in the doctor's ear. He had a hurt look, a surprised look. Some people . . . so damn rude! A fraction of a second later he became aware that the alarm rattlers were sounding, an appalling din, and then the ship seemed to come alive with pounding feet.

149

FOURTEEN

Hampton reached the bridge as the alarm rattlers started. Kemp was in the port wing, with Williams. He put Hampton in the picture. 'This is it, Captain. Sounds like a whole hunting pack. I'd like your engines to stand by for maximum power – it'll be needed within the next minute.'

'Aye, aye, sir.' Hampton nodded at his messenger, who went at once to the wheelhouse. The word went down to the engine-room, to Chief Engineer Burrows already on the starting-platform. On the bridge Kemp gripped the rail ahead of him: so many U-boats, so many torpedoes to be loosed among the ships, too big a target – they couldn't possibly miss if they simply fired blind into the mass. In Kemp's view the time had come for the extreme order: with misgivings he gave it in a firm voice.

'Scatter the convoy, Williams. Inform cs29 and Captain(D).'

Williams passed the order to Mathias, who got busy with his shaded masthead lamp, remote controlled from the bridge. Now the ships would begin to move into independent sailing, diffusing the target while the warships went into the attack. In a few minutes would come the testing time, the time when collisions might well be almost inevitable as the ships altered course and speed, some this way, some that, a great disintegrated monster flailing about the North Atlantic.

'Rendezvous, Williams. Work out a position on the chart, south-east from Cape Farewell. Thirty-six hours' steaming.' Kemp searched the surface through his binoculars, eyes straining through the moonlit night. Nothing to be seen, but signals were coming again from the flagship. There were some twenty contacts, all of them on the port bow but some of them now moving across. The convoy, course having been altered east-wards after the four hours stipulated by the Rear-Admiral, was steaming virtually slap into the packs. As Kemp watched out, a message from the radio room was reported to him: the Rear-Admiral had broken wireless silence to the Admiralty, reporting the HX about to come under potentially heavy attack. Still nothing showed, no feather on the surface, not in the *Ardara*'s vicinity.

'Buggers are taking their time,' Kemp said.

Hampton asked, 'What about that battleship?'

'Sitting duck. Useless! But I'd hate to see her go. Part of Britain's history.'

'Psychological effect?'

'Precisely. At home as well as here. Household names, all those battlewagons. Remember the sense of doom when the *Hood* went?'

Hampton said, 'Yes, very well indeed. My wife . . . she had a nephew aboard, an RNR snotty. Went down with the ship.'

'I'm sorry,' Kemp said.

'Not to worry, sir. It's in the past now.'

They were talking for the sake of talking, a human reaction as they waited, since all they could do was wait now. The relevant orders had been passed, the formation of the convoy was breaking up, the cruisers of the escort were moving across with the destroyers, the protective greyhounds of the seas, steaming fast into the attack, following their Asdics, the depth-charges ready in the racks and throwers aft, their main armament manned to finish off anything that was forced to the surface, to shatter the U-boats with gunfire. No survivors on either side would be picked up: the remnant of the convoy, if it came to that, would steam at its best speed, independently, for the rendez-vous. Then would come the count.

'Hey there, Commodore.'

Kemp turned: Brigadier O'Halloran, conspicuous by his ab-sence after the contretemps about orders, had come back to the bridge. Kemp said, 'This is it.'

'Sure, I know that. I'm reporting all my soldiers ready, Commodore.'

'Thank you.' Ready? Kemp wondered: what for? Ready to slide over the lifted side of a stricken transport, ready to gasp their lungs out in spilled oil fuel, to try to swim for the lifeboats, to die horribly in a series of explosions and escaping steam if they failed to make the boats before she went, or die more slowly, trapped, carried down into the depths until the water pressure crumpled all that was left? He gave himself a shake: those were defeatist thoughts. But it was the waiting that gave rise to them, the sense of helplessness, of being a sitting duck like that pathetic old battleship with her maximum speed of around twenty-one knots.

And the *Ardara* had little more. Perhaps, with luck, twenty-three with the holding-down bolts in danger of shearing under the stretched thunder of the shafts. Below in the engine-room, the chief engineer was bringing her up to that maximum, standing on the starting-platform, watching his dials and gauges, a mess of cotton-waste in his hands, his white overalls spotless in a hell of heat and din and spider's-web ladders criss-crossing the space above his head, right up to the airlock into the engineers' alleyway.

Burrows thought about what was going on up top, in the fresh air. He was thinking about some of the things that could happen – they didn't often, but there had been a time in his experience when they did, and aboard a certain merchant ship, not the one he was in himself but he had imagination enough to see it all, the engineers and greasers and firemen had suddenly found steel bows knifing in, with ton after ton of seawater pouring in around them as the plates buckled. The engine spaces would have filled, lifting the engine-room complement to the deckhead far above, lifting them to impact and drown. The normal procedure when one ship hit another was for the hitting ship to remain in the hole to act as a kind of collision mat, something to plug the damage until, say, a cement box could be prepared as a running repair; but that hadn't happened in the case Burrows had in mind. The hitting ship had been a neutral that had attached herself to the convoy without invitation – that had often happened in the earlier days of the war – and she'd hauled off to the accompaniment of panic-stricken shouts and wails, a load of native crewmen dancing about on her bridge and rushing up and down the deck getting in each other's way and the Captain literally tearing at his hair.

Nasty!

There had been just a couple of survivors from that engine-room, two greasers who'd managed to find the air-lock and get through with seawater acting as a thrust . . . and soon after that the ship had been torpedoed anyway, and had gone down.

Burrows turned over the starting-platform for a while to his senior second engineer and moved around, having a word here and there, eyes darting, looking at bearings and such, ears attuned to every sound, any small interruption to the sweetness of the running that might be a forewarning of trouble. A chief engineer needed all his senses alert, sight, sound, smell, touch. Machinery was Burrows' life but he knew it had a life of its own and was very temperamental. To be a good chief engineer you had also to be a machine doctor, a diagnostician first class.

[ii]

Hampton was conning the ship: that wasn't the Commodore's job. Hampton was having his work cut out: in the circumstances of convoy scatter, the precise letters of the regulations for preventing collision at sea didn't always apply, simply because they couldn't. No ship could alter three or four ways at once and still obey the regulations, and often three or four ships could come close and need to be stood clear of.

If possible.

It was when it became impossible that collisions happened; avoiding one ship, you stood foul of another.

Fortunately Captain Hampton had a cool mind and a clear brain with a capacity for instant decision. Just once during the early stages of that scattering operation did Commodore Kemp feel his blood run cold. A big freighter loaded to her marks with high explosive came suddenly across the *Ardara*'s bow, surging from port to starboard as she attempted to give clear passage to another ship that in its turn had come across her own bow.

Kemp had to bite back the order, but Hampton gave it in good time: 'Engines emergency full astern, wheel hard-a-port!'

The telegraphs were hauled over on the bridge, from full ahead to full astern twice, two pulls being the emergency signal. Bells rang and were repeated from deep down in the ship as Burrows, back on the starting-platform, reacted. There was a momentary lull in the spinning of the huge steel shafts that ran through their tunnels to the screws, and then they went into reverse and a shudder ran through the ship, a shudder that became a violent vibration, and water boiled beneath the *Ardara*'s counter. Churned sea, milky white, rushed for'ard as the way began to come off. On the bridge the Captain ordered the wheel amidships. Below, Burrows wiped his cotton-waste across his sweaty forehead and waited for the crump. Throughout the ship the tension had mounted. The *Ardara*'s crew guessed the score: the soldiers didn't. To them the sudden vibration that had taken their steel box in its grip brought another dimension of the unknown. Anything could be about to happen – like an explosion. They stood fast because they were soldiers and not boys or women, but a good many prayers were said and a good many stomachs got the runs until, as suddenly as it had started, the vibration ceased and a member of the transport's crew came shouting along the alleyways and troop decks: Master-at-Arms Rockett.

'It's all right, no panic.' The loud voice carried and brought comfort. 'The ship's all right, just a near miss, almost hit a silly bastard but didn't.'

Rockett was brought to a halt by a sergeant-major, an infantry RSM resplendent with the Royal Arms on his right sleeve. 'You, there!'

Rockett stopped. 'Yes?'

'Who are you?'

'Ship's master-at-arms, Sar-Major.'

'What actually caused the vibration?'

'Engines going astern.'

'You'd think,' the RSM said, 'the Captain'd have given some bleeding warning,' He looked shaken, grey in the face.

Rockett stared at him, face blank. 'Waste time doing that and he'd have hit. Result – you might be bloody swimming now.' It was an exaggeration but it seemed to put the RSM out of his misery. He wiped his face and marched off, left-right-left, and began shouting at his troops. Rockett moved on, no longer on the snoop for sin but helping to spread confidence. Moving through the troop decks and then down to the working alleyways he found Mr Portway and his fire parties, standing by the fire hydrants and their hose connections.

'All well, Mr Portway?'

Portway nodded, seeming oddly startled to be confronted by

the master-at-arms. Maybe not so odd; Rockett had heard funny rumours . . . things always circulated aboard a ship, nothing could ever be kept entirely secret, and Rockett was aware that there *was* a secret though he couldn't get at the truth. Nothing had been said officially so there had to be a cover-up in progress. God alone – or God and a handful of others perhaps – knew what the facts were re Portway. But the buzzes! Portway had got rotten drunk and attacked the purser, Portway had attempted rape, Portway had attempted buggery against a young private of the army draft, Portway had seven wives like the man who'd been going to St Ives and he'd gone round the bend with the strain, gone berserk and tried to jump overboard . . .

Never mind, Rockett thought. One day it would come out and since whatever it was had never been reported to him it would be no skin off his nose. What intrigued him was where the sod the buzzes had started. In his view it all added up to Crump's section, and he'd interrogated Crump and Crump wouldn't say a thing, not even when Rockett approached him on a man-to-man basis, an ex-RPO to ex-colour-sergeant basis. Crump was always like a clam. Obstinate old twit.

Rockett went back up the ladders, feeling the tension again as he moved for'ard along the troop deck. The soldiers were all ready, all fallen in with their kitbags and rifles as if about to go on parade – and they might just as well ditch their ruddy kitbags here and now, Rockett thought, because no deck officer was ever going to allow the lifeboats to be cluttered up with personal possessions if they had to abandon.

Through the troop deck, up three decks to the purser's office in the for'ard square, along the port alleyway past the surgery and the purser's accommodation and then, away ahead and dimly seen in the blue police lights, the unsteady lurch of a figure out of a cross-alleyway followed by its total collapse to the deck.

Bloody Norah, Rockett thought, it's the quack! He put on speed and shone his torch down on the heap. It was the doctor, all right, out cold but breathing, breathing noisily. Poor old bugger, Rockett thought, all grey and rumpled, always with soup-stains down the front of his uniform . . . but he should have known better considering he was a qualified quack. Rockett clicked his tongue, bent and grabbed the doctor's shoulder.

'Come along now, sir. Come along, get up. I'll take you to your cabin, sir.'

There was an indistinct utterance that sounded like 'splurge' but couldn't have been, but no other response. The doctor was physically inert.

Pemmel came along from aft. 'What's that?' he asked.

'The doctor, sir.'

'Oh, my God,' Pemmel bent. 'Out for the count.'

'Yessir. Wonder what did it.'

'Don't try to be funny, Rockett.'

'Sorry, sir. Just thought it might be tactful like.'

'Oh – yes! I see what you mean. The sudden vibration, a fall and a bump on the head. Give me a hand, will you?' They lifted and dragged, the heels slid along the polished corticene, and the doctor was sick. They got him into his cabin, lifted him to his bunk, removed his tie, loosened his collar and took off his shoes. He appeared lifeless though he still breathed.

'Nasty colour, sir. His face.'

'Yes. Get Sister Ord here, Rockett. Fast.'

Rockett lifted the telephone. 'She'll be in the surgery, sir.' He called the surgery, passed his message and rang off. 'On her way, sir.'

'Right, thank you, Rockett.'

'Want me any more sir?'

'No. I'll cope. Er . . .'

Rockett understood. 'Soul of discretion, sir.'

Pemmel thought: I wonder! That remained to be seen. Rockett was inclined to be bolshie at times but he was basically an arse-crawler whose future lay in the hands of the ship's officers. Soon after Rockett had left the cabin, Jackie Ord came in.

She looked at the bunk and said, 'Lovely sight. I did warn him.'

'He's past heeding.'

'He is at this moment.'

'I mean all the time.'

'Yes, I'm afraid that's right.' Jackie examined the motionless body, pulling back the eyelids, feeling heart and pulse. Pemmel asked if they shouldn't get Dr Barnes along, but she said that wasn't necessary. 'Just drunk, nothing else. He'll live.'

'And the less that know . . .'

'We all know already,' she said crisply. 'It's not that. It's just . . . well, I've got a lot of time for the old soak, Andy. I just

156

don't want to expose him to a junior who's not long out of medical school, that's all.'

Pemmel nodded. 'Yes, I get you, Jackie.' He paused. 'Look, isn't it about time you got out of all this? I mean . . . pissy-arsed doctors in charge, all the social boozing . . .' His voice tailed off. 'I know I'm not the one to throw stones.'

She looked at him, a quizzical expression showing. 'Are you suggesting I ought to retire?'

'In a way, yes, I am.'

'Bit young, aren't I?'

He said, 'If you got married, Jackie . . .'

'Is this a proposal?'

Pemmel sounded defensive. 'Yes.'

'Weird setting – quite original!' Mid-Atlantic, convoy scattering, attack likely at any moment . . . one drunk doctor and a lot of work potentially looming. But she laid a hand on his arm and her answer was gentle. 'I'm a qualified woman, Andy, an SRN, and I'm needed. Even if I did get married, I'd want to carry on.'

'But surely –'

'Andy, there's a war on. Remember?'

There was a smell of vomit again. Already Jackie had turned the doctor's face to one side so that the vomit wouldn't remain in his throat and suffocate him. Pemmel left her to clean up.

[iii]

Before the convoy had moved very far apart the officers on the *Ardara*'s bridge had heard the series of explosions from the port bow of the original line of advance, the explosions as the depth-charge patterns blasted the ocean aside in their search for the submerged attackers. They seemed to go on without cease and Kemp wondered how any U-boat could survive. Wondered, but knew they would. Submarines were not easy targets to find and not all that easy to sink when found. They could go deep, and silence could be ordered throughout the boat, not even a rattle against the hull that might be picked up. Always the settings on the depth-charges were a matter of guesswork: they could go off too near the surface or too deep, and submarines were capable of surviving quite a number of close explosions. Also they could fool their attackers into thinking they had been hit, fool them by disgorging quantities of oil and bits of wood and clothing to rise to the surface so that the attack would be broken off.

But tonight could be different: Kemp knew this was the massive attack, the one scheduled to halt the convoy in its tracks and destroy the troop lift before it could be deployed against the armies of the Third Reich. There would be many targets and the attack would be kept up indefinitely, or at any rate until the dispersal of the convoy was complete and the ships away on their separate courses. Even so, many of them were going to be sunk. That was inevitable. Certain of the ships were going to be marked by the U-boat captains, the bigger units, the troopships especially.

The *Ardara* was one of those most at risk.

Kemp watched for torpedo trails. All the lookouts were glued to their binoculars. The moon was bright now, an unkind quirk of fate that illuminated the targets for the Nazis. Each ship stood out sharply, silhouettes inviting attack. The destroyers were concentrating around the area of the most echoes, but Kemp knew that not all the U-boats would be in that area – some would have sneaked away to carry out isolated attacks. The cruisers were moving around, apparently aimlessly but doing their best to stand between the heavy ships and the likely direction of the enemy, a constant movement in and out, a tricky and dangerous movement calling for a consummate ship-handling skill. Away now on the port quarter as the *Ardara* steamed on her new course away from the attack concentration, the old R-Class battleship could be seen pushing her great bulk through the water, slow and solemn and stately with her battle ensigns hoisted – before the *Ardara* had moved farther off Kemp had seen the huge, over-size White Ensigns creeping to the mastheads in glorious defiance of Adolf Hitler's killers. The old battlewagon could possibly succumb to just one torpedo if the Nazis aimed a lucky shot clear of the anti-torpedo bulges that ran along both her sides in protection of her magazines and engine spaces. But not all the way along: if she was hit in the bow or stern she could flood and never mind the watertight doors and bulkheads, never mind the efforts of the damage control parties. Certain things had been rumoured about Britain's ageing battle fleet, the old-timers from the last war. Their so-called watertight divisions were said to leak like sieves . . .

Kemp wasn't looking towards the battleship when the first torpedo hit was scored for Germany: he was looking right ahead and had in fact spotted the torpedo trail seconds before it hit. He had called an automatic and totally useless warning, and then hell appeared to lift from beneath the living world and shatter it into an inferno. Immediately ahead of the *Ardara*, an ammunition ship went sky high as something approaching twenty thousand tons of high explosive blew up.

FIFTEEN

Heat blasted back; Kemp's eyebrows singed and his exposed skin felt red-hot. All the windows of the wheelhouse shattered. Debris, flung into the air from the ammunition ship, began falling from a great height. Slivers of steel had sliced across the *Ardara's* fo'c'sle and bridge, some of them at white heat. Hampton was lying on the deck, quite still and bleeding. Two other of the ship's officers were reeling about. Kemp ran for the wheelhouse. The quartermaster was all right, a lucky man.

Kemp shouted the order: 'Wheel hard-a-starboard!'

'Wheel hard-a-starboard, sir.'

Kemp ran for the engine-room telegraphs and once again the bells rang and the indicators, the tell-tales, ordered full astern. The heat was increasing, could be felt all along the open decks. Petty Officer Frapp felt it, though he was to some extent protected as were the guns' crews by their anti-flash gear. Frapp looked for'ard, saw Lieutenant Williams on the bridge with the Commodore. It didn't look as though Williams was coming down to start fussing and that was something to be thankful for. Frapp looked with horror at the shattered, blazing freighter so close ahead, beginning now to draw away as the *Ardara's* helm took effect and the engines thundered her astern and clear. He saw men, ablaze themselves, jump from what was left of the decks. He fancied he could hear screams even over the roar of the flames, coming back to him through rolling clouds of red-licked smoke. It was total devastation, total obliteration of a big ship that had been steaming intact only seconds before, carrying some fifty men each with his own hopes and thoughts of homecoming. Many of those men would have been fried by now, reduced to running fat or blackened crisps. And many were in the sea, the red-lit sea, some swimming, some lying motionless with their heads down in the water.

As Frapp looked in horror and anger, he saw the next torpedo trail. On the port beam and headed straight for the *Ardara*. He cupped his hands, yelled a warning to the bridge, then followed it up by use of the telephone, the communication between gun and bridge.

Kemp, too, had seen it. As Frapp put down the telephone the *Ardara*, with sternway on her and with her bows swinging, presented her counter to the approaching torpedo. Kemp, watching closely from the port wing of the bridge, checked the swing so as to maintain a position stern-on to the torpedo trail.

'Wheel amidships . . . hard-a-port. Stop engines . . . engines to full ahead. Midships . . . *steady*!'

Sweat streamed down his cheeks, not from the heat of the burning ship alone. For a moment he lost the torpedo and stood with fists clenched, waiting for the stern to blow out of the ship. Then he heard Williams' voice.

'It's all right, sir! You've done it!'

Kemp felt far away. 'Done what, Williams?'

'Torpedo passing down our port side, sir.' Williams pointed; Kemp looked. Down the port side was right – the tin fish could be seen, or its trail could, a matter of half a dozen feet from the *Ardara*'s plating.

Kemp said, 'Thank God.'

'Yes, sir. But that'll be the first, only the first.'

'I know.' Kemp stared down into the water, at the men struggling for their lives, men now drawing astern fast but still visible in the bright glare from the ammunition ship. Not for long: the light went quite suddenly as the rising water doused the fires, and left a hiss of steam behind as the freighter sank, steam and a great bubble of air. No one spoke of picking up survivors: no one would expect to hazard a troopship for the sake of a handful of men who might well have little longer to live in any case. The *Ardara*'s task now was to keep floating and clear the danger area – but that danger area extended across many square miles of the ocean depths. Kemp said, 'We're not the only target, Williams.'

'No, sir.'

'And I don't mean that as a kind of hope for ourselves.'

'I realize that, sir.' Williams spoke with sincerity; he knew the strains on the convoy Commodore, knew that Kemp was thinking of all the others, of his responsibility that continued overall even though each shipmaster was now under individual orders. The Commodore couldn't be everywhere at once. But that wouldn't lift the weight from a man like Mason Kemp. Williams had learned quite a lot about Kemp since the convoy had left the Clyde; Kemp had proved he was no has-been, no dug-out like Brigadier O'Halloran. O'Halloran, to give him his due, had remained quiescent in a corner of the bridge wing throughout, but now, as the *Ardara* drew away on a zig-zag course to the south, he thrust himself back into the picture.

'Somebody's balls are going to be had for garters,' he said.

Kemp turned and stared briefly. 'Whose, may I ask?'

'Oh, not yours. The skipper of that freighter.' O'Halloran seemed to realize he'd said something out of place. He coughed. 'Poor bloke . . . he'll be dead most likely.'

'Yes. And not to blame in any way, Brigadier.'

'That torpedo should have been spotted.'

'Try it some time. It's all luck. We could get one at any moment.'

O'Halloran said, 'All that wasted ammunition!' He sounded disgusted.

Kemp turned his back: inside, he was boiling. What did a man like O'Halloran know of the war at sea? Then Kemp took a grip and simmered down. The answer to his unspoken question was: about the same as he, Kemp, knew of the war on land. The difference was that Kemp, if caught up in a land battle, wouldn't shoot his mouth off.

Kemp looked at his watch: the whole thing had taken no more than two minutes. Now there were things to attend to: the transport's Captain and the two watchkeeping officers. Kemp said, 'Williams, get the doctor up at once.'

'Message already sent, sir.'

'Good. Have you had a look at them?'

'Yes, sir. Captain Hampton . . . he's dead, sir. Caught in the neck . . . a steel splinter by the look of it.'

Kemp reeled a little: an old friend and shipmate. He asked, 'The others?'

'Just knocked out I believe.' A minute later Dr Barnes, the

162

assistant surgeon, reported to the bridge. Kemp, with sharp memories of the slurred telephone call, refrained from asking why his senior wasn't attending. Barnes made his examination and confirmed what Williams had said. Barnes had Sister Ord with him. Kemp recalled the last time they'd met on the bridge, the time he'd had to deliver a broadside at her. She had been ill at ease then. Now she was the spirit of confidence, the ship's nursing sister doing her professional job.

Barnes said, 'The chief officer, sir. He'll need rest in his bunk.'

'See to it, then, Doctor. What about the senior third?'

'Fit enough, sir, just knocked about a bit by the blast.'

'Fit to take over the watch?'

'I think so, sir.'

Kemp nodded. 'Right. I'll be here myself, of course.'

Barnes looked at him critically. 'You need rest yourself, sir. I –'

'I'm all right, Doctor.'

'But you –'

'I said, I'm all right. Doctor's orders don't always apply at sea.'

Barnes was stubborn. He tried again. 'Benzedrine, sir. A tablet would keep you going.'

'*Drugs?*'

'You could call it that, yes. But with a difference.'

'You can put them where the monkey put the nuts,' Kemp said tersely.

'Waste of much-needed medical stores,' Barnes said with a grin. 'The point is, benzedrine helps concentration when you're tired. As Commodore, you need –'

'Don't you tell me my duty, young man!'

'It's *my* duty to do so, sir.'

'God . . .' Kemp came near to an explosion but held on to his temper. Barnes was persistent, and certainly he had a duty as much in his own sphere as the Commodore in his. One should not be too old-fashioned in this war; keep-awake drugs could help. And Kemp respected anyone who did his duty and stuck to his opinions in the face of seniority and rank. He came to a decision, for the good of the convoy. He said, 'Very well, Doctor. Produce your confounded bloody tablet!'

Barnes fished in a pocket and brought out a phial. He also produced a flask. Kemp asked, 'What's in that? Whisky?'

'Water, sir. For sending down the Benzedrine.'

163

Kemp laughed. 'You come prepared!' He put a tablet on his tongue and took a swig at the flask. A pity it wasn't whisky . . .

[ii]

Hampton's body was taken down from the bridge by two seamen with a Neil Robertson stretcher and laid upon his bunk in his sleeping-cabin. Kemp wondered about committal: it would have to be done, of course, but not before they were clear of the danger zone. He could not risk stopping engines while the body went overboard. So that was something for the future, a grim and unwelcome business that he didn't want to think about too much. He put it from his mind. There were other considerations: Staff Captain Greene would now take over command as master of the *Ardara*. Greene was in general charge below during action stations and had better remain there until he was relieved by another officer. Kemp sent Williams down to report the facts and ask Greene to make his arrangements. Kemp himself would do no more, could not interfere with the master's conduct of his ship. Poor Hampton . . . Kemp took a grip on his mind, forced down thoughts of pre-war days, of a lasting friendship, of a first-class shipmaster who very likely, if he'd been given the chance, would have preferred death at sea while still in command to the slow disintegration of old age and the gabbling of senility, the repetition of stories of old times that no one wanted to hear any more. Kemp thought suddenly of his grandmother: if she survived much longer she too would probably outlive her wish to go on. He knew all her yarns by heart, had often prompted her in the telling, bored stiff but not wanting to hurt. It was hard to grow old. Well, Arthur Hampton wouldn't be doing that. Kemp would find time to write a letter to Hampton's wife, for posting in the Clyde if ever they got there. Hampton had lived not far from Meopham; Mary would go and see her, do what she could – they'd liked each other and there was the sea's and the Line's bond between them . . .

The *Ardara* moved on, zig-zagging at full speed, coming clear of the convoy as the ships scattered in all directions. The senior second officer had come to the bridge to take over the watch; the senior third remained to act as second watchkeeper. Distantly there had been more attacks, more torpedo hits: Kemp had counted no less than thirteen and currently had no information as to whether the ships concerned were afloat or sunk. There had been only three mayday calls and it could be assumed that those three ships had gone down: the calls had not been repeated.

Greene came to the bridge and saluted the Commodore. He reported, 'Taken over command, sir.'

'Thank you, Captain. I'm sorry it had to be this way.'

'Yes indeed.'

'What's it like below?'

'Everything under control. No panic. All troops at their boat stations, sir.'

Kemp nodded, lifted his binoculars and once again studied the sea's surface, sweeping all around. So far as could be seen, there were no torpedoes running. He could have chosen a lucky course, but that couldn't be banked upon. He looked away towards the destroyer escorts: he couldn't pick them out now, but he saw the evidence of attack, the results of the exploding depth-charges. Some of them must surely reach their targets, the U-boats wouldn't get away without losses. Kemp thought ahead: such ships as remained to re-form the convoy at the rendezvous later would still not be in the clear. Soon after they had re-formed, they would come within the range of Goering's *Luftwaffe*, the reconnaissance Focke-Wulfs and the bombers and the torpedo-bombers that in many ways were worse than the U-boats. Kemp sent up a prayer that the aircraft-carrier from the Home Fleet would reach them in time. Her fighters would be more than welcome as a better bet than the anti-aircraft fire from the escort.

[iii]

'All right, Crump?'

'Yes, Mr Portway, thank you.' At emergency stations, Crump became one of the below-decks fire parties working in the second steward's section. Currently he was standing by a fire hydrant, ready to spin the handwheel and bring the water to swell out the hoses.

'Nasty, that ammo ship,' Portway remarked. The word had spread to the troglodytes below decks as to what the vast

165

explosion had been due and all hands were expectant of something similar happening at any moment to themselves; but Portway's thoughts were still centred mainly around his personal problems and he was being nice to Crump, just in case. He said, 'I could do with a drink.'

Crump made no comment.

'Care for one yourself, would you? In my cabin.' Portway, in charge of his section, had a fairly roving commission and wouldn't be missed if he made it a quickie. He said as much.

'No, thank you, Mr Portway. Not in action.' Crump's whole bearing was a rebuke. Portway flushed and turned his back, stifling a temptation to tell Crump to fuck off.

[iv]

The purser's staff had all the cash checked and balanced, a nightly routine at sea in wartime, and ready in bags to be sent aboard the lifeboats if they had to abandon. There was plenty of it, in Canadian dollars and sterling, notes and coins, the notes largely fivers all ready for paying off the crew when they reached their home port, preparatory to re-signing the same hands, in the main. Pemmel took personal charge of the Articles of Agreement and the as yet uncompleted Portage Bill, the basis of the crew accounts. These were in his briefcase, and the briefcase was close by his side as he sat in his private office taking sips from his whisky flask.

His telephone went: it was the surgery calling. 'Purser speaking . . . yes, Jackie?'

'It's the doctor, Andy.'

Pemmel sat straighter in his chair. 'What about him?' If the doctor had been taken bad . . . Jackie could be for it, not having called Barnes in. 'Bad, is he?'

There was a brittle laugh. 'Not that! Better if anything – mobile, anyway. He's not in his cabin.'

'Where is he, then?'

'That's just it. I don't know. He's certainly not in the surgery or the sick bay. No one seems to have seen him.'

'Heads?'

'Not there either. Not his own, anyway – bathroom's empty.'

Jackie's voice gave away her anxiety. 'I was wondering if I should let the bridge know?'

'Why, Jackie? They'll have enough on their plate – Captain dead, ship in the middle of a bloody great mass of U-boats –'

'Yes, I know all that. Can't you guess what I've got in mind, Andy?'

Pemmel's lips framed a whistle. 'You mean he could be suicidal?'

'Yes! The state he was in, the state he's been in so long, come to that. I'm terribly worried . . .'

'All right, Jackie. I'm all ready here and the DP can cope if the bridge wants anything, which I doubt if they will. I'll have a look around myself, do some questioning. I'll ring you later.'

Pemmel put down the receiver, picked up his cap and briefcase and left the office. He'd talked of questioning but that would take too long and might lead nowhere. He went straight up on deck, to the open section of C deck alongside the square ports of the peacetime staterooms to port and starboard. No sign of the doctor; and the same on B deck, where he looked into the big main lounge, empty but for duty hands. In the lounge he did ask questions: no one had seen the doctor.

He climbed to the boat deck, one deck up from the embarkation deck that was crammed with troops. The boats had been swung out earlier on, their gripes cast off and the lowerers standing by the falls ready for such orders as might come from the bridge. Again, no one had seen the doctor. Pemmel shrugged: the old soak could be anywhere and Jackie was panicking. In Pemmel's view one of the heads was the obvious answer; Doc had done that before, he could do it again. Lavatories meant privacy and a cloak against having to perform duties, a cloak against decision and a drunken state. But this wasn't a time to mount a search of all the heads in the ship – there were so many of them. Another point: suicidal doctors had better means of self-disposal than jumping overboard.

Or had they?

To get at drugs or whatnot would mean a visit to the surgery. The doctor might keep a stock in his cabin but that was unlikely to be the case without his staff knowing of it. There were such things as drug checks, and keys to drug lockers.

Pemmel blew out his cheeks in uncertainty. He looked out

from the boat deck, past the naval gunnery rates at the close-range weapons mounted before and abaft the funnel casing and at the after end, looked out at the moonlit sea that covered the menace below, the submarines that even now might be coming to periscope depth to line up their torpedo-tubes on the *Ardara*. Along the deck came Petty Officer Frapp, making contact with his close-range gunners.

Pemmel stopped him. 'Have you seen the ship's doctor, by any chance?'

'No, sir, not that I know of. Wouldn't know him by sight, not unless I saw his uniform like.'

'Oh, well . . .' Pemmel shrugged.

'What would he be doing up here, sir?'

You didn't say the doctor was being half regarded as a potential suicide. Pemmel said, 'I wouldn't know. Taking the air, perhaps.'

Frapp nodded and turned away. Then, suddenly, he turned aside and went at the rush to the port guardrail. Pemmel followed, his heart beating rapidly. 'Christ Almighty,' Frapp said.

'What is it?'

'Man overboard, port side aft.' For the second time that night Frapp raised his voice in a bellow to the bridge, repeating what he had just said.

'Lifebuoy,' Pemmel said, looking about him.

'No, sir.'

'No? Why? What the devil d'you —'

'Prolong the agony, sir, that's all it'd do. Skipper won't stop engines, nor will any other ship, stands to reason. Anyway, likely he'll have been drawn into the propellers by now.'

Feeling sick, Pemmel looked out astern. He couldn't see anything. Frapp said, 'You was asking about the quack, sir.'

'Yes . . .'

Frapp jerked a hand aft. 'I reckon that was him. I just see the gold stripes. Don't know about the red cloth. Not enough light.'

Pemmel turned away and climbed to the bridge. The *Ardara* was still moving ahead – as Frapp had forecast, no checking of her way to look for a man gone overboard. War was war. Pemmel made his report to the acting master. Kemp was listening when Pemmel told the story, and he said, 'Frapp was right. And if what *you* feared was right, then he wanted to go. If it was the doctor.

How sure can we be?'

They couldn't; but Pemmel was certain in his own mind. Staff Captain Greene said that a full search of the ship would be made as soon as conditions permitted and if the doctor was found aboard then there would be a roll-call against the crew list. The army units embarked would be told to carry out their own muster.

But that was not to happen.

SIXTEEN

The King was in his counting-house, counting out his money . . . the line from the nursery rhyme was going through Pemmel's mind as he returned to his office and walked past the bagged cash in the main office. Why had he bothered, why did anyone ever bother? It was only money and if it was lost recompense would presumably be made by the Admiralty. But you still didn't lose the Line's money if you could avoid it. Pemmel had looked in at the surgery and told Jackie what had happened and he'd left her very upset and blaming herself. If only she'd reported to Barnes, or done something to ensure that the doctor hadn't been left alone. Pemmel said if he wanted to go, why not let him? He was better off now than if he'd lived to get the push, the push into a living death with no money to keep himself boozed up. Jackie hadn't liked that; she was dedicated to saving life. So often, Pemmel thought, the medical profession simply didn't use their imaginations.

He had left the surgery and gone back to his office just four minutes before the two torpedoes hit the *Ardara*, one for'ard, the other aft.

[ii]

The concussion, the flame and smoke, were tremendous. The two torpedoes had hit almost simultaneously. The hit for'ard was immediately below the bridge on the starboard side and a lot of the blast swept upwards. Kemp was sent flying: he had been in the starboard wing, braced against the guardrail and using his

170

binoculars. For a moment he lay stunned, then felt Williams sitting him upright.

'Are you all right, sir?'

'Yes.' Painfully, his head muzzy, Kemp got to his feet with the assistance of Williams' steadying arm. 'Reports, Williams. State of damage. God! All those troops. Where's the brigadier?'

'Here,' a voice said. The bridge was becoming enveloped in smoke and there were screams coming up from below. 'Guess you'd better get the boats away, Commodore. Or the Captain had.'

'We'll assess the damage first,' Kemp said. He gave his head a shake. 'Signalman?'

Leading Signalman Mathias was already in attendance, waiting for orders. 'Yes, sir?'

'Make to cs29 from Commodore . . . am hit fore and aft. Will report damage soonest possible.'

'Aye, aye, sir.' Mathias ran for his sp and began clacking out the Rear-Admiral's call-sign, raising him at the extremity of vs range. cs29 would get the unspoken part of the message: U-boats in the *Ardara*'s vicinity. It wouldn't be long before the destroyers altered course and began an attack. By now the reports were coming in from the various sections of the ship and to Kemp's ears they sounded bad. There were big holes in the plating and plenty of water had come inboard; but the watertight bulkheads and doors were holding, leaks apart. There was fire fore and aft but the fire parties were in action and coping – that was something. The engine-room was itself more or less intact; the hit aft had not penetrated but it had been close and there was a heavy weight of water piled up against the fore bulkhead. Chief Engineer Burrows couldn't guess how long it might hold. If he was forced to give an answer, it would be that it wouldn't last all that long. The chief steward was one of those who reported by telephone to the bridge: most of the watertight doors had been shut earlier but a few had been allowed open until the torpedoes had hit, for the handling of the hoses and so on. These had now been closed by automatic control from the bridge: and a number of the chief steward's department were shut in behind them. Was there a chance they might be opened to let through those that hadn't drowned already?

Greene looked at Kemp. Kemp, his face a grim mask, said,

'Very briefly, by sections. They'll have to be fast . . . we could be hit again. And if water comes through, they're to be shut again immediately.'

[iii]

They said that when you drowned all your past life flashed before your eyes, a sort of fast-run film show just for your personal benefit. Mr Portway just didn't want to know if and when the time came, although it would be a way out. Thurrock, Grays and Tilbury just wouldn't matter any more. Mabel and Mrs Portway would be left to get on with it and Mrs Portway would inherit the house. She'd be glad about that. Mr Portway, fat and flabby and very far now from being any sort of Romeo, pushed ahead of the rising water, or rather through it as it started to reach his armpits, making for the nearest watertight door, all ready to bang and bang and shout himself hoarse. Luck was with him: just as he reached the sealing door, it opened and he flung himself into the gap before it could shut again. Hands dragged him through and a gush of seawater flooded along the alleyway before the door was once again shut. No one else made it. In the section behind the watertight door many men were trapped: soon their bodies would be forced upwards by the rising water to impact against the deckhead and all air would be displaced by the sea's encroachment. One of them was ex-Colour-Sergeant Crump, thinking, as his last moments came, of that other war when he had manned a heavy gun-battery aboard a cruiser. He had little to remember other than his service at sea.

[iv]

In his office Pemmel supervised the transfer of the cash and his briefcase to the embarkation deck, ready to be put into the boats. He and his staff mustered at their various boat stations, where they would be in charge of embarking the troops in their sections under the overall command of the deck officers. That was, if the order came to abandon.

Pemmel was shaking like a leaf. He wished to God Jackie was

with him. He'd looked out for her in the awful confusion, the milling of too many bodies, but hadn't found her. She had her own station, her own part to play. Again – if they abandoned.

Pemmel said in desperation, 'Why the sod don't they give the order?' They would be better off in the boats; you didn't stop the ship in the middle of a U-boat pack to pick up one man gone overboard – true; but the naval escort, and the other ships in the convoy if they were close enough, would certainly mount a rescue operation for the *Ardara*'s vital passengers.

[v]

Kemp didn't believe the time had yet come to abandon. The ship still had power and although she was going lower in the water they might get away with it so long as there was no further attack – the pumps might overcome the apparent leak of the water through sprung plates and watertight sections damaged by the explosions. Kemp knew the *Ardara* and her capacities well enough; but for form's sake he asked Greene's opinion.

'What d'you think, Captain?'

'The same as I believe you do, sir. She's not a goner yet.'

'Right! We'll hang on.' Kemp lifted his binoculars to the *Ardara*'s starboard quarter. 'They're coming. The destroyers. Now we'll see some action.' He picked up the microphone of the Tannoy and switched on. 'This is the Commodore speaking to you all. The destroyers are moving in. If you hear explosions, they'll be the depth-charges. In the meantime the ship is still seaworthy and we're going to try to bring her through.'

He switched off. His face was sombre, the lines more deeply etched than before. It was going to be a long haul to the safety of the Clyde anchorage.

Below in the sick bay Jackie Ord, hearing Kemp's voice, taking in his words of encouragement, was thinking similarly: for many of the men who had been brought to her care the haul was going to be far too long. They wouldn't see the welcoming arms of the land, far from it. Mangled bodies . . . as on the outward voyage there had been screams as the quivering, burned flesh had been brought in. The horrible sounds had died by now; the pain-killing drugs had had their effect. There were too many injured for the sick bay to accommodate; Dr Barnes and the second nursing sister, helped by the army medics, were treating people where they lay throughout the ship and the enclosed decks had taken on the air of a casualty clearing station. Soon after the Commodore had been on the Tannoy the crump of explosions was heard, close explosions that seemed to ring throughout the ship as the depth-charges reached their settings and went up. They clanged through the engine-room where Burrows and his staff were watching the bulkhead and noting the seepage, the water running down the strained seams, a few places where there was a stream of water zipping through holes left by sheared rivets. These were being plugged but Burrows feared there would be more, feared that he detected an ominous bulge that could mean the entire bulkhead might give under the weight and pressure of the water. The section immediately before the engine-room had had the pumps working but the sea was winning.

He got on the telephone to the bridge. Greene answered.

Burrows reported. 'I'm worried about the fore bulkhead. Too much strain. If that goes . . . we all go.'

Greene said, 'I'll send assistance. Shoring-up beams might do the trick.' Orders were passed to the bosun: as many seamen as could be spared, to reach the engine-room at the double, taking timber for the ship's carpenter to rig shoring-up beams, well chocked down to take the strain. Just as Greene had passed the order, there was a shout from Mathias.

'Starboard beam, sir – U-boat coming to the surface!'

They all looked. A cigar shape was breaking surface, bows angled upwards. A gun was seen on the casing, then the conning-tower with water streaming white from the washports. Kemp called for the searchlight to be switched on. When the beam steadied blindingly, men were seen emerging from below, through the hatch into the conning-tower. Some climbed down to the casing and ran for the gun. The U-boat's stern remained beneath the water: she had damage aft. Kemp called for Williams.

'Sir?'

'Open fire, point of aim the gun.'

'Aye, aye, sir!' The message went to all guns; at the after six-inch Petty Officer Frapp, who had already laid and trained on the

174

emerging U-boat, opened fire on the instant of receiving the order. There was a flash, an ear-splitting crack and a stench of cordite.

'Bloody miss,' Frapp snarled. He brought his range down a little: the next fall of shot was short. By this time the U-boat's gun was itself in action, and a shell went close above the *Ardara*'s bridge, its wind making all the personnel duck. It whined away to port, harmlessly. Kemp saw one of the destroyers moving in at speed, her 4.7-inch guns blazing away from before her bridge. The U-boat hadn't a chance: her gun vanished in a red flash, and when the smoke cleared Kemp saw that the conning-tower, too, was shattered and lifeless. A moment later the bow's angle increased sharply, and then the submarine slid back beneath the surface, stern first.

'One gone at all events,' Kemp said.

Now the destroyer was calling by lamp. Mathias reported: The destroyer was asking if the *Ardara* was seaworthy.

Kemp said, 'Answer: Yes.'

[vi]

Dawn came up: the *Ardara* was still afloat, the engine-room was still intact and the ship was steaming at reduced speed so as not to strain the watertight sections further. There had been no further attack: apparently it had been just the one U-boat that had despatched the two torpedoes. The escort reported no less than twelve U-boats believed destroyed. It was anyone's guess how many more remained; contact had been lost. The Nazis could have gone deep to lie doggo with the intention of mounting another attack later, or they could have drawn off, preferring not to take further risks against the exceptionally strong escort. They had had an impressive enough bag as it was: Kemp believed, from reports received, that eighteen ships had gone or were severely disabled. The count would be made finally at the rendezvous. Before dawn had come up, the reports of casualties aboard the *Ardara* had been made to the Commodore: thirty-seven of the ship's company dead, forty-one wounded. The troops had been luckier, since they had almost all been on deck at their boat stations: two officers and four NCOs had died

175

whilst on their rounds below, checking that all men had cleared the troop decks. There was a corporal with a leg broken when he'd been knocked endways during a mild stampede along the embarkation deck when the torpedoes had hit.

Kemp had stayed on the bridge throughout the night; the ship had remained closed up at emergency stations. When the reports had come in from the escort that there were no more contacts, Kemp stood the men down and the galleys produced breakfast. Williams said, 'You could do with some sleep, sir.'

Kemp had been almost reeling about the bridge: because of this he had wedged himself into the corner of the wing. He said, 'I think you're right, Williams.'

'I'll call you at once if necessary, sir.'

'I'm not much use as I am.' The effect of the benzedrine had worn off and left Kemp with something like a twitch: he was dead tired physically but mentally he was racing away on a cloud though not thinking constructively: he knew he wouldn't in fact find sleep but his body cried out for rest. He went below to his cabin. His steward brought breakfast: he felt better after he had eaten, but his mind was still too active for sleep. So many things to worry about . . . things big and little. One of the lesser ones was the trouble with the second steward . . . but Pemmel had said he could sort it out on his own. Kemp hoped he could. That young nurse; Kemp felt immense sympathy for her. Not much older than his own sons – somewhere around the early twenties, he'd have said. His thoughts went homeward, ahead of the stricken ship, covering the sea miles to the London River and a small Kent village. He wondered if the dead ship's surgeon had had anyone to worry about him, wondered what the effect might be on someone at home when the news went through of a suicide. But that could be covered and if Kemp had anything to do with it, it would be. 'Lost at sea' was always a useful phrase.

[vii]

In the engine-room Burrows stood on the starting-platform feeling rather like the boy who stood on the burning deck except that in Burrows' case no one had fled. He looked down at a slop of water across the deck plates, water that rolled from side to side in

176

time to the rolling of the ship. The level had increased but only a little. The pumps were just about coping. It was a matter of time alone. They might make it and they might not: the bulkhead was shaky, and it alone stood between safety and disaster. If it went, it would go fast, very fast, one fell swoop as they said. If the rate of leak continued to rise, it would be much slower but it would end the same way: a flooded engine-room. Then they would have either to abandon or be taken in tow. The *Ardara*, in the absence of proper ocean-going rescue tugs, would be a heavy tow. Kemp, who thought of everything before anyone else did, had already asked via cs29 for such specialist tugs to be sent out from home waters – just in case. But it was still a matter of time, Burrows knew. Time and the enemy, who would be in a position to make short work of any tugs. And of the *Ardara* come to that . . .

The following day they made the rendezvous, the point where what was left of the convoy was under orders to re-assemble. Still there had been no further attack, at any rate on the *Ardara*. Something of a miracle, Burrows thought, or maybe there was a better target somewhere else – Churchill coming back across the Atlantic perhaps, or had he already made the return passage aboard the *Prince of Wales*? There was, of course, a massive security clamp-down on the battleship's movements.

One by one the ships of the hx convoy converged on the rendezvous and signals were exchanged between cs29, Captain(D) in the destroyer leader, and the Commodore. Kemp and Williams made a count as the ships appeared from their different directions under a bright blue sky: sixteen ships. The losses had been even heavier than they had feared. The hx had left Halifax with in fact more ships than the outward ob from the Clyde and other ports. Ships for home had been tagged on to them, fast ships that could maintain the speed required of a troop convoy. Two of the liners had gone: one was the *Aratapu* of the Mediterranean-Australia Line. The men aboard the *Ardara* would have lost many friends and shipmates. Kemp himself had sailed with her master, then staff captain, on many peacetime voyages through the Suez Canal to Sydney.

'A bad day for you, sir,' Williams said.

'Yes. But now we have to get the *Ardara* home. I wonder where those bloody tugs are!' Earlier a signal had come in cypher, indicating that the Commodore's request was being met but giving no further information. Kemp thought about the water rising in the engine-room . . . if the engines flooded, they would wallow around the ocean, more than ever a sitting target for the Nazis. By this time their position on the chart was well eastward of Cape Farewell and every turn of the screws brought them closer to the enemy's air and U-boat bases along the coast of occupied France. Kemp paced the bridge as he had done for so many days, deep in thought. As he saw it, there were three alternatives open to him: as Commodore it was within his decision to alter the convoy's route and he could order an alteration further south, to avoid the danger zone that lay between the convoy and the approaches to the Bloody Foreland on the north-western tip of County Donegal or to the Lizard for the northward passage of the Irish Sea for the Clyde. He could drop south and then make his northing from a safer position; or he could do the opposite and go north to start with, and then drop down past Iceland and Cape Wrath for the Clyde.

But each held its own dangers.

The southerly approach would bring him too close in to the French airfields; the northerly one opened up the possibility of a German pocket-battleship or such lurking in the Denmark Strait, ready to pounce.

The third alternative was to maintain his course and chance the Luftwaffe. In this war, there was no safety anywhere at sea. All you could do was to try to peer into the minds of the enemy, of Hitler's high command or his own personal hallucinations. The Führer was well known to have those brainstorms that he called visions or premonitions sent by God to direct him aright. And only God could tell what he had put into the Führer's mind in regard to the *Ardara* and her consorts. In the meantime there were other considerations to be borne in mind: any deviation north or south would extend the time spent at sea, and the *Ardara* might not make it. Also, there could be no question of breaking wireless silence again – not now the convoy had re-assembled – to divert the ocean-going rescue tugs or the aircraft-carrier presumably now well out from her home base . . .

Kemp turned. 'Williams?'

'Sir?'

'Make to cs29 repeated Captain(D) from Commodore: Propose

no alteration to route. Convoy will proceed as ordered for the Clyde.'

'Yes, sir –'

'And then inform individual masters.'

'Yes, sir.' Williams stood there, pencil poised over his naval message pad. 'Sir, the engines.'

'What about them, Williams?'

'We're not maintaining the normal speed of the convoy, sir, and –'

'No. Not at this moment. But we shall. I propose to risk the bulkhead, Williams. If I dropped out, I would need to split the escort – our troops can't be left without proper protection. To split the escort would be to put the other ships at too much risk. We must proceed in company.'

'But –'

'That's all, Williams. See that my signals are made at once.'

Kemp turned away and walked to the starboard wing of the bridge. He had made his decision: like many a man before him, he could only hope it was the right one. So much, as always, depended upon luck.

SEVENTEEN

Mr Portway had had luck and he knew it: luck, plus a certain amount of personal physical push. He was sorry for the poor blokes that hadn't made it, but he preferred not to think too much about them. He thought, nevertheless, of night steward Crump, Crump had bought it, his body wouldn't be retrieved from behind the watertight section until the ship was in dockyard hands for repair. That was a bit of luck too: the principal witness for the prosecution would never give evidence now and Portway reckoned he was safe from all that. No official report had ever been made and Mr Pemmel could go and stuff himself.

Which was how Pemmel himself was seeing it. Better to let the whole thing drop: better for Jackie Ord, better for the Line. Let Portway crow if he wanted to. He certainly wouldn't broadcast anything and the crowing would be between the three of them. And Portway could sort out his matrimonial affairs all by himself and good luck to him. From what Jackie had said, it looked as though Portway's wife would be the one to sort him out. Pemmel had visions of an empurpled face and a raised umbrella and a hand deeply in the till of house ownership after the divorce.

On the bridge, Brigadier O'Halloran, much concerned by the loss of many of the troops aboard the *Aratapu*, was kept busy with signals to and from the ships of the convoy that had mounted a rescue operation to bring the survivors scrambling up the nets either from the lowered boats or from the sea direct. He was in a carping mood, hinting that the British Navy was to blame for the loss of the troopship. The army, he seemed to suggest, wouldn't have let it happen. Kemp shrugged it off; they were closing home waters and soon the brigadier would leave the ship, taking his curious attitudes with him. Kemp's hopes were rising; the engine-room bulkhead was taking the extra strain of higher speed and the pumps were still just coping. The sea was clear of contacts and so far no German aircraft had appeared. It wasn't long before Kemp knew why: the coded weather reports came in on the wireless routines, bringing tidings of adverse conditions ahead. It was likely enough the Luftwaffe would be grounded – good news so far as it went.

But Kemp and Greene, and Chief Engineer Burrows, had a strained bulkhead to worry about, a bulkhead open to the sea via the hole that had proved impossible to plug effectively.

[ii]

Burrows was watching carefully; like Kemp and Greene on the bridge, Burrows hadn't left his place of duty for very many hours past. The engine-room was his kingdom and when the kingdom was threatened the king must be there. Burrows would never have it said that he'd skulked from a bulkhead that in his view might go at any moment. He could be wrong and he knew it; he wasn't Jesus Christ. And he understood the reasons given by the bridge for keeping the engine-room manned and the screws turning. A hell of a lot of troops depended for their lives . . . a lot of generals spread around an empire under threat depended on a supply of cannon-fodder. All true.

But still!

The water continued to slop from side to side, deepening almost imperceptibly, and there was the sea sound from immediately the other side of the bulkhead, a surge and slither and a curious drumming as the weather deteriorated as promised in the met reports. Bloody bad luck . . . what was good against the dive bombers was a sight less good for damaged bulkheads and Burrows didn't like the way the plates were sending up a sort of groan, a real sound of impending doom.

Burrows looked upwards, through the maze of steel ladders. It was a long way to the air-lock and the exit to the engineers' alleyway.

Kemp put down the telephone from the engine-room, his face deeply troubled. 'Where are those God-damn tugs!'

Williams decided no response was required. With the Commodore he looked out ahead. The day was darkening unseasonably early thanks to the filthy weather they were steaming into. Cold and clammy and soon the rain would come. The seas were high and the *Ardara*'s stem was butting in deep and sending back heavy spray. Some hours earlier Kemp had ordered a reduction in speed once again, had slowed the whole convoy for the sake of the *Ardara*'s engine-room. There was little risk now from the enemy: Hitler had been cheated by the weather. And the weather was the *Ardara*'s enemy as well.

Kemp was speaking again, referring to that last report from Burrows. 'Sooner them than me!'

'Sir?'

'Down below, Williams. Talk about guts! The men who choose to go to sea in engine-rooms . . . up here we're in touch with the elements, with the fresh air.'

'I see what you mean, sir.'

'Do you?' Kemp gave a harsh laugh. 'I doubt if even I do! That damned engine-room . . . it could become a coffin inside a few seconds. I've a good mind –' He broke off as an excited shout came from the signalman on watch. 'What's that?'

'Vessels ahead, sir! Fine on the port bow, sir!'

A moment later identification came from the masthead lookout who should have seen anything before the signalman lower down. The telephone whined and Kemp answered it himself. As he slammed it down again he said, 'The tugs. And the aircraft-carrier.' He took up the telephone to the engine-room, this time not waiting for Greene. 'Commodore here, Chief. Clear the engine-room. The tugs are coming up. We won't risk it any longer.'

Burrows put down the phone and once again looked up through the network of ladders. As a precaution he had sent as many hands as possible up those ladders, just to give them a better chance of making it to the air-lock. Himself, he had remained on the starting-platform with his senior second engineer. He passed the order that had come down from the bridge.

'All hands, clear the engine spaces! Out and away!'

As he said the words, he looked again at the bulkhead. He could have sworn there was a more pronounced bulge, even that the shoring beams were starting to bend, and the run of water down the sprung seams was becoming a river. Just about in time, he thought, just about in bloody time . . . he ran for the foot of the nearest ladder, just behind his number two. The senior second went up fast while the others, already half-way up, climbed at the rush for the air-lock. As Burrows put a foot on the bottom tread of the ladder, his other foot slid on a patch of oil and he lurched sideways, his grip came off the ladder uprights and he spun along the plates just as one of the shoring beams bent and broke with a crack like gunfire, followed by the others, and the bulkhead bulged inwards. A solid wall of water suddenly released crashed into the engine-room, thunderously, devastatingly, smashing ladders and steam pipes, gauges and dials and machinery, breaking electrical circuits. The chief engineer's body was hurled away to pulp itself against the still-spinning shafts.

With the engine spaces flooded, and the ship down by the stern but held in the care of the tugs, Kemp came back once again to the Clyde with the remnant of the HX convoy steaming between the lines of the warship escort. Up the Irish Sea to the North Channel under leaden skies and a blustery wind, turn to starboard short of the great rock of Ailsa Craig to enter the Firth and move on past Turnberry and Ayr away to starboard, Arran and Inchmarnock

Water to port, through the narrows of the Cumbraes, past Toward Point at the entry to the Kyles of Bute beyond Rothesay Bay, through the boom to proceed slowly for the anchorage at the Tail o' the Bank. There was a press of troops and ship's company along the open decks as the convoy moved towards journey's end. Today Scotland looked grim and grey beneath its rain, no hint of the glories of snow-capped winter mountains and deep blue lochs, no hint of the skirl of the pipes to welcome the convoy in, the convoy that arrived as anonymously as the OB had left less than a month earlier.

Not much in terms of time elapsed. Plenty in terms of war-lost men and ships, plenty to be laid eventually at Adolf Hitler's door.

Many thoughts went out across the sullen waters off Greenock as the *Ardara* moved in towards her temporary anchorage as signalled by the King's Harbour Master. Williams looked at clouded skies and rain-slashed water and the depressing sight of Greenock on a wet day. He would get some leave before he accompanied Commodore Mason Kemp on another convoy; or he might get a new and different appointment. As to that he couldn't prophesy. But he knew that he faced an uninspiring leave in Hounslow, listening to tales of ARP and the office – that was if he went home and he saw no other prospect unless he managed to pick up a popsie in Greenock or Glasgow *en route* for the south . . . like Petty Officer Frapp, he was more or less doomed to a home leave. Not that Frapp felt quite that way, home was home and he was fond of the missus but he shrank from hearing her voice after the initial welcome to a returning hero from the sea. He knew her thoughts were of heroism or some such bunk, but she never wanted to hear the details – maybe they'd be too mundane and she didn't want her illusions shattered, but whatever it was she preferred her own moans to his. Frapp's son-in-law, if he was around, might be some solace, someone to have a pint with in the local even if he was a Brylcreem Boy. And after leave, what? Frapp knew the answer to that one: another bloody convoy, and another, and another after that, world without end. You just soldiered on, hoping for the best every trip until bloody Adolf wrote your name on a projy or a torpedo. Or you got through the war and then got chucked back on the civvy scrap-heap.

Mr Portway, like the deceased ship's doctor before him, had

been having trouble with his bowels for some days and was not far off wishing he'd copped it behind that watertight bulkhead. If it wasn't for the house, he'd leave his wife – transfer, like an appointment to a new ship, to Mabel. If she would have him now; in fact he knew from her letter in Halifax that she wouldn't, daft bitch.

Mr Portway had no loopholes at all. Maybe he would cut and run from the whole bang shoot and find another willing woman, up north. But there was still the house . . .

And Kemp?

Commodore Kemp had tried to keep his thoughts at bay: the death of Burrows had shaken him. If he'd given the order to clear just a few seconds before, Burrows might have lived. That was something that was due to remain with him for a lifetime. There were others too: so many ships lost, so many other lives – even that sad suicide. Perhaps he, Kemp, couldn't be blamed, but you always did blame yourself and wonder if you'd handled things right. He recalled how the doctor had rung the bridge, asking for Williams . . . the natural reaction was anger but perhaps there could have been another response, a request to someone, say the purser, to go and keep the doctor company till he'd sobered up and simmered down. As the *Ardara* crept on past Princes Pier and Albert Harbour, other painful thoughts came to Kemp: Leading Signalman Mouncey, by now presumably home to a wife dead in Devonport; Redgrave . . . but Redgrave of course was only one among so many, it was just the fact that his name had come to Kemp's attention over the desperate efforts of the *Stephen Starr* to catch up with the convoy and not be what she was, a perishing nuisance. And the people ashore? The British public at large would never know about the HX convoy. No news would be released about the losses . . .

Williams approached the Commodore, looking troubled. Kemp asked, 'What's the matter, Williams? You look thoughtful.'

'Yes, sir.'

'Out with it, then, but don't take too long.'

'It's all right, sir, thank you.'

'Very well, Williams.' Kemp stood motionless as the tugs took the ship up to her anchorage, the second offiicer watching the bearings on the azimuth circle. Any moment now the tugs would

185

be cast off, the Captain would lift his red anchor flag and when he brought it down the anchor would rattle out on its cable in clouds of rust-red dust. Just before that happened someone switched on the BBC News and Kemp heard something about air raids over England. He caught Williams' eye. 'Did you hear the start of the news, Williams?' he asked.

'Yes, sir.'

So that was it, Kemp thought. He said, 'Tell me.'

Williams said, 'Heavy air raids on London, sir. Widely dispersed.'

'I see. Anywhere else?'

'Kent, sir. They weren't specific. And Portsmouth.'

Kemp nodded, his face expressionless. Kent was a large area, so was London. Meopham, Hounslow . . . and Frapp lived in Portsmouth. You came in from a convoy, from a sea at war, to enjoy the blessings of the land for a spell, and all you could do was hope the blessings were still there and not scattered to the wind as in the case of Redgrave's wife and children. Well – they would all know soon enough. Kemp brought his mind back from Meopham to see Greene lift his anchor flag and bring it sharply down in the final unspoken order of the convoy.

CAMERON
ORDINARY SEAMAN

1

IT was all plain sailing still: all the way out from Scapa the Atlantic had been as clear as the skies. No U-boats, scarcely any wind – a winter miracle if a frozen one. This early morning, Dawn Action Stations had just been fallen out and the officers and ratings on the destroyers' compass platforms and on the navigating bridges of the wallowing merchant ships of the convoy flapped their arms to keep the circulation going beneath the heavy duffel-coats and balaclavas; behind the gun-shields the crew stamped warmth into their sea-booted feet and thought of home and girls or beer in the pubs of Queen Street and Commercial Road in Pompey. Winter of 1940–41; and this weird respite in the almost continuous foul weather that harassed the North Atlantic convoys but at the same time gave them a strong measure of protection against U-boat attack. The hidden menace lay powerless in gigantic waves, but came eagerly to periscope depth the moment the weather was fair.

On the port side of HMS *Carmarthen*'s compass platform, Donald Cameron, ordinary seaman on lookout, scanned his allotted arc through binoculars. His sector was from right ahead to the port beam, and God help him if he missed so much as a leaping fish. The trick was to spot what was there to be seen before the Officer of the Watch had done so; and on his vision, and that of the other lookouts scanning the other sectors in full protection – theoretically at any rate – of HMS *Carmarthen* and her charges, depended the lives of very many men. A split second could make all the difference to the

5

destroyer's ability to dodge torpedoes and to turn effectively to the attack herself.

On this occasion, however, there was nothing: only the other escorts from time to time as they altered course to weave in and out of the convoy lines, chasing stragglers, passing orders by loud hailer; and the merchantmen themselves, their masters and mates normally unaccustomed to sailing the seas in company. The station-keeping was naturally poor enough; merchant ships were not equipped for small alterations in engine revolutions such as kept the warships easily in station.

But apart from a few near misses as the mass of ships weaved about it was peace, perfect peace in the midst of war; and it couldn't possibly last. Donald Cameron, straining aching eyes through his binoculars, seeing things after a while that were not there, removed the binoculars for a spell of naked eye work, then went back to the binoculars to check. Again and again, and still nothing but the ships and the sea, which was covered with white horses, just the sort of sea condition that best suited a U-boat captain's purpose, though in point of fact attack normally came during the night watches: at night the U-boats could cruise on the surface and make better speed – and, when surfaced, they enjoyed an immunity from the Asdics of the escorts. It was not unknown for daring captains to take their boats right into the middle of a convoy at night before despatching their torpedoes.

But today fate had decided differently: the conditions were perfect for submerged day attack. *Carmarthen*'s Asdic picked up a contact and almost simultaneously the signalling started from the Senior Officer of the escort: more contacts had been established. A hunting pack of U-boats was in position. As aboard *Carmarthen*, to the orders of Sub-Lieutenant Stephenson, Officer of the Watch, the action alarm sounded throughout the ship and brought the upper deck alive with officers and men, Cameron spotted a feather of water, standing out a little above the small, breaking crests. Keeping his glasses on the feather he reported in a voice high with excitement, 'Dead ahead, sir, a periscope!'

Stephenson's glasses moved to the bearing. 'Right! I have it.' He bent to the voice-pipe connecting with the wheelhouse beneath the compass platform. 'Full ahead both engines, steady as you go!'

The reply came up, metallic-sounding, phlegmatic. 'Full ahead both engines, sir, steady as you go, sir.' As *Carmarthen*'s Captain, a young lieutenant-commander carrying an immense responsibility, reached the bridge, a 45-degree turn to starboard was ordered by signal from the Commodore of the convoy, and as the convoy swung the warships increased speed, their wakes deepening and widening. The first casualty came within minutes: a three-island 10,000-tonner, in ballast for North America to bring home war materials, suddenly spouted water and smoke and flame from her starboard side for'ard and began at once to go down by the head. As her speed came sharply off, she was cut into astern by a tanker altering course to the Commodore's orders, and then came a second explosion. Cameron saw more trails of torpedoes running through the lines of the convoy.

It was to be a massive attack.

Instinctively, Cameron felt for the inflated lifebelt nestling round his body beneath his duffel-coat, and pulled his steel helmet more firmly down upon his ears. As he listened to the quickening pings from the Asdic he felt he could congratulate himself on having beaten the set to it by giving the Officer of the Watch a visual bearing to attack. . . .

Cameron had joined the Navy on a hostilities-only engagement some seven months earlier. At the age of nineteen, he had enlisted at the first possible opportunity, as a volunteer who had not waited to be called up for service. He had joined, not in the first place in the seaman branch, but in the rating of ordinary signalman. The first weeks were to prove that he would never be able to get the hang of flag-wagging, Aldis lamps and the Morse code, but he was a good seaman – his

7

father had seen to that – and on being recommended for a commission in the executive branch had been transferred to the rating of ordinary seaman. That had been at the former Butlins' holiday camp at Skegness in Lincolnshire, right on the wind-swept Wash, now a naval shore establishment known as HMS *Royal Arthur*. Cameron would not forget his arrival there, in a coach that had met the train from Portsmouth, where he had enlisted along with a number of other new entries.

Over the gate was still set, in very large letters, Butlins' welcoming message to holiday-makers: OUR TRUE INTENT IS ALL FOR YOUR DELIGHT. And an equally large and loud Chief Gunner's Mate, the Navy's equivalent to a Regimental Sergeant-Major, had drawn the draft's attention to it with a wave of a hammy hand.

'Now then. See that sign?'

There had been a chorus of polite yesses.

'Well, it doesn't bloody well apply to you lot,' the Chief Gunner's Mate had said with a certain degree of satisfaction in his voice. 'Get fell in properly. . . .'

They had shambled into some sort of line and had been taken by a petty officer and marched beneath the sign of welcome. Cameron was to find that its message certainly did not apply to the establishment's wartime occupants. The training routine was hard, the life rigorous, the day long – it started at 0630 hours when the trainee sailors were turned out from the chalets in which they slept to muster for inspection by their petty officer instructor, and then set to 'scavenge' – scrabble about among the chalet lines and pick up any piece of paper or other un-Naval objects that might be lying around. The chalets themselves were more spartan than the holiday-makers had known them: each contained three men in two bunks, the double one being for decency's sake split in half by a deep board. Here they washed and shaved in cold water which had afterwards to be emptied. After scavenging there was breakfast in a vast, noisy building, one of several that were known by such names as York House, Kent House and

8

Gloucester House; and after breakfast Divisions, in the course of which the various classes marched behind a Royal Marine band playing, daily, 'Sussex by the Sea' and 'Heart of Oak', marching past the Training Commander and the First Lieutenant to be dispersed to the different classrooms or other training areas. Much of the daily routine was taken up with square-bashing and with long route marches into the surrounding countryside; the rest was devoted to instruction in Naval routine, shipboard organization and the art of signalling; the latter included many sessions at the semaphore flags, when the arms of the assembled trainees moved rhythmically to the tune, never to be forgotten, of 'The Teddy Bears' Picnic'. Every fault, however small, of work, dress or behaviour was pounced upon hard by the PO Instructor, one Yeoman of Signals Possett, a small, wiry man, a Fleet Reservist who had been called back for active service after some eight years on the beach. A kindly enough man when off parade, he tended to ramble on about the past when he had served in the old *Iron Duke*, Lord Jellicoe's last-war flagship in the Grand Fleet.

'You young lads,' he would say fairly often, 'you've got it soft compared to what we had at your age. Bloody soft! I tell you something, though.'

'Yes, Yeoman?'

Possett would give a characteristic hitch to his trousers. 'Never had a good *laugh* ashore I didn't! Not till I got back in the andrew. Then I laughed again. And every time I sees you lot I laughs again till I splits me sides.'

It was not encouraging, but it was not unkindly meant. Cameron learned, as he was to continue learning throughout many facets of the war, that the chiefs and petty officers of His Majesty's Navy were mostly the salt of the earth, hard but fair, utterly dependable, utterly honest. They chased and chivvied the new entries but the new entries, as their service proceeded, quickly realized that it had all been for their own good and that of their seagoing mates: one piece of bad seamanship, one signal read too slowly, one moment of slackness,

9

could mean real danger. Yeoman of Signals Possett and his fellow petty officers were not going to have that happen. And many of the new entries needed a good deal of chivvying: they were a mixed bunch, some volunteers, some conscripts – some keen, others far from it. There were plenty of mutinous mutters about hardship. And the backgrounds were just as mixed. The majority were of the working class, from any number of trades from bricklaying to farming. There were clerks, waiters, bookies' runners, shop assistants . . . men from banks, solicitors' offices, Town Halls, slaughterhouses. There were those who stood out on account of their appearance and their accents: the sons of professional men, of service officers, even of peers of the realm. Cameron was one of those who attracted attention from above, and after a couple of months of being observed discreetly by his Divisional Officer, he was summoned for a word in private. His Divisional Officer was a lieutenant of the Wavy Navy, the RNVR, named Stubbs.

'Sit down, Cameron,' Stubbs invited – or ordered.

'Thank you, sir.' Cameron sat.

Stubbs said, 'I've been looking through your service certificate.' The reference was to the 'parchment' that was started when a man joined and accompanied him as a continuing life-history throughout his lower-deck service. 'You were at a public school, I see.'

'Yes, sir. A minor one, sir.'

Stubbs looked up sharply. 'Not apologizing for that, are you?'

'No, sir,' Cameron said, flushing. 'It's just that – well, it's not the thing to confess to –'

'Amongst your messmates. So you try to minimize it. I think I understand, but try to drop the habit. You're who you are and that's that.' Stubbs looked down at the service certificate again, then up at Cameron, seeming to stare right through him. 'School certificate, six credits, Matric exemption. Going on to college, were you?'

'No, sir.'

'What, then?'

10

'I'd have gone into my father's business, sir.'

'Ah, I see. Trawlers, isn't it?'

'Yes, sir. He owns a small fleet sailing out of Aberdeen.'

'Yes. Yet you joined in Portsmouth, I see. How come?'

Cameron said, 'I was staying with an uncle, sir. He was in the Navy ... invalided out before war started. I had my nineteenth birthday while I was there, sir –'

'And joined. I see. Like it?'

Cameron smiled. 'Yes, sir, I do.' There was a pause, and he filled it. 'I'm used to the sea, sir. My father often sent me away with the trawlers in the holidays.'

'Yes, I was wondering,' Stubbs said reflectively. 'Yeoman of Signals Possett tells me you've taken to boat-handling like a duck.' He grinned. 'Knowing Yeoman Possett, the "duck" could be taken two ways, of course ... but I think I got the right translation. Tell me this: if you'd gone into your father's trawling fleet, which I take it would have been on the management side, would you have got yourself some kind of seafaring qualification?'

Cameron said, 'Yes, sir. My father would have insisted on that.'

'He has one himself?'

'He's a master mariner, sir.'

'I see.' Stubbs paused, then said rather sharply, 'You're a pretty rotten signalman, aren't you?'

'I'm sorry, sir, I just can't get to grips with it.'

Stubbs nodded. 'That's honest. Why did you join in that rating?'

'The Chief PO at the recruiting office said there was a shortage of signalmen, sir, and I'd be likely to get to sea quicker than as a seaman.'

Stubbs laughed. 'Yes, and it's true, oddly enough. I'm afraid the Navy's a bit of a shambles in some ways ... seamen can spend months sweeping the parade at RNB while signalmen always go to sea. However, since you're no signalman, how would you feel about a transfer?'

'I'd like it, sir.'

'Good! If you wish, I'll put the wheels in motion. And something else: a commission. How about that?'

'A commission, sir?' Cameron looked startled.

'That's what I said. I'm sure you've envisaged the possibility, haven't you?'

'Well, sir—'

'Of course you have,' Stubbs said briskly, and stood up. 'That's settled then. In my view, and in the view of the Training Commander, you have the right qualities of leadership and common sense and personality ... they're all summed up in the service phrase, Officer-Like Qualities or OLQ for short. I'm prepared to put it to the Captain that you should have a White Paper started.'

'Thank you, sir—'

'Don't thank me, thank yourself – and Yeoman Possett. Once it's all put through, you'll be sent to *Ganges* at Shotley for seamanship training, along with your White Paper, and after a course there you'll be drafted to RNB Portsmouth and thence to sea. You'll need to do a minimum of three months' actual sea-time and get your Captain's recommendation for a commission, then you'll be put before a board at Portsmouth. Pass that, and you go to *King Alfred* in Sussex as a cadet rating. All right?'

Leaving the Divisional Office, Cameron knew that henceforward life would be a little different. Harder; for he had to prove himself even more and repay Stubbs's confidence that he could make it. He had to show not only seamanship but the vital elements of leadership and initiative. OLQ would loom very important, and his ships and establishments would have eagle eyes on the White Paper, the avenue to a commission that would carry every detail and every report upon his character and abilities. He was now what was known officially as a CW Candidate, CW standing for Commission and Warrant, the hawse-hole in effect through which every member of the lower deck must pass to the warrant officers' mess or the wardroom. And he would pass through it in the hard and bloody world of war.

12

Within the next two weeks Cameron was drafted to *Ganges*, the former boys' training establishment opposite Harwich at the mouth of the River Stour. Here he learned to climb the great mast on the parade-ground and sit nonchalantly on its truck; learned to scavenge as at *Royal Arthur* but this time with brooms and squeegees along the sloping covered way that ran between the seamen's messes; learned elementary gunnery and torpedo work and how to handle whalers and cutters under oars and sail and how to take charge in his turn as coxwain. After six weeks he was drafted with his class to Portsmouth, with more words of praise on his White Paper. In RNB he loitered, in a seafaring sense, as a seaman of the Commodore's Guard, belted and gaitered and slamming to the Present Arms with a ceremonial rifle made simply of wood. Time-wasting though this might be, a couple of weeks of it gave him a better insight into the Navy than he had so far acquired, for his guard duties included acting as escort for miscreants at Commodore's Defaulters, and as gaoler in the Detention Quarters housing men under such punishments as ninety days' detention for various offences. It also improved his parade-ground efficiency to the satisfaction of the Chief Gunner's Mate of the Guard.

'Know something, Cameron?'

'What, Chief?'

'It's always said, though never in my hearing, that the order is, Royal Marines will advance in column of fours, seamen will advance in bloody great heaps. Now laugh, cos it's true.'

Cameron laughed.

'But you're better than that. White Paper, eh?'

'Yes, Chief.'

The Chief Gunner's Mate clapped him on the shoulder, 'Go to it, lad, and the best of luck. I'm putting in a word that you should get to sea pronto, and put your time in.'

He was as good as his word; within the next week Cameron was on his way from Portsmouth Harbour Station to Thurso in the far north of Scotland, to go from there by the aged ferry *St Ninian* across the Pentland Firth to Lyness in the Orkneys, to join His Majesty's destroyer *Carmarthen* on North Atlantic convoy escort duty. Her task was to shepherd the America and Canada bound merchant ships as far as was possible taking into account the limited availability of escort vessels, whence the convoys would chance their luck alone; and to bring in the laden vessels homeward bound. He found life in the fo'c'sle messdeck of a lurching, water-shipping destroyer to be different again from Skegness, or the *Ganges*, or the Pompey barracks. Life here was real and tough and largely filthy, both as regards language and the few amenities: the seamen's heads, or lavatories, containing only five cubicles for some eighty to ninety men, were continually blocked, had no doors, and opened into a space below the break of the fo'c'sle right alongside the messdeck and the galley. The stench was foul and wrecked the appetite. The messdecks were usually awash at sea, and water swirled about below the slung hammocks and around the lockers upon whose tops those unfortunates who had no slinging billet had to sleep. Cameron was one of these: all the billets, fitted for peacetime requirements and not enough for a full war complement, had been taken long before his arrival. His accent, he found here, was against him: it yelled White Paper. The *Carmarthen* already had another would-be officer in the seamen's messdeck.

A fat able-seaman, a man with three good conduct badges on his left arm, apprised him of this. 'WC candidate, aren't you, Lofty?'

Cameron admitted the fact, accustomed by now to the inversion of CW.

'Join the other little sod,' the three-badgeman, whose name was Tomkins, said with a belch. 'Know what? When you 'ears the pipe, 'ands to dinner, it includes wot it don't say, wot is, WC candidates to *lunch*.' He gave a loud laugh and thrust Cameron into a stanchion with his stomach as he moved past towards his locker. 'I s'pose somebody 'as to be officers. . . .'

Carmarthen sailed out through the boom to pick up her convoy before Cameron had been aboard four hours. She

14

sailed into vicious weather, to be thrown about like a cork on vast waters that rose sheer like hillsides and then ebbed away as the destroyer lurched into the troughs, leaving her suspended while her men stared down into a great valley. Cameron, despite his experience in trawlers, was as sick as a dog for the whole ten days of the escort, out and home. He stuck to his duties because he had to, but he couldn't eat anything beyond an occasional biscuit.

A few hours from Scapa inward bound, during the morning watch, the weather moderated as the ship steamed into the lee of the land, and the waters lay flat. Hunger returned very suddenly. *Carmarthen* was a canteen messing ship, as opposed to the general messing system in use aboard big ships; this meant that each mess prepared its own food, which was then taken to the galley to be cooked. This morning there was nothing Cameron wanted so much as fried eggs, fried bread and bacon. These he acquired when he came off watch and took them to the galley with his mouth drooling in anticipation. They were beautifully cooked, and he carried the plate to the long scrubbed table in his mess and set it down beneath the bottom-bulge of an occupied hammock overhead. Before he had taken so much as a bite, a stockinged foot emerged from the hammock and plunged straight into the bacon and eggs. There was a shout of anger from above, and Able-Seaman Tomkins glared down. No matter that he had worn the sock for no less than six weeks, day and night; it was spoiled and would have to be washed.

'You bloody little perisher!' Tomkins yelled down at Cameron. 'Jus' look wot you gorn an' done to me fuckin' sock!'

There was no come-back on that; Able-Seaman Tomkins not only had three badges but some forty-odd years against Cameron's not quite twenty. Hunger simply had to endure; but there was always a laugh around the corner. One came that morning: a leading-seaman had gone ashore from the battleship *Rodney* in search of women, of which Scapa held none. Desperation and long abstinence had driven the leading-seaman to make use, so rumour said, of a sheep, an act of bestiality which had been observed and reported. When the miscreant had been brought under escort to Captain's Defaulters, his excuse had been that he had got drunk in the shore canteen – where in fact each man from the fleet was allowed two pints only of Brickwood's beer sent up from Portsmouth – and thought the sheep was a Wren with a duffel-coat on.

After this interlude, and a run ashore in the Orkneys' bleak desolation, it was back to sea again. And again after that, in continuously filthy weather. Again and again, until Cameron's necessary sea-time was almost up. There had been some action, but nothing very spectacular; there had been the rounding-up of stray merchant ships whose engines had failed them, or whose steering was erratic. There had been false alarms from the Asdic, and false sighting reports from the lookouts that had sent the ship's company to action stations and caused plenty of sour comment and swearing. And now, on this current run out of Scapa, it was apparently as peaceful as ever even though a highly important convoy was due to cross eastward with valuable cargoes from Halifax, Nova Scotia, a convoy that would be escorted home by *Carmarthen* and the other destroyers of her flotilla – an exceptionally strong escort that had drained other convoys of their protection – once the outward-bound merchantmen had passed beyond the area of attack. Placidly, in their eight columns – five of four ships each, three of five, the longer columns steaming in between the shorter ones at the convoy speed of seven knots – the ships advanced. With five cables between columns and three cables between individual ships in each column, the mass covered some five square miles of the Atlantic.

No attack until now: not until the busy Asdics had spoken and Cameron had sighted that feather of water made by a periscope. *Carmarthen* hurtled on under full power, Cameron still on lookout since his action station as per Watch and Quarter Bill happened to be the same as his three-watch

16

cruising station, still sweeping his arc as the Asdic continued with its ghostlike wailing pings.

A moment later, nightmare burst.

With her captain, Lieutenant-Commander Hewson, now in charge on the compass platform, *Carmarthen* was streaking up to overtake one of the merchantmen on her way to engage the sighted U-boat with depth charges, and passing close, when a shout from the captain of Number Two gun on the fo'c'sle, looking like a daylight ghost in his white anti-flash gear, indicated a torpedo coming in from starboard, slap across *Carmarthen*'s hurtling bow. Just as the shout came, the torpedo struck the great wall-sided merchant ship. There was a huge explosion and a blast of super-heated air swept the destroyer's bridge, bringing with it more lethal matter: slivers of blasted metal moving at the speed of light. Cries came from the decks, from the compass platform itself. Something bounced off Cameron's steel helmet, which went spinning out into the Atlantic wastes. Hewson sagged in a corner with the top of his head missing; on the deck the Yeoman of Signals lay with his neck spouting blood, his head nowhere to be seen. Stephenson, Officer of the Watch, was lying across the guard-rail with his entrails spread wide. As Cameron looked in sheer horror, the body slid away into the sea, leaving its bloody trail.

Cameron looked all around in disbelief, then took in the fact that no officer was now on the compass platform; no petty officer either. Below in the wheelhouse, the quartermaster would be able to see events through the ports, but would be in need of orders. The other bridge lookouts had a dazed, uncomprehending look. Cameron went, shaking in every limb, to the binnacle and the voice-pipe. In action, the Torpedo-Coxwain would be at the wheel, and thank God for it. Cameron spoke down the voice-pipe. 'Cox'n, it's Ordinary Seaman Cameron here. Both officers are dead, and I –'

'All right, lad, I'll keep her clear of the convoy. You just stay where you are and act as a communication number. I'll send a messenger and get Jimmy on the bridge pronto.' Jimmy was the time-honoured lower-deck name for the First Lieutenant. And for Cameron's money he couldn't get there fast enough. As Cameron looked across towards the stolidly-steaming merchantmen of the convoy, a deafening noise and a blast of flame came from *Carmarthen*'s fo'c'sle. Jags of metal glowed red where the breakwater had been, and Number One gun leaned drunkenly to starboard.

2

'PETTY Officer Thomas!'

Thomas, Chief Boatswain's Mate, turned as he heard the First Lieutenant's shout. 'Sir?'

'Damage Control report, fast as you can.'

'Aye, aye, sir.' Thomas doubled for'ard, sea-booted feet sliding on the iron-deck's slippery metal. Seymour, the First Lieutenant, followed, making for the bridge ladder. Reaching the compass platform, he paled as he met the carnage, but controlled himself as he saw Cameron's eyes watching him.

'It's my first time, too,' he said. 'They say you get used to it.'

'Yes, sir.'

Seymour stepped to the binnacle and the voice-pipe. 'First Lieutenant here,' he said. 'Stop engines, Cox'n.'

'Stop engines, sir.'

Bells rang below as the telegraph handles were pushed over. Seymour said, 'Warn the engine-room, I may go astern.'

'Aye, aye, sir. Engines repeated stopped, sir.' There was a pause. 'Do I take it you've assumed the command, sir?'

'I'm afraid so, Cox'n. Get the Leading Signalman up here pronto, will you – the Yeoman's bought it.'

'Aye, aye, sir.'

Seymour moved away from the binnacle and stared down at the wreckage of the fo'c'sle, at the dead and wounded seamen gunners, the latter being attended to by the Surgeon-Lieutenant, then away to port at the convoy where more shattering explosions were taking place and where the other destroyers of the escort were carving wide swathes with their

19

wakes as they raced to drop their depth-charge patterns on the attacking U-boats. Seymour clenched his fists in frustration: if only they could join in! In fact all they could do was to retreat; as a merchantman loomed on the destroyer's port side Seymour passed the word to put the engines half speed astern, in order to take his broken command clear. As *Carmarthen* gathered sternway, Petty Officer Thomas came up to report.

'It's a shambles for'ard of the collision bulkhead, sir, all gone in fact. The bulkhead's leaking, but it's holding.'

'Not well enough to go ahead?'

'No, sir, definitely not, sir.'

'Casualties?'

Thomas wiped the back of a hand across his forehead: he was sweating despite the intense cold. 'Number One gun's crew, sir, all dead. Two dead on Number Two gun, and three wounded. No others, sir.'

Seymour nodded: with the ship closed up at action stations, there would have been no one below for'ard of the collision bulkhead, which was something on the credit side. He said, 'I may have to abandon ...'

'Yes, sir. Let's hope not, sir.'

'It all depends on that bulkhead.'

Thomas said, 'Shipwright's doing his best, sir, rigging shoring beams.' Seymour reflected that no shoring beams would be likely to permit headway being made and if they didn't sink then they would complete the escort stern first. By now *Carmarthen* was on a safe course astern, clear of the merchant ships, and Seymour passed helm orders to turn the ship and keep her on station abeam of the convoy. From now on, he would be virtually unable to leave the bridge: with the Captain and the senior sub-Lieutenant dead and *Carmarthen* having sailed short of one officer landed sick at the last moment – he was left with a sub-Lieutenant RNR and a midshipman RNVR. The RNR Sub could be relied upon, but the RNVR snotty had held his rank for six weeks only and before joining the Navy had been a bank clerk. ... As the Leading-

Signalman, replacing the dead Yeoman, clattered up the ladder and saluted, Seymour, with the whole responsibility of the ship now on his shoulders, gave himself a physical and mental shake. He must ask for orders in the first place.

He said, 'Signal to the Senior Officer of the escort, repeated for information to the Commodore of the convoy, from *Carmarthen* First Lieutenant. My Captain is dead and I have assumed command. Damage to the fo'c'sle by torpedo leaves me able to move astern only. Request instructions. I do not require assistance at this stage.' He paused. 'Got that?'

'Yes, sir.'

'Right. Make it by Aldis immediately.'

'Aye, aye, sir.' The Leading-Signalman took up the Aldis lamp, already plugged into its socket on its wandering lead, identified the Senior Officer's vessel away ahead of the convoy, and clacked out the call-sign allocated to the leader. The acknowledgement came quickly and Seymour's message was passed. Seymour, reflecting on his own responsibility so suddenly assumed, took some comfort in the knowledge that the leader's responsibilities were infinitely heavier: not only had the Senior Officer in *Raglan* to guard and chivvy the valuable merchant ships and their crews, direct the escort and supervise the current counter-attack on the U-boat pack, but he had to worry about the damage to individual ships, both merchant and Naval, make an assessment from necessarily scanty information, and issue orders accordingly after a fast decision. And after that again, if anything should go wrong, he would have to justify his decision to the Admiralty in London, to high-ranking, largely costive officers who could take days or weeks to arrive at a judgement on a man who had had little more than seconds to make the on-the-spot decision . . . and indeed the Senior Officer's answer was received aboard *Carmarthen* within five minutes of Seymour's signal being made. *Carmarthen* was ordered to leave the convoy and make independently for Belfast. Hard on the heels of the order a message from the W/T office, where a listening watch was maintained constantly, brought the weather report: gale force winds were imminent ahead of the convoy's westward track. The *Carmarthen* would be well out of that lot, Seymour thought as he took his departure from the convoy. The North Atlantic, having relented thus far, was once again back to its full winter fury.

Before contact had been finally lost, eight more ships of the convoy had gone to the bottom. Ten large vessels out of thirty-five, a good bag for the Germans, a heavy loss for Britain: ten ships whose cargo-carrying capacity could not be spared, a worrying delay to vital war material waiting to be brought across from America; and a loss of crews who were not easily replaced. No further attack was made on the *Carmarthen*; the U-boats evidently preferred to concentrate on the convoy and then conserve the rest of their torpedoes for the eastbound ships due through the area shortly. The weather was still good as *Carmarthen* began her lone stern-first voyage back to Northern Ireland and the Belfast repair yard. After the convoy and its attackers had vanished over the western horizon, Seymour had all hands who could be spared mustered along the iron-deck so that he could inform them of the position personally. Rumour was never a good shipmate; 'buzzes' and the 'galley wireless' too often got things badly wrong.

'I'm reducing to second degree of readiness,' Seymour said after he had indicated his orders from the Senior Officer of the escort. Second degree of readiness meant a two-watch system. 'Things won't be too bad unless the weather moves easterly faster than we do, and I've no information on that at the moment. God knows, we're a slow enough target, but I don't expect any further attacks just yet. I repeat, just yet.' He paused. 'The eastbound convoy out of Halifax will rendezvous with the escort in two days' time, and the Germans will know that. They'll be waiting – and don't forget the FW 200s out of Bordeaux as we close the UK. Because of them and the U-boats I intend to move south until I'm out of the shipping lanes, then east.' He turned to the Chief

Boatswain's Mate. 'That's all, Petty Officer Thomas. Carry on, please.'

'Aye, aye, sir.' Thomas detailed the starboard watch to close up and the port watch to fall out for part-of-ship duties, while Seymour went back to the compass platform and sent the RNR Sub below for a spell. Later that morning a boatload of merchant seamen was encountered, and engines were stopped whilst they were picked up. They turned out to be from a fast, independently routed tanker, sunk some days earlier. There were some grim sights: dead men without arms or legs, men with severe stomach wounds, many of the living on the point of death from sheer loss of blood if nothing else; men cruelly burned by blazing oil fuel floating murderously on the water, men who still cried out in agony as they were brought aboard the destroyer and continued crying out until the Surgeon-Lieutenant and his sick-berth attendant brought the relief of morphia.

The day passed peacefully into night. The lookouts and the guns' crews flailed their arms to keep out the bitter cold, everyone on deck watchful for any surfaced, battery-charging U-boat. Breakfast next morning was cocoa and tinned herrings in tomato, known to the Fleet, either with affection or disgust, as 'herrings-in'. The mixture was a revolting one to a gourmet, if nourishing, and all CW candidates were expected to have fastidious stomachs and palates. Able-Seaman Tomkins, known as Stripey on account of his three good-conduct badges, remarked on this to Cameron.

'Not wot Your Lordship normally 'as for breakfast, I take it?' The accent was mock middle class. 'Not wot the bloody butler brings – wot?'

'I've known worse, Stripey –'

Tomkins became belligerent. ''Ere, wot's this – Stripey! I'm Stripey to me proper mates, see, not to bleedin' ODs on their first five minutes of the bloody war, all right?'

Cameron shrugged. 'All right. *Mr* Tomkins, then.'

Tomkins looked baffled, and bafflement worsened his

temper. 'Don't you be bloody cheeky. Not unless you want a thick ear, that is. Bloody little perishers ... WC candidates my arse! Ponces, that's what they are.' He assumed a mincing tone. 'Not good enough for 'em, we common seamen ain't. Oh, no. We bloody eats orf of our bloody knives, we do. And we eats 'errings-in.' He jerked a hand aft. 'Down there the officers eats caviare all day long till it comes out o' their bloody lug-'oles.'

Cameron continued eating calmly, which irritated Able-Seaman Tomkins. He said threateningly, 'Don't act dumb with me, Your Lordship.' He returned to an earlier theme. 'Wos that wot you wos, before you joined, eh? A bleedin' ponce?'

'No. I've done time as a deckhand aboard a trawler,' Cameron said. He finished breakfast and got to his feet: he towered over Tomkins, six feet to five-foot-five. 'It was a hard life and it kept a man fit. You should try it, Mr Tomkins. You're all gas and gut, too fat by half. You've been eating too well ... and you couldn't give a flea a thick ear. Not that I wish to be disrespectful.' There was a smile on his face as he pushed past Tomkins, but it was a tight one and his eyes were hard. As he walked away he heard titters at Tomkins' expense. He had made an enemy but you never went through life without doing that. Behind him the titters subsided as Tomkins uttered loud threats as to what he would do to WC candidates as soon as he got the chance. Men could vanish overboard during night watches in bad weather, and a time would come. Cameron put Tomkins out of his mind as the boatswain's calls piped the watch to close up; coming out from the break of the fo'c'sle to the iron-deck amidships, he stood back for the acting Captain as Seymour came down the ladder from the bridge. He saluted smartly, and Seymour, returning the salute, paused.

Seymour said, 'I've had a word with the Cox'n, Cameron.'

'Yes, sir?'

'I gather you stuck to your post yesterday. I'd expect no less of any man, of course, but you faced up well to your first

experience of action and casualties – and you didn't panic.'
Seymour smiled. 'Well done.'

'Thank you, sir.'

Seymour moved away aft. From below the break of the
fo'c'sle Able-Seaman Tomkins emerged, his face twisted in
anger. He might have overheard, or he might not. If he had,
then there would be remarks later about arse-crawling to the
officers.

Half-way through the forenoon watch a black line of cloud
began to form like a mourning ribbon a little above the
westward horizon; Humphries, the RNR Sub-Lieutenant,
reported to the Captain, whose head was under the chart-
table canopy, and Seymour emerged to study the cloud formation briefly through binoculars.

'It's coming,' he said. 'Not unexpected, Sub!'

'No, sir. It's moving faster than we thought, though.'

'Too true. Well, there's always the silver lining – the
U-boats don't like it any more than we do.' Seymour swept his
glasses round all the horizons. Already the line of black was
extending out towards the labouring destroyer. The air was
different now: a curious calm and silence over an oily swell, a
swell that took the ship and lifted her, only to slide back and
wallow as though at the foot of a craggy Scottish mountain. As
Seymour passed the orders for battening-down to meet bad
weather, and warned the shipwright's team on watch by the
weakened collision bulkhead that their reserve shoring beams
might be needed, the wind took them in a preliminary grasp
and white horses appeared on the water. Now the cloud
extended with extreme speed, seeming to race out towards
the lone vessel and place a threatening pall over her head.
Then the rain came, a torrential downpour not unlike that of a
tropical storm but with the cold of ice in it, rain that brought
the visibility right down so that the horizons closed in around
them. But just before the visibility went Cameron spotted
something and made an instant report:

'Submarine on the surface, sir, fine on the port bow!'

Up came the binoculars of the Captain and Humphries. Seymour said. 'Sound action stations, Sub!'

As the alarm rattlers blasted out through the ship, Seymour passed the helm and engine orders to bring the after guns to bear; but the German had the advantage and was the first to open fire. She fired almost from invisibility, only the orange flame of the discharge marking her position. A shell whistled across, close above the bridge, so close overhead that Cameron felt its wind as an extra force in the gathering Atlantic storm. A second shell sliced through the fo'c'sle debris left by the earlier torpedo attack, and exploded to bring a tremendous blast of hot air and a rain of metal down upon the reeling destroyer. A good deal fell on and around the bridge and by nothing short of a miracle caused no harm although Cameron found his oilskin sleeve torn by a fragment that pinged against his binocular-stand. By this time *Carmarthen*'s after guns were in action, fired virtually blind by the gun-layers aiming at the German's flash. *Carmarthen* kept up the fire, but it was not returned, and Seymour decided to break off the action rather than waste ammunition upon an unseen target.

'She's probably dived,' he said. A binocular sweep had revealed nothing. 'If so, she'll wait her time and try again as soon as the weather moderates.' He lowered his glasses. 'I'll stay at action stations for a while, Sub, but I've a feeling that U-boat's bedded down.' He turned his head. 'Cameron?'

'Yes, sir.'

'Nicely spotted. She almost caught us with our pants down.' Seymour was about to say something further when the destroyer gave a violent twisting lurch, heeling hard over to starboard as a heavy sea took her, everything movable on the bridge sliding across. Cameron, torn from his position, seemed to drop like a stone, then fetched up hard against the starboard plating with all the breath knocked from his body. As Seymour shouted urgent orders down the voice-pipe to the wheelhouse, *Carmarthen*'s stern swung uncomfortably round so that the shattered bow began to come close to the wind and sea; and along the wires of the sound-powered telephone rigged from the collision bulkhead to the compass platform the shipwright's urgent voice came, doomladen.

'Bulkhead's giving way, sir!'

3

It was utter chaos below in the seamen's messdeck, and in the stokers' messdeck below again. The shipwright and his gang, sweat-streaked, wet and dirty, fought like madmen to place more shoring beams in position and to stem the increasing leaks. As the full force of the North Atlantic was flung against the bulkhead, water was forced through, the many jets like a gorgon's head of hoses; *Carmarthen*'s messdecks were never dry when any sea was running, but now they were well and truly awash with water that slopped from side to side as she rolled and dipped her broken bows under.

Petty Officer Thomas was below now: Robens, the RNVR Midshipman, was there too but it was Thomas who made the suggestion. 'Hammocks, sir.'

'Hammocks?'

'Yes, sir.' Thomas' voice was brisk and confident. 'Plug the leaks, see.'

'They'll just saturate, won't they?'

'Every little helps, as the old lady said when she piddled in the sea.' Petty Officer Thomas was already passing the orders. There were plenty of hammocks available, belonging to those men who had slinging billets; the others had already had their hammocks removed to act as extra shelter – as substitute sandbags, in effect, against machine-gun attack and blast – around the bridge and the close-range weapons' crews. The lashed hammocks were now brought out from the nettings and passed forward to be battened down with timber and held

28

fast against the many leaks. This brought some improvement though it would have no actual strengthening effect: the bulk-head's future must depend on the ship being brought round again to lie stern first to the wind and sea. Constant reports reached Seymour on the compass platform as he attempted to do just that, cautiously, knowing that he might all too easily broach-to on the turn, and lie broadside to the mounting waves. With the engines still moving astern he tended the ship's head and inch by agonizing inch *Carmarthen* swung, bringing her counter round to ease the bow to a degree of safety. Seymour appeared to be succeeding when disaster came: a big wave rolled beneath the stern and lifted it in a twisting motion; and the ship's head came round to take once again the full force of the sea's battering. Then it happened: there was a tremendous noise from somewhere below and the remains of the bow dipped very suddenly. In the same second the sound-powered telephone whined into the wind and the Chief Boatswain's Mate's urgent voice reported the bulkhead gone in the stokers' messdesk.

'Sea's coming up the hatch, sir, into the seamen's mess, like a waterspout.'

Seymour's response came as a death-knell: 'Batten down the hatch cover, Thomas, evacuate the seamen's mess and clip down the watertight doors behind you.' His face was set hard as he put the telephone down. He had given the only possible order, but it meant that any men working in the stokers' messdeck who had survived the inrush of water would now be left under hatches to drown. In the seamen's messdeck, Petty Officer Thomas himself ran through deepening water to the hatch and, with the assistance of a leading-seaman and two ABs, fought the cover down against the spouting Atlantic and pulled the clips across. As the upper part of the bulkhead began to break up, all hands cleared the messdeck at the rush and Thomas, having shepherded them all through into the galley flat, closed the watertight door and slammed the clips on. Moving through the galley flat for the iron-deck, he found himself climbing uphill past the engineers' store by the fore funnel. The destroyer was stopped and helpless, the weight of water in her for'ard section having lifted the screws clear of the sea; she had fallen off the wind and now lay broached-to, broadside to the great racing waves. For Thomas' money, the old girl couldn't last long now.

A sea-anchor had been rigged with much sweat and foul language: three spars lashed together in a triangle and covered with canvas, with a three-legged bridle heavily weighted at one corner. It had been the very devil to construct, was awkward to handle, and in the event didn't appear to help very much. After a few hours it had carried away. Nevertheless, when that day and night had dragged away and the next dawn had come, *Carmarthen* was by some miracle still afloat, though still stopped and wallowing dangerously. Seymour, hunched into a corner of the compass platform which he had not left for more than a minute or two throughout, stared across the wave-crests, knowing he must assess, and assess in good time, when the moment might come to abandon. A second's delay would make the vital difference between losing perhaps a whole ship's company and allowing them to live a little longer in the boats and Carley floats. Cameron, on lookout again for the morning watch, thought about that clipped-down hatch and the dead who surged about below, drifting into lockers and mess tables as the destroyer wallowed in the ocean's grip. He had known all of them for better or worse; some had been his friends, others merely faces met in the course of duty. *Carmarthen* had carried a total war complement of almost two hundred men; now fifteen seamen lay entombed. Thirteen including the Captain and Sub-Lieutenant Stephenson had died in the earlier U-boat attack: the sea and the enemy together had already exacted a heavy toll, and the ordeal had only just begun. God alone could tell what lay ahead on the long haul back to the UK. And even though so many had gone, the ship was now vastly overcrowded as a result of the two main messdecks being flooded. The burned and wounded men picked up from the tanker were being accommodated in the tiny sick-bay and in the officers' cabins and wardroom. When off watch, the officers just used the deck of the wardroom flat and the ratings dossed down where they could find shelter, the galley flat just aft of the seamen's messdeck being the best billet if a man could squeeze in and find a space on the deck, with just the watertight door and its surrounding bulkhead holding off the Atlantic. Fires had been drawn in the galley itself as a safety precaution and there would be no more hot food. They would exist on cold bully beef out of tins, ship's biscuits and cold herrings-in plus the daily rum issue made by the Torpedo-Coxswain and the Supply Petty Officer. Cameron, dead tired, cold and hungry and wet through beneath his oilskins as he searched the seas of his arc for signs of the enemy or indeed of a friendly ship, thought somewhat bitterly of the days before he had joined. How eagerly he and others had gone to war! Not, according to his father's accounts, as eagerly as that older generation had flocked to the Navy and Army to give the Kaiser what for – but eagerly enough. This time there had been no thoughts of it all being over by Christmas: Hitler had asked for it and now he was going to get it. It was going to be a pleasure to give it to him.

So far, it hadn't worked out quite that way. On land, the Army hadn't yet recovered from the blow of retreat from Dunkirk, though thanking God they had got so many men away to fight again. As for the sea war, Hitler appeared to be winning that as well: the sinkings in the North Atlantic had been far too many for an embattled island to bear. Men and ships took time to replace, and the cargoes were desperately wanted: food, arms and ammunition, oil fuel, the very sinews of war and the ability to continue an unequal struggle. Cameron had passed some of the 'phoney war' period in Portsmouth, doing that spell in the Commodore's Guard at the Naval barracks. Phoney it had been, all right. Pompey Town had been full of uniforms, predominantly Naval, the uniformed sailors with slung gas-masks – and woe betide you if a chief gunner's mate heard you referring to them as anything but anti-gas respirators. The barracks, crammed with eight thousand men, vastly more than it had been built to hold when at about the time of the Boer War it had replaced the old barrack hulks in the dockyard, disgorged its liberty-men each evening to roister, until their pay ran out, in the many hundreds of public houses. The civil police didn't mind much when a rating got drunk; the Navy was honoured in Portsmouth and they looked the other way. All too soon, the drunken man might die in grotesque agony on the seas, in the flame and thunder of the guns – in agony and in honour and glory too, like the memorials to the last war said. In the meantime, he was well entitled to enjoy his fling. The girls helped, too; there was plenty of talent in Portsmouth, a good deal of it in the women's services. Cameron had drunk his half-pints of Brickwood's bitter in the brasserie bar of the Queen's Hotel in exclusive Southsea along with three or four other CW candidates – in a bar where before the war a rating in uniform would have been directed elsewhere – and had met a Wren there. Mary Anstey had been brought in by a sub-lieutenant from the gunnery school at Whale Island, but the sub-lieutenant had become filthy drunk and passed out and somehow or other the girl had attached herself to Cameron and after that he'd seen quite a lot of her when guard duties had permitted. . . .

'Cameron!'

'Yes, sir?'

Seymour snapped, 'Keep your mind on the bloody sea, man! You've been staring at one spot for the last three minutes.'

'Sorry, sir.'

Portsmouth and Mary Anstey faded: the phoney war stage was of the past now and danger was real. Somewhere out there, that submarine might lurk yet, might be manoeuvring into her firing position and never mind the weather.

The same thought appeared to be in the mind of the RNR Sub as later he came up to take over the watch, relieving decks for the Midshipman to snatch a quick, cold breakfast:

32

Seymour ate his in his corner of the compass platform – a cup of cocoa and two slices of bread and marmalade, brought with a butlerish air by his seaman servant. Humphries asked, 'Do you expect that U-boat to attack submerged, sir?'

'I doubt it,' Seymour answered. 'She probably wouldn't waste a tin fish on a ship that must look about to sink.'

'She could have fired off her stock, I suppose, sir.'

Seymour said, 'Could be. Could be one of the bastards that attacked the convoy.'

Cameron overheard this. It was on the cards, he fancied, that the U-boat might come to the surface to finish them off by gunfire, and in that event they wouldn't have a chance, hadn't had a chance ever since the flooding of the for'ard decks. The after 4.7-inch guns could surely never be depressed to an angle that could hit the target, at any rate if the submarine surfaced close and astern, which she would obviously do after a look through the periscope. And currently *Carmarthen*, with her silent engines, was a sitting duck, unable even to steer, broadside to the sea. A sitting duck some four hundred sea miles from base ... the prognosis was not good. In the meantime, however, she was being urged by the action of wind and sea in the right direction, more or less, and that was on the credit side. When Humphries, who had the duty of navigating officer, took the noon sight, then an assessment could be made. Cameron had gathered that it had not been possible to obtain a sight during the night hours: there had been no stars visible.

They wallowed on sideways in a strange and somehow forboding silence. A destroyer at sea was normally vibrant with her engine-sounds and now there were none; only the hum of the generators that kept the electric circuits going.

In a two-watch system there was scant time for the hands to work part-of-ship when off watch; sleep was necessary so that the watchkeepers could be alert when their watch came round again. Thus the routine work of the seaman divisions – fo'c'sle, iron-deck, quarterdeck – was held in abeyance and

33

only the daymen, those who kept no watches – the supply ratings, the cooks and so on – worked normally. Though dead tired when he came off watch, Cameron found that sleep did not come. His mind was too active. Alongside him in the galley flat lay his fellow cw candidate, by name Lavington, a former medical student who had failed his second MB examination and had thus, aged twenty-one, come into the age group for call-up. No doubt Lavington's public school education had led to the starting of his White Paper; but he did not strike Cameron as good officer material. He was inclined to dodge the column when possible and had approached the leading hand of his watch, unsuccessfully, with a plea that his seasickness was bad enough to have him excused watchkeeping. Currently, Ordinary Seaman Lavington was looking like death warmed up and was as sleepless as Cameron.

'What d'you think is going to happen?' he asked in a strained voice.

Cameron said, 'Oh, we'll make it, don't worry.'

'I'm not so sure.'

'I am! Seymour knows what he's doing.'

'Well, I hope so.' Lavington was shaking like a leaf. 'If we're attacked . . . look, what happens when we get into the air attack zone? You know those Focke-Wulf Condors – four engines, long range. They're way beyond anything Coastal Command's got, aren't they? They can blow us out of the water at the drop of a hat!'

Cameron laughed. 'Six trips out and we've never seen 'em yet! Why should we this time?'

'There's always a first time,' Lavington said. There was a whine in his voice now. 'God, how I wish this bloody war was over!'

Once again Cameron laughed and softly sang under his breath: '*When this bloody war is over, Oh, How happy I shall be . . . no more bullshit from the wardroom, no more draft chits off to sea . . .*'

'Shut yer muckin' mouth!' an angry voice said.

Cameron said obligingly, 'All right, Mr Tomkins. Sorry.'

'One more muckin' word and you'll get filled in.'

Alongside Cameron, Lavington said disconsolately, 'They're all so awfully coarse, these men.' He hadn't intended anyone but Cameron to hear this, but Stripey Tomkins did. The fat AB levered himself to his feet, his eyes red with lack of sleep and now with anger, and bent threateningly over Lavington.

'On your feet, sonny.'

Lavington stared back glassily, looking like a ghost in the blue light on the bulkhead. 'What for?' he asked.

'I'm going to give you a lesson in bleedin' politeness,' Tomkins said, and reached for Lavington's duffel-coat. Gathering the material in his fist, he heaved the sick-looking ordinary seaman to his feet and then drew back his other fist. Cameron got quickly to his feet and grabbed the fat man's arm.

He said, 'I wouldn't, if I were you, Mr Tomkins, even though he asked for it.'

'Don't be bloody cheeky!' Tomkins, still baffled as to how to react to the 'Mr Tomkins' but well knowing it was said sardonically, glared at Cameron. 'What if I do, eh?'

'Then I'll send your false teeth through the back of your throat, Mr Tomkins.'

'You an' 'oo else?'

Cameron smiled. 'Just me.' He towered, head bent away from the deckhead. He extended his two hands, big hands now bunched into fists. 'This one,' he said calmly, indicating his right, 'is hospital. The other's sudden death. There was a trawlerman once ... thought he could take liberties with a green youth. He never tried again. Go back to sleep, Mr Tomkins.'

'You 'it me and you'll be up before Jimmy. Then you can kiss your bleedin' commission goodbye.'

'I'll chance that,' Cameron said quietly.

Tomkins let go of the duffel-coat and Lavington almost collapsed back to the deck of the galley flat. Tomkins, eyes furious, said in a thick voice, 'Sod you, Cameron. I'll get you one day, see if I muckin' don't.' He turned away and flopped back into his billet. Cameron also got down on the deck and once again tried to sleep. He couldn't; Lavington seemed to be talking to himself or something, a low dirge of self-pity that grated badly. Tomkins' reaction hadn't been all that surprising, but Tomkins had all the instincts of a bully and Cameron didn't like bullies, however justified they might be on occasions.

Meanwhile, Lavington worried him: he was no advertisement for cw ratings, already much unloved by their lower-deck shipmates, and he sounded now as though he might well be about to crack up. He had a sensitive face, much too sensitive for the war at sea; he was over-careful of his hands, never bent his full weight to the falls, for instance, when the pipe came for the lower deck to be cleared for hoisting the whaler in port. Cameron's own hands had not been fully toughened up when he had his first experience of Up Whaler and afterwards he had found them badly blistered, but they had soon got their hardness. Minds had to be as hard as hands in the fo'c'sle of one of His Majesty's destroyers on war service. It was perhaps the toughest assignment in the Navy.... Sleep came at last as Cameron drifted off into a nightmare jumble of thoughts and fancies in which Mary Anstey was at one moment about to jump from the after deck of a blazing oil-tanker and the next was on the pier at Lyness in Scapa, welcoming him back from sea, now wearing on her left sleeve the blue fouled anchor of a Leading Wren and thus his superior officer. He was holding Mary in his arms when the shattering sound of the alarm rattlers broke into what was after all only a surface sleep and he came fully awake on the instant.

Already dressed and lifebelted as all hands always were at sea, he joined the mad scramble for the iron-deck and doubled up the ladder to the compass platform just as the three-inch gun amidships blasted off starshell. There was a tremendous crack and seconds later the shell burst off the starboard bow, cascading brilliance to illuminate the seas in

36

the vicinity. In this brilliance could be seen the surfacing U-boat, long and low and menacing as the water foamed from her casing and men scrambled from the conning tower and fore hatch, running for the gun-mounting on the casing. This went immediately into action, belching smoke and flame and sending its projectiles screaming towards the helpless destroyer.

4

MORE starshell went up; the Lewis gunners were in action now, sweeping the U-boat's conning tower and casing. So were the pom-poms and the machine-gun's crew. From the U-boat a man went over the side of the conning tower, plummeted screaming down to the casing, then bounced off. On the whole the German seemed to be getting the worst of it, at least until a shell from her 3.5-inch gun took *Carmarthen*'s aftermost 4.7-inch fair and square, burst on the gun-shield and almost took the mounting out of the lifted deck. The gun itself vanished as though it had never existed and the casualties were heavy: strips of flesh and entrails lay with shattered dismembered limbs among the wreckage or flew, in the starshells' light, like bloody pennants, from the standing rigging aft and amidships. Number Three gun's crew, just for'ard of the gaping hole that had been Number Four gun, had been caught by the lethal spread of the explosion and the flying metal and all were dead except for the gun-layer who, miraculously, had survived without a scratch.

Then, as *Carmarthen*'s close-range weapons kept up their stuttering fire, there was a swirl in the heavy sea and the U-boat had gone back into the uneasy depths.

Seymour said savagely, 'We haven't heard the last of the bugger. Go aft and have a look ... let me know the casualties and damage, Sub. I'll keep the ship closed up at action stations for a while yet.'

'Aye, aye, sir.' Humphries went down the starboard ladder at the rush. When he returned, his story was a mixed one: the only further structural damage was to Number Four gun and its mounting and once the hole in the deck had been plugged and covered the ship would be little less seaworthy, if such was the word, than before – except that, as Seymour had already noted, the removal of Number Four gun's weight from aft had put her a little farther down by the head. The really bad news was that ten more men had died and the Surgeon-Lieutenant had four more wounded to attend to, three of them unlikely to survive into Belfast Lough. *Carmarthen* drifted on, lone and stricken; and during the next forenoon watch the dead were sewn into canvas shrouds and committed to the sea. This was in fact the second committal, for those killed in the initial attack on the convoy had been disposed of as soon as *Carmarthen* had been well clear of the area. Seymour once again read the short, simple service in a voice that rang defiance out over the heaving Atlantic wastes, his face grey with strain, tiredness and sorrow for the men he had sailed with for many months. As each shrouded figure was laid upon the plank beneath the folds of the White Ensign, and the plank was tilted, the Captain's voice followed it:

'Man that is born of woman hath but a short time to live ... in the midst of life we are in death ... our dear brother here departed, we therefore commit his body to the deep. ...'

It was soon all over and the hands were fallen out. Normal routine was resumed; rum was issued, three-water grog for junior ratings, neat spirit for the chief and petty officers who were presumed to obey the Admiralty's instruction that it should not be bottled for subsequent over-indulgence, but who in fact seldom took any notice of that, preferring to chance their arms. Birthdays cropped up now and again, and needed to be properly celebrated. On the compass platform Seymour brooded, thought again about that U-boat: he would not have expected her to surface in such foul weather, weather that was scarcely conducive to good gunnery – the shot that had taken out Number Four gun was sheer luck – but then of course all submarines needed to charge batteries and no doubt that was what the U-boat had been doing.

When that day's noon sight was taken, using a false horizon – the visibility had come down a little further before noon and the horizons were too close – it showed bad news. The destroyer had in fact made some unwelcome and unexpected northing and although she was somewhat closer to home, she was being taken by the drifting action of the wind and sea into the area where the Germans might be expected to operate the Focke-Wulf 200s. Seymour's hope of making a little south had died with the flooding of the for'ard decks and the consequent lifting of the twin screws out of the water....

It was no time before the buzz had reached the lower deck: they were not making a good heading.

'It'll be bloody cold if we head up too far,' Stripey Tomkins said. 'Know what?'

'What?' Lavington asked, blue with cold already.

'Freeze the balls off a brass monkey. Know something else, do you, eh?' Tomkins scratched under his right armpit. 'I was off Greenland once, up the Denmark Strait. Fishery protection, back in 1934 it wos. Skipper, 'e'd made a cock-up and we wos right off course like. Just before Christmas. Talk about cold! One o' me mates, 'e lost 'is wherewithal.'

'Wherewithal?'

'Wherewithal to enjoy life. Got frostbite in it, see. Quack 'ad to amputate it.' Tomkins gave a coarse laugh. 'Bloody fine officer you'll make, without a pr—'

'All right, skip it, Stripey.' This was Leading-Seaman Farrow, a gloomy man with a long, horse-like face. 'We all know your yarns. We don't have to believe 'em, but don't try to make things worse, it don't 'elp at a time like this.'

'I—'

'I said, put a sock in it, Stripey. That's an order.' Farrow's voice held the snap of authority and Tomkins subsided, muttering about jumped-up killicks, killick being the sobriquet for leading hands, deriving from the rank-badge of the fouled anchor. Farrow turned his head. 'You there, Cameron?'

40

'Yes, Killick?'

'You've done time in your old man's trawlers, right?'

Cameron nodded. 'Right.'

'Denmark Strait?'

'No, not that far up. Off the Shetlands ... well north of Shetland as a matter of fact.'

'What's it like?'

'Cold but bearable,' Cameron said, and added, 'Just. That's if you're kept busy on deck and warm below.'

'Which we aren't bloody goin' to be,' Tomkins said, and said with truth: there was no warmth below at all, other than maybe in the silent engine-room and boiler-rooms where steam was being maintained throughout, and watchkeeping duties on deck were never exactly active physically. You stood about and stamped your feet behind the gun-shields or at the tubes or on lookout, and prayed you wouldn't freeze to a statue. When it snowed, you became a temporary snowman, and the wind turned you blue. Of course, they all had their cold-weather issue gear: knitted balaclavas, thick socks, duffel-coats and long johns extending from waist to ankles which protected wherewithals but could all too soon get soaked through with seawater or driving rain that could penetrate any amount of oilskin. Life at sea in the world's extremities both north and south was a cold hell and that fact couldn't be denied, Farrow or no Farrow. Stripey Tomkins said so, and was again told to put a sock in it.

'All right, all right, *Bleedin*'-Seaman Farrow.' Tomkins scowled. 'Me, I'll put two pairs of woolly socks *on* it,' he said. 'Me old woman, she wouldn't expect less ... nor would a couple of popsies in Pompey, come to that.'

Cameron glanced across at Lavington: the former medical student looked almost on the verge of tears. He'd been, Cameron understood, at Cambridge and hoping to go on to Barts in London. Life as an undergraduate at Cambridge must have been a lovely soft billet and a privileged one too. Set of rooms, servant, good food, soft bed and all that went with all that. A very far cry from the fo'c'sle of a destroyer, even a destroyer that wasn't in a half-sinking condition in heavy seas and under constant and increasing danger of attack. At Cambridge, there wouldn't have been any Stripey Tomkinses, and the lascivious talk wouldn't have been so bald, probably. Cameron was mighty glad his father had made him sail in the trawlers: at least he'd had some sort of preparation for what he was now facing. Like Kipling's soldiers, trawlermen at sea didn't grow into plaster saints. But Lavington had had no preparation at all; he was certainly not alone in that, but there was a softness, a basic softness about him that was making it far, far worse to bear. When Leading-Seaman Farrow left the galley flat to go aft, Stripey Tomkins resumed the baiting of Lavington. This time, Cameron didn't interfere, and wouldn't do so short of physical threat. He couldn't be nanny all the time, and it wouldn't help Lavington if he was. The baiting would only become worse.

Three days before *Carmarthen* had left Scapa to pick up her convoy, Mary Anstey had been suddenly drafted from Portsmouth, where she had worked in the office of the Captain's secretary at HMS *Vernon*, the anti-submarine and torpedo school. She had been given a draft chit and a railway warrant, third class, from Portsmouth to Rosyth on the Firth of Forth in Scotland, to serve on the staff of the Commander-in-Chief, Rosyth, whose dockyard frequently contained some of the Home Fleet battleships – the mighty *Nelson* and *Rodney*, and the battle-cruiser *Hood*. Never for too long, for Hitler and Goering were in the habit of despatching aircraft to bomb the Forth Bridge, and if they ever happened to bring its great network of spans and girders and railway tracks down, then an important part of Britain's battlefleet might well be hemmed in for the duration. They hadn't got it yet, and Rosyth was in good heart, and able to laugh heartily over the story of the American destroyer captain, dangerously entering the war zone even though his country was not yet at war, who was given by signal an anchorage 'beyond the Forth Bridge'. When he had hit some rocks fair and square he had complained bitterly that, gee, he'd only passed *one* goddam bridge.... Apochryphal the story might be, but the Navy in Rosyth enjoyed it as they watched the great ships proceed in safety back to Scapa with their destroyer escorts. Mary Anstey, when she had a moment to spare, thought of writing to Donald Cameron to tell him she was somewhat closer to him, but she didn't; she really didn't know why, though she had a confused sort of idea that to let him know she was closer might disturb him and deflect his concentration on the all-important target of his commission, which meant a lot to him. He had talked in Portsmouth about possibly seeking to transfer to RN after the war, if there was an after. She felt there might not be, despite a popular song of the moment that drooled stickily about after and said, *There's a land of begin again, On the other side of the hill, Where we'll learn to love and live again, When the world is quiet and still.* If Donald wanted to transfer to RN, than an RNVR commission was a first essential; and in any case he would get no leave till – if he got his recommend – he went back to Portsmouth for his commission board, so why bother him now?

Donald Cameron was much on Mary's mind and it showed in pensiveness; she opened her heart a little way to a buxom, motherly Leading Wren almost twice her age when the latter gave her the opening on her first day in Rosyth.

'Boyfriend trouble, love?'

Mary smiled. 'Not trouble exactly.'

'Oh, I get it. Absence! Down in Portsmouth, is he?'

'No, he's at sea.'

'Well, I hope he loves you in return, love, that's all. They don't all, not by a long chalk. Love 'em and leave 'em, that's the motto of some.' The tone had suddenly become a shade bitter and subsequent conversation revealed that back in 1914 the buxom lady had loved – too well – an able-seaman who had deserted her for another just before he had sailed under Rear-Admiral Sir Christopher Cradock in the armoured cruiser *Good Hope*, to be sunk at the battle of Coronel. There had been issue, fathered by a hero, which was something; and the lady had subsequently married a grocer's assistant from Clapham who had been willing to accept the child, a girl. 'Don't go and get caught like that, love.'

'I don't think Donald would do that.'

'No. Well, I'm sure he wouldn't, love, but there's them as do, that's all I can say. What's the young man's ship or shouldn't I ask?'

Mary told her.

'*Carmarthen*, eh. First Destroyer Escort Group, out of Scapa.'

'That's right. How did you know?'

The motherly woman laughed. 'My job to know, and yours too from now on.' Leading Wren Davis was in Operations, for which Mary also had been detailed. 'You'll see. It's interesting, I'll say that for it, but there's times when it gets you down terribly, love. The sinkings and that.' She added, 'You feel responsible in a kind of way. Not personal exactly ... but you're one of the team that sends them out and gives them their routeing orders.'

Mary did find it interesting, the more so as *Carmarthen* was involved from the word go. She saw the ship indicated on the plot, watched its progress as estimated across the Atlantic with the slow west-bound convoy, day by day. Saw, too, the likely positions of the hunting packs of U-boats out from the Fatherland to attack and sink British ships and seamen to the greater glory of the Reich. She found her nails digging hard into her palms: along with everyone else in Britain she hated Hitler, but now more so because she had that personal stake and was where she could watch by proxy of the Staff Officer (Operations) the progress of the convoy and its escort. If only they could have air cover, she heard so (o), a Commander, say through set teeth – but the aircraft-carriers were all too few and could not be spared from other war theatres; and the aircraft of the RAF's Coastal Command hadn't the fuel capacity to extend far enough from their bases and then return.

Then came the shattering news: the Commodore of the OB

44

convoy had broken wireless silence, since his position was now known to the enemy, to report the U-boat attack and the condition of HMS *Carmarthen*. Severely damaged and with casualties, the destroyer was limping home, alone and untended. Mary Anstey's fingers shook as she worked at her place on the plot. The hours dragged; no more news came. SO(O) was non-committal: he'd seen all this many times before, and presumably he had no close ties aboard the *Carmarthen*. At last news of a sort, not directly about *Carmarthen*, did come through: the eastbound convoy, the HX out of Halifax, Nova Scotia, had come under U-boat attack some four hundred miles west of the Bloody Foreland in County Donegal. Two ships, both crammed with munitions, had blown sky-high; the escort was counter-attacking but with no known success so far.

SO(O) said, 'They'll be attacked all the way in, for my money.' He scanned the plot, his face worried, desperately anxious. 'The HX is bearing down on where *Carmarthen* should be by now. Near enough, anyway.'

Mary Anstey didn't need to be told what that meant: the battered destroyer would come into the dead centre of a heavy attack if the inward-bound convoy should overtake her, and she wouldn't have a hope. She felt cold and dead inside. Those evenings in Portsmouth came back to hit hard. She stared at the impersonal, impassive plot, at the counters that indicated the ships at sea. The one that represented *Carmarthen* took on, in her eyes, the outline of the ship itself, and she tried to pray.

By now the word had reached Seymour: his W/T office had intercepted the signal from the eastbound Commodore and the Petty Officer Telegraphist had brought it personally to the compass platform; the Surgeon-Lieutenant had been sent for to perform his deciphering duties, such as normally fell to the lot of the doctor in a small ship. The great heavily-laden convoy was, as estimated, some twelve hours' steaming westward; it was almost due west of *Carmarthen*, and Seymour reckoned it was likely to come up dead on his drifting track.

He called down the voice-pipe to the wheelhouse. 'Chief Boatswain's Mate to the bridge, immediately. And the Engineer Officer.'

'Aye, aye, sir.'

Petty Officer Thomas was the first to report. 'You sent for me, sir?'

'Yes, Thomas.' Seymour paused, running a hand across his chin's stubble. Shaving often enough went by the board at sea. 'The HX is due to pass us within, I'd say, twelve hours.'

'Yessir. That makes it the dark hours, sir.'

'Right. Now, she's come under attack already. That makes me believe the weather's moderated westerly. If so, then we may come into flatter seas ourselves before long.' Seymour's breath hissed out. 'You know what *that* means, Thomas.'

'I do, sir. Continuing attack, sir.'

'Exactly. Warn all hands, if you please ... full alertness and be ready to abandon if we have to. I don't suppose we're likely to have trouble over lifejackets, but just in case, warn them that any man found not wearing one will be in cells ashore the moment we reach Belfast. That's a promise,' Seymour turned as the Lieutenant (E) reported: Matthews, ex-lower deck, was a prickly character but as dependable an engineer as Seymour had ever met. 'Chief, we've been into this before, but I'm coming back to it again: I've half a mind to flood some after compartments and get those screws down.'

'There's only the after magazines available—'

'Yes. But I've a feeling that to be able to move might be more profitable than an availability of gunfire – our arc's pretty well non-existent anyway. In the meantime, we're a sitting duck, and soon we're going to be slap in the middle of a concentrated hunting pack.'

Matthews eased his cap on his forehead and said, 'Well, the engines are ready whenever you want them. But if we flood aft there'll be bloody little freeboard left.'

'You still don't like the idea, Chief?'

46

'On balance,' Matthews answered in a sour tone, 'no. But it's your decision.'

Seymour stared bleakly out across the angry seas: everything, always, was the Captain's decision, and he had come suddenly and without warning to command and the sobering knowledge that it was *his* decisions, along with those of God and chance, that would bring the *Carmarthen* back to base or send her to the bottom of the North Atlantic. He had a feeling that Matthews had sensed some indecision in him; the Engineer Officer went on, 'We could overdo it and lose buoyancy. Touch and go ... it might work out but I don't believe it would.'

'All right, Chief, we'll carry on as we are for the time being. And I'm glad of your advice,' Seymour added.

'Any time,' Matthews said with a grin, and went down the ladder to the iron-deck and below again to his engine-room.

Later, when the watch on deck was relieved, Cameron found Seymour in a gritty mood, snapping at the RNVR Midshipman and the Leading-Signalman, hunched in his corner of the compass platform, eyes salt-reddened and tired. So much of this was a waiting game, waiting for the unseen enemy to strike and then coping as best possible with the result of that strike. Cameron could begin to understand a captain's anxieties: his own father had held command at sea, and he himself had sometimes seen the trawler skippers under stress in filthy weather. True, they had not had to face the human enemy, but the fight against the sea itself was universal to mariners and the sea at its worst could be as terrible as anything the human hand could do. And Seymour was considerably less experienced than any trawler skipper when it came to fighting the sea. Cameron began to feel a sense of unease; already the buzz had gone around the lower deck that Seymour wanted to put the ship still lower in the water to correct the trim, and that the Chief had said that was bloody daft. Argument, most of it singularly ill-informed, had blossomed: some were for Seymour, others for the Chief. Most in fact were for Seymour. As Stripey Tomkins had said, loudly and with embellishments of speech, they were currently going nowhere and they might just as well take a chance.

The dark came down thick and black; but with its coming the weight of wind began to slacken and the waves, though they would remain high for a while yet, no longer lost their crests in blown spume. The destroyer still lay sluggishly at the sea's mercy but the water no longer broke across her or slammed into her as viciously as before though she continued wallowing in the troughs and then climbing the hillsides to slide away into the next rolling water-valley. Life was as uncomfortable as ever. The wind dropped more as midnight approached and the seas began to become oily, developing an uneasy ocean swell as the wind fell away. All the lookouts were alert to spot the eastbound convoy as the estimated time of sighting drew close. Once again, Cameron saw things that were not there and Seymour's responses grew more snappish as he searched the reported bearings time and again through his binoculars and found nothing. Snappish but not quite reproving: you didn't scare lookouts from their duty of reporting even what they thought they had seen. In the event it was not until just after a bleary dawn that the convoy out of Halifax was seen away to the north-west, and even then it was heard rather than seen in the first instance. It was heard as long-drawn thunder following the roar of an explosion, then seen as a vast sheet of flame, red and orange and white, and a great plume of black smoke rearing into the overcast sky.

Seymour said bleakly, 'Must be an ammunition ship. Poor sods. Snotty!'

'Yes, sir?' The RNVR Midshipman saluted Seymour's back.

'Sound action stations.'

'Aye, aye, sir.' The alarm was pressed and the rattlers screamed out around the ship; men just fallen out from dawn action stations pulled themselves from sleep and hurried back to their positions, cursing. To the north-west debris was still falling from the sky and the smoke was pouring yet. No one in that ship could possibly have lived; and the British Army in the Middle East, the RAF fighter and bomber airfields in Britain, and the seabound ships of the Navy, would feel the loss of her cargo. One more feather sprouted in Adolf Hitler's bloody cap; within the next ten minutes, as *Carmarthen*'s company watched in helpless horror, another vessel was hit and vanished in an individual holocaust. Seymour's voice shook a little as he lowered his glasses.

'That looked like a troopship,' he said. 'Canadians, I suppose ... God knows how many.'

No one else spoke, but minds filled with images, images of upwards of a thousand men, probably a good deal more, either mangled when the ammunition-filled holds went up beneath them or cast into the sea to flounder and freeze to death within minutes. Soon the convoy, or what was left of it, was seen clearly, moving now from north-west to north and slowly closing nearer to the *Carmarthen*: Seymour counted twenty merchantmen, all biggish ships, four deep-laden tankers amongst them bringing desperately-needed oil from the United States. Around them the escorting naval ships could be seen, *Carmarthen*'s own group now returning with their charges to the Clyde, whence they would break off for Cape Wrath and the Scapa base. As Seymour watched, one of the tankers was hit by a torpedo. Again there was an almighty explosion and thick black smoke rose in a pall that seemed to blot out the entire sky to the north. Fire spread out over the sea, sizzled around any men who might have survived the initial explosion. Then came indications of a depth-charge attack by the escort: the Atlantic erupted in a pattern of waterspouts. In the prevailing swell it was not possible to see the result from *Carmarthen*, but a cheer went up spontaneously from the destroyer's up-ended decks as her company watched the attack. If hopes could help, the Third Reich would now be missing at least one U-boat from Grand Admiral Raeder's lethal packs. . . .

Once again Seymour lowered his binoculars. He said, 'Yeoman, call up the Senior Officer of the escort by lamp.

Make: am flooded forward and unable to use my engines currently but do not repeat not require assistance.'

'Not, sir?'

'Not.' God knew, the assistance of a tow was desperately required; but it could be neither asked nor given unless the vital convoy was to be held up or deprived of a part of its escort. 'This is war, Yeoman, not a bloody peace-time exercise!'

'Sorry, sir.' The Leading-Signalman, acting now as Yeoman, moved across to the signalling projector in the starboard wing of the compass platform and clacked out the leader's call-sign. The acknowledgement came, the message was passed, and Seymour waited for the response. It was more or less what he had expected; the Leading-Signalman reported: 'Answer, sir: God be with you.'

'God,' Stripey Tomkins said bitterly, 'is all very well but he's not a flippin' tow. Them bastards, they could've taken us right out of this lot!' The convoy and its escort had passed on by now, hauling away to the east together with the U-boats that would in all likelihood harry it until it came beneath the umbrella of the Commander-in-Chief, Western Approaches – or met attack by the FW 200s. Once again, there was a naked feeling. The sight of the escorts had provided, very briefly, a kind of companionship. Now they were alone again. It was good that they had come under no further attack themselves, but many of them tended to share Stripey Tomkins' view even though they knew in their hearts that there was nothing else that could have been done. Lavington seemed closer now to going to pieces. He sat in a corner of the galley flat, hugging his knees, his face dead white and his eyes shining curiously. Suddenly he blurted out, 'We're all going to die. You know that. We can't possibly get home. We—'

'Shut up,' Tomkins said threateningly. 'Bloody spreadin' alarm and despondency! Course we'll get 'ome, we're bloody *British*. Stands to reason. Senior Officer, 'e'll report our position and they'll send out an ocean-going rescue tug.'

50

'Why didn't he say so, then?'

Tomkins raised his eyebrows. 'Wot, an' let the muckin' 'Uns read 'is lamp and then wait for the tug and put a fish in her? Bloody likely!'

Lavington swallowed almost convulsively and went back to his theme. 'We're done for, whatever you say. We can't—' He broke off as Tomkins swiped a fist at him, catching him a hefty blow on the ear. He began sobbing. Cameron watched in pity mixed with disgust: Stripey Tomkins had probably done the right and proper thing. Lavington said no more, but went on crying and shaking. Fear and stress were building up inside him and before long would have to come out. Cameron felt a kind of responsibility for him as a fellow CW rating, and would be watching out for trouble, trouble of a particularly nasty sort if Lavington should crack. The start of panic was something that could not be tolerated in the circumstances. There were a number of hostilities-only ratings aboard who might well be affected; mostly they hadn't the phlegmatic, philosophic steadiness of the experienced RN hands who had been trained from boyhood for war and its dangers. A firm word in Lavington's ear might not come amiss: Lavington might consider reporting sick – in fact it was a wonder, really, that he hadn't already done so since it might get him out of work and discomfort. For the future safety of the ship, he might be much better in the doctor's hands, though of course a lot depended on the doctor himself; Lavington might well be considered as lead-swinging, but Cameron fancied the doctor might take note of his mental condition and come to his own conclusion about ship safety. Cameron was about to have a quiet word when the order was piped:

'Clear lower deck . . . all hands fall-in along the iron-deck!'

5

THE reports had been received by now in the operations room in Rosyth: HMS *Carmarthen* had been contacted, still afloat but without the use of her engines. It had been Mary Anstey who had taken the report and passed it to SO(O). The Commander had nodded non-committally and in a dismissive manner, but Mary wanted to know more and, her heart beating fast, she had stood her ground and asked questions.

'Sir, I was wondering ...'

'Yes? Well, go on, out with it, I won't eat you!'

'No, sir. The *Carmarthen* ... will anything be done for her, do you think?'

'You'll have to ask the Admiral that.' The Commander gave her a shrewd, searching look. 'Have you a special interest, or something?'

She said, biting her lip, 'Yes, sir.'

'Yes, I see.' The Commander smiled in a friendly way, and put a hand on her shoulder. She was a good-looking girl and he understood well enough. He said, 'Now look, do try not to worry. It's no good to anyone. Have confidence in the ship and her company – there's plenty of experience there. If you want to know what I think, it's this: the Admiral will send out an ocean-going rescue tug to have *Carmarthen* brought in under tow. She's around three hundred and fifty miles out ... say, twelve hours' fast steaming for the tug. Okay?'

'Yes, thank you, sir,' she said, and went back to her work. The work needed her full concentration and she tried her best to give it, but didn't succeed too well. The *Carmarthen* was with her all the time. It might be silly, but she couldn't help it. They hadn't even an understanding, and it might all be in her own mind alone for all she knew, but she desperately wanted Donald back safe and sound . . . and damn and blast the war! It was terrible to think of all the young men, so many of them only just out of school, who were suffering and dying already. More than a year of war now, and Hitler looked very much like winning, and if he did, what then? The Gestapo in English streets, and sudden midnight arrests, and concentration camps and all that went with that?

It didn't bear thinking about. They just had to win this war.

'I'm going to flood the after magazines,' Seymour said, addressing his ship's company from the searchlight platform amidships. 'That holds dangers and I won't disguise them. We'll lose the use of our main armament once the backed-up ready-use ammo has been fired, but the 4.7s are largely useless already.' The Gunner's Mate had already had hands below, bringing up ammunition for the close-range weapons, plus a box of hand-grenades, and all this would be stowed by the guns handy for use as required. Seymour went on, 'The principal danger is that we'll settle too far. I consider that a danger worth risking. We can't stay here indefinitely, that's certain.' He looked at his wrist-watch. 'I shall flood in five minutes from now. All hands not required will remain on the upper deck and stand by to move fast if things go adrift and I have to abandon. Petty Officer Thomas?'

'Sir?'

'Have the Carley floats made ready for immediate release, and swing out the whalers port and starboard. We'll have one hell of a job lowering them in this swell, but we'll do it, and we'll need to do it fast if and when the moment comes. All right?'

'All right, sir.'

'Good. Well, I think that's all. Carry on, please.'

Thomas saluted and turned about and began mustering the

boats' crews and lowerers of the whalers, and detailing hands to stand by the Carley floats that in the event of abandoning ship would be slid down into the sea while men dived in and then swam to grasp the lifelines looped along the sides of the floats, and clamber in. Seymour went to the compass platform, outwardly calm but, inside, a bag of nervous reactions and doubts, largely due to something of a scene with Matthews. Because the exchanges had been in public, the scene had been subdued but the antagonism to Seymour's order could be felt. Lieutenant (E) Matthews was a forthright man and had been at sea a good deal longer than Seymour: all the way from apprentice and Engine-Room Artificer Fifth Class to Chief Engine-Room Artificer and Warrant Engineer until he had made the wardroom with his two gold stripes and purple distinguishing cloth in between. He knew, he had said, all about buoyancy and ship stability and to flood aft was bloody dangerous. He would take no responsibility, he declared flatly, and Seymour answered in cold tones that he didn't expect him to. Go ahead then, Matthews had said, and see what happens. Was it not better to remain afloat and wait for rescue which was sure to come when the Senior Officer reported their position?

Of course, he had a point.

Nevertheless, Seymour had made his decision and it stood. It would be implemented. Taking a deep breath, Seymour, after a final look around the sea's surface, passed the order down for the flooding to begin. It was a simple enough operation, quickly carried out by the opening of a valve. From the quarterdeck lobby, word came back that the compartments were now flooding. Seymour held his breath: the effect seemed little enough so far, barely noticeable in fact from the compass platform. But reports from the quarterdeck, where the RNR Sub was in charge, indicated that the ship was coming down a little in the water although taking into account the sea that was running it was impossible to be precise....

'Magazines flooded, sir,' the communications number reported.

'Thank you.' Seymour moved to the engine-room voice-pipe. 'Chief!'

'Speaking.'

'Magazines flooded. I can't say if it's done the trick. I want you to turn over the main engines ... gently, just for a trial run, all right?'

'All right,' came Matthews' voice, grudging and surly. Seymour stepped back. Within the next few moments he could feel the subdued throb of the main engines as the shafts were geared in and began to turn at dead slow astern. He let out a long breath of relief and mopped at his forehead which was damp with sweat despite the intense cold: there had been no sudden surge, no racing of the screws, and that must mean they had bitten into water. The engine-room voice-pipe whined and Seymour answered it.

'Captain here.'

'Chief. She's all right, anyway for now.'

'So it paid off, Chief.'

'Right, it did. I'll still not speak for the buoyancy if the weather worsens again.'

'We'll be all right,' Seymour said tightly. 'Obey telegraphs, Chief.' He slammed down the voice-pipe cover and spoke down the tube to the wheelhouse. 'Cox'n, telegraphs to slow astern together, wheel amidships.'

'Slow astern together, wheel amidships, sir,' the Torpedo-Coxswain repeated. The engines throbbed, and very slowly *Carmarthen* began inching astern through the water, coming back to life. That life spread throughout her company: there were smiles in the wheelhouse and along the upper deck, even though the sea was now so close that the swell was surging inboard from time to time, rushing along below the search-light platform and pouring past the engineers' store to pound against the bulkhead of the galley flat, where the after watertight door had now been clipped down. The ship was moving once again; but she had a far from healthy feel – she was sluggish and wallowing as the swell took her and flung her about, the kind of reaction that said she might not rise to it if

55

the weather should deteriorate again. One of those off watch who now thought she might not was Able-Seaman Tomkins.

'She's buggered if you ask me,' he said, although no one had. 'What are we making, eh? You, Your Lordship. You've just come off the bridge, right?'

Cameron said, 'Three knots maximum is the Captain's estimate.'

'An' all that bleedin' way to go,' Tomkins said in disgust. 'It's askin' too much. One whopper of a sea would send us under if we don't die of cold first. Or if the 'Uns don't get us.' After this he lapsed into silence and soon was snoring loudly. He was, Cameron thought, only too right about the bitter cold. Down here in the galley flat it was only a degree or so warmer than the compass platform, for the fires still remained drawn, the only warmth coming from the physical proximity of the packed, sleeping bodies. The atmosphere was almost fetid, with a fug that came from unwashed personnel and the foul condition of the seamen's heads with their doorless openings. It was a miracle that human beings could suffer it all and not mutiny; but hard-lying, as it was known officially, brought a small amount of extra pay called hard-lying money, and the discomforts were accepted as paid for and as a part of naval life, part of the normal lot of the lower deck while the wardroom officers lived in comparative luxury in their cabins aft – except when, as now, those cabins were occupied by the less fortunate survivors of the convoy attack. Lower-deck conditions aboard *Carmarthen* were worse than Cameron had known in his father's trawlers, though the same didn't go for all trawlers. Cameron grinned to himself as he thought of his father: the old man wasn't too well liked by his brother owners. They complained that he made his boats too soft, thus spoiling the trawlermen and encouraging them to expect similar conditions from other fleets. That had never worried Captain Henry Cameron: one of his sayings was that the labourer was worthy of his hire.

Next time off watch, Cameron had his self-promised word with Lavington and found total opposition. Lavington was

56

oddly adamant; there would be no reporting sick, because he wasn't sick and would be seen through at once. There was a curious underlying insistence that somehow spoke of an inner knowledge that he was on the brink of a breakdown but didn't want anyone to know it. He wanted a commission at all costs; he couldn't go on taking the lower deck, it was bestial and his messmates were morons, working class to a man. Cameron realized it was useless; he was more worried than ever as a result and a little diffidently – the CW label was often inhibiting – he asked Petty Officer Thomas if he might raise a problem.

'Go ahead, lad,' Thomas said, holding one nostril closed and blowing hard down the other to leeward. 'What's it all about, then, eh?'

'Ordinary Seaman Lavington, PO.'

'Him, eh.' Thomas sniffed and adjusted his sou'wester. 'Well?'

'I think he's sick,' Cameron said.

'What of?'

'I don't know, PO, but I think he's going to crack up and that may mean trouble. I was wondering ...'

'Well?'

'Perhaps he should report to the sick-bay.'

Thomas laughed. 'Up to him, isn't it? Why not say so to him?'

'I have,' Cameron answered, and told Thomas the result. 'I'm worried both for him and everyone else.'

'It's not your concern, young Cameron,' Thomas said admonishingly. 'His leading hand should raise it if he wants to. You're not a bloomin' officer yet, you know.'

'No.' Cameron found himself flushing. 'Nor am I a do-gooder, normally! I'm sorry, PO. I expect I should have gone to Leading-Seaman Farrow if anyone—'

'It's not *up* to you! It's Farrow's job to see for himself, and he won't thank you for doing it for him, will he now?' Thomas laid a hand on Cameron's shoulder. 'All right, lad, you've done what you thought best, now leave it, all right? I'm not

57

blind either . . . maybe I'll talk to Farrow and then drop a word in Jimmy the One's ear. Off you go now.'

He had to leave it there; Jimmy the One – the First Lieutenant, now the RNR Sub – might act or he might not. It would be in his lap. Cameron had his dinner of cold bully beef and turned into his billet in the galley flat. It was two bells in the afternoon watch, and Cameron was dead asleep when the alarm came. The urgent rattlers jarred him awake and he scrambled with the others out from the galley flat to the iron-deck and his action station. It was almost a repeat of the last surface attack: as Cameron went fast up the bridge ladder he saw the U-boat just coming to the surface on the port bow with the water cascading from her casing and her close-range weapons coming into action already. A stream of machine-gun bullets zipped across the span of water and ricocheted off the steel-work of the bridge and midships superstructure, a sweeping arc of fire that scattered the men as they ran to their stations and left a dozen dead or wounded. Cameron watched helplessly as the inboard-sweeping swell took three men, dead or alive he knew not, and swept them willy-nilly into the sea to vanish. There was no time to think about them, how-ever: as he climbed the ladder, a body crashed down from one of the four Lewis guns, then another. Blood poured; Cameron, climbing on, dashed for the Lewis gun which was swinging, crewless, on its mounting. As machine-gun bullets flew about him he seated himself at the Lewis, brought his sights on, and fired a sustained burst towards the U-boat's conning-tower. He seemed to have taken the Germans by surprise: a cap flew, and a body slumped over the side of the conning-tower. Cameron sent another burst on to the same target. Simultaneously, as the U-boat's casing-mounted 3.5-inch gun opened, another Lewis crew caught the German gunners fair and square and sent them reeling over the side. They were not quite in time: the shell from the U-boat smashed into the *Carmarthen*'s searchlight platform, and shell fragments scattered fore and aft. The Lewis gunners, joined now by the pom-pom crews, depleted their ready-use

58

ammunition in keeping up a sustained fire over the German's conning-tower and gun-mounting. Unable to send men to man the gun, and unable to use the machine-gun in the conning-tower, the German captain evidently decided to retreat. There was a swirl of water and the casing began to vanish.

Seymour ordered, 'Cease firing!'

The U-boat disappeared beneath the surface. Seymour leaned over the compass platform guard-rail and called down. 'Well done, Cameron. Quick thinking on your part.'

'Thank you, sir.'

Stock was taken of the situation: fifteen men dead, twenty wounded. It was a heavy toll and there was more bad news to come: an unwelcome quantity of the ready-use ammunition had been expended. With the after magazines now flooded as well as the forward ones, *Carmarthen*'s teeth were being drawn. She would soon be able to fight no more.

Making her three knots' sternway, wallowing in the swell that would not leave her, *Carmarthen* moved slowly eastward. The galley fires had been flashed up again when the weather had moderated further and the off-watch surroundings were that much more bearable. The hot food was welcome: bangers and mash were a sight better than cold bully beef, and thick, hot cocoa went down well too. Cooked food in the stomach lifted spirits and revived optimism, though by now there was little to be really optimistic about. On the compass platform Seymour, who had had only briefly-snatched sleep for many days – a sum total of maybe four hours, no more – still stared bleakly from his corner, wrapped in oilskins and duffel-coat, the hood of the latter pulled well down around his unshaven cheeks. Constantly he did his sums, praying always that he was wrong. Three knots meant something like a hundred hours of steaming – it was a simple enough sum to do, but the result was unreliable since so many imponderables could intervene and extend the voyage almost to infinity. The weather was one imponderable, the Germans were another,

59

the chance of rescue from the United Kingdom yet another and not to be counted upon. The Navy was over-stretched, badly. Certainly no fighting ship could be spared to search, locate and tow a battered destroyer across upwards of three hundred miles of the U-boat infested convoy lanes, though an ocean tug might be despatched – perhaps. *Carmarthen* would not be the only damaged warship in northern waters, and if, say, a battleship or cruiser was in similar difficulties then all efforts would be directed towards her rather than towards *Carmarthen*. *Carmarthen* had seen better days; she was elderly, having been completed just in time to see service in the last war. If it hadn't been for Hitler's war, she would have been scrapped by now. As it was, she had been withdrawn from the Reserve Fleet to be refitted and sent again to sea. She was expendable if more valuable ships called; that was a simple fact of war and the exigencies of the service. Seymour, as his eyes searched the sea for either trouble or assistance, found his mind drifting back to the piping days of peace. The peace-time Navy manned by the caretakers, as the reservists liked to call the RN, had been a very different service. The youthful Seymour – and by God he felt pretty aged now at the age of twenty-three – had emerged from the Royal Naval College, Dartmouth, to join the Fleet as a midshipman and had been appointed for sea training to the great battleship, HMS *Nelson*, wearing the flag of the Commander-in-Chief, Home Fleet, a ship that swarmed with gunner's mates afloat on a Whale Islandish sea of gas and gaiters. Everything aboard the flagship was immaculate, from the Admiral's summer-season white cap cover to the pipe-clayed turks'-heads on the hatchway guard-rail stanchions. Everything was done by the bugle calls of the Royal Marines; and when the Home Fleet came to anchor, perhaps in Scottish waters, perhaps off Portland or in Spithead, everything was done to split-second timing: the great bower anchors went down, all ships together, to smash into the water as the brakes came off the cable-holders, and in the exact same instant the duty boats were lowered on the falls and the lower- and quarter-booms were swung out. Woe betide any officer or man who reacted a second late to the Admiral's order. The Home Fleet was a proud institution; so was the Mediterranean Fleet, in which Mr Midshipman Seymour next served on appointment to the *Renown*, also wearing a flag, this time that of the Vice-Admiral Commanding the Battle-Cruiser Squadron, under the overall command of Admiral Sir William Fisher, Commander-in-Chief, Mediterranean, whose flag flew in HMS *Queen Elizabeth*. None of this meant a total unbendingness; the Navy was reasonably tolerant of, for instance, a seaman's sense of humour: when *Nelson*, undergoing dry-docking in Portsmouth Dockyard, found herself a main exhibit of one Navy Week, her telegraphists dreamed up sample telegrams that could be sent from her transmitting room to the relatives of the visitors to the ship. The best-seller was the one that read: HAVING A LOVELY TIME WATCHING NELSON'S BOTTOM BEING SCRAPED.

There had been happy, carefree days in Malta and Gibraltar; combined manoeuvres of the Home and Mediterranean Fleets when the harbour had been crammed with British warships of all sizes and the air had been vibrant with the bugle calls from the Army barracks as well as from the ships themselves. There had been regattas, there had been cruises to strange ports to show the flag and give the ships' companies a run ashore. There had been women and there had been drink, although a young officer was well advised, for the sake of his career, to treat both the latter with reserve. There had been sport – cricket and football, shooting, sometimes hunting in the right sort of country: Seymour had borrowed a horse and hunted with the Calpe hounds in Andalusia in Spain, just across the isthmus joining the rock of Gibraltar to the mainland. There had been dances aboard the quarterdecks of the Fleet, romantic affairs under scrubbed white awnings with the Royal Marine band playing softly around the great fifteen-inch or sixteen-inch turrets of the *Queen Elizabeth* or the *Nelson*.

There had been odd interludes, infuriating at the time but

laughable at in retrospect: Mr Midshipman Seymour had an uncle who owned a coal-mine in Fife, and while serving in the *Nelson*, visiting the Firth of Forth, his uncle had invited him ashore to have a look around his coal-mine. After this interesting visit, Seymour had returned to the Rosyth dockyard to embark aboard the officers' boat for his ship – and had met the battleship's Commander who had been playing golf. The Commander, bound for a night's entertainment and not wishing to be encumbered with his golf clubs, had asked Seymour to take them back to the ship for him; Seymour had naturally done so.

Upon his return to the quarterdeck, he had met the majesty of the Commander-in-Chief pacing for his evening exercise.

'Ah, Snotty,' the great man said genially. 'Been playing golf, I see.'

'No, sir,' Seymour corrected in all innocence. 'I've been down a coal-mine, sir.'

The result had been a fourteen-day stoppage of leave for impertinence, and no mumbled explanations accepted. Officers never made excuses and that was that, at any rate until the Commander put it right. It had been, all in all, a happy time and a hard one, with much work to be done, but Seymour wondered, as he stared from his shattered command, whether it had really fitted a man for modern war.

It was a totally different service by now: it had been flooded out by the Royal Naval Reserve and the Royal Naval Volunteer Reserve. RN stripes were becoming a rarity ashore and afloat. The RNR, both officers and men, were of course professional seamen though they didn't necessarily know a lot about RN methods; the RNVR were certainly enthusiastic, but basically they were Saturday-afternoon sailors. The time-honoured saying had it that the RNR were sailors pretending to be gentlemen, the RNVR were gentlemen pretending to be sailors, and the RN were neither pretending to be both. No one took it seriously, of course, but there was a basis of some truth. The plain fact was that the reserve officers had risen to the challenge and were every bit as good as the straight stripers of the RN, without the supposed benefit of the peace-time bull and bugles and all that went with them. The lower deck was a rather different kettle of fish: the volunteers among the hostilities-only men were first-class material, but the majority of the intakes were conscripts, as was inevitable in the case of those who, when war had been declared, had been over the minimum age and automatically liable to call-up; and a number of them were unwilling ones. The peace-time Navy had not contained conscripts since the evil days of the press gangs and it didn't take all that kindly to them now. The unwilling ones among them stood much in need of the stiffening provided by the long-service men, especially the chief and petty officers, as ever the real backbone of the Navy, many of them comparatively elderly men called back from the Royal Fleet Reserve to which all naval lower-deck pensioners were attached on retirement from active service. And they were the salt of the earth; many had served in the Grand Fleet under Jellicoe and Beatty. It was they, not the officers, who turned raw green youths into seamen.

Then there was that new fish, the CW candidate, the White Paper rating, such as Cameron. Seymour, coming back from the past and once again facing the tense reality of war, thought about Cameron. Hewson, his dead Captain, had been impressed from the start and had fully intended giving Cameron his necessary recommend for his commission. He, Seymour, would honour that, and with pleasure, if nothing happened in the future to make him decide the other way. Cameron was reliable and could think for himself without waiting for orders: that was one of the attributes of an officer, or should be. Then there was Ordinary Seaman Lavington, and Seymour's mouth turned down at the corners as he thought about him. An unforgivable mistake on someone's part that he should ever have been given his first recommend, and that recommend would not be repeated. Lavington didn't pull his weight and appeared to be as soft as soap. He was also a little obsequious, a quality that Seymour didn't admire; arse-crawlers were not to be trusted. However, this was not the

time to be worrying about that sort of thing. Proper consideration of Ordinary Seaman Lavington would have to wait till
this lot was sorted out; it was essential to be fair, and before
making a final decision the other officers, and Lavington's
divisional petty officer, would have to be consulted. But as it
turned out, events were to force Seymour's hand.

The weather worsened again later that day; once more the
galley fires were drawn and the wind came back strongly to
balloon out men's oilskins and fill their sea-boots with a salty
drench. That wind was bitterly cold, hinting at ice and snow,
and it cut through to the bone. Now more than ever before,
with the destroyer so low in the water, the ship's company was
constantly soaked. There was no respite from it as the increasing seas swirled aboard to carry all before them; hands and
faces became blue, bristly cheeks became more haggard as the
terrible voyage home progressed, hour after dragging hour
with the ship yawing badly and making her pathetically slow
sternway.

Cameron felt he would never be warm again, and thought
of home in Aberdeen with a coal fire burning in the sitting-
room and his father worrying about his trawlers, all of them
now taken into Naval service for the duration. The old man
had been too old for sea service – unless you were a regular
officer, the Admiralty had no use at sea for anyone over fifty –
and after his trawler fleet had been taken over he'd found a
management job in the port. Thus he was in touch with the sea
still, and though he hadn't liked being ashore he could at least
keep warm, and fed too, so far as the ration books permitted.
In point of fact the civilians weren't having it all that easy; last
time home, even though some food items were easier in
Scotland, Cameron had been shaken by the small food ration
and the way his mother had had to skrimp and save on basic
essentials, going without herself so that the returning hero
could be fed. He'd put a stop to that pronto; the Navy, he said
with truth, was going short of nothing except ships themselves. But that was before he had joined *Carmarthen* and

suffered drawn galley fires and all that went with that; right now, the shore-side ration seemed like a cornucopia. So did that cheerful fire.... Cameron, his eyes busily scanning the seas, thought of Mary Anstey. She was a nice girl, if a little possessive; they'd had some good evenings down in Southsea – it was like another world now, all the difference between the seagoing Navy and the chairborne warriors of RN barracks, HMS *Vernon*, Whale Island and all the rest. He wondered who Mary would be going out with now; she would have the pick of many officers in Portsmouth. Like him, she had been hoping for a commission but he had a feeling that a commission would change her. Officers of the WRNS were a different breed, largely, from the ratings; and it was said that many a Third Officer WRNS turned up her nose at anyone under the rank of commander. It was also said that WRNS officers were borne on the books as officers' mattresses. Well, it would be up to her; there was nothing much between them. They had parted friends, and that was all, really. Nevertheless, he missed her and hoped he would see her again. She was the sort of girl you didn't forget even though there was nothing all that special in her looks. It was a case of personality: a general merriness and companionability, a ready smile and freckles. Warmth ... and right now it was bloody perishing.

Relieved at last from his watch, Cameron went below and was given news by Leading-Seaman Farrow.

'Your mate Lavington,' Farrow said heavily.

'What about him, Killick?'

'Gone sick. By order, like. Know what I mean, don't you?'

Cameron nodded.

'Buffer told me.' Petty Officer Thomas, Chief Boatswain's Mate, was known as the Buffer, as were all Chief Boatswain's Mates, possibly because they acted as buffers between wardroom and lower deck. 'Gettin' a shade big for your bloody boots, aren't you?'

'I'm sorry,' Cameron said, wanting only to get his head down and find a little warmth.

'It's all right, I'm not that worried. Anyway, Jimmy sent for

Lavington, gave him an ear-bashing and told him off to report to the quack. We're short-'anded enough already . . . now this 'as buggered up what's left of the bloody watch and quarter bill.' Leading-Seaman Farrow sucked at a hollow tooth, managing to look aggrieved even though his face was only partially visible beneath the wool of his balaclava. 'I'm takin' you off lookout and puttin' you on three gun which will also mean seaboat's crew if and when required. Buffer's orders. All right?'

'All right,' Cameron said, pleased enough at the shift from the never-ending eye work. Farrow went off and Cameron flopped down on the deck, so dead tired that he found sleep immediately and never mind the wet beneath his body, scarcely kept out at all by his oilskin. Not that it made much difference; like everyone else aboard, he was already soaked to the skin. He came awake very suddenly about an hour later. It wasn't the alarm rattlers this time: it was a running man, a man who burst wildly into the galley flat from the iron-deck: Lavington, visible in the police light, bloodstained and waving a scalpel that he must have snatched up from the sick-bay.

6

'WHAT the hell!'

Cameron was on his feet, leaping over the recumbent bodies. Lavington fell back against a bulkhead, his eyes blazing madly. Cameron grabbed for the hand holding the scalpel, but Lavington squirmed away. Blood was all over him, he was waving the scalpel, and now he was screaming out obscenities. Stripey Tomkins scrambled up, swiped at Lavington, missed, and fell flat on his face on the deck. The destroyer lurched, sagging into a heavy sea, and the savage whine of the wind outside the galley flat came like the very sound of doom. As Tomkins got up again and charged towards Lavington, the scalpel sliced across his right arm, cutting through the sleeve of his duffel-coat, and blood spurted. Cameron got a grip on the man's shoulder and forced him back against the bulkhead, hard, flattening him with his own weight and then gripping both upper arms so that Lavington was helpless.

'What the bloody hell!' he said furiously. 'What have you done, you bloody little fool?'

Lavington shook in his grip; tears were streaming down his cheeks. There was no fight left in him now; the scalpel dropped to the deck, and another seaman picked it up and stared at it wonderingly. Lavington moaned. Thickly he said, 'I couldn't help it. I couldn't go on.'

Cameron gave him a violent shake. 'What have you done, for Christ's sake?'

Lavington's lips trembled. 'The SBA.'

'What about him?'

Lavington said, 'He ... laughed at me. He taunted me. I couldn't take any more ... everything went red, I don't know if you understand that, but it did. Then I saw the scalpel. I'd used one often in the dissecting room.'

'What did you do with it, Lavington?'

Lavington said unsteadily, 'I think I killed him. Oh, God. What's going to happen now?'

Cameron gave no answer; the answer was only too plain. He thought to himself, the bastard hadn't even the guts to go overboard afterwards and put a quick end to it. From now on, *Carmarthen* was going to be a marked ship in the Scapa base, the ship where murder had been done. And worse was to follow fast: Cameron was moving at the double towards the sick-bay when the urgent pipe was heard along the upper deck:

'Away seaboat's crew and lowerers of the starboard watch! Man your boat!'

It was a case of man overboard: afterwards, when the whaler had been hoisted again on the falls and secured at her davits, the victim unrecovered, Lavington was taken by the Torpedo-Coxswain into the engineers' store and grilled. When the Torpedo-Coxswain emerged, Lavington was locked into the store and a man of the watch on deck was armed with a rifle and detailed as sentry; *Carmarthen*'s cells were, along with the seamen's and stokers' messdecks, submerged. The Torpedo-Coxswain, his face grim, went immediately to the compass platform to report to the Captain. Seymour turned from his cold, windswept corner.

'Well, Cox'n?'

'The man's made a full statement, sir.'

'Let's have the facts, then.'

'Aye, aye, sir.' The Coxswain spoke formally as if at Captain's Defaulters. 'Ordinary Seaman Lavington, sir, was interrupted by the Surgeon-Lieutenant whilst attacking the Sick Berth Attendant, sir. He brandished the scalpel at the Surgeon-Lieutenant, who retreated out of the sick-bay. The

68

Surgeon-Lieutenant was followed by Lavington to the quarterdeck, sir, where he was attacked. He was washed over the side whilst attempting to disarm Lavington.'

Seymour swore. 'A *double* murder!'

'Yes, sir. Sick Berth Attendant Platten, sir, did not die immediately. He crawled out from the sick-bay and witnessed what happened, sir. It was he that gave the alarm, before he died, sir.' The Torpedo-Coxswain paused. 'As soon as the alarm was given, the seaboat's crew and—'

'Yes, yes, I know all that, Cox'n, thank you. I take it Lavington's in close custody?'

'Yes, sir.'

Seymour nodded. 'He'll remain in close arrest, of course, back to Scapa ... if we ever get there!'

'Yes, sir. And Defaulters, sir?'

Again Seymour nodded. 'It'll be done by the book, Cox'n. All the way ... he'll have to be brought before the Officer of the Watch and put formally in the First Lieutenant's report. Then I'll see him at Captain's Defaulters.'

'Yes, sir.'

'And there'll need to be a full transcription of all statements and evidence. Word for word.'

'Aye, aye, sir.'

'That's all, thank you. See to the charge, Cox'n.'

'Yes, sir.' The Torpedo-Coxswain saluted and clattered down the ladder from the compass platform. Seymour turned wearily and stared out across the surging, hostile seas. Neither he nor the Torpedo-Coxswain – nor anyone else aboard probably – had encountered a charge of murder before. It was an open and shut case, of course, but with such a serious charge King's Regulations and Admiralty Instructions must be followed to the letter. When, within the next few minutes, Lavington was brought in handcuffs to the compass platform to be charged, Seymour withdrew. As Captain he must in due course hear the formal case for the first time at his own Defaulter's table and should not be present at the first proceedings. He felt a pang of sympathy for the RNVR snotty,

Officer of the Watch, who would be watching his P's and Q's and hoping desperately to get it right. Going back to the compass platform when the initial statements and evidence had been given, Seymour's mind was filled with the thought that now they had neither doctor nor SBA and there was a hell of a lot of unfriendly ground to cover yet. Any further, unattended, deaths from wounds in action, or from the sea, could also be laid at Ordinary Seaman Lavington's door.

Next day one of those further deaths became a distinct possibility: a leading-stoker named Crucible developed severe stomach pains. He reported, more or less bent double, to the sick-bay where Midshipman Robens had been detailed to study the quick-reference manuals supplied to all ships, especially intended for the use of those not carrying medical officers. He had coped reasonably easily and efficiently with a number of cut hands, boiler-room burns (fortunately perhaps for themselves, the worst burn cases from the convoy had died) plus some sea-sores and boils, when he was faced with Leading-Stoker Crucible and his obviously serious complaint. Conscientiously, manual at the ready, he asked all the set questions and was able to eliminate both diarrhoea and constipation. The cure-all at sea was a liquid known as Black Draught, which worked wonders. But, Robens thought, not this time. As a youth, he had himself suffered from appendicitis and he played safe.

'Trousers down, Crucible, and lie on the settee.'

'Aye, aye, sir. If I can, sir.'

'Just try.'

Crucible did; but lay with his knees drawn up, in obvious pain. Sweat-beads formed on his forehead and he said, 'It's bloody agony, sir.'

'I'm sure it is, but we'll do what we can.' Midshipman Robens felt gingerly around the stomach. He couldn't identify any swelling or obstruction by touch and wasn't sure whether or not he should be able to; but Crucible left him in little

70

doubt. The man yelled in extreme pain as Robens' fingers probed and the sick-bay was filled with obscene language uttered in a very heartfelt manner. The makeshift doctor gave a brisk nod intended to instil confidence, told Crucible to remain on the settee, tucked him firmly in with blankets, put a lashing round his body to keep him intact against the destroyer's roll, and then went at once to the compass platform. He approached Seymour.

'Captain, sir.' He saluted.

'What is it, Snotty?'

'Acting as Medical Officer, sir.'

Seymour gave a tired grin. Robens, beginning to see himself as a real doctor, noted the signs of strain and felt the Captain, acting like himself, was not so far off cracking up. Seymour said, 'All they ever get is VD. Can you cope?'

'It's not VD this time, sir. I believe it's an appendix.'

'God!' Seymour blew out a long breath. 'Bad?'

'I don't know, sir. It could be burst, sir. That makes it peritonitis, and that's very serious indeed.'

'I know.' Seymour grinned again, but with no humour at all. 'I suppose it's no use ordering you to operate, Snotty!'

'If you give an order, sir—'

'I know, and I don't. God, this would go and happen on top of everything else!' Seymour clenched his fists in something close to despair, and turned away so that the Midshipman should not read that despair in his face. Of all people aboard, the Captain must remain serene, at least outwardly. So many lives depended upon him . . . as did the man with the appendix. That was his duty and his alone; in the old days of sail, the merchant shipmasters had had to cut off arms and legs and mend gashed stomachs, all with the sole aid of a medicine chest and a publication known as *The Ship Captain's Medical Guide*. Yes, it was the Captain's job; and, as Captain, he had to choose between one of his ship's company and the ship herself. An operation, which he would almost certainly botch, would take time; and he should not be absent from the bridge of his wallowing command. He temporized; the decision would not be made immediately. An operation might not become necessary.

'Morphia,' he said abruptly. 'Or whatever's in the medical stores – the drugs cupboard, isn't it? The pain must be stopped. Can you cope?'

'I'll do my best, sir. For a start ... may I find out if there's any medical knowledge among the ship's company?'

It hit Seymour like a blow in the guts. Lavington, who was responsible for the loss of the doctor and the doctor's assistant, had done two years as a medical student. He would know something – he would know his anatomy, if that could be considered a help. From what Seymour had seen of Lavington when he'd been brought to the bridge to be charged, he wouldn't be fit to operate but at least he might be able to advise the hand that made the incision. It wouldn't make any difference to the charge against him – or would it? It would be open to Lavington's defending officer at the Court Martial to plead diminished responsibility and it might be a sound enough plea in the circumstances; but could you plead diminished responsibility in the case of a man who had subsequently advised on an appendectomy? Would not Lavington's defence be automatically voided? Seymour had a duty to be fair and not prejudice any man's case whatever the facts might be; on the other hand, another man's life was at risk.

He made his decision. 'Yes, you may. If there's no one else, and I'm pretty sure there's not, try Lavington.' He turned to face aft again as the Midshipman left the compass platform. The weather had no look of moderation about it; the North Atlantic was not a kindly sea when roused and it held no compassion for the sick or injured. The cold, made worse by the keen, icy wind, was like a knife. At least Crucible would be reasonably warm in his sick-bay blankets, but the weather and the resulting motion of the ship would make an operation that much harder and more risky.

The vessel was sighted just as Seymour had made up his mind

72

that he must turn the compass platform and the ship over to Sub-Lieutenant Humphries, and go below to operate. Robens had come again to the bridge: Crucible was worse in his view. He was sweating, was deathly pale, had a high and rising temperature and Robens had no idea how much morphia he should give to douse the pain – with the result that he had probably not given enough and the agony was showing through. Well, you wouldn't leave a dog like that; Robens had gone through the ship seeking medical knowledge and had found none. Seymour was about to give the order to have Lavington taken under armed escort to the sick-bay when the report of the sighting was made and Seymour brought his binoculars up on the bearing. Through poor visibility he was able to make out the vessel, which he fancied was lying without way on her. He saw the Red Ensign aft, saw one funnel and two masts, and saw too that the ship was listing heavily to starboard and was down by the stern.

'Probably a straggler from the HX convoy,' he remarked to Robens.

'Another sitting duck for attack, sir?'

Seymour nodded. 'No doubt ... when the weather moderates.'

'What do we do, sir?'

'Do?' Seymour's harsh laugh blew along the icy wind. 'What the ruddy hell *can* we do, Snotty?' For a while he delayed going below; in the last resort, the ship came first and the lame duck ahead could spell trouble if some submerged U-boat decided to go for a kill despite the weather. Within the next half-hour he was able to see her upperworks clearly through his binoculars: she was a three-island merchantman, a dry-cargo carrier, probably of around ten thousand tons. And she was undoubtedly in a bad way; her list to starboard must be affecting her stability seriously in the heavy sea that was running. Seymour turned to the Leading-Signalman, already expectant at his side. He said, 'Call her up, Yeoman. Ask who she is and what happened.'

'Aye, aye, sir.' The signalling projector clacked out busily while Seymour and Robens waited. The reply was a long one; taken down by the signalman of the watch from the acting Yeoman's dictation, it was handed to the Captain on a signal pad. Seymour read:

SS WESTWARD BAY TORPEDOED AND THEN ATTACKED BY GUNFIRE WHILST IN EASTBOUND CONVOY. DAMAGE SERIOUS AND AM DRIFTING WITHOUT POWER ON MAIN ENGINES. AM CARRYING CARGO OF MILITARY VEHICLES FOR THE MERSEY. ALSO HAVE ON BOARD SURVIVORS FROM HMS ABERDARE SUNK DURING U-BOAT ATTACK.

Seymour's face showed shock. *Aberdare* was a sister ship, one of their own escort group who had accompanied them out from Scapa and then left to rendezvous with the eastbound convoy only a matter of days before. 'God, if only we could have a real smack at those bloody U-boats ...!'

Robens said suddenly, 'Doctor, sir!'

'What?' Seymour stared.

'She reports picking up survivors, sir. She could have *Aberdare*'s doctor.'

Seymour smashed a fist into a palm. 'By Christ, you're right! Yeoman, make: have you a doctor aboard and if so can you put him aboard me for urgent operation.'

'Aye, aye, sir.' The signal was made; the reply came quickly: SURGEON-LIEUTENANT FROM ABERDARE ABOARD BUT ALL BOATS SHOT AWAY. CAN YOU COLLECT.

'Answer yes,' Seymour said crisply. He bent to the voice-pipe. 'Cox'n, call away the seaboat's crew and lowerers of the watch – at the double!' In fact they always doubled, but the addition of the words would put an extra urgency behind their movements.

The seaboat was slipped with considerable difficulty and danger in the rushing seas and high-blown waves and was almost taken and lifted on a surge of water back on to *Carmarthen*'s quarterdeck. Sheer luck and the roll of the ship the right way brought her clear again, and she plunged into

74

the valley whence her crew could stare upwards at their ship until another surge of water lifted her high above. The men, bulky in their heavy cork lifejackets, held their breath as the whaler swooped down again, clear by some miracle of the limping destroyer. Cameron at one moment felt his oar strike fresh air and he almost flew backwards into his next astern; then it bit deep and he heaved as the whaler's coxswain, Leading-Seaman Farrow, gave the orders to bring them on course for the merchantmen. Seymour had not slipped the seaboat until he had closed the *Westward Bay* enough to give them the shortest possible pull across, but it was still a desperately long one in the heavy Atlantic gale. The exertions almost cracked their muscles and their straining backs as the men pulled on the oars and thrust with their feet against the stretchers. Up and down, rise and plunge, then rise again, kept efficiently on course by Leading-Seaman Farrow, slowly closing the great wall-like side of the *Westward Bay*. A small party of men could be seen, wrapped in oilskins, waiting by the starboard after rail where a Jacob's-ladder was coiled ready to be sent down. Despite the list, the climb down for the doctor would be a long one and held its hazards: a rope suspended in space, with a man on its end, could sway dangerously; but it was still much less of a hazard than sending him to scramble down the lifted port side.

After what seemed an eternity the whaler came under the lee of the *Westward Bay*, which was lying dangerously across the seas, broached-to at their mercy. With the roaring wind cut off, there was easier work; here the crests had temporarily flattened and there was a reduced amount of blown spindrift to sting the eyes and to blind. Carefully Farrow tended the whaler in, holding her off the steel sides of the 10,000-tonner as the listed deck loomed above. When he was ready he cupped his hands and shouted up:

'Right, send the officer down now!'

A hand waved from the guard-rail in response and the Jacob's-ladder with its wooden-stepped ropes was sent snaking down, to dangle and sway a few feet above the whaler.

With no time lost the Surgeon-Lieutenant, wrapped in oil-skins and duffel-coat, a balaclava helmet beneath his sou'wester, was helped over the guard-rail and held until his reaching feet found the first step of the ladder. Then, taking a grip with his hands, a grip like very death, he started gingerly down, reaching, feeling, finding. Farrow stared up, eyes narrowed, assessing the moment when he should call for the ladder to be lowered with the doctor on its end, lowered so that the officer could be grappled safely into the whaler and not plunged to his death in the foaming sea that still lifted and dropped the boat as the Atlantic rose and fell against the merchant ship's side plating. The slap and thunder of the restless water formed a backing of sound to the orchestral whine and roar of the wind: a combined sound of savage fury.

'Lower four feet!' Farrow yelled as the doctor reached the end of the ladder. 'Hold tight, sir, and wait till we 'as you safe!'

The doctor looked down, his eyes wide. There was stark fear in his face as the whaler appeared to jump at him and then in the next instant fell away to show a great yawning pit of disturbed water far below his swaying body. Cameron reckoned he was going to cling to that rope ladder till he was forcibly snatched away from it: it was his lifeline, all that stood between him and drowning, however insubstantial it might feel.

The boat rose again, swift and sharp. '*Now*!' Farrow yelled, and two able-seamen made a concerted grab for the doctor. No good: Cameron's guess had been spot on. The doctor didn't let go and the down-drop of the seaboat brought the grasp of the seamen away from his body.

'Stupid bastard,' Farrow said, not too softly, then called out, 'Next time, sir, and do try not to make a cock of it again.'

The face, as once again the boat swooped up, was whiter than ever, but this time the doctor let go as he felt the hands grab for him. The result was disaster; a leg took one of the grabbing seamen hard in the face and he staggered back, still grasping the doctor, and lost his balance. He just stopped himself going over the side, but the doctor went over head first and vanished. At the same moment a sea took the boat and swung her in towards the ship, to be borne off at the last vital moment by the ready oars and boathooks. Farrow, swearing horribly into the eddying wind below the ship's side, stared frantically around for the doctor. He said, 'Bet the bugger can't bloody swim!'

Then Cameron spotted the white, frightened face, carried by now some twenty feet clear of the boat. It was pretty obvious the doctor was no swimmer. Not waiting for Farrow, Cameron dived in. As he did so, he heard Farrow yelling at him not to be a bloody fool. Taking the water, he swam strongly for the drowning man and, reaching him, seized him below the arms. By this time Farrow had the whaler turned and making out towards him and within minutes both rescuer and rescued were being heaved, gasping, over the gunwale into the bottom of the boat. Farrow was withering. 'Bloody hero! Might have got drowned an' left us short, then none of us might 'ave got back alive!'

'Sorry, Killick ...'

'Disobeyed orders, what's more.'

'I didn't hear you,' Cameron said with a grin.

'Bloody Nelson.'

The trip back was made in safety and the whaler was hooked on to the falls; the lower deck was cleared for hoisting and the Surgeon-Lieutenant stepped shakily out to a comparatively safe deck. Seymour called down from the bridge. 'Glad to have you aboard, Doc.'

'I'll be only too pleased to help out,' the doctor called back, 'but what's up with your own MO?'

'It'll wait,' Seymour said, then added, 'He's dead.'

'I'm sorry.'

'What about your lot?'

The doctor, who was an RNVR named O'Connor, said, 'Captain's gone, so's Number One and the Sub.'

Seymour nodded, his face hard. He said in a controlled voice, 'All right, Doctor. Get along to the sick-bay – an appendectomy awaits you. I propose hanging on to you afterwards, seeing as you're part of the flotilla.' He then left the rail and resumed his never-ending vigil at the after end of the compass platform. *Aberdare* being of their own group, he had known her officers well. Her Captain had been a close friend; her First Lieutenant had been coming up for a command of his own. The Sub had been RNVR, a solicitor in pre-war days, with the makings of a useful officer. The war was bloody awful.

It became bloodier: suddenly, the engines stopped.

7

'WHAT the bloody hell are you up to, Chief?'
Seymour snapped down the engine-room voice-pipe. Tempers, by now, were somewhat more than frayed.

'I'm not up to anything,' the Chief snapped back. 'The bloody engines have stopped, that's all.'

'All! Jesus –'

'It can't be helped. You'll not be unaware, I presume, that the shafts have been racing from time to time?'

'Yes, I know!'

'Well, then. That's not done 'em any good –'

'So what's gone wrong?'

'I don't know yet,' Matthews said with exaggerated calm that Seymour found highly irritating. 'I'll be finding out just as soon as I can and then I'll be seeing if I can put it right.'

'It's a damn fine time for you to stop engines without warning. There's one of your own men –'

'I know, I know. *I* didn't stop engines, the sods stopped themselves. I'll be as quick as I can and I can't do more than that.' Seymour heard the cover slam back below, and he gave the bridge end of the pipe a vicious slam in return. God help Leading-Stoker Crucible if the destroyer broached-to and came beam-on to some bloody great wave just as the doctor had started to make his incision. Seymour, scowling, sent a messenger from the wheelhouse to warn the doctor of what had happened and what might happen. Maybe he could take some kind of precaution, maybe he couldn't; in this ruddy war, all life was at risk and uncertain in any case, but it would be bloody hard luck if Crucible should be killed, or at any rate not saved, because of the God-damn engines! This trip, Seymour had begun to yearn for the days of sail. With sail, he could probably have made better speed and would certainly have remained steadier, and if he'd had any canvas to speak of he would have had the Chief Boatswain's Mate at making and rigging sail on the yards of the fore- and mainmasts, but he hadn't, only enough to provide shrouds for sea burial and too much of that had been used up already. Mental note if ever they returned to UK: stores indents to include canvas for shrouds.

He stared aft towards the *Westward Bay*, as useless and as derelict as himself. The *Westward Bay* might carry some canvas – just might. There would be a need to replace the tarpaulins on the hatch covers, and the deck hatches of a 10,000-tonner would be nice and big. It was likely that the master of the *Westward Bay* had spared a thought for the use of sail to propel himself along, but it would take more than hatch tarpaulins to move a 10,000-tonner laden with military vehicles. Thinking of that cargo, so much wanted by the Armies in Britain and North Africa, so much wanted for the build-up that must surely come one day for the landing of an expeditionary force to retake France and Belgium, Seymour pondered the fact that he was now the *Westward Bay*'s sole armed escort and never mind that he had little ammunition beyond the torpedoes in his tubes amidships. It was his duty to stand by her, and God damn Lieutenant (E) Matthews and his failed engines. At the moment he was as helpless as he had been when the screws were lifted clear of the water. He might yet ask the *Westward Bay* for canvas.

In the meantime, there was Leading-Stoker Crucible.

Below in the sick-bay, Robens was looking green. The operation was not a very spectacular one and not particularly messy, but the atmosphere was close and there was a strong smell of chloroform and the ship's motion was diabolical. She was heaving and twisting, rising and falling, and making

80

Surgeon-Lieutenant O'Connor's task a difficult one, but he was coping well enough. Blood welled from the incision into the towelling placed by Robens around the site as indicated by the doctor; O'Connor probed around with a finger, then with his whole hand, drew something to the surface, and then used his scalpel again. Crucible's remaining innards went back into place. O'Connor looked up as he dumped something like a piece of smoked salmon into a kidney dish.

'That's it,' he said.

'All done, sir?' Robens was surprised.

The doctor nodded. 'Just the stitching to do yet.'

'He'll be all right?'

'No reason why not. He'll need nursing, that's all.'

'Me?' Robens asked in some alarm.

O'Connor smiled faintly. 'I rather think not. Your other duties are more in your line, aren't they? I'll see to the nursing myself.' He was busy making ready for the stitching. 'I congratulate you on your diagnostic powers, young man. If you hadn't been quick off the mark, he'd have died. I got to him only just about in time.'

Robens, his services no longer required in the sick-bay, reported to the compass platform. Seymour asked, 'Well? How is he?'

'All right now, sir. He'll pull through.'

'Thank God for that,' Seymour said, and meant it. One worry was past, though the others remained. So far there had been no further reports from the engine-room and Seymour was in a fever of impatience, having to force himself not to chivvy Matthews. Matthews knew his job and would report as soon as he had something to communicate. He was the sort who reacted badly to chasing. Seymour attempted the impossible task of trying to forget his engines, and stared across the heaving grey sea wastes towards the *Westward Bay*. The relative positions of the two ships were shifting as the waves buffeted them; the merchantman was now lying across the destroyer's bows, distant some six cables, maybe a little more. Distances were hard to assess in such sea conditions. . . .

Seymour's mind went to another worry: Lavington. That was a horrible business, and Seymour shrank from the thought of carrying a man across the seas to his certain death by hanging. Or almost certain; the state of Lavington's mind might save him, as he'd thought earlier. He had to be mentally sick; and Seymour could feel pity for him. Life in a destroyer's fo'c'sle would be hell for a sensitive man. Seymour, trained for the Navy at Dartmouth from the age of thirteen and a half, was no stranger to harshness and a tough routine. The Divisional Lieutenants and Chief Petty Officer Instructors at Dartmouth had never been easy to satisfy and the days had been physically hard. But Seymour, who had never in fact had to live in a destroyer's fo'c'sle as an ordinary seaman, had to use his imagination to assess what Lavington had gone through, living cheek by jowl with companions not of his own choosing, men with whom he would have had nothing in common, men who were capable of a merciless hazing of someone of a different class. It was a test of character and Lavington hadn't come through it. ...

The engine-room voice-pipe whined. Seymour reached for it and jerked back the cover. 'Captain here.'

'Chief speaking,' came Matthews' aggrieved tones. 'We won't move for a while, if ever. I'm sorry, but there it is.'

'What's the trouble, Chief?'

'Bearings running hot – both shafts seized up. There's been a leak of oil from—'

'Why?'

'Give me a chance,' Matthews snapped. 'I reckon there was a fracture when Number Four gun was taken out. I checked round afterwards, checked personally ... I found nothing amiss, certainly, but I think the trouble probably started when that shell hit and it's worsened.'

'Yes, I see. How long before—'

'I don't know,' Matthews said. He sounded bloody stubborn, Seymour thought with a flash of anger. 'We'll be working on it. I'll let you know as soon as I can, but it's going to take time, that's for sure. We may yet be unable to do it at all, as I said.' The metallic, disembodied voice stopped and Seymour heard the rattle as the cover was replaced below in the engine-room. He turned from the voice-pipe and looked again towards the *Westward Bay* and thought once more about canvas; there was plenty of wind to drive them home if they could only rig sail. He was about to tell the Leading-Signalman to call up the merchantman when a messenger reported from the W/T office. A radio signal had been received from Rosyth, in Naval cypher. Seymour sent down for the Surgeon-Lieutenant, whose customary duty it was to decipher signals when not medically engaged.

Half an hour later the plain-language version was in Seymour's hands. Seymour read it with much relief: OCEAN-GOING RESCUE TUG FORCEFUL HAS BEEN DESPATCHED TO YOUR ASSISTANCE AND SHOULD REACH YOU BY 0600 HOURS 24TH.

That was tomorrow's dawn. Seymour, feeling a good deal happier, had the news piped around the ship. It brought joy mixed with many doubts. On the iron-deck Leading-Seaman Farrow said gloomily, 'She'll come if she finds us. It's a bloody big if, an if as big as the bloody North Atlantic, almost. Eh? An' what about *that*?' He indicated the *Westward Bay*. 'One tug can't tow two ships, right?'

'Perhaps,' Cameron suggested, 'another's been sent to take her in. They won't know in Rosyth that we've come together, so they wouldn't have included the *Westward Bay* in the signal to us.'

Farrow lifted his sou'wester and scratched his head through the balaclava. 'So quick you catch yourself coming back,' he said with heavy sarcasm. 'If they don't know where the *Westward Bay* is, where do they send the flippin' tug?'

There was no answer to that; if indeed only the one tug turned up, a difficult situation could arise. Presumably the *Westward Bay* and her cargo were currently of more value to the war effort than a crippled destroyer. If that was the way the decision went, then all they could do aboard *Carmarthen* would be shrug their shoulders, wave goodbye, and continue wallowing around until another tug came out for them.

That evening a somewhat macabre routine event took place, as it would take place daily whenever the weather and the exigencies of the service permitted: prisoners in cells had to have their exercise period, and Lavington was brought out under escort to walk up and down the iron-deck's leeward side. He stumbled rather than walked, looking grey and haggard, with haunted eyes that stared wildly but seemed to see nothing. The reactions of the ship's company were mixed; most avoided looking at the pathetic rating but some stared with naked hostility and with a clear desire to hurt. But Lavington was oblivious, almost automaton-like. There was still blood on his duffel-coat, now dried brown, a grisly enough sight. Cameron, looking down from his station at Number Three gun, which still had a small reserve of ready-use ammunition in the racks, wondered just how alert the escort was expected to be. It would be a relief to everyone aboard, he fancied, if Lavington were to go over the side. But he made no move in that direction; he was clinging hard to the lifeline and keeping as far inboard as possible. The sea was his enemy, and even in his present condition he had no wish for a confrontation. Up and down he went, forlorn and lonely. Cameron looked away: the degradation hurt. He was glad when Lavington was put back in the engineers' store, out of sight. So was Seymour, into whose vision Lavington had come continually as he kept his vigil on the compass platform. To Seymour, the whole thing was ghoulish, like curing a sick man so that he could live for the execution. Looking out towards the *Westward Bay*, another anxiety that had plagued him ever since the engines had stopped struck more forcibly: the two ships were a little closer. A little, not much, but if they went on closing a highly dangerous situation was going to arise. And neither of them, with their silent engines, would be able to do a thing about it.

Seymour went to the voice-pipe and called the engine-room. An ERA answered; the job would take a long while yet, he said. Seymour said, 'Tell the Engineer Officer, we're in some danger of collision with the *Westward Bay* until the engines can turn over. I'll give you good warning to clear the engine-room and boiler-rooms if it looks likely.'

Night came down and still the ships lay silent, heaving in the swell, with the wind keeping up its eerie sigh and whistle around the masts and yards, making the wire of the triatic stay between mainmast and foremast sing weirdly. *Carmarthen* was like a ghost ship; below in the engine-room the work proceeded without respite, all hands bent to the urgent task of getting the shafts turning again. Not too much reliance was being placed on the arrival of the rescue tug; they were by now well away from their previously reported position, and it was known throughout the ship that the Captain had decided not to break wireless silence to report his present whereabouts. To do so during or immediately after an attack was one thing and was acceptable and often necessary; but not in present circumstances. Two sitting ducks could be very quickly and easily despatched if any surfaced U-boat should pick up the signal and alter towards them, or if the monitors in the German naval or air bases in France should intercept and order an attack. The risk was too great: as ever, the various risks had had to be assessed and the lesser chosen. That was a captain's responsibility, and everyone knew it; but there were those who criticized and said that the fastest possible tow back home would have been better than hanging about in cold and danger, waiting to be found, as found they very likely would be, by a stray U-boat on the prowl. Every minute they were out here increased that danger. That was how Lieutenant (E) Matthews was thinking while he worked, but he didn't voice his opinions. As an experienced man he knew that if you undermined the Captain's authority, you undermined your own at the same time, for your own derived from his.

On the compass platform Seymour stared with aching eyes through his binoculars, watching the *Westward Bay*'s great bulk – watching with difficulty, for the night was dark and in wartime no ship burned navigation lights or any other kind of light that would be visible on deck. The night was playing tricks: sometimes the *Westward Bay* seemed to be in one place, at other times elsewhere. It was devilish hard to determine whether or not she was closing; even the old lookout's trick of looking away for a while, or skirting the watched object, failed to work.

At Number Three gun, Cameron, acting as communication number from the gun to the control tower at the after end of the bridge, chatted with the gun-layer, Able-Seaman Hodge. Hodge was a two-badgeman who had once been a leading-seaman but had been disrated for bringing drink back aboard after a night's leave. That had been some four months earlier and having behaved himself in the meantime Hodge hoped soon to get his killick back. Hodge was a small man, dark and skinny, with a perky manner. He was married and had two children, living in Pompey, where the German bombs were inclined to fall now and again, and he was perpetually worried, this showing in a creased forehead and puckered eyes. He was rather like a monkey, Cameron thought. He was talking now about his family, rather less well-off now he had reverted to an able-seaman's pay, which was basically four shillings a day and a little more with his hard-lying money, his badges and his non-substantive rating of seaman gunner, plus an insufficient marriage allowance. It all added up to little enough, as he remarked.

'Navy's all right if you're single,' he said. 'Just don't get hitched, that's all!'

'I won't,' Cameron said with a grin.

'Not till you get that ring, eh?'

'Ring?' The word held marital connotations at first, then Cameron ticked over. 'Oh – commission. Not then either, so far as I know at present!'

'No popsies?' Hodge asked with an invisible leer.

Cameron said, 'No, not really.' Mary Anstey was there in

86

his mind, all right, but no more than that. Things might develop if he saw more of her, but very likely he would not. Both of them were subject to draft chits, to the whims and requirements of the service, and they might be ordered anywhere where there was a naval presence and that meant half the world. His home was in Aberdeen, hers in London. Since joining, Cameron had had one long leave of fourteen days and he'd gone home for it; that was a pattern he had decided to stick to, anyway for the foreseeable future. He felt he owed that to his mother and father. Also, he knew a number of girls in Aberdeen whom he would be glad enough to see again, and they him for that matter. Hodge continued talking – dripping, in the lower-deck phrase for complaint – about his enforced absence from Pompey and his home comforts, but very suddenly he stopped and said, 'Christ!'

'What?'

Hodge yelled, 'That merchant ship, she's bloody near on top of us!'

A moment later the alarm rattlers sounded throughout the ship.

Seymour, cursing himself and the bridge lookouts for not having seen the *Westward Bay*'s proximity much sooner, grabbed the cover off the engine-room voice-pipe. 'All hands on deck!' he shouted. 'Clear the engine-room and boiler-rooms, fast as you can.' He looked aft through his binoculars; the big ship had loomed very suddenly, seeming to thrust without warning through the poor visibility, through the night's total blackness, right aft. Seymour sent a warning by Aldis, a fairly useless warning since she couldn't stand clear with her defunct engines any more than he could himself. As the ratings poured up from below, Seymour cupped his hands and shouted down to the upper deck.

'Stand by to abandon ship! Petty Officer Thomas, are you there?'

'Here, sir,' came the Chief Boatswain's Mate's voice from the iron-deck.

'Get fenders out and a party to the sick-bay at once.' Seymour turned as someone came up the ladder at the double. 'Ah, Robens. Take charge of the sick-bay party, will you, and stand by to get the sick to the boats and Carley floats.'

'Aye, aye, sir!'

'How's Crucible, d'you know?'

'Making progress, sir.'

'Well, I hope he'll be able to keep it up. Off you go, Snotty.'

Robens clattered down the ladder again. Seymour gripped the compass platform guard-rail tight, waiting for the bump. It would be more, much more, than a bump, and never mind the pathetic fenders. The two ships would grind together and *Carmarthen*, half under already, wouldn't have a dog's chance of surviving. The battering effect of the waves would see to that, as they churned her plates against the side of the *Westward Bay*. Riveted seams would go and that would signal the end. Once again Seymour's task was to assess the moment when he should abandon; that must not be left too late, for men would be mangled between the two hulls if they hit before he gave it; nor must it be given too soon, for to abandon would mean inevitably that many would die in the freezing cold of the water before they could be hauled aboard the boats, and to cause men's deaths unnecessarily would be unforgivable. They might never need to jump at all. A miracle could happen at the last minute.

Seymour stood and sweated as he heard the orders being passed for the whalers to be swung out and lowered. The ships were coming closer now: had the moment come? He believed not yet; the *Westward Bay*'s bulky profile was altering and he believed she was swinging away and might stand clear with any luck.

Yes, she was swinging. . . .

Seymour scarcely breathed.

Then the *Westward Bay* showed her starboard side, the side to which she was listing, and in the same moment a surge of the sea, some cruel fate, took the semi-waterlogged

88

Carmarthen and seemed to lift her and throw her towards that great listed steel side. Seymour cursed savagely: the moment to abandon had gone, if ever in fact there had been the time at all. He shut his eyes and prayed. Then the crunch came, a tremendous impact that threw men to the decks throughout the ship. There was a great shudder and an ear-splitting shriek as steel met steel, and the destroyer gave a curious whipping motion as she came broadside against the merchantman. There was an agonized cracking noise from overhead as the *Carmarthen*'s masts impinged against the bulwarks above, and a tangled mess of metal came down with a resounding crash on the upper deck, on the guns and torpedo-tubes and on the compass platform itself: Seymour jumped back as something whizzed past his face and smashed down atop the chart table at the after end of the bridge. It was all hell now; the *Westward Bay*'s listed side loomed overhead like the lid of a coffin, a coffin that was about to close. There were screams as men who had been thrown to the destroyer's side were caught and nipped between the two ships, nipped and flattened as though taken by a steam-roller. From the deck above, someone shone a light down, a bright light on the end of a wandering lead, taking a justifiable risk. In the beam Seymour saw stark horror: his whole starboard side seemed to be red with blood and, as he watched, a man's severed head came rolling for'ard along the iron-deck, to fetch up at the foot of the ladder leading to the break of the fo'c'sle.

There was nothing to be done now but wait and carry on praying. Then he heard a voice shouting strongly into the wind against the noise of the grinding metal; he fancied it was Cameron's but couldn't be sure. 'Bearing-out spars!' the voice called. 'It's worth a try!'

Bearing-out spars . . . Seymour blew out his cheeks. Useless in these conditions – they worked alongside a jetty in a flat calm, but hardly now. Yet that voice was still shouting, urging the hands on to bring out the big lengths of timber and lay their ends against the side of the *Westward Bay*, then back themselves up against the superstructure and shove and push

89

with every last ounce of their strength. But why Cameron? What had happened to his officers and petty officers? Seymour, realizing his own uselessness on the compass platform, went down the ladders at the rush to lend a hand himself. Cameron could be right after all; it was worth that try in the absence of anything better. At the foot of the starboard ladder the severed head had now rolled away again but Seymour found a body being gradually ground to fragments as *Carmarthen*'s gunwale scraped against the *Westward Bay*: Robens, the RNVR snotty, nineteen years of age. Lurching aft, Seymour·found Petty Officer Thomas, his arms around a stanchion, clinging like death, both legs taken straight off above the knees as clean as a surgeon would have done it.

Then he saw the bearing-out spars being sent into position, and as four men moved past him, staggering and sliding on the bloody deck, he joined them. The spar was laid against the merchantman's plating in the streaming light from above and along the starboard side other bearing-out spars also went into action. Seymour, his back against one of the torpedo-tube mountings, thrust with all his strength. Incredibly, after a while, *Carmarthen* began to move outwards a little. It was the devil's own task to hold the ground won, but they did it, and Leading-Seaman Farrow and a party of ratings appeared on deck with more fenders which they lowered over the side and made fast to cleats and bitts. These acted as a protection to the hull itself, but the superstructure was still smashing hard into the tilted side of the *Westward Bay* and all manner of damage was being done; but this would be mostly superficial. As the destroyer was held off, Seymour handed over to one of the men who had brought the fenders, and took charge of the bearing-out operation as a whole. He shifted the spars for'ard, working almost inch by inch, and inch by inch *Carmarthen* was borne away astern, moving with agonizing slowness towards the bow of the *Westward Bay*, where she was taken by the full force of the wind. Her stern came round quickly, and at the same time the huge looming bow above her decks came round to starboard, swinging into the wind, and smashed into

90

Carmarthen's sunken fo'c'sle. There was a lurch and a twisting motion that was felt throughout the whole ship; *Westward Bay* appeared undamaged as she swung away and clear. The ships moved apart; fate alone would keep them that way. There was nothing any man could do.

Seymour, making his way back to the battered compass platform to survey the damage there, met Sub-Lieutenant Humphries and ordered a full report on the destroyer's seaworthiness.

The casualties had been little short of catastrophic: Robens had been joined by no less than fifty-three seamen and stokers crushed to death or drowned. The Torpedo-Coxswain, who had remained on duty in the wheelhouse to do what he could to tend the helm, was the only senior seaman rating left, apart from the badly-smashed Chief Boatswain's Mate, Petty Officer Thomas, who was under sedation in the sick-bay and would never go to sea again. The Gunner's Mate had gone, as had the Torpedo-Gunner's Mate and all the divisional POs. There were any number of injuries, many of them serious. It was a holocaust, and had been largely due to the parting of the lifelines when the superstructure had been damaged. Seymour's face was like dead ashes as a dim and watery dawn came up and the gale continued to blow at full force. It wasn't the casualties alone: there had been further damage to the ship's structure during the grinding together of the hulls and a number of leaks had started. Also, the quarterdeck had buckled slightly under the heavy gale-driven impaction; and when the masts had gone – and there was any amount of clearing away to be done along the upper deck and compass platform – the transmitting and receiving aerials had gone, so had the H/F D/F, and all of them were lying in a thousand pieces where they had not gone overboard altogether. The Petty Officer Telegraphist was not hopeful in regard to a repair. It would prove beyond the ship's capacity; it looked more like a dockyard job, he said.

'Just do your best, Wilkins,' Seymour said.

'I'll do that, sir. I may be able to rig something up, but it'll not have much range, sir.'

Seymour had to be content with that; and he got no more joy from the Engineer Officer. In fact the news from that quarter was hopeless and final: during the violent battering against the *Westward Bay*'s side, or more probably when the merchantman's swing had carried her into the *Carmarthen*'s fo'c'sle, the ship had taken a twist and the shafts themselves had bent the stern tubes. Not much, but enough: the shafts wouldn't turn again. Seymour listened bleakly to the mad roaring of the wind, and the sound of the spume-topped sea as it dropped aboard and raced along the decks to turn the destroyer into something resembling a submarine.

8

LEADING-Seaman Farrow was now acting in the room of the drowned Petty Officer of the iron-deck division, men known collectively as iron-deckmen. He had a word with Cameron while the latter was at work around Number Three gun.

'Reckon you did all right, lad,' he said. 'Gettin' out the spars ... it was good work, was that.'

'I've seen them used before.'

'Maybe. Well, I reckon you saved the ship—'

'Oh, not—'

Farrow put a hand on his shoulder. 'I don't believe anyone else was going to think of it, lad. Me – *I* should have done, for one. I didn't. You did. Might even say the skipper should have done or Jimmy. I reckon we was all taken flat aback as you might say.' He paused. 'Anyhow, I've had a word with the 'swain. He'll see that Jimmy knows where the credit's due.' He slid down the ladder to the quarterdeck, vanishing before thanks could be uttered. Cameron appreciated what Farrow had said and what he had done, too. It was utterly unselfish: Farrow, as a long-service RN rating having to stand by and see an HO ordinary seaman vault over his head to a commission, might well have sucked his teeth and said nothing to anyone. It would have been understandable, but it hadn't happened. Cameron got on with his work which, this early morning, was to help in clearing up the general debris of a terrible night. There was mess and confusion everywhere; and during that morning watch some of the ratings had the shattering experience of finding limbs buried beneath the remains of the masts and top hamper. Cameron himself was one of these: his gruesome find was an arm still in a seaman's blue jumper-sleeve, both arm and sleeve ripped off at the shoulder. It was a right arm, as could be seen from the red woollen non-substantive badge upon it: it had belonged to a seaman torpedoman second class. Was he dead, or was he below in the wardroom, now acting as an overflow sick-bay? It didn't really matter which, Cameron supposed. Arms couldn't be stitched back on again, muscle, sinew, bones, nerves, flesh ... one day perhaps, but not yet. Whoever it belonged to, the arm was just 'gash' now, seagull food.

Cameron pushed it overboard along with the rest. A sea took it and surged it for'ard, tossing it above the sunken fo'c'sle and those other dead in the submerged stokers' messdeck. It was a bloody awful war, all right.

Just then Stripey Tomkins manifested behind Cameron. 'I 'eard what the killick said, Your Lordship—'

'Put a sock in it, Stripey. The joke's an old one by now and you're getting tedious.'

'Tedious?' Tomkins' mouth sagged open; the action revealed that he stood in need of a toothbrush. 'What's that, then?'

'What you are – boring.'

'Now look 'ere,' Tomkins began belligerently. 'Boring! No one calls me that an' gets away with it, no one. You, you're just a puffed up little bleedin' poofter wot thinks 'e can stamp over everyone's 'eads to a muckin' officer's billet ... you know something, Mister bleedin' Cameron, Your Lordship? You could say you're bleedin' 'oistin' yourself to a commission over the bodies of the dead, couldn't you, eh?'

Cameron wanted nothing so much as to smash a fist into Tomkins' unpleasant face, but that way lay First Lieutenant's report and a cw rating had above all to keep his nose clean and not appear at Defaulters on serious charges, or any charge at all preferably. So he shrugged and took no notice;

94

Tomkins continued his baiting but Leading-Seaman Farrow came back and it stopped.

Men who go down to the sea in ships are frequently believers in the Almighty without being what a landsman would call religious. Divine Service in barracks and in capital ships might well not have been attended at all if it were not a matter for compulsory parades. But something about the very fearfulness of nature and the sea itself tends to make a man believe in something greater than himself controlling it all. And miracles at sea are not entirely absent from the reckoning; God's hand appears when most needed. Cameron had found this sense of the presence of a superior force among the trawlermen; and this morning, as dawn began slowly and reluctantly to break into something approaching day, the look of deliverance hove in sight from the eastward.

She was seen first by the starboard lookout on the compass platform. 'Ship fine on the starboard quarter, sir!'

Seymour's binoculars came up; he was half expecting a surface raider – perhaps the *Scharnhorst* or the *Gneisenau*, perhaps one of the German pocket-battleships (or as the BBC had rendered it in the case of the burning *Graf Spee* off Montevideo, German bottle-packetships). Thus his look was a long and careful one.

He said, 'I believe it's the rescue tug.' He turned to the Leading-Signalman. 'She's not calling – I doubt if she's seen us.' They were somewhat too low in the water to be seen from the tug's range, while the *Westward Bay*, who was certainly big enough, had been out of sight for most of the night after the collision. 'Call her up. Use the general call-sign.'

'Aye, aye, sir.'

The general call-sign went out by lamp, and Seymour waited impatiently. The reply was just what he hoped to hear.

RESCUE TUG FORCEFUL. ASSUME YOU ARE HMS CARMARTHEN. SECOND TUG WILL ARRIVE FOR WESTWARD BAY WITHIN TWELVE HOURS. DO YOU KNOW WESTWARD BAY'S CURRENT POSITION.

Seymour almost threw his sou'wester into the air. 'Answer: she is somewhere astern of me. Congratulations on a good rendezvous.'

The signal went out; within minutes the word had gone round the ship that rescue was imminent. Seymour passed the order: 'Prepare to tow aft,' and the hands worked like demons to be ready to take the tug's tow-line. *Forceful* was soon seen clearly, steaming fast towards them and sending up great gouts of water that were flung back over her blunt bows as she bit her stem into the sea. She had a pugnacious look that fitted her name – pugnacious and strong. She came up on *Carmarthen*'s lee quarter and began signalling again, this time to say she now had *Westward Bay* in view distantly on the horizon. The visibility was improving as the daylight increased, and the tug's higher bridge gave her master a longer view. Seymour brought up his glasses but was as yet unable to see the *Westward Bay*. However, now that she had shown up and was available, he knew well enough what he had to do: she was the more valuable ship to the war effort, because of her military cargo. And he was the escort. The shepherd ... and the shepherd didn't leave the sheep to drown.

He took a deep breath and called, 'Yeoman!'

'Sir?'

'Make to *Forceful*: I shall await the arrival of the next tug. Your tow should be passed to *Westward Bay*.'

The signal was made and acknowledged; the tug hauled off at once, passing down *Carmarthen*'s side towards the listing merchant ship, butting through the seas, disappearing into the valleys and rising again to the crests. It was going to be the devil of a job for her to get a tow across to the merchantman, Seymour thought, and a continuing foul job to make the tow all the way home with seas such as they were experiencing ... but his thoughts were bitter as hopes of rescue faded towards the west. And along his leaky decks the obscenities flew; heroics were all very well, but disappointment was cruel. They all had families to get home to. There was a grudging acceptance that the skipper had been right, but now a total despondency came down like a cloud over the destroyer. They couldn't possibly make it back to UK. One rescue tug had got through, but to expect another was asking for the moon. There were plenty of Jerries around, above as well as below the North Atlantic waves. This pessimism was to prove only too well founded: as in due course the tug, now with the *Westward Bay* under tow behind her, moved slowly past *Carmarthen* to the east, a lamp began flashing from her starboard bridge wing to be read off by the Leading-Signalman.

He reported, grey-faced, to the Captain. 'From *Forceful*, sir. Rescue tug *Alacrity* has broken wireless silence to report strong air attack. Last message indicated she was about to abandon.'

Seymour nodded. 'Acknowledge,' he said. That was all; there was nothing else to say. The ship's company watched in grim silence as the *Westward Bay* moved past, the towing wire with its rope spring lifting and dipping between the wave-crests; too much lifting and it would part, Seymour thought. A tow should remain submerged, but in seas like this it was asking a lot of it. Below on the iron-deck Stripey Tomkins lifted a fist and shook it, first towards the compass platform, then towards the passing *Westward Bay* from which a farewell signal was coming.

'Bastards,' he said savagely. 'Bastards the lot of you!'

'Shut your bloody gab,' Leading-Seaman Farrow said, and turned to the rest of the hands standing by the guns and torpedo-tubes. 'Poor sods'll likely come under air attack soon enough,' he said. 'Let's give 'em a cheer, right?'

Farrow led the cheers as the sou'westers were waved in the air. It was probably, certainly in fact, unheard aboard the *Westward Bay*; but Seymour heard it and it warmed his heart a little, and he waved his own sou'wester towards the departing vessels. They were all seamen together, after all. Farrow's action and the response to it made him more proud than ever of his ship's company.

The next day's noon sight put *Carmarthen* some fifty miles

97

nearer the Bloody Foreland; the eastward drift, however slow, was continuing, thanks to the wind. In Rosyth, the last reported information for the plot was that *Carmarthen* was lying in latitude 18 west, longitude 55 north. This was only an estimate and it was recognized that it could be inaccurate; and in any case it was out of date. Of recent events Rosyth knew nothing, and would have no further information until the tug *Forceful* was able to report in home waters, which would not be for some days since the tow could proceed only slowly. It was known that *Alacrity* had come under heavy air attack by the German FW 200s and had been forced to abandon. Any survivors would now be rolling about in the floats; and the ship she had been despatched to take in tow would now remain where she was unless and until another tug could be despatched. Currently, this ship was believed to be the *Westward Bay*; it was assumed that *Carmarthen* was already under tow of *Forceful* or soon would be always providing that the dead reckoning of the destroyer's position was not too far out.

The Staff Officer (Operations) was on the closed line to the Admiralty in Whitehall. He was making urgent representations that another tug be made available to bring in the crippled *Westward Bay*. There was no other tug capable of the job available in the Forth or in the Orkneys either; and the Clyde had been unable to help.

'Sorry,' the remote voice of Admiralty replied. 'Awfully sorry, old chap, but we can't help either. We're over-stretched as it is.'

'Portsmouth dockyard –'

'No. Portsmouth has nothing available, nor has Devonport. Sorry.' It was no use; so(o) banged down the scramble line. He hadn't had many hopes – for one thing, the whole Navy in home waters, give or take a few ships, had moved north into Scottish bases soon after the outbreak of war and the southern dockyards were virtually empty. If the Forth and the Clyde had nothing, then that was more or less that, but the formal request had had to be made. There was one more line that could be tried, and so(o) tried it: he called the Admiral direct and outlined the situation.

He said, 'We have *Nottingham* available, sir.'

'*Nottingham*? This isn't a cruiser's job!'

so(o) agreed, up to a point. 'Not for the tow, sir, but she could provide anti-aircraft cover at least.' *Nottingham*, a County Class cruiser of some ten thousand tons, had recently been converted to an anti-aircraft ship; just recommissioned as such, she was on working-up exercises from the Rosyth base. 'First-class practice, sir,' the Staff Officer urged.

'Damn it, she's working up! She's not yet operational, Commander.'

'That's true, sir. But ack-ack cover could be absolutely vital to the *Westward Bay*'s survival. There's the *Carmarthen*, too, presumably coming in under tow. We don't know her latest state, but it's a fair assumption she's in a very bad way by now. *Nottingham*'s cover could make all the difference, sir ... as you know, destroyers don't make very good ack-ack ships. And it's not as though we'd be taking *Nottingham* off other duties, seeing she has none at this moment.'

The persuasive voice went on; Mary Anstey listened to it, hoping against hope that it would get through effectively to the Admiral. Although she hadn't been long in Rosyth, just a matter of days, she had gathered that the Admiral was not easy to shift. He was an admiral who worked by the book – by King's Regulations and Admiralty Instructions. That could mean that ships supposed to be working-up didn't get operational orders. On the other hand the Admiral had once been a destroyer man himself; that had been his speciality, and he had advanced to command of a flotilla as Captain (D) before his promotion to the Flag List. That might weigh, which was why so(o) was stressing *Carmarthen*'s predicament; Mary Anstey went on listening and hoping and found her heart going at a tremendous rate that seemed about to stop her breathing. Then so(o) put the telephone down and caught the eye of a lieutenant-commander. 'Orders for *Nottingham*,' he said briskly. 'She's to prepare for sea immediately. Detailed

99

orders will reach her within the next hour, by hand of officer from the Admiral.'

Mary Anstey breathed again and realized that her eyes were wet. Off duty that afternoon, she was watching as *Nottingham* steamed outwards beneath the Forth Bridge.

The leaks continued through the sprung plates, but seemed to be coped with by the pumps and the baling-out efforts of the seamen, slopping about the wardroom flat. The ship was a sieve. In fact, according to Matthews who came to the compass platform to say so, the pumps were *not* coping adequately.

'She's lower in the water,' he said. 'Much longer, and we'll submerge.'

Seymour detected blame in the Engineer Officer's tone, blame still for his action in flooding aft. Matthews sounded sourly vindicated. He went on as Seymour didn't respond, 'I reckon we may have sprung more bulkheads below – round the magazines, for instance – when we were bouncing off the *Westward Bay*. If so ...' He raised his arms eloquently.

'If so,' Seymour said, 'there's nothing we can do about it and you know it, Chief.'

'Yes. More's the pity.' Matthews proceeded to underline, verbally, what Seymour had noted already in his manner. 'If we'd never flooded aft—'

'All right, Chief, that's history. I could have been wrong. If I am, I'll be told so by the Admiralty, don't worry! In the meantime I stand by what I did and we all have to make the best of it. Understood?'

'Understood,' Matthews said ungraciously. 'It's just a bloody pity, that's all.' He turned away, the wind blowing out his oil-stained white overalls, which were soaked through after just a couple of minutes of the upper deck and compass platform. As he reached the ladder he was sharply called back.

'Chief.'

'Yes?' Matthews turned.

100

Seymour walked towards him and kept his voice low. 'You and I, Chief ... we're the senior officers. Bridge and engine-room. But I'm the Captain. Let there be no mistake about that. Don't let's fall out, right? It wouldn't be good for the ship – would it?'

Matthews stared him in the face, sour and arrogant, then turned away without a word and clattered down the ladder. Seymour's hands balled into fists and his grey, weary face suffused for a moment. He stared down at the departing figure of his Engineer Officer. Matthews vanished into the battered superstructure aft of the compass platform, making for the engine-room hatch to dry out. Seymour turned away, still angry, but in control of himself. He found his thoughts had come close to murder; in a captain, such thoughts could be dangerous. Dangerous to a hell of a lot of men.

Damn Matthews. Damn him to hell.

By now the wardroom flat was no use for dossing down; it was much too wet. More than a foot of water slopped from side to side, pouring over the coamings of the cabins as the destroyer lurched and rolled. The galley flat was just about the only place left for men off watch and here, too, leaks were starting as the bulkhead separating the flat from the seamen's mess began to show signs of strain. Leading-Seaman Farrow set men to plug the leaks; Cameron found himself working along-side Stripey Tomkins.

'Sod the ship,' Tomkins said savagely as he struck a thumb with a hammer. He put the thumb in his mouth and sucked away the pain, plus some blood which he spat out again. Then he said, 'It's all that Lavington.'

'How come?' Cameron asked.

'Jonah.'

Cameron laughed. 'Bullshit!'

'Bullshit, is it?' Tomkins glowered. 'My arse! Jonahs are real, and Lavington's one – little ponce! Takin' 'ome a bloody murderer, it's askin' for trouble.'

'You'll just have to put up with it, Stripey.'

'I don't know so much. An' don't be bloody cheeky, tellin' me I 'ave to put up with it.' Tomkins dripped on, sounding dangerous. Cameron knew that to some of the older seamen jonahs were indeed real. They could be made to take the blame for all manner of sea ills and misfortunes, and there was no doubt whatsoever that Lavington was generating a very nasty taste. Tomkins' loudly expressed views could find a fruitful seed bed. Yet it was hard to see what anyone could do about this particular jonah. Lavington was safe in the engineers' store, still under a sentry, and his daily exercise period was very well supervised. If anyone – say Tomkins – had the idea Lavington could be shifted overboard, then that person wouldn't have a hope of getting away with it. But men like Stripey Tomkins were wily enough, up to all the dodges even though they had a fairly limited intelligence. Tomkins just might fancy he saw a way that he could manage. Tomkins was going to need watching. There was nothing over-fanciful about it; Cameron had heard of unpopular petty officers vanishing on dark and stormy nights and afterwards the whole ship's company clammed up and knew nothing, hadn't seen or heard a thing. He knew beyond any doubt that the majority of *Carmarthen*'s ratings would see a watery grave as being a far better end for Lavington.

He worked on, wet through, cold, tired, hungry; they seemed to be making little progress with the plugging. The leaks continued, spurting icy water across the galley flat. Beyond the bulkhead were curious sounds: trapped mess stools and tables surging about and banging against the plates, ominous noises not unlike the ship breaking up. Farther down in the stokers' messdeck the waterlogged, bloated corpses would still be floating unless they had drifted out past the broken collision bulkhead, drifted out to sea to find peace. Cameron forced his mind away from thoughts like that: all too soon, they might all be the same, drifting corpses.

Beside him, Tomkins dripped on about Lavington.

Far to the eastward, HMS *Nottingham* had cleared the Firth of

Forth past the Bass Rock, altering northward off May Island for Duncansby Head and the passage of the stormy Pentland Firth for Cape Wrath. From Cape Wrath she would head westerly across the top of Northern Ireland to take her departure from the Bloody Foreland out across the Atlantic on her search for the *Westward Bay* and to watch out for *Carmarthen* believed to be under tow; there had still been no word in Rosyth or anywhere else that the *Westward Bay* was coming slowly in.

Nottingham was steaming fast, her high decks riding nicely clear of the seas as she came up the east coast of Scotland. Her ship's company were currently in two watches, with the anti-aircraft batteries manned for immediate action, action that could always be expected from the hostile French coast in German hands. Her Captain had informed all hands over the tannoy as to what their mission was; the eyes of the lookouts would be keen enough and the newly-fitted RDF aerials would be on constant search as well. The area where the *Westward Bay* was expected to be found would be well and truly quartered but the Captain's hopes were not particularly high. There was far too much water around and if success came, it would come largely as the result of sheer luck.

As *Nottingham* began to approach the Pentland Firth, it seemed that something of that luck was in fact already on the way. A signal was received in her W/T office, a signal from Rosyth: this signal reported that an aircraft of Coastal Command, searching an area out in the Atlantic from the west coast of Ireland, had sighted a vessel under tow and had made contact by light. The vessel under tow was the *Westward Bay*, the towing vessel was the *Forceful*. The tug had passed the last known position of *Carmarthen* drifting helpless in the westerly gale. So now the facts were known in Rosyth.

Nottingham's captain put a finger on the reported position on the chart. 'She'll have drifted somewhat,' he said to his Navigating Officer, 'but she'll not be too far off. We shouldn't have too much difficulty now.'

'We make direct for *Carmarthen*, sir?'

The Captain nodded. 'We do. The *Westward Bay* should be all right now she's under Coastal Command's umbrella, Pilot.' He looked out through the chart-room ports; the weather was foul still and the passage of the Pentland Firth would be a nasty one. The weather reports for the area west of Ireland were currently bad but a break was expected as a high-pressure area was coming in across the Atlantic. He could only hope the destroyer would last until the weather moderated and until he reached her. Going back to the compass platform high above the sea he called the Engineer Officer of the Watch on the starting-platform below.

'Captain here. Maximum revolutions ... we have *Carmarthen* virtually in our sights now.'

9

ABOARD *Carmarthen* they were very far from
knowing that they were in anyone's sights. There were indications now that the ship was going to succumb; she had a
deader-than-ever feeling, a feeling of complete rigidity and
unresponsiveness. Even the waves were not really shifting her
about much; she was half under. The engine-room, that silent
place, had been abandoned long since and to Seymour's contained fury Lieutenant (E) Matthews was sharing his vigil on
the compass platform, his very presence and his monosyllabic
utterances, when they came at all, a reproach; Matthews
assumed the proportions of a ghoul, there to criticize and
remind his Captain of his mistake in flooding the after compartments.

Cameron, back on lookout following another re-shuffle of
the watch and quarter bill, such as it now was, could almost
feel the hostility. It cut the atmosphere like a knife – or a
scalpel. Lavington was still on Cameron's mind; he couldn't
free himself of the man, try as he might. Lavington wasn't his
concern; Petty Officer Thomas, days ago, had made that very
plain. Yet they had been shipmates, messmates – mates in the
struggle for a commission. Lavington had lost that struggle, of
course; there would be no future for him ... Cameron jerked
his head, trying to clear it of a consuming desire for sleep.
Future! That was a stupid word in the circumstances. He
stared through his binoculars, feeling the uselessness of his
watch. What was there to look out for now? Certainly they
themselves were too low in the water to be seen from other

ships and if, for instance, the *Queen Mary* or the *Queen Elizabeth*, sailing independently as fast troop transports, should be crossing the Atlantic now and loom up ahead, they could do nothing about it other than wait for the huge knifing bows to cut right through them and bring an end to it all.

The eyepieces looked blank; blank and black. Cameron used all his efforts to bring his eyelids up. He succeeded, but lapsed again. Then again. The compass platform looked horribly close to the water, which was surging right up to it now and threatening to engulf both the Captain and the Engineer Officer, who had now come together in a deathly embrace.... Cameron jerked awake, sweating. To fall asleep on watch, especially on lookout, was the cardinal sin. Short of murder ... fall asleep and be spotted and *he* wouldn't get his commission either. Now the Chief had his hands round the Captain's neck and was squeezing ... it was all very odd behaviour for two officers aboard a sinking ship in wartime, but in some way it seemed at the same time absolutely logical, and became more so when the roles were reversed in the next nightmare-sequence and the Captain seemed to be laughing at the Chief's vain struggles to free himself. ...

· Then something else appeared: a body. A horribly bloated corpse that lifted and fell and seemed to loom towards him from the sunken fo'c'sle. Lavington. Stripey Tomkins had done it. Cameron made an enormous effort and his eyes blinked. He was sure he was awake but the corpse was there still. Lavington had gone overboard. But it wasn't Lavington after all; Cameron came fully awake and saw the corpse, horribly bloated, moving towards the half submerged Number Two gun for'ard, where for a while it stuck and bobbed about. Some quirk of the sea, some movement of the ship, must have dislodged it from the stokers' messdeck and sent it swirling out through the broken bulkhead.

The first of the aircraft showed a little after the next dawn: it came in high and alone from a sky that was becoming a good deal clearer and the silhouette was quickly recognized aboard the *Carmarthen*: one of the Focke-Wulfs, the FW 200s, out from the French coast. There was still some ammunition available for the close-range weapons – the Lewis guns, the pom-poms, the machine-gun – but the FW was unlikely to approach all that close. The three-inch AA gun amidships had been put out of action when the searchlight platform had been hit earlier. Seymour manned his available guns, but hoped the destroyer might not be seen. She would not be presenting a normal destroyer shape and the seas were confused and spume-covered enough, perhaps, to make the outline invisible.

No such luck.

Within minutes of being sighted, the bombs were seen to fall. A stick of six, dropping like eggs to take the sea in a line of explosions some four cables clear of *Carmarthen*'s port side, near enough to send shudders through her leaking plates. The air was blue; the Focke-Wulf's aim was bloody hopeless but it must be just a question of time now. The next stick came down an equivalent distance off to starboard. The third was very much closer: it came down right ahead and the last of the six exploded close to the sunken fo'c'sle. Gouts of water rose to fall back on the compass platform and the ship shuddered violently. After that, inexplicably unless all the bombs were gone, the Focke-Wulf turned away and vanished back towards the east. Within ten minutes of its departure, something curious happened aboard *Carmarthen*: there was a vicious clanging and tearing noise from ahead of the compass platform and the whole ship lurched. When she righted, she was seen to be riding on a more even keel, much less down by the head than before.

'Always look for the silver lining!' Seymour said to Humphries. 'That bomb's sheered away some of the fo'c'sle and taken some weight off.'

'Not much use,' Humphries said sadly, 'without the engines.'

'Don't drip, Sub! She has a better feel and that's something.' Seymour brought up his binoculars and scanned the horizons all around. Those horizons were much farther out now, and that, together with the clearing skies and a drop in the wind's weight, was good indication of fair weather coming in at last from the west. But there was little comfort in that prospect; with fair weather they would be much more liable to come under attack, and the appearance of that solitary Focke-Wulf, which would now summon up its fellows without a doubt, must surely prove the last straw. Seymour had his depleted ship's company mustered along the iron-deck and spoke to them.

He said, 'I haven't much for you to cheer about, frankly. There's no knowing whether or not another rescue tug will be sent, nor if she'll ever find us if she is. From the point of view of seaworthiness, I believe we have a chance of lasting after all, especially if better weather overtakes us. We're riding easier – you'll have noticed that for yourselves, of course. But from now on we must expect air attack at any moment. The Luftwaffe isn't going to allow us home if it can stop us. But I'm going to do my best to get us home – that is, to keep afloat until we find a friendly ship.' He paused. 'It's not much of a prospect, is it, but I know I can rely on all of you not to give in now. We've already come through quite a lot.'

Platitudes, of course, but what else was there to say? As the hands were fallen out Seymour admitted to himself that he was no orator. He wondered if he inspired any confidence at all. There was much that could be said about loyalty, about fighting back for King and country, about the embattled Empire, about the vital importance to Britain of the Atlantic convoys and the need to preserve every vessel capable of acting as their escort. But this wasn't Nelson's Navy and perhaps they wouldn't go much on oratory in any case. Others could do it without indulging in sentiment. Lord Louis Mountbatten, also a destroyer man, could lead his men anywhere and his choice of words was always right. Seymour felt his own inadequacy like a knife in the heart and felt he had read in the dour faces of his ship's company their inner doubts as to his capacity to see them through anything, let alone get a powerless ship home. In this, he was in fact wrong; and it was Leading-Seaman Farrow who put it best.

He said to no one in particular, 'Skipper's all right. Command was flung at him and he took it. Not done so badly either. What more could he do without the bloody engines?'

The Focke-Wulfs came back; this time, two of them, their great four-engined bodies menacing as they came on with the sun behind them. The engine sounds came like pulse beats as they passed over the wallowing destroyer, then turned to release their bomb-loads. *Carmarthen*'s close-range armament was once again manned, more as a gesture than anything else. The first stick of bombs landed well off target, the second was closer – just like last time. But then came a difference, a shift in the mode of attack. The aircraft parted company, one machine remaining at a high level while the other circled and lost height and then came roaring in towards the destroyer. She passed down the port side, and the men behind the stuttering pom-poms could see her crew in the perspex-enclosed cockpit and the air-gunner squinting along the sights of his machine-gun. When that machine-gun opened, both pom-poms fell silent: a spraying burst of bullets had found its mark, and the bodies of the gunners hung in their seats, spilling blood.

As Farrow shouted orders, Cameron made a dash for the pom-pom mounting. With another man he dragged the bodies of the dead gunners clear and within half a minute had the gun ready for action. By now the Focke-Wulf had passed astern and was turning to come in for another attack, this time heading to fly along the starboard side. As she came abeam, the German machine-gunner opened up once more. Bullets zipped around Cameron as he pumped the two-pounder shells blind towards the aircraft without any apparent effect. He had just brought his sights fully on when the pom-pom jammed and fell silent. The Focke-Wulf passed on in safety, with the Lewis guns wasting ammunition as she moved out of their range. *Carmarthen*'s superstructure was pockmarked by the machine-gun bullets from aft to for'ard and three more men lay dead. Also an officer: on the compass platform Humphries had taken a bullet through the throat and had choked on his own blood. There were just three officers left now: Seymour, Matthews and the Surgeon-Lieutenant. Cameron had seen the happy grin on the face of the German air-gunner as he had passed by. The Germans, he believed, were treating this as a game, a sport in which the British were to be picked off singly and the *Carmarthen* finally left to lurch about the North Atlantic without a crew. As the Focke-Wulf flew ahead to make yet another turn, the gunnery rates worked fast to free the jammed pom-pom; but this time the aircraft's turn was wider and she was seen to be regaining height. Stripey Tomkins waved a fist in the air and bawled out, 'Bastards! Too muckin' 'ot for you, I reckon!'

There was amazement on deck when both Focke-Wulfs were seen to be departing eastwards. But Seymour had a theory about that and he shared it with the ship's company: 'They could have got word of something more worth while in the area, a better prize. That could be our rescue tug ... we'll keep our fingers crossed that the buggers don't get her.'

Seymour had been partially right: the *Nottingham*, coming in on a course well north of the enemy aircraft's flight from Bordeaux, was now within some twenty miles of the destroyer; and she had in fact been sighted by the Focke-Wulf that had kept her height. The second aircraft had been re-called from the attack on *Carmarthen*. Inside the next few minutes the FWs had been sighted from *Nottingham*'s bridge and the Royal Marine bugler had, via the tannoy system, sounded her ship's company to action stations on the Captain's order. *Nottingham* was travelling fast, sending up a big bow wave; she would not prove any easy target. She was no sitting duck like *Carmarthen*. As the attack came in, her Captain watched the fall of the bombs and reacted with per-fect timing: *Nottingham*'s helm was put over and she swung hard to starboard, away from the likely line of drop. In the

110

meantime her heavy ack-ack armament was pumping away, keeping the Focke-Wulfs high: the screen of fire would be suicide to penetrate. The ship was virtually obscured by the smoke of the discharges and the bursting of the shells as they sent their fragmented shrapnel hurtling out in all directions. The noise was ear-splitting, with every gun in action. *Nottingham* twisted and turned in violent helm alterations as the bombs came down, but luck was with the Germans: the end came very suddenly and unexpectedly as an alteration of course carried the cruiser slap into the path of a falling stick of bombs and every one found its mark. *Nottingham* seemed to erupt from stem to stern as the bombs exploded on fo'c'sle, bridge and quarterdeck; and then from deep down in the ship, as a bomb sped straight down one of her funnels to explode in total devastation in a boiler-room, there came the shattering upheaval that spelled out the end.

Nottingham went up in a sheet of flame and a tremendous roar, broken open like a can. Debris filled the air along with the acrid smoke and flames from burning oil fuel, and fell back on an empty sea.

The FWs flew back to France. The pilots had a need to watch their fuel tanks, and the *Carmarthen* wasn't worth the risk.

A final signal had been picked up by Rosyth, a brief indication that *Nottingham* had come under air attack, and then there had been complete silence. A sinking was virtually certain and it was possible to make accurate deductions: the sinking must have been rapid, leaving no chance to send out further signals. That would have meant a sizeable explosion, something that would have blown the bottom out of her. Thus the question of survivors was extremely uncertain. It was not wartime practice to despatch valuable ships to search for survivors alone; bringing in a crippled ship such as *Carmarthen* or *Westward Bay* was a different matter. In any case, there were no more ships to spare. And that was that. Along with any survivors from the *Carmarthen*, those from *Nottingham* would now have to take their chance. No one liked it, but the facts of war

111

and ship availability dictated. Mary Anstey, off duty soon after the *Nottingham*'s signal had come through and had been assessed, went for a walk by herself, out of Rosyth towards Inverkeithing, which was dreary enough and in line with her mood, though she refused to give up hope.

'Lavington,' Seymour said to the Torpedo-Coxswain, then stopped.

'Yes, sir?'

'I don't like it. We all know we're right inside the zone for air attack. I should have thought about him earlier. If we're hit, it'll be fast. No time to release him, perhaps, before we go down. Follow?'

'Yes, sir. He could be let out whenever there's an attack, sir.'

Seymour nodded. 'I don't see any point in keeping him locked up at all, frankly. We're in a bloody dicey condition structurally – anything could happen fast. What d'you think, Cox'n?'

The reply was doubtful. 'His own safety, sir. The hands might react.'

'D'you really think so?'

The Torpedo-Coxswain was emphatic. 'Yes, sir, I do. The SBA was well liked, so was our Surgeon-Lieutenant. And what Lavington did ... no, sir, it wouldn't be fair on the men. There'd be a temptation, and we don't want unnecessary charges of anyone striking anyone, sir.'

'Well, I take the point,' Seymour said reluctantly. The Torpedo-Coxswain could perhaps have added another: favouritism to a CW rating might be suspected, ridiculous as any such suggestion might be. Class rankled a little in the Navy; the gulf between officers and men was so wide that some men – men like Able-Seaman Tomkins, for instance – saw class everywhere. Seymour was well enough aware that collectively Naval officers were referred to as pigs by certain bolshie types of ratings. He went on, 'All right, he stays where he is. He's to be released in action, all the same, Cox'n.'

112

'Aye, aye, sir.' The Torpedo-Coxswain paused, looking at the Captain through eyes that showed concern. 'You're just about all in, sir. That's not good.'

Seymour smiled. 'It's far from good!'

'Yes, sir. I meant – for the ship, sir. What's left of it.'

'Yes, I take that point too. But I have no officers, Cox'n – no executive officers. So there's no alternative, is there, to my remaining on the compass platform?'

'You'll collapse soon, sir. Then what?'

Seymour answered irritably. 'I've already said, there's no alternative.'

'With respect, sir, I believe there is. There's me. The ship has no way on her. Even if she had, I've enough experience not to do anything bloody daft, sir. Why don't we work watch and watch, Mr Seymour, sir?'

It was said in almost fatherly fashion; in fact Chief Petty Officer Groves, Torpedo-Coxswain these many years, was quite old enough to be Seymour's father. Seymour suddenly felt a sense almost of being overwhelmed, of gratitude that someone had even noticed his terrible weariness, that someone had realized that a captain was only human after all. He knew that he couldn't go on for ever, couldn't go on much longer in fact; and the suggestion was a sensible one. There would be complications, however, if anything should go wrong when the Torpedo-Coxswain was on watch. King's Regulations were not unbending in themselves and according to some senior officers were intended only as a guide; on the other hand, other senior officers were capable of their own interpretations and regarded King's Regulations as a bible to be obeyed come what may. They could in fact be quoted either way that suited – as guide or as orders. And any Court Martial would be likely to find a captain guilty of hazarding his command by neglect of duty if trouble came when that captain had allowed a rating to assume his place.

It couldn't be done and Seymour said as much. This the Torpedo-Coxswain had to accept, but did so with an expression that said some bastards were born stupid. He went down

113

the ladder muttering and shaking his head and going aft towards the quarterdeck he met Matthews.

Matthews said, 'You look upset, 'Swain. And you've just come from the bridge. What's the trouble now, eh?'

'No trouble, sir.' The Torpedo-Coxswain spoke stiffly; he was aware of friction between the officers of bridge and engine-room, though that was none of his business, and he was also aware that Lieutenant (E) Matthews was quite capable of trying to make use of the fact that he had been a lower-deck man so as to be, when it suited him, matey with senior ratings. This the Torpedo-Coxswain did not much like. As Matthews stood there slap in his path, blocking him, he added, 'No trouble at all, sir.'

Matthews smiled. 'Sure?'

'Quite sure, sir.'

'I see. How's the First Lieutenant?'

'Captain, sir.' Reproof showed.

'All right, all right. I asked, how is he?'

'Captain's all right, sir. Tired, but plenty of fight. And that's what we need.'

'I doubt if he is all right. I doubt it strongly. No man can keep going day and night indefinitely.' Matthews paused, stroking his jaw and looking a little sideways at the Torpedo-Coxswain. 'I'm not too sure ... in regard to Admiralty law, that is ... how would I stand to take over?'

'Watch on the bridge, do you mean, sir?'

'No, no. Command – if necessary, that is. As an Engineer Officer. You're well versed in that sort of thing, or should be.'

'Yes, sir.' The Torpedo-Coxswain spoke briskly. 'I am. As an Engineer Officer, and this I think you do know very well, you cannot have any executive authority—'

'But in special circumstances? What I'm asking is this: would I be able to count on your support if—'

'Against the Captain, sir? Most certainly *not*, sir. And now, if you don't mind, sir, I have matters to attend to.' The Torpedo-Coxswain pushed unceremoniously past, his face scandalized. Bloody black gang. The Captain would have his

114

full loyalty and never mind his daft stiff-necked attitude about sharing the watch. Funny that the Chief should have come out with it now, just when he himself had been having a go at the skipper ... and of course Matthews knew the score well enough and hadn't in fact been seeking any information at all – it had just been an attempt to line up allies.

Behind the Torpedo-Coxswain, Matthews scowled and turned away. In his view, Seymour was a danger to those of them that by some miracle were still left alive. Fighting back now, when another attack came, would be nothing short of suicide. Far better to call it a day and throw themselves on the mercy of the Germans the first time a U-boat surfaced. That wasn't disloyalty; it was prudence. The ship was a bloody wreck. You could go too far in keeping the flag flying. Matthews glared towards the White Ensign, blowing in the diminishing wind from the ensign staff aft. High time it was replaced by a plain white one.

'Leave it, Tomkins,' Farrow said. Tomkins was on again, on about jonahs. Farrow fancied the man might be starting to go round the bend as a result of what was fast becoming an obsession with Lavington and his presence aboard. Tomkins had been hanging about around the door of the engineers' store, looking threatening and muttering away like all hell. God alone knew what he expected to gain by it all; but Farrow had seen to it that the guard on Lavington, when the man was taken out for his exercise periods, was on the alert for trouble. As it happened, Tomkins hadn't tried to interfere with him – yet, anyway.

Tomkins said, 'Get stuffed.'

'Watch it,' Farrow warned, his long, gloomy face hardening. 'You and me, we're long service ... we sets an example, right?' He added, 'Now more than ever. It's important, is that. Try and remember it.'

Tomkins sniffed and flapped his arms against the penetrating cold. The weather was better right enough, but the perishing cold was as bad as ever. If ever he got back to Scapa ... but if ever he did, it would be out again next run with the next perishing convoy, time after time, world without end amen. The seas wouldn't leave a man alone, not in wartime. It was a dog's life. Tomkins was about to slope off and never mind the killick, and dodge into the galley flat for a burn if he could find a fag that wasn't wet through, when he heard the throb of more aircraft engines. Then the alarm rattlers went and Tomkins saw a sight that at first angered him and then pleased him: Lavington was being brought out from the engineers' store.

10

ONCE again it seemed to be a case of attempted attrition; *Carmarthen* would be showing a very small target to high-level bombers, and raking machine-gun fire seemed to appeal more to the Focke-Wulf pilots. Down they came, risking the return fire from the close-range weapons. Puffs of smoke from the pom-poms filled the sky but the Focke-Wulfs penetrated and roared parallel to the destroyer, peppering her decks and superstructure, killing, wounding. Three of them this time, but soon reduced to two: Cameron, now at one of the Lewis guns, found the aircraft slap in his sights, more or less by sheer chance, and fired a burst that shattered the perspex of the cockpit and killed the pilot. As the Focke-Wulf veered right across the destroyer's decks, the pilot's blood could be seen spread like a red mist across the remains of the perspex shield; and as the plane took that course across the decks, Leading-Seaman Farrow, his face murderous, swung his pom-pom to follow her and pumped straight into her belly. Smoke poured from two of the four engines and the Focke-Wulf twisted, losing height until her port wing took the sea. The starboard wing came up and she turned over, to sink within a couple of minutes, some half mile from the destroyer. There were no survivors. There was no time for cheering their first victory; the ship's company were at once engaged by the two remaining aircraft.

Seymour, dodging bullets along the iron-deck, made his way aft as *Carmarthen*'s fire slackened: neither the machine-gun nor the pom-poms were in action. The last of the ready-use ammunition had been expended. As he contacted Leading-Seaman Farrow, the Lewis guns also fell silent.

'Get all hands below, Farrow. Wardroom flat. Quick as you can,' Seymour ordered.

'Sit it out, sir?'

'Right!'

Seymour looked up at the sky, bitterly: no British aircraft. It was always the same old story. *Where the hell was the RAF?* Never there when they were wanted ... yet that wasn't quite fair. The pilots and aircrews wouldn't have held back; there simply weren't enough planes, that was all. And when there were, some solid-brained bastard at the Air Ministry usually decided that there were better uses for them than supporting the Navy. Carriers were what was needed, more carriers; just now, the Navy had all too few. Keeping in cover, Seymour remained on deck until the Torpedo-Coxswain and Leading-Seaman Farrow had shepherded the men below to the ward-room flat, then he went down himself. Water slopped around; there was nowhere dry, not even in the officers' cabins or in the wardroom itself, but at least the German bullets couldn't reach them. The bombs might, if the Focke-Wulfs decided to climb and drop their bomb-loads. This, Matthews pointed out sourly.

'Nothing we can do by remaining on deck, Chief,' Seymour answered. 'There's no ammo left. None at all.'

'Except in the flooded magazines.'

Seymour flushed; by now he would have tried to pump out, but that, too, was impossible. Along with the bent stern tubes, the pumping system was buggered. He said, 'Let's keep to practicalities, shall we?' Disregarding angry mutterings from the Engineer Officer, he turned to the assembled men. 'We stay here,' he said, 'and ride it. There's no other way.' He knew he had no need to remind any of them of the stark facts: no engine power, no fighting capacity, no means of communication. Those few facts had to render a warship totally useless and now it was a simple matter of survival until, as they drifted the seas like a ghost ship, someone found them.

118

'Suppose it's a U-boat?' Matthews asked. 'What then?'

Seymour said, 'We'll cross that bridge when we come to it.'

Matthews fished around for a cigarette and lit it. He said, 'Isn't it best to have a plan for all eventualities? Isn't that what Commanding Officers normally do?'

The tone had been sarcastic; the atmosphere became tense as the ship's company took in the overtones of hostility, of wardroom factions coming out against each other. The men looked anywhere but at Seymour, lifting eyes to the deckhead, waiting to see what might now develop. Seymour said quietly, 'You're right, Chief. Let's say, it depends what the U-boat captain does ... if you follow?'

'No, I don't.'

'Then I'll spell it out. He may decide to attack. If he does, then we've had it. Just like when a submarine's under depth-charge attack, you sit it out and hope for the best. We're in no position to fight, Chief – I've already made that point.'

'Yes. And if he doesn't attack? I'm not sure what you mean. If he doesn't attack, what the hell *does* he do?'

Seymour said, 'He'll see for himself what sort of state we're in. We'll look abandoned, right? So it's on the cards he may decide to board. If he does, well, then we'll be ready for him. We fight to the last man if that happens. I'll be watching. We won't be taken unawares, Chief.'

'Watching? From here?'

Seymour said, 'No, I'm going to the wheelhouse. You're in charge here, Chief.' He caught the eye of the Torpedo-Coxswain. 'Yes, Cox'n?'

'I'll come with you, sir. To the wheelhouse, sir. That's my place in action.' The Torpedo-Coxswain added, 'On your own, sir, you'll not be able to keep awake. We can share the watch.'

Seymour nodded and smiled. 'All right, Cox'n, you've got your wish at last. Leading-Seaman Farrow?'

'Sir?'

'You're the senior seaman rating left below. Remember that.'

'I'll remember it, sir.' Farrow was puzzled, uncertain what the Captain meant by his remark, which could in a sense be considered an order. Cameron, watching him, saw his uncertainty; in Cameron's mind there was no such uncertainty at all: he was convinced that the Captain had passed a warning that the seaman branch must if necessary act independently of the engine-room. It would be up to Farrow to decide when that moment might come.

Before the Focke-Wulfs turned away for France they dropped their bombs in a farewell gesture. They scored no hits, but some of the bombs dropped close enough. Seymour, from the wheelhouse, watched them fall, helpless to do anything about them. In the wardroom flat the detonations were felt like the thuds of sledgehammers and Cameron believed that more leaks had started; the water seemed to be gaining even though Farrow, his long face gloomier than ever as he pondered that remark of the Captain's, had set the hands to bale out, using any utensil they could find – cups and bowls from the wardroom pantry, even the chamber-pots from the officers' cabins – and emptying them through the opened wardroom ports. Cameron had been detailed by Farrow to stand by the sound-powered telephone from the wheelhouse so that any word from the Captain could be reported without any delay. Lavington was being employed to assist the Surgeon-Lieutenant in the cabins, using his embryonic medical knowledge to keep the tanker survivors and *Carmarthen*'s own wounded as comfortable as possible. Most of the burns cases would have been better off dead; some had little visible flesh left and the eyes seemed to scream with pain that ate even through the morphia. Lavington moved like an automaton, a person quite without volition. His face was virtually expressionless, his mouth hung slack, the lips parted. He looked like walking death.

Soon after the bomb explosions had died away, the sound-powered telephone whined. Cameron took the instrument from its hook.

120

'Wardroom flat, sir.'

'Captain here. Is that Cameron?'

'Yes, sir.'

'The aircraft are leaving. How're things down there?'

'All right, sir.'

'Good.' The line went dead. The destroyer rolled and wallowed, heavy, soggy, all but waterlogged now. The water rushed from side to side as she rolled, slopping and dirty, carrying odds and ends from the cabins and other spaces. In the pantry the officers' cook prepared a makeshift meal: fish-paste sandwiches made from stale bread, cold bangers and tinned tomatoes that looked like red lead.

'Sandwiches, all nice an' bleedin' dainty,' Tomkins grumbled none too quietly. 'Officers' grub! Officers' wives 'as pudden and pies, while sailors' wives 'as skilly.'

'Shut up,' Farrow ordered.

'Soddin' class distinction.'

Farrow loomed angrily. 'I said, shut up, Stripey. So you shuts up or else.'

'Else what?' Tomkins responded with a jeer.

'I'll have you before the Officer of the Watch.'

'What Officer of what Watch, may I enquire?'

Farrow breathed hard. 'Just shut up. Just watch it, that's all.'

There was a sardonic laugh from Matthews. 'All right, Farrow, he has a point, you know.'

'Sir?'

'We're all on a level now, Farrow. I think you'd do well to bear that in mind.'

'If you says so, sir.'

'I do, Farrow, I do.'

Leading-Seaman Farrow wiped the back of a hand across his nose and frowned. He thought the officer was talking balls; officers and ratings were never on a level till they were dead, then they were accorded the same burial unless they were admirals who died ashore heavy with honours and decorations. In the meantime those present in the wardroom flat

121

were not dead, though they might well be close to it. Until they were, the conventions held. And Farrow didn't like having his own authority eroded, which was what that Matthews had done. For an officer, Matthews was a bloody bolshie, though Farrow had a shrewd idea that if he failed to come up with the 'Sir' each time he opened his mouth, the bolshie aspect would vanish fast. Anyway, he didn't open it again; you didn't argue with officers if you valued the hook on your left arm, the fouled anchor that gave you your authority, whether or not you were on a level.

Farrow moved away but before doing so met Tomkins' eye and gave him a look that said he'd better watch it and never mind what the officer had said. Again he thought about the Captain's stricture. Funny, that . . . almost as though the skipper didn't trust the bloody engine-room. For that matter, neither did Farrow. Stokers – they were all right; they didn't virtually join the service right off in the rating of petty officer, which the tiffies did – the Engine-room Artificers. The ERAS might be good at being tiffies, but as petty officers they were about as much use as Farrow's left tit.

'Weather's improving, sir,' the Torpedo-Coxswain said.

Seymour nodded; it was. The day was moving towards evening and the skies were clear and bright; the seas had gone down considerably, which eased the strain on the hull. There was little wind left; it all added up to good U-boat weather, of course. Seymour racked a tired brain, trying to remember, to assess when the next outward-bound convoy would be due to pass through the area. Not just yet, he fancied, though there might be convoys on the move to and from Gibraltar, and their tracks would take them well westerly of the direct peace-time route – the French coast had to be stood well clear of. Even if there was no convoy due, the U-boat packs could be gathering, to lie in wait submerged and then surface during the night once the ships were in their sights.

'What d'you make the chances, Cox'n?' Seymour asked suddenly.

'Fair, I reckon, sir. Jerries always permitting, of course.'

'Yes. We've got this far, we should last in better weather. Someone'll find us.' Seymour rubbed at his eyes, which were red and swollen from lack of sleep and from constant vigilance. If ever they were found, he would be faced with the final decision: unless they could be taken in tow, which was scarcely likely except in the event of the finder being an ocean-going rescue tug, he would have to consider abandoning so as to get his ship's company to safety. That would come hard, very hard; his ship was still technically afloat and from a seamanship point of view could certainly make it home and could be refitted. Where would his first duty lie? To a ship that could be got home but almost certainly wouldn't be if they met the enemy again, or to men who could live to fight again another day? A captain's decision; and much as Seymour would have liked to, he couldn't share it with his Torpedo-Coxswain. When the decision was made, the order would be given and that was all. It hadn't to be made yet, but it was a captain's job to have his mind ready, to have the alternatives assessed ahead taking into account all foreseeable factors, so that instant orders could be passed. Matthews had been dead right. It was a case of weighing likelihoods and possibilities. Seymour's brain was moving in circles now; his mind was as tired as his body. There were times when he would have welcomed the final blow from a torpedo: at least no more decisions would be required. Until he had assumed the command, he had never really appreciated how a captain's day was made up of constant decisions both large and small.

God, he was tired. So tired it didn't seem possible that he could last out. The effort to keep his eyelids open was shattering, taxing all his strength of will. Sagged into a corner of the wheelhouse, he pulled himself upright; the best way was to keep on the move. He took a couple of steps, meaning to walk around the steering position, and was asleep before he had taken two more, asleep on his feet and in motion. The Torpedo-Coxswain caught him as he fell, and laid him flat on the deck.

'Sleep it out,' the Torpedo-Coxswain said, knowing his voice wasn't penetrating. 'Sleep it out. Christ, you've done all you can and that's a fact!'

The U-boat, cruising at periscope depth a little before the light went altogether, had the *Carmarthen* in her sights; the German captain was watching carefully, frowning as he did so. It was very strange; there was no sign of life whatsoever. No one on the bridge, no one along the decks, no one at the after gun. One of the after guns seemed to have gone and the destroyer was in a very bad way. Abandoned? The British Navy didn't normally abandon so long as a keel was afloat beneath their feet.

The Captain moved away from his eyepiece and gestured to his First Lieutenant. 'Take a look,' he said. 'Tell me what you think.'

The First Lieutenant took a long, slow look. He said, 'There is no one visible, sir. That does not mean they're not there, out of sight.'

'But why?'

The First Lieutenant shrugged. 'Sick? Some spreading disease?'

The Captain made a contemptuous noise. 'Come, Franz! That is not likely. More likely it's a trap.'

'To what end?'

'That depends what is in their mind. What is certain is that there are no boats or rafts in the vicinity ... no survivors. That's odd.'

'The weather has been bad till now, sir,' the First Lieutenant reminded. 'They could have been separated. They could be miles away by now.'

'Possibly,' the Captain said. He frowned again; the British still didn't abandon. He looked again through the periscope. With the stem so well down in the water, it was impossible to see the destroyer's pennant numbers painted on either bow, so no positive identification could be made. Also, she was so damaged above the upper deck that it was almost impossible to be certain of her class, but it seemed likely that she was of the *Raglan* class. Perhaps in due course this would fit with the situation report from Hamburg, broadcast to all U-boats at sea in the area and picked up whilst charging batteries, which the U-boat would do once the full security of the dark came down. Time would tell and the Captain could afford to wait.

'Down periscope,' he ordered. 'We will hold our present depth – and we shall see.'

The periscope, unseen by *Carmarthen*'s Torpedo-Coxswain in the fading light and ruffled sea, slid down below the waves.

Once it was dark, the two men in the wheelhouse could be fed from aft so long as no light was shown, but care would have to be taken to move discreetly just the same. There was a moon now and the visibility was good. Leading-Seaman Farrow whirled the handle of the sound-powered telephone and it was answered from the wheelhouse.

' 'Swain here.'

'Farrow, 'Swain. I'm sending grub up.'

'Right. Whoever brings it, tell him to watch it, Farrow.'

'Will do, 'Swain.' Farrow hung the instrument back on its hook. 'Cameron!'

'Yes, Killick?'

'Grub to the wheel'ouse. Keep low, keep against the super-structure – keep on the side away from the bleedin' moon, too. All right?'

'All right,' Cameron said, glad enough to escape for a while from the claustrophobia of the crowded wardroom flat. He went to the pantry and collected the food from Hemming, the officers' cook. More sandwiches and some herrings-in, plus tinned peas, all cold. A bottle of lime-juice from the ward-room wine store and some water. Cameron lifted an eyebrow and said, 'What about a bottle of whisky? They could do with it.'

The officers' cook shook his head. 'Not Mr Seymour. Late Captain's standing orders: no drinking while at sea. Kept to rigid. Seymour, 'e won't go against that.' He paused. 'Not unless it was an issue, like, to the whole ship's company ... and they're only authorized to drink the rum issue. It's not on, lad.'

'Okay,' Cameron said. 'It was just a thought, that's all. Is the Captain as rigid as that?'

'Yes,' Hemming answered briskly, and polished up the glasses for the lime-juice and water. Cameron watched the meal being packed into a metal container normally used to keep food hot for transport to the compass platform. He was glad of that; he might prove unhandy with a tray and even the noise from a dropped plate was to be avoided if they were to keep up their appearance of abandonment – the U-boats had long listening ears. With the box held tightly in front of his body, Cameron climbed the ladder to the deck hatch and with one hand pulled back the clips. He emerged on to the quarterdeck, circumspectly, looking all round in so far as he was able before coming right out into the open. Bending, he dropped the hatch back into place and applied two clips, loosely. Then he faded against the after screen and came round on the moonless side. The Atlantic stood empty so far as he could see. He made his way for'ard as fast as he could and climbed the starboard ladder to the wheelhouse. Seymour was still asleep, looking like a drugged man.

The Torpedo-Coxswain took delivery of the food, gratefully. 'Thanks, lad,' he said. 'I reckon this'll do the Captain a power of good.' He gave his lips a preliminary wipe; like those of everyone else, they were salt-encrusted and unwashed for many days past. Then his eyes widened as he saw Cameron look through the port and stiffen. 'What's up?' he asked.

'Periscope,' Cameron said. 'Or I think so ... fine on the port bow.'

11

SURFACING in the darkness to recharge batteries and take routine transmissions from base, the U-boat's Captain had received information that HMS *Carmarthen* was lying helpless after an initial torpedo attack on the last westbound convoy to pass through and subsequent bombing and strafing attacks by the Focke-Wulfs. It was clear enough that the vessel he had seen through his periscope was the *Carmarthen*; now, his duty was equally clear. The wireless reports had not indicated any abandonment though the FWs had indicated that the British destroyer's guns had fallen silent during the last attack and it was assumed she had expended all her ammunition.

Thoughtfully, in the glow of the lights of the control room below the conning-tower, the German Captain studied the charts; then called, 'Franz?'

'Sir?' The First Lieutenant came to his side.

'We must attack, of course. The destroyer is worth sinking. She is not yet a total loss, and could make port. The question is, how do we attack? I have to bear in mind that another convoy is due to pass through the area and we haven't many torpedoes left.'

The First Lieutenant laughed. 'Sink her by gunfire!'

'Yes. That's obvious, of course.'

'Then—'

'But no. I have another idea, Franz. The destroyer intrigues me ... no one moving, no signs of life at all. It's like the *Marie Celeste*. I shall find out more.'

Orders were passed to bring the U-boat back towards the *Carmarthen*'s last observed position; before surfacing earlier, she had been withdrawn some ten miles easterly so as not to be spotted. Now, making back towards the destroyer, she submerged again to remain until further orders at periscope depth. About an hour later her periscope had picked up the dark blob that was *Carmarthen*, a blob standing out clearly from the moonlit water that broke gently against the base of her forward superstructure. Still there was no one visible; the U-boat captain examined the silent, motionless ship carefully with his motors stopped, then came cautiously nearer. With a better view, he still found no life whatsoever.

'Captain, sir!' The Torpedo-Coxswain's voice was urgent against Seymour's ear. In emergency the regulations had to go by the board: Seymour was dead to the world and the Torpedo-Coxswain did what no rating should do: he reached out, laid hands on the Captain and shook him awake. 'Captain, sir –'

'All right, Cox'n.' Seymour came awake and stared about as though he had no idea where he was. 'What is it?'

The Torpedo-Coxswain repeated Cameron's sighting. 'Periscope, sir, fine on the port bow. I believe it's closing, sir.'

'All right, thank you, Cox'n.' Seymour pulled himself to his feet, staggered a little, then steadied his weary body against the useless wheel. He brought up his binoculars and stared through the port, searching. After half a minute he said, 'I've got it. You're right, Cox'n, she's closing. I doubt if she'd do that if she meant to send off a fish, somehow.'

'Gunfire, sir?'

'More likely. Warn the wardroom flat, Cox'n.'

'Aye, aye, sir.' The Torpedo-Coxswain took up the sound-powered telephone. 'Orders for aft, sir?'

'Tell Lieutenant Matthews to remain where he is unless he gets word from me. Tell him that if the Jerries don't open with their gun, they may board. If they do, we fight back. In the

128

meantime all men below are to be armed with rifles from the racks. I'll pass the word if they're to come out.'

'Aye, aye, sir.' The Torpedo-Coxswain passed the message down. Below in the wardroom flat, Able-Seaman Tomkins passed it to the Engineer Officer. In the wheelhouse the three men watched the slow, cautious approach of the periscope and its small feather of disturbed water. The tension was immense as they all waited for the German to show his hand; it was clear by now that there was not to be a torpedo attack.

Seymour said suddenly, 'Bare fists for you and me, Cox'n. No bloody rifles!'

'Beg pardon, sir.' The Torpedo-Coxswain gave an apologetic cough. 'I took it on myself to bring up two for us, sir, beneath my oilskin.' He bent and produced the rifles from beneath one of the hammocks used as blast protection at sea, now lying discarded on the deck of the wheelhouse. 'We'll fight, sir, never fear.'

Seymour grinned tightly. 'You're a ruddy pirate, Cox'n, but thank God you are!' Then his tone altered. 'She's surfacing. Tell the wardroom flat to stand by. Cameron – man the phone and act as communication number.'

'Aye, aye, sir.' Cameron went to the telephone and wound the handle fast. Below, Tomkins answered once again. Crisply Cameron said, 'Stand by. The U-boat's surfacing.'

'Yes, sir,' Tomkins said before he could stop himself; he could have sworn it was an officer's voice, until the recognition had come. His face went a deep, mortified red: bloody wc candidates! 'Anything else, you little perisher?'

'Not yet. Wait for the Captain's order.' Cameron put back the telephone and stared out through the port towards the U-boat. Her conning-tower was in view now, with water pouring from the wash-ports. Cameron glanced down at the meal he had brought up, now abandoned. It hadn't been up to much anyway; now it had a forlorn look. The U-boat's casing came into view, streaming water as it rose through the seas, silhouetted beneath the moon, long and low and black. Men emerged in the conning-tower and a moment later all hell

129

seemed to burst upon the *Carmarthen* as the U-boat opened at point-blank range. There was an immensely bright flash and almost in the same instant there was a violent explosion at the base of the destroyer's wheelhouse and the metal bulkhead at the fore end grew red-hot. The concussing effect was immense: the three men were thrown violently into a corner and everything flew around them – cork insulation from the bulkheads, slivers of metal, the wheel and its mounting came adrift. The fire at the base of the superstructure was put out almost at once by the sea's action, but before this happened the German had opened once again. The next shell took the angle of the wheelhouse in the port for'ard corner, but failed to explode. The passage of the projectile, however, twisted the metal into a shambles, leaving a gaping hole in the bulkhead – leaving, too, the broken bodies of Seymour and the Torpedo-Coxswain. Cameron stared in horror at the result, felt a complete paralysis of the mind come over him. Now he was all that was left in the fore part of the ship, the only one in the command position. He had no idea what he should do. There was no further firing from the U-boat, which was now moving closer. Cameron, feeling that to remain hidden was even now the best thing to do, dropped to the deck where he was concealed by the remains of the port bulkhead. As he did so the sound-powered telephone whined and the need to silence it before its noise could reach the Germans overcame his mental paralysis. He grabbed for the instrument, remaining flat on the deck as he did so.

'Engineer Officer here,' the voice came up. 'Who's that?'

'Ordinary Seaman Cameron, sir—'

'Yes. Well, what's happening?'

'We've been hit by gunfire, sir.'

'I know that, you bloody idiot, what's the damage?'

'Not too serious I believe, sir. Nothing that'll affect our stability and seaworthiness.'

'So far as *you* know,' Matthews said sourly. 'Is the Captain still expecting the Jerries to board?'

'Yes, sir,' Cameron answered almost without thinking. He

was about to make the report that he alone remained alive in the for'ard superstructure when the Lieutenant (E) cut in on him.

'Tell the Captain we're all armed with rifles but it's *my* opinion the time's come to pack it in. Tell him that, Cameron.'

'Aye, aye, sir.' Again the automatic reaction, much to Cameron's own surprise. The instrument was banged back hard in the wardroom flat and Cameron replaced his end on its hook. Matthews was assuming the Captain and the Torpedo-Coxswain were still alive; well, let him! With the ship still, so far as Matthews would know, under command, the wardroom flat would continue to obey orders from the compass platform or wheelhouse. That was fine, if ultimately dangerous. One did not play ducks and drakes with officers. But if Matthews was for giving in, Seymour had not been. Seymour had intended to fight it out and had had the full backing of the Torpedo-Coxswain; Leading-Seaman Farrow, too, would back that decision willingly. Cameron intended that the wishes of the dead Captain should be followed out: there would be no surrender if there was anything he could do to prevent it. If the ship couldn't fight back any longer, at least her company could, and take as many Germans as possible with them in the process.

Cameron tried to project himself into the mind of the U-boat captain: what would the German be deciding currently? He would probably board; the present manoeuvrings seemed to indicate that he intended to lay alongside. Not an easy task despite the sea's flatness – there was still a swell running, left behind by the recent gales. There would be a need for much care or the submarine could damage her casing, even her pressure-hull, Cameron fancied. Submarines were a closed book to him as yet, but simple seamanship was always to be observed. But what would the German gain by boarding? It could be assumed that the Jerries knew – or thought they knew – that the destroyer had been abandoned; men would have emerged under gunfire, most likely, ready to abandon had they still been aboard. But so what? Sure, the

Germans would believe they could board without opposition, but what would be the object of that, for God's sake? A submarine, operational in an operational area where convoys were expected through, could scarcely take a crippled destroyer in tow! She probably wouldn't have the engine capacity or towing points to do it, operational or not. So why? True, it would be a feather in any submariner's cap if he could bring an enemy destroyer back to base as a prize of war. But it couldn't be feasible. On the other hand, a skeleton crew could perhaps be put aboard, and the German might risk breaking radio silence to make a report of his action so that a tow could be sent post-haste from Hamburg or one of the French ports to bring her in from under the very noses of the British. Hitler would rave with sheer joy at a well-cocked snook, and the U-boat captain would have his brass hat the next day.

That had to be stopped.

Cameron watched from cover, saw the U-boat was now lying off with her starboard side parallel to the *Carmarthen*'s port beam. He saw the conning-tower personnel, saw both Captain and First Lieutenant studying the destroyer's ravaged decks and superstructure through binoculars. So far there was no closer approach. The moon shone down brilliantly, bringing everything up clear and stark. That was unfortunate: the moment the seamen and stokers emerged with their rifles from the wardroom hatch, they were going to be spotted. And when they did emerge, they would do so on the word of an ordinary seaman, a word supported only by the dead.

'Leading-Seaman Farrow.'

'Yes, sir?'

'A word in your ear, Farrow. Come over here.' Matthews beckoned. Farrow went across to where the Engineer Officer stood just inside the doorway of his own cabin, now occupied by two of the sedated burns cases, one in the bunk, the other on the settee. 'You heard what came down from the Captain, I take it?'

132

'Yes, sir, I did.'

'It's bloody suicide!' Matthews snapped.

'Maybe it is, sir.'

Matthews gave him a sweeping look. 'You don't mind?'

'Yes, sir, I mind all right. I've some living to do yet.' Farrow drew the sleeve of a jersey across his nose. 'But it's orders. Orders from the bridge, like.'

Matthews glared. 'Is that supposed to mean something, Farrow?'

'Oh no, sir, no,' Farrow answered, all innocence, eyes wide. It was a good act. 'Nothing at all, sir. Just statin' facts, that's all. Orders are orders, aren't they, sir?'

'Yes! But I don't believe the Captain's in a fit state to make decisions, Farrow. So many days and nights up there – no sleep to speak of, cold food—'

'We're all in the same boat, sir.'

'Don't you damn well interrupt me when I'm talking to you, Leading-Seaman Farrow!' Matthews' eyes blazed redly; in Farrow's view it was he, not the Captain, who was showing the strain-signals. 'Try that again, and I'll have that hook off your arm the moment we reach Belfast.'

Farrow sighed. 'Sorry, sir, I'm sure.'

'All right, all right. Now just listen. Don't get me wrong, but I'm not willing to risk my stokers in a bloody daft attempt at heroics. What's left of the ship's not worth it – just not worth men's lives, understand?'

Farrow nodded. 'You may be right, sir, but—'

'I *am* right and there aren't any buts, Farrow. Trained men are more use to the war effort than a boat that's damaged to the extent we are. So my stokers don't take any part in trying to repel boarders or whatever it is Seymour has in mind to do. Right?'

'It's your decision, sir.'

'Thank you very much!' Matthews snapped rudely. 'I know it's my decision, and you'll abide by it.'

'If you say so, sir,' Farrow said for the second time that night. Inside, as the Engineer Officer uttered a curt dismissal,

Farrow was seething. True, it was easy enough to appreciate his point: men were men and often enough throughout history it had been plain daft to throw their lives away. 'Repel boarders' had an old-fashioned ring about it, certainly; in Nelson's day hardy tars had followed their officers often enough, cutlasses in hand, when the old wooden walls of England had laid alongside the French, to cut and thrust into bellies and chests, arms and legs and necks, or to hack away the rigging so that the canvas descended to envelop the enemy and leave them without their motive power if they lived. That had been commonplace, then. Not now. Farrow, going back towards the wardroom pantry where he had taken up his station, sucked angrily at his teeth. God knew, the Navy was crammed to the gunwales with bull, but it was a proud service and the White Ensign was still, even now, floating out from the ensign-staff aft. Surrender was a dirty word to Farrow. In any case, that Matthews had overstated his case; the old *Carmarthen* was far from lost yet. Given time and a bit of luck, an ocean-going rescue tug would appear over the horizon from the east and would bring her in, bring her home again. That would be a wonderful moment, one well worth fighting for. Farrow intended to fight for it. Like Seymour.

He frowned thoughtfully. The seaman ratings had been very badly hit. Very heavy casualties ... and no stokers or tiffies had been lost, not yet. Farrow wished them long life but had to face the fact that without them his fighting capacity would be sadly small, not to say negligible. He pulled at his jaw and glared towards Lieutenant (E) Matthews, who was talking to his Chief Stoker, a little fat man named Peters. Chief Stoker Peters didn't seem to be liking it any more than Farrow. It would reflect badly on the department afterwards. You couldn't keep buzzes at bay, and word always spread like lightning round any naval base. *Carmarthen*'s engine-room complement would come in for any amount of crap and Peters knew it.

Farrow, his nails digging hard into his palms as he waited for the sound-powered telephone to whine again with orders,

134

decided that he might have to stick his neck out. He was very unsure of his ground, but he did remember the Captain's remark just before he'd left the wardroom flat, and he remembered the appeal that had seemed to be in it. Mr Seymour, with command suddenly thrust upon him, was doing his best. It was up to the rest of them to give him proper backing and sod Matthews. Farrow, in advance of the expected orders which still hadn't come, was about to start to stick out his neck and make a formal approach to the Engineer Officer, who strictly speaking had no executive authority at all, when he saw a man make a dash for the ladder leading up to the deck hatch: Lavington, with a rifle in his hand.

Farrow came out from the open door of the pantry, yelling. 'Stop that man! *Get him before he makes the muckin' hatch!*' He was moving fast himself as he spoke, running as fast as was possible with all the impediments both structural and human, but was beaten to it by Able-Seaman Tomkins. Farrow had seen murder in Tomkins eyes and he pushed forward to stop tragedy, tragedy that might – indeed would, once Lavington was through the hatch – wreck any plans the skipper might have to continue hoodwinking the Jerries. Farrow was too late: ahead of Tomkins, Lavington made the quarterdeck and began a mad, pointless rush for'ard along the iron-deck towards the sunken fo'c'sle. Tomkins had enough sense not to pursue him once he had been spotted from the U-boat's conning-tower; Tomkins stopped and took cover in the lee of the after screen, and it was Lavington alone who ran into the Germans' machine-gun fire. He lurched, his rifle clattered to the deck, and he went overboard with his brains spilling.

Shaking like a leaf, Tomkins went below.

'Tried to stop the stupid bugger,' he said to Farrow, but didn't meet the Leading-Seaman's eyes. Everyone in the wardroom flat knew what he'd intended to do. In the circumstances he might have got away with it, and anyway he hadn't stopped to think it through, not really. ''E bought it from the Jerries.'

Farrow nodded. The machine-gun fire had been heard. He said, 'Well, that's that, then.' It was the best way out for Lavington, without a doubt.... The sound-powered telephone from the wheelhouse was whining again. Tomkins answered, then reported to Farrow.

'Wheel'ouse says the buggers look like boarding – they're coming alongside and a party's mustering on the casing. You're to act in execution of previous orders.'

As Tomkins finished the message there was a bump along the destroyer's port side and a noticeable lurch. Farrow lost no time. He called, 'All hands, up on deck. That includes the engine-room.' He caught the furious eye of Lieutenant (E) Matthews and said, 'By my reckoning, sir, the Captain meant me to take charge aft as the senior seaman rating left. So I'm taking charge, sir. And afterwards I'll take my chance that I acted right.'

He turned away for the ladder, ordered the seamen and stokers to fix bayonets, and climbed fast. Out through the after screen and on to the quarterdeck, he heard rifle fire coming from the wheelhouse, heard it being returned, and then saw the U-boat's crew jumping in swarms from the casing to the iron-deck whence some moved for'ard and the rest aft. Farrow fired round the angle of the after screen in an attempt to hold the Germans until he had all his men on deck: he was successful. The rush aft halted, and a body went over the side to be pulped between the two hulls. The Germans, as Farrow fired again and scored another hit, became much more circumspect, seeking cover. The fire was being kept up from the wheelhouse too, though Farrow fancied it was coming from one rifle only; and the moment all the seamen and stokers were mustered behind him, Farrow ordered the counter-attack.

Half his force ran for the starboard side of the iron-deck under Chief Stoker Peters, while Farrow himself took the port side, doubling from behind the after screen with all rifles blazing away. The U-boat crew seemed taken utterly by surprise: the attack was much stronger than they had expected.

136

While the bullets from Farrow's seamen thudded into flesh, the starboard-side attack came at the boarding-party from over the shattered remains of the searchlight platform and the midships superstructure. As Farrow came to close quarters he reversed his rifle and smashed away with the butt, grinning like a bloodstained demon. At his side Àble-Seaman Tomkins did the same and appeared to be enjoying every moment. Aboard the U-boat, an attempt was being made to man the gun; but Cameron in the wheelhouse was in an excellent position to stop this happening. From cover, he was able to pick off each man as the gun was approached. Bullets pinged around him, ricocheting off the wreckage of the bulkheads. Blood poured from a near miss that sliced a lobe from an ear. From the upper deck came screams of agony as wounded men slid over the side to become fenders for the U-boat. The German Captain, keeping prudently below the lip of his conning-tower, was shouting orders through a megaphone, but no one seemed to be taking any notice as the slaughter continued. Cameron believed that most of the casualties were German; the destroyer's seamen and stokers were fighting like maniacs, giving no quarter at all, determined to save the ship and themselves. After a while it looked as though the Germans were retreating: as their commander's megaphone shouts continued, they began jumping back across to the casing, which was slippery with blood, some of which had dripped over from the conning-tower.

Second thoughts were in the air now; the U-boat would probably withdraw and attack from a distance by gunfire.

That must spell the end.

Then Cameron remembered something: the grenades. They had been stowed in the ready-use ammunition locker aft, by Number Three gun. They would still be there and there might just be time. He went down the starboard ladder to the iron-deck, ran like lightning towards Number Three gun-mounting, and opened up the ready-use locker. There they were, a box of them, lethal pineapples. As he lifted the box out and clambered back down to the iron-deck he found

Tomkins kneeling on a German seaman and struggling to pull his bayonet out from the chest.

Cameron said, 'Leave it, Stripey.'

Tomkins looked up, his face smeared with blood. ''Oo's givin' 'oo orders, then?'

Cameron grinned and said, 'Simple request, that's all. Something more important. How about a coconut shy ... down the conning-tower? As many as possible, in as short a time as possible before they get away. Two hands are better than one – right?'

'Right,' Tomkins said, and got to his feet, leaving his rifle and bayonet to sag from the German's rib cage. Together they ran for the wheelhouse and from there into the port wing with its now useless close-range weapons. Here they were almost immediately above the conning-tower: it was just too easy.

'Ready,' Cameron said, and began counting as he released the lever of the first grenade. Tomkins did the same. Both were thrown together, both found that easy, impossible-to-miss target. One landed in the conning-tower itself, the other fell straight through the hatch into the U-boat's control-room. Before the first two had exploded, four more had gone down. The results were horrible: the conning-tower looked as though a bacon slicer had been at work, strips of bloody flesh hanging everywhere. Below it must have been far worse. Smoke came up through the hatch, and with it the death screams of mangled men. Somewhere, an electrical fire had probably started. It was highly unlikely that the U-boat would be able to submerge until the fires had been dealt with.

Tomkins said as much, in tones of awe. 'Poor soddin' Nazi bastards! They'll fry. I reckon they've had it good an' proper now. Won't have done the periscope much good an' all, eh?'

'I rather think not, Stripey. Nor the circuits. I think we can call it a victory.' Cameron, now in cover behind the mangled metal of the destroyer's control tower, took a cautious look down to the iron-deck. Farrow's hands were in full control and the deck was littered with bodies. The U-boat was bumping the side plating and lurching about as though she was no longer under command. Cameron said, 'Well, that's it. Let's get down.'

He went into the wheelhouse, followed by Tomkins. For the first time Tomkins seemed to realize that there was no one else present and he asked, 'Where's the skipper, then, eh?'

Cameron pointed. 'There, Stripey. And the Cox'n.'

'Strewth!' Tomkins appeared shaken as he saw the bodies. ''Oo did the orders come from, then?'

Cameron said quietly, 'Someone had to give them.'

'You, eh?' Tomkins screwed up his eyes. 'Bloody little OD, makin' out 'e's the skipper! Just you wait till that Matthews get to 'ear, then watch out. Cor! Muckin' WC ratings ... you even said "Cox'n" like a bleedin' officer.' He minced the word; to the lower deck, the Torpedo-Coxswain was customarily the 'Swain. Just one of the differences ... Tomkins went down the ladder to the iron-deck, muttering.

12

THE hands remained ready to return any further fire, but no fire came as the U-boat continued lurching against the side plating. The remainder of the grenades were ready too, ready to be lobbed across if the need should arise. From the compass platform Farrow could see that the conning-tower hatch was open still – it looked as though its closing mechanism had been fouled up by the first of the grenades. Netting had been rigged over it to prevent the ingress of more grenades but Farrow didn't reckon that would help the Jerries much; it could be blown away, he thought. As he looked down, he saw the kerfuffle starting below the U-boat's counter; the main engines were turning over and she was buggering off at last.

That was something; it remained to be seen whether she could use her surface armament, her gun. With any luck, the firing circuits would be out of action ... but even so, she could probably still fire by local control.

Hearing a step behind him, Farrow turned. Matthews had come to the compass platform. The Engineer Officer looked sour. He said, 'I'm taking over command, Farrow. It's my entitlement.'

'Very good, sir.'

'You'll obey my orders or you'll face trouble.'

'Yes, sir.'

'Don't sound so damn defiant!' Matthews said loudly.

'I'm sorry, sir. I didn't mean to.'

Matthews, breathing hard, swung away, then swung back

again. 'As Damage Control Officer, I know the ship inside out, know her capabilities. In this situation, that's what counts, right?'

'Yes, sir.'

'Any fool can be a seaman . . . especially in a ship without power.'

Farrow held on to his temper and said, 'It's a matter of opinion, is that, sir.' He wanted to smash a fist into the Lieutenant (E)'s face but that would never do. 'The hands haven't done all that badly, sir. Ordinary Seaman Cameron—'

'Yes, quite. That lad's in for trouble, Farrow. He passed orders as from the Captain, who was dead. Those orders resulted in a good many men being killed – my ERAS and stokers among them. That's something you have to answer for as well and I give you fair warning you'll do so.'

'Very good, sir.' Matthews was in a foul mood, a highly dangerous and far from sane mood in Farrow's opinion, but something had to be said and Farrow said it. 'Ordinary Seaman Cameron, sir. Maybe he did exceed himself . . . but I reckon he's saved what's left of the ship, sir. He crippled the U-boat, sir, him and Tomkins between them—'

'That's enough, Farrow.' Matthews was shaking.

'Yes, sir. And I intend to state all that, sir, to Captain (D) when we get back to base.'

Matthews' fists clenched. 'Get below, Farrow. Get below before I lose my temper. When you're wanted, you'll be sent for.'

When the U-boat had pulled away clear, which was shortly after Farrow had been ordered below, she went into action with her gun. The aim was poor, and the shell went well over. After that, there was no more firing. Farrow believed that the gun had probably jammed. Whatever it was, the end came suddenly and spectacularly: the U-boat blew up, torpedoes and all, a tremendous blast that sent shock waves ringing through the destroyer. Brilliant flame, red, white and orange,

141

lit the area like day for a brief while after which even the moon seemed to have lost its brilliance. The hands on deck stared in awe.

Farrow said, 'They won't have known much about it.' His guess was that the electrics, damaged by the grenade explosions, had caused further fires. Those fires had reached some vital part, maybe a torpedo warhead. Anyway, it was one U-boat less to harry the convoys and it could be chalked up to young Cameron, whose idea it had been. Farrow grinned to himself: U-boat destruction by grenade was a damn sight cheaper than using depth charges, less of a strain on the munitions factories, but it was never likely to happen again, not in this war. The Nazis would have learned a lesson now, if the facts ever penetrated back to the Fatherland: never put your boat alongside anything that still floated, no matter how beaten it appeared to be. Adolf Hitler would be biting a few carpets when he heard, and taking it out on Grand Admiral Raeder, the bastard. In the meantime, the old *Carmarthen* could settle back into her new routine, the routine of being closeted out of sight below in the wardroom flat. That, and waiting for the base staff to pull their fingers out and send a tow. Farrow spared a thought for Lieutenant (E) Matthews, solitary on the compass platform or more likely in the wheelhouse. He had a word with Cameron, a word of warning of what might come when they made port.

'I wouldn't worry too much, though,' he said. 'The Navy doesn't come down too hard on success, never mind how it's brought about.' He paused. 'Initiative ... that's part of Officer-Like Qualities, isn't it?'

Cameron smiled. 'So they say!'

'They say right, Lofty.' Farrow laid a friendly hand on his shoulder. 'You'll make out all right, and it'll take more than Matthews to stop you.'

Now that Lavington had gone, the atmosphere in the wardroom flat was a good deal easier. Carrying a virtually condemned man, a murderer, had cast a blight; Lavington had

142

indeed been a jonah. Yet the fact of the Engineer Officer's sour-tempered reactions, and his taking over the command, affected the ship's company in various ways that could lead to renewed tension. There was argument as to whether or not Matthews was entitled to take over. True, he was, apart from the Surgeon-Lieutenant, the only officer left, and that presumably gave him some rights. But the belief among the seamen at any rate was that when all executive officers were dead, the command devolved upon the senior lower deck rating of the seaman branch, which was Leading-Seaman Farrow, who happened to be a good hand and a popular one, one who carried authority well and didn't chuck his weight about unduly. Engineers were all very well, but they weren't seamen and didn't think and react as seamen; they had a job to distinguish port from starboard, said some. Tomkins was one of these; and Tomkins was incensed that his and Cameron's grenade-throwing efforts had come in for criticism because they hadn't been authorized by an officer.

'Black gang bleeders,' he said bitterly as he lit a fag. 'Useless lot, they just don't savvy. Me and me mate did the job an' that's wot counts, ain't it, eh?'

Farrow grinned to himself: *me and me mate* ... quite a change, was that! Tomkins had accepted Cameron now; they'd done a job together and it looked as though they might both go down in naval history, for what they had done was certainly unprecedented. The night, what was left of it, passed amid a bedlam of snores from weary men. At a little after 0800, when the officers' cook was preparing the breakfasts, the sound-powered telephone whined from the wheelhouse. Tomkins answered.

'Wardroom flat, sir. Able-Seaman Tomkins.'

'Send Leading-Seaman Farrow to the compass platform,' came Matthews' voice, followed by a bang as the receiver was replaced. Farrow, who was asleep, was woken and went straight up.

'Ah, Leading-Seaman Farrow.' Matthews looked frozen, and was throwing his arms about his body in an attempt to find

143

some warmth: compass platforms were less comfortable than engine-rooms, Farrow thought uncharitably. 'First, burial of the dead.' Matthews stared around vaguely, as though looking for the bodies of Seymour and the Torpedo-Coxswain; they had been taken below immediately after the action against the U-boat and were lying in the tiller flat aft of the wardroom. 'Hands to muster at four bells and I shall read the religious service.'

'Aye, aye, sir.'

'Next, I intend to pump out aft. Or try to. Not pump exactly – that's not possible. Bale.'

'Bale, sir?'

'That's what I said, Leading-Seaman Farrow. Bale. By hand.'

'Bale out the after magazines, sir?' Farrow stood there amazed.

'Yes. We'll ride easier when that's been done, in my opinion. We're far too waterlogged at the moment and with the main shafts out of line there's no point in keeping the screws under. We'll make a start immediately after the committals.'

Farrow sucked his teeth. It would take a bloody week, and it seemed wholly pointless except as an exercise to keep the hands occupied, which might be sensible perhaps. From a stability point of view ... well, they'd ridden out one storm with the stern down and hadn't done so badly. Any interference with the trim might have unfortunate results, but Lieutenant (E) Matthews, who could be presumed to know something about trim and stability, had spoken and that was that.

Once again, the dreadful duty of committing bodies to the deep; and this time the corpses, sewn into their canvas shrouds, floated alongside the stationary destroyer's decks and by some hideous quirk would not move away; nor, even with the firebars sewn into the canvas at their feet, would they sink. Air, trapped in the canvas, kept them afloat. Feet down, there they remained, heads and torsos moving sluggishly to the slight scend of the Atlantic.

'Bring a rifle,' Matthews ordered. When the rifle was brought he sent several clips of .303 ammunition into the corpses and after that they slowly disappeared. The shots had scattered the seagulls, come as usual to scavenge amongst the 'gash' thrown overboard from the wardroom pantry, but they were soon back, wheeling and crying. Farrow looked at them sardonically; like the albatrosses of the Southern Ocean, maybe they bore the souls of mariners dead and gone and couldn't keep away from ships.

The bodies disposed of, the long business of baling-out the flooded after spaces was put in hand. As the magazine was opened up, Farrow drew Matthews' attention to the western horizon.

'There's a change coming in the weather, sir.' The customary menacing line of black was forming, low down as yet but increasing, and there was a curious oiliness on the sea, too flat a calm for Farrow's peace of mind.

'Then the hands'll work the faster,' Matthews said.

'Aye, aye, sir. But if –'

'Just get on with it, will you?' Matthews ordered testily. Farrow turned away and got on with it; there was no option, but he believed that if the stern was allowed to lift again, then the coming wind might use it, as it were, to drive the sunken stem down farther into the water. They'd been riding well enough; better to leave it. But Matthews seemed obsessed with the idea – Farrow thought – that he must reverse everything that Mr Seymour had done, Mr Seymour who was at this moment somewhere below them, spiralling down in the Atlantic wastes, Mr Seymour who'd been determined to get the old ship back to base. Matthews, he hadn't quite the same determination; he'd wanted to chuck it in earlier, the bastard. Farrow wouldn't forget that.

As the distant black loomed higher, chains of men, seamen and stokers together plus the daymen, a case of all hands, lifted water from the magazine shaft in buckets, balers, galley

145

saucepans, leather charge cases, anything that would hold water for tipping back into the sea. Under the sour-tempered lash of Matthews' voice, they worked hard. At least it kept out the bitter cold and that was something. But their labours appeared to have no effect on the trim of the wallowing hull, and the Engineer Officer's mood grew worse.

'If anything,' he said to Farrow, 'she's going deeper.'

'Seems like she is, sir. Could be the tiller flat's leaking, sir.'

'Oh, rubbish, everything's tight down there, has been ever since we sounded round after leaving that merchant ship.'

'Worth checking again, sir?'

Matthews breathed hard down his nose. 'Oh, all right, send a man down.'

Farrow called up Cameron, told him off to check right aft. On his way below, Cameron met Chief Stoker Peters: the Chief Stoker had made his own investigation of the tiller flat which was undoubtedly flooding through a sprung plate. 'God knows how *that* happened,' he said, sounding professionally aggrieved, 'unless something was shifted while we were being bashed about and it's just worsened.'

He reported to Matthews. 'I'll do what I can to caulk it, sir. I'll need some hands below.'

'Right you are,' Matthews agreed. 'Take 'em from Farrow's party. And be as quick as you can, Chief. That weather's closing in. We can't afford to be put further down in the water.'

The work continued, above and below decks; there was a real urgency now to get as much water as possible out of the ship before bad weather struck yet again. With the tiller flat flooding, the position had changed. Farrow was gloomy, and confided as much in Cameron and Tomkins. A lot was going to be up to them, he said. Stripey Tomkins was about the most experienced seaman rating now left, and Cameron had proved himself to be quick thinking and not prone to panic.

'I'll be relying on you two,' Farrow said. 'Don't let me down.'

It was soon after this that the full force of the weather hit

them; Farrow estimated the wind at Force Ten. The White
Ensign, still bravely flying from the ensign staff, cracked
several times like a whip and then stood out as though
starched, held like a board by the shrieking, tempestuous
gale. The sky was black with heavy, low cloud and such
visibility as remained was further cut by the blown spindrift
that lay across the breaking crests. Water boiled along
Carmarthen's decks and the baling-out of the flooded after
spaces was at once suspended by Farrow without waiting for
orders from Matthews. There was a sound like thunder as one
wave after another, waves that seemed to be growing larger
every minute, smashed into the base of the superstructure and
broke in spray that covered the compass platform and the
wheelhouse ports and sent its sting aft to lash the men still on
deck. Farrow's voice roared out, ordering all hands back to
the wardroom flat; they could serve no useful purpose now.

As Matthews fought his way for'ard to the wheelhouse,
Farrow made for Chief Stoker Peters in the tiller flat aft.

'Need any more hands, Chief?' he asked.

Peters shook his head. 'Thanks, I've got enough.' He was
slopping about in a foot of water. 'It's not men I need now, it's
new stern plating and a D2 bloody refit in Pompey!'

In the operations room at the Rosyth Naval base more convoys were indicated on the plot by now: the next westbound
and the next eastbound, with their escorts who would change
from the one to the other as the westbound convoy passed
into the 'safe' zone and the eastbound one left it.

The name *Carmarthen* wasn't there any more among the
escorts; she had been presumed lost and already she was past
history, her place now taken by one of the four-stackers, the
elderly United States Navy boats handed to Britain under the
Lend-Lease agreements, weird-looking craft but more than
welcome and, so it was said with tongue in cheek, capable of
ten knots on each funnel, a statement that landsmen found no
reason to doubt. HMS *Pennsylvania* was there instead of
Carmarthen, though this was a fact that Mary Anstey simply

147

refused to accept. Each time she saw *Pennsylvania*'s name, it was to her *Carmarthen* as it had been in the last convoy-escort pattern. Crazy, perhaps; but she had an inner feeling that to admit the destroyer's loss to herself would in some way ensure that it *would* be lost and somehow she had a strong belief that *Carmarthen* was still afloat somewhere out there in the wild Atlantic gale. That gale was already sweeping in across Northern Ireland and into the Firth of Clyde; according to the reports, it was a bad one, the worst for many years. For the convoys soon to depart, this was good enough news, of course; but Mary's mind was not on the convoys. If only the Naval Command didn't assume a loss so readily ... if only there was a better availability of ocean-going tugs ... if only there were more long-range aircraft, such as Goering had at his command ... there were so many 'if onlys' about this war. There was another: if only she and Donald Cameron had managed to see more of each other when they had both been in Portsmouth. She'd heard it said that the dead go fast when they hadn't had a long time to become deeply known and she was finding it something of an effort to recall the set of his face ... she forced the thought down and away. She mustn't think in terms of death. *Carmarthen* would come through if she kept faith.

That afternoon, with twenty-four hours off duty, Mary took the train into Edinburgh. As the train left Inverkeithing and passed on to the Forth bridge, the battleship *Rodney* was coming in, and as she approached the bridge a single shaft of sunlight, thinly breaking for a moment through the overcast, lit upon the nine great sixteen-inch guns in their triple turrets for'ard of the superstructure, and upon her ship's company fallen in fore and aft for entering harbour, with the Cable Officer standing motionless in the eyes of the ship ready to bring her to her buoy off Rosyth dockyard once the order came from the compass platform to send away the buoy-jumper. With the battleship were her escorting destroyers and astern of her the elderly county-class cruiser *Norfolk* with her high freeboard and thin, raked funnels, a gracious lady from the past. Mary's eyes filled with sudden tears as the warships passed in solemn state below the great dark-grey span of the bridge and from below a bugle-call rang out, sounding clear above the rattle of the train.

They were all one Navy, with the same unvarying basic routine from ship to ship: dawn action stations, change of watches, hands fall in, breakfast, stand easy, Up Spirits, hands to dinner ... all the way through to dusk action stations and Pipe Down. There was a security about sameness, like the Church of England's matins and evensong; wherever in the world you found an English church, you found the comforting familiarity of the unchanging order of service. Ships were the same.

For no real reason, she felt cheered by the sight of the ships below, passing from danger and foul weather into the port's safety.

Every plate, every rivet seemed to be straining its guts out to keep the *Carmarthen* afloat, almost as though she were a wounded animal, facing death but filled with a determination to die in home surroundings. The wardroom flat was a cheerless place, a place of no hope despite the best efforts of Leading-Seaman Farrow and Stripey Tomkins, who was now proving a tower of strength. From some recess in his bulky clothing, Tomkins had brought out a mouth-organ. His repertoire was limited, but adequate. He played 'Tipperary', 'Keep the Home Fires Burning', 'Roll Out The Barrel', and then went into sundry hymn tunes to which generations of British seamen had put words never dreamed of by the clergy. Tomkins got them all singing, but not for long. The future was much too bleak, as were the current discomforts. And Lieutenant (E) Matthews, sod him, used the sound-powered telephone every few minutes to ask about the tiller flat – his line to Chief Stoker Peters had, it seemed, packed up on him. Able-Seaman Tomkins, interrupted in his mouth-organ playing for the hundredth time, grew bitter.

'Pity this soddin' line doesn't pack it in an' all,' he said as he banged the telephone down. 'I don't know what bloody use 'e is up there, buggered if I do.'

'What is it this time?' Cameron asked.

Tomkins wiped the back of a hand across his lips. 'There's a ship in sight and 'e don't know what it is. Comin' up from the west, visible jus' now and again like.' He called out to Farrow, passing the report. Farrow moved fast for the ladder and the hatch and Cameron went up behind him. Emerging on to the quarterdeck, now lower than ever in the water, they stared out towards the west. Their world seemed bounded by the great rearing waves and the breaking crests; from aft no ship could be seen in those heaving, spindrift-filled waters.

Farrow said, 'Come up to the wheelhouse, Lofty. Two pairs of eyes are better than one.'

In the wheelhouse they found the Engineer Officer slumped like a zombie against a bulkhead. Matthews said, 'You took your time, didn't you?'

'Sorry, sir. I looked around from aft first, sir. Didn't see anything.'

'Well, look now, then. Here.' Matthews handed over his binoculars and indicated the bearing. Farrow took a long look; two masts and a funnel were occasionally visible as the unknown vessel rose to a sea.

Farrow said, 'I don't know, sir. She's a merchantman, that's all I can say. Can't see her flag, sir.'

'Cameron? You reckon to be an officer, I'm told. See what you can make of her.'

'Aye, aye, sir.' Cameron took the binoculars, found the vessel, and steadied the glasses on her. He said, 'I agree with Leading-Seaman Farrow, sir. And I can't see a flag either.' He paused. 'She could be a stray from another convoy – or she could be one of our armed merchant cruisers, I suppose, sir.'

'That's what I thought,' Matthews said. 'On the other hand, she could be a bloody Hun surface raider ... one of the converted merchantmen.'

'Right, sir,' Farrow said.

'So what do we do? That's the question now, isn't it?'

150

'Yes, sir,' Farrow said again. There were the two alternatives in his view: one was simply to hope not to be seen – and it was highly unlikely they would be, in fact – and let the ship go; the other was to attract the attention of her Officer of the Watch by signal or rocket. Either way was a risk. To let a British or allied ship pass by would be bloody hard; but to attract a Jerry would mean the end. 'I reckon we'd do better to wait, sir,' Farrow said. 'Wait till she closes and we get a better look.'

'*Is* she closing?'

'I fancy she is, sir, yes.'

'Uh-huh.' Matthews brought himself upright and moved across the lurching wheelhouse, grabbing for handholds. He looked sick, dead weary, at the end of his tether. 'All right then, we wait. On the other hand ...'

'Yes, sir?'

'Heroics are finished. That part's over and done with, all right?'

'I'm not sure what you mean, sir,' Farrow said. He sounded uneasy. In his opinion the fight wasn't over yet, at any rate the fight against the sea. Let them remain afloat, let the weather improve, and they could make it yet with a bit of luck. But Matthews?

'I mean what I said, damn you!' Matthews snapped. 'We can't fight anyway, whether we want to or not. That's out and we all know it. That ship ...'

'Yes, sir?'

'If she's a German, the worst that could happen would be that we'd be taken prisoner for the duration. The way things are now, we're probably going to drown. Either that, or be finished off by bombs once the weather clears enough for the FWs to have another go at us. That's not good enough. If you ask me, it's just plain daft.'

'The Captain –'

'The Captain, Leading-Seaman Farrow, if you mean Hewson or Seymour, is dead. I'm in command now.'

'Very good, sir. But as the senior seaman rating left, sir, I'd

151

like to ask a question,' Farrow said doggedly. 'And it's this: do you intend to attract that ship's notice, sir, whether she's British or neutral or German ... and kind of see what happens?' He paused. 'Because –'

'Because nothing. You'll do precisely as I say, Leading-Seaman Farrow, and remember you're a rating.' Matthews lurched back across the wheelhouse, his eyes blazing in the fading light. Cameron noted that the Engineer Officer's hands were shaking badly, that his whole body seemed to be in a fit of the tremors. His look was wild, far from reassuring in one who had said he was in command. 'I have the welfare of the ship's company to consider – their lives, man, don't you understand that? It's not for me to sacrifice them for nothing – nor you nor anybody else!'

'In my view, sir,' Farrow began stolidly, 'I –'

'To hell with your view.'

'I'm going to say it nevertheless, sir. In my view, to bring a German vessel towards us would be an act of surrender. I don't believe there's any of us would go along with that, sir. Not when we've come so far.'

'The vessel,' Matthews snapped, sensibly enough, 'could be British, couldn't it?'

'Yes, sir. We have to try to make sure first, sir. That's why I suggested waiting.'

'While the light goes, and we can't bloody well see her? Is that what you suggest?'

'There's time yet, sir. We aren't going to lose the light yet, sir. Meanwhile, she's closing.' Farrow was looking through the binoculars again, frowning over them as he studied the silhouette each time the vessel rose to view above the gale-lashed waves. The wind howled eerily around the superstructure, like the voice of clustering devils out to send them to the depths. Farrow could understand the dilemma Matthews found himself in; lives were always a heavy responsibility, but in the exigencies of war an escort destroyer must be considered the more vital: escorts were so desperately short and the convoys with their troops and supplies so badly in need of

152

such protection as could be given them. The old *Carmarthen* could live to fight yet, if only she could be found by friendly hands and brought safely to port. She was badly damaged, certainly, but there was nothing a dockyard refit couldn't put right, Farrow believed, and believed truly. She couldn't be abandoned to be sunk by Nazi guns and Farrow wasn't going to be a party to any surrender. Mr Seymour had intended to bring the destroyer in; and Mr Seymour had said something that had at first puzzled him but which had since begun to make sense. Mr Seymour hadn't wanted that Matthews to give in to the bloody Nazis. What he had said, it had been like his last will and testament.

Well, then!

Maybe he was obtuse, maybe he was over concerned with Mr Seymour's intentions as last known, maybe many things. But he'd been a good few years in the Navy and he was a tenacious man. And when recognition came to Leading-Seaman Farrow, recognition that the ship coming in from the west was a German surface raider, a former merchant ship that was probably returning home after harrying the South Atlantic shipping routes with her six-inch guns, he knew beyond doubt what he had to do.

13

'GERMAN?' Matthews repeated. 'You're sure?'

Farrow handed over the binoculars. 'See for yourself, sir.'

Matthews focused. 'Yes,' he said. 'Yes, she's German, all right. You're aware of my views, Farrow.'

'I am, sir, yes.'

'Right.' Matthews was still shaking and his face was an unhealthy colour. He licked at dry lips and looked away from Farrow's accusing eyes. 'I'm acting for the best.'

'I don't think you are, sir.'

'I wasn't asking you.'

'No, sir. I believe we can get her home, sir. We're sure to be found before long ... we're not far off the convoy routes, can't be.'

Matthews said, 'That's as maybe, Farrow. I'm now ordering you to make contact with that German ship. You'll fire rockets, until she alters towards us, all right?'

'No, sir. I'll not do that, sir.'

'I repeat my order,' Matthews said in a stony voice.

'I'm sorry, sir.'

The Engineer Officer turned to Cameron. 'You heard that, lad. You're a witness to an act of mutiny, all right?'

Cameron made no response to this; Farrow spoke again. He said, 'There's no mutiny in my mind, sir, none at all. I'm just not going to see surrender, that's all. If Cameron's a witness to anything, it's to the fact you wanted to ditch the ship, sir.'

Matthews' face had gone a deathly white and he seemed to be having difficulty with his breathing. He began to mouth incoherent words, and spittle ran down his unshaven chin. Then, suddenly, he seemed to crumple. He put his head in his hands and staggered backwards. Farrow caught him before he fell. 'That's it, then,' Farrow said. 'Go down and fetch the Surgeon-Lieutenant, Lofty.'

Wallowing so low in the heavy seas, *Carmarthen* remained unseen as the enemy vessel passed them to the north and faded into the approaching night. But a little before the next day's dawn, heavy gunfire was heard distantly, and then an almighty explosion, the flames of which lit the northern horizon for many minutes before they died away.

'Convoy under attack,' Tomkins said. 'Probably that bleedin' raider.' U-boats wouldn't mount an attack in the current weather conditions. Over the next hour gunfire was heard almost continually: there was quite a battle in progress, and it ended in another violent explosion with more flames to light the sky. Speculation proliferated: how many ships would have gone? Why had that last explosion ended the gunfire – had the convoy escorts managed to get in under those six-inch guns and sink the German? Such ships were certainly vulnerable enough, with their high freeboards and unprotected hulls. They didn't, in fact, normally attack escorted convoys, preferring to hunt for the lone ship or the straggler. Yet on this occasion the raider must have been lying in wait for an unexpected target, the passage of the convoy. Uneasily, *Carmarthen*'s company awaited the dawn, fearing what they might find: survivors, most probably, wounded men beyond their reach. It would come hard, not being able to help. The faces of the men were blank from sheer weariness; there had been little sleep and no release at all from tension for so long. As for Matthews, he was lying wrapped in a blanket on some pillows placed on the wardroom pantry's servery; the cabins were still occupied by the burns cases and the deck still held its surging slop of seawater. Matthews was securely lashed with rope against the destroyer's lurching movement and he lay with his eyes open but his face expressionless, saying nothing but looking haunted by his thoughts. Farrow, in the wheelhouse with Cameron, was now indisputably in charge. Cameron asked what was likely to happen in regard to his refusal of Matthews' order.

'When we get home, Lofty?' Farrow scratched his chin and gave a harsh laugh. 'I don't reckon much is going to happen, somehow. There's only you and me – and Matthews – knows, eh? It'll all come out in the wash – you'll see!'

'How?'

Farrow laughed again and said, 'Me, I don't want to be charged with mutiny. Matthews won't want it known that he was meaning to hand over to the Jerries. Nothing'll be said at all. And I've already had a word, quiet like, with the doctor. He's going to say Matthews wasn't fit to exercise command even in his own engine-room. He was right on breaking point, was Mr Matthews.'

'So –'

'So you needn't bother your arse about it, Lofty. All right?'

Cameron nodded, much relieved. He was well aware he had been placed in a potentially tricky situation. To have had to give evidence against Farrow at a Court Martial would have gone strongly against the grain; to have had to give evidence against an officer might have prejudiced his chances of a commission – the armed forces were in many ways curious institutions, class-structured and rigid to the point at which to acquire notoriety however blamelessly could count against promotion. He was about to speak again when there was an exclamation from Farrow, who was staring northwards through his binoculars.

'It's a bloody cruiser! Sod me if it's not the old *Emerald* ... I did a commission up the straits in her years ago.' Farrow left the wheelhouse at the rush and climbed to the compass platform. Cameron followed. The cruiser, scarcely visible to the naked eye through the filthy weather, appeared to be turning to the east. Farrow, using his binoculars again, reported the

156

ships of the westbound convoy in sight now. ~~H~~ ~~glasses to Cameron,~~ he took up a battery-fed Aldis, ~~c~~n fast to the compass platform, and began flashing the general call-sign towards the *Emerald*. To Cameron he said, 'Get on the phone, Lofty. Have a bunting-tosser sent up pronto. I'm no bloody signalman!' Before the signalman had reached the compass platform, *Emerald*'s acknowledgement was seen. *Carmarthen*'s pennant numbers were flashed across to her and inside three minutes Farrow, through his glasses, saw the cruiser's stem swing round to starboard.

He gave a whistle of relief: she was coming in.

The *Emerald* swept up to them, cutting through the heavy seas and flinging great gouts of water back from her bows. The signal lamps grew busy; *Emerald* would stand by until the weather moderated enough for a tow to be passed. When the towing pendant was sent across, back-up hands would also be sent and these would include a shipwright's party to help seal leaking plates. Medical assistance would be provided and the sick taken off to the cruiser's sick-bay if necessary. The cruiser's captain added words of congratulation: *Carmarthen*'s depleted company had achieved a near miracle. She would be brought back to UK if it was the last thing the Navy ever did. Relevant news was also passed by lamp: the German raider had despatched three ships of the westbound convoy before being sunk herself by the destroyer escort. *Emerald* had been in the vicinity on patrol and had heard the gunfire, but had arrived too late to add the weight of her armament to the battle. She was now proceeding to Rosyth, which was where *Carmarthen* would be taken.

Six days later *Carmarthen* was approaching May Island off the Firth of Forth. Once in safe waters, *Emerald* had broken wireless silence to send her report ahead. That report included the names of the survivors. Almost disbelievingly by now, Mary Anstey saw the name *Carmarthen* appear again on the plot in the operations room. The news had already swept the dockyard and the Navy was jubilant; and it was not long before the officers and men and the dockyard mateys were able to give exuberant voice to their feelings.

As *Carmarthen* passed under tow beneath the great bridge, the cheering started; as she was turned off the dockyard to be handed over to the care of the tugs for placement between camels – big deep-draught floating pontoons that would be pumped out to act as lifts – the whole yard went mad. Mary Anstey was there with the rest, her face tear-stained. It wasn't entirely with relief and joy: there was the worry that Donald Cameron mightn't be as delighted to see her as she would be to see him. The possibility had to be faced. In any case, his qualifying sea-time for his commission was just about finished now. He wouldn't be long in Rosyth.

After the wounded men had been brought ashore the dockyard took over and the ship's company was marched to the depot ship to be accommodated prior to entraining for Portsmouth barracks and re-draft after leave. Until the fresh draft chits came through from the Drafting Master-at-Arms in Pompey, those that were left would remain together, then they would go their separate ways and might never meet again.

Cameron took his leave of the ship with real regret: his first ship, brought to safe harbour after much ordeal and bloodshed. He would never forget her; nor would he forget the men he'd shared the ordeal with, particularly Farrow and Stripey Tomkins. On arrival aboard the depot ship, various matters were sorted out. Nothing was going to be said about mutiny or a wish to surrender, just as Farrow had forecast; and Matthews was removed to hospital for observation. Ordinary Seaman Lavington was not so easily disposed of, even though he had been killed: his victims had had families, after all. And nothing on God's earth could prevent the ship's company talking about what had taken place out in the Atlantic.

The staff officer who had taken the reports from

158

Matthews and Farrow had a brief word in Cameron's ear afterwards.

He said, 'If you're worried about your Captain's recommendation, don't be. It'll go through even though he's been lost. From what I've heard you showed all the right qualities for a commission, and I've no doubt at all you'll get it – I'll be having a word with the Admiral as soon as possible, and you can take it you'll be drafted to Portsmouth for the Admiralty board.' The staff officer grinned. 'It must surely be the first time in history that a U-boat's been blown up by an ordinary seaman with a hand-grenade!'

Mary Anstey had her ear to the ground and was outside the dockyard gates when, twenty-four hours later, after a weary ship's company had almost slept the clock round, local overnight leave was piped for the men ex-*Carmarthen*. Cameron saw the WRNS uniform; he had to look twice before he recognized Mary, since he hadn't expected her to be in Rosyth, *Carmarthen*'s mail having not yet been sent down from Scapa, but he was pleased to see her. He said as much, and she smiled in relief.

He said, 'We've got just tonight, that's all. I'm for Pompey tomorrow.'

'I know. What shall we do?'

'How about Edinburgh?'

She fiddled with the black silk bow of his uniform jumper, the black silk worn in perpetual mourning for Nelson. 'What about a film in Inverkeithing?'

'What's on?'

'Oh, I don't know,' she said. 'Some old pre-war thing, I expect. Does it matter?'

He grinned. 'Not in the back row. All right, come on, then.'

They went to a cinema and Cameron was quite unconscious of what was showing. He didn't see it; all he could see was *Carmarthen*'s lurching, half-under decks and the gun-flashes and the dead faces, and the imagined carnage in the U-boat after the grenades had been thrown. That, and Lavington and,

159

in his mind's eye, the opening up of *Carmarthen*'s fo'c'sle messdecks and the retrieval of the submerged bodies. When the film ended he realized he must have been a disappointing companion and so he remained for the rest of their evening together; he hadn't the stomach, yet, for socializing. The bloody awful war kept obtruding.